GRAVE PROPHECIES

Prophecies of Angels and Demons

Book Two

CASSANDRA ASTON

For every girl who sought strength from others but found it in herself

TABLE OF CONTENTS

Content & Trigger Warnings

This book is a work of fiction. No part of this book should be construed as true or accurate; no people or animals were harmed in the creation of this story. Grave Prophecies is intended for mature readers and is recommended for 18+. Mature content and triggers are listed below.

Descriptions of torture and death

Allusions to rape and other acts of sexual deviance

Necromancy and reincarnation

Biblical and other related references

References to angels, demons, heaven, hell, and consequences for human actions

Explicit language

Witches, magic, and other magical, fantastical beings

BOOKS BY CASSANDRA ASTON

Prophecies of Angels and Demons

Grave Secrets – book 1
Firefly – Simon's Novella – book 1.5
Grave Prophecies – book 2
Light – Gabriel's Novella – book 2.5
Grave Revelations – book 3
Parable – Peter's Novella – book 3.5
Fated – Sanura's Kindle Vella

Deadly Fae Duology

Whispers Among Thorns – Coming June 2025
Book 2 – Coming December 2025

Cowritten Novella

The Darkest Star – A standalone cowritten vampire novella – Coming 2025

Vicious Villains: A Twisted Fairytale Reimagining Anthology Series

Book 1 – Coming 2026

PROLOGUE

She flew up in her hammock, icy dread shooting down her spine. Holding her breath, she waited, listening for the sound that had woken her. The twinkle of Hyades in the night sky, her only light on this moonless night, pulsed in time with the rhythm of her heartbeat. The red glow of Aldebaran, usually almost too dim to make out this late in May, was glowing brightly.

She knew it was a sign.

Had this been what had awoken her? A sign from the stars? No. She was certain she had heard something.

She lay back, nestling into her hammock, and closed her eyes.

Ears tuned to the night air, she opened her third eye and let it float on the wind until she spied the blue haze hovering just a few meters away.

Although she had never met one of the night-beings in her very long life, her family had many legends of them. It would be foolish not to fear it.

"Are you here for me?" she breathed, knowing it could hear even from this distance.

"Are you Maria?" The light voice drifted on a phantom wind.

"I am."

"Maria Kavraz?"

Maria sat up again, blinking her eyes open. A yellow-eyed girl stood before her. "No one has called me by that name in a long time."

2

GRAVE PROPHECIES

The yellow-eyed night-being smiled. "You were hard to find."

The red eye of Taurus had everyone in an uproar, but Pythia didn't need to attend another meeting of the coven leaders to know what it meant. She'd had the same dream each night for a week.

The stars had spoken. The prophecy was upon them. But Maria had disappeared, and several of the Graia were making predictions of their own.

"Pythia, come here, child," her mother called. She joined the other women on the sacred rock overlooking the Gulf of Corinth.

Pythia placed a hand on her mother's, but her grandmother's wrinkled fingers wrapped tightly around hers and pulled them to her mouth. She kissed each finger and gazed with milky eyes at the sea.

"Tell us what you dreamed, Pythia," her grandmother rasped in the old Greek tongue, and all chatter died. Even the wind seemed too quiet as her grandmother squeezed her fingers once more.

She took a breath. She was the youngest Pythia in the history of her coven, and the gravity of her new position weighed heavily on her.

"The end times are near." Several women gasped, and a few crossed themselves. "The war that will be waged for all human souls is upon us, and one who was born under Hyades will decide the fate of us all."

CHAPTER 1

Simon

A dark shadow fell across his path, stretching up the adjacent wall.

Simon Carey slid the blade from its sheath, reveling in the weight resting in his palm.

It was close, right behind him.

He didn't need to surprise it. Not one this weak. He spun, slicing through a dark shape. A thin green arc of blood sprayed the opposite wall. The demon gave a cry of outrage, charging him.

He dropped the sword, lunging for it. They met, midair, as he tackled the demon to the ground, sinking his teeth into her neck.

It wasn't like human blood. It was thicker, sweeter, but the life force siphoning into him as her feeble cries faded was intoxicating. Strength bled through him; recharging limbs drained by weeks of sleepless nights.

The creature would regenerate, as they always did, but each time he drained them, he drained their source just a bit.

It might be that he still needed their energy to survive, it might not, but if he was expected to continue in this manner, the boost was necessary.

His phone buzzed. The timer reminded him he was expected in Bath in thirty minutes.

His sleeve had demon blood on it. A minor complication, but one that would delay him.

He sped into the dusky evening, stopping at the old boat dock where he stored his car when he was away from the Graves Estate. Opening the back door, he lifted the false floor he had carefully constructed and slid the sword in, gently returning it to cover the weapon.

He checked his phone again. He was late. Knowing Allie, she would be too. He sent a quick text, slipped his phone back into his pocket, and ducked into the front seat.

Outside the Graves mansion, Simon went to the trunk, pulled out a fresh black button-down, and changed quickly. His heart thrummed in his chest, nervous anticipation making his palms slick.

Every time he saw her, she stole his breath. The last time they'd seen each other, he asked her to be his girlfriend. She hadn't given an answer. It was old-fashioned, and the title didn't do his feelings justice, but he wanted her to know this wasn't just a summer fling for him.

But tonight wasn't about him. It was her night, and he wouldn't push things if she wasn't ready for titles. They were meant to be together. They were forever.

CHAPTER 2

Allie

A llie glared at the counter littered with glasses, plates, and bowls of various sizes. Buying them had been fun. Scrubbing those tiny little price tags off each one would not be. She tapped her fingers on the polished marble countertop. She could ask Rhea to do it, but Rhea already did *everything* in this house. Besides, she had resolved not to be a messy slob anymore, and that included cleaning the brand-new dishes she bought for herself.

With a sigh, she reached for the stopper, stuffing it into the sink before turning on the hot water. Maybe if she let them soak for a while, it would make the job easier. Or *maybe* Rhea would come by and do it for her. No, she would do it herself. She squirted dish soap into the rapidly filling sink and watched as bubbles bloomed. She put in the new plates and bowls and wedged in as many of the glasses as she could without overflowing the sink.

"You need to get ready for your date, miss thing, or you'll be late."

Allie jumped and dropped the glass she was holding into the sink. "Geez, Rhea, you scared the shit out of me!"

Rhea quirked an eyebrow. "I'll take care of this." She motioned in the general direction of the sink full of dishes. "Go get ready. You need to shower."

Allie considered objecting for all of two seconds before she turned and bounded from the room. "Thanks Rhea! If I haven't told you yet, you're the best person in the entire world!"

"Mmhhmm," Rhea called from the kitchen, but Allie was already sprinting up the stairs, two at a time.

In her bathroom, now updated with bright white tile and blush pink paint, she twisted on her luxurious new showerhead, holding out a hand to catch raindrops as they fell from the ceiling. She sighed, watching the mirror fog as it warmed.

It was hard to believe this was her life now. Big, impressive mansion on a country estate, more money than she knew what to do with, and a boyfriend who seemed too good to be true.

Boyfriend.

Her stomach did a little somersault. It was still hard to accept that a guy as perfect as Simon wanted her. He was so much more put together than she was. Polished, accomplished, and handsome.

She stripped off her clothes, tossed them into her brand-new laundry basket, and stepped under the spray. Steam invaded her nostrils as warmth pelted her skin.

"Alexa play my favorite songs," she called to the device now mounted in her bathroom ceiling.

Reaching for the shampoo, she lathered it through her shoulder-length locks and inhaled the lavender and eucalyptus scent. How could one girl be so lucky? If she died right now, she would have said she had everything she wanted.

"Girl, you are going to be late!" Rhea's voice shouted over Allie's singing as the words to 'Flowers' died on her lips.

She dropped the back scrubber she had been using as a microphone and turned both shower faucets off.

Poking her head around the glass, she said, "What time is it?"

"It's six-twenty-five, aren't you supposed to be there at seven?"

"Shit!" Allie stepped out of the shower and into Rhea's waiting towel.

"He's going to be mad at you."

"He's never mad at me."

"He's a good one." Rhea grinned.

Allie wrapped the towel around her chest and sighed again.

"Alright, stop drooling and go get ready." Rhea shooed her out of the bathroom and began picking up items from the floor and placing bottles back in their place.

Allie turned and hugged Rhea. "I am grateful for you."

Rhea hugged her back, squeezing just a little too tightly, but Allie didn't mind. Rhea was like the friend, sister, mom she'd never had. Had she really only known her for three months? It felt as though they were kindred spirits meant to find each other across lifetimes.

"Hush," Rhea whispered into her hair. Allie wished she could remember more about her mom, either of her parents, but she only had vague memories of them from her childhood. She had been five when they died in a car accident, leaving her with only a backpack full of mementos from their time on the road and an old leather journal she forgot she owned half the time.

Allie selected a red belted sundress from her closet and a pair of leopard print heels. One of the best things about dating Simon was that even at five-ten, heels were not a problem. She'd only had one other boyfriend before and she towered over him, even without heels.

She crossed the room to the pink vanity table and plugged in the blow dryer, combing her fingers through her wet curls. It had cost a small fortune to run electrical outlets into this room, but it had been worth it.

With her hair dried, she tugged the strands into a loose side braid and ran a bright red lipstick that matched her dress over her lips. With thick dark lashes framing sapphire eyes and porcelain skin, a little went a long way.

"You'll be late," Rhea said as she left the bathroom, moving behind Allie to the closet and began organizing her clothes.

"You don't have to clean up *all* my messes, Rhea."

Rhea clucked her tongue but said nothing and stooped to pick up a shirt.

Allie stood from the vanity and grabbed her phone from the bedside table. How was it already six-fifty? And she had two missed messages. She bit her lip and clicked the message icon.

"Hey beautiful. I'll pick you up, so you don't have to watch the time."

Why was this man so perfect?

The second message was from a number she didn't recognize. Frowning, she clicked the number to open the message.

"Did you think I would never find you, Ms. Graves? Leaving Atlanta won't keep you safe from me. I'll see you soon." Allie dropped her phone on the bed, stumbling back. Her heart pounded a staccato rhythm in her chest.

Rhea came to her side. "What's wrong? What happened?"

Allie sank into the chair at her vanity, swallowing. She opened her mouth, but words failed her. How had he found her?

Cathedral bells pealed through the house, startling them both. Rhea moved away from her, going to the door.

Allie found her voice. "Don't" she breathed. "Don't answer it." The bells rang through the house again, followed by a loud knock. Allie's heart was in her throat, the thrum of its pace suffocating her. The door opened downstairs.

"Hello?" called a male voice.

Her breathing leveled out as her heart slowed its frantic pace.

Rhea left the room and called from the hall, "We're up here, Simon."

Allie attempted to school her features into something resembling calm as she continued to breathe in and out. When she felt steady, she stood, bracing an arm on her armrest. Then Simon's shape filled the doorframe and their eyes met.

"What's wrong?" He crossed the room and reached for her hand. Slight shocks of electricity danced over her fingers, and, for a moment, she forgot her problems, thinking only of his soft lips on hers. She leaned forward. He dropped her hand and stepped back. "Allie, what is it?"

As if a spell were broken, fear flooded her veins once more, and she dropped back into the chair. "It's... it's nothing."

Simon looked at Rhea, who was now leaning in the doorway, her face drawn. "She was fine one moment, singing her heart out, and then she checked her phone and started acting like this."

Simon moved to the bed and picked up her phone at the same moment that Allie got control of her emotions.

"No, stop. I was surprised, that's all." She reached for her phone, attempting to swipe it from Simon's grasp, but he held it over his head, just out of her reach.

"That wasn't your surprised face, Allie. That was the face you make when something has scared you."

Allie pushed up onto her tiptoes, leaning into Simon as she attempted to grab her phone again.

He wrapped an arm around her waist and pulled her closer to him, pressing his nose to her ear. "I like this," he purred. She felt the rumble of his words all the way to her toes and turned her head, inhaling his scent. He nuzzled her ear. "Please, firefly, tell me what has you so worried."

Even as she melted at his words, she knew she couldn't tell him. Not this. He was a lawyer. It had to be against some kind of legal code. He kissed along her earlobe, still not relinquishing her phone. Rhea turned and left the room.

"I can't," she said, even though she desperately wanted to give in.

Simon pulled away from her, cataloging whatever emotions played across her face. He handed her the phone and leaned down to kiss her hand as she took it.

"Very well. Shall we go?"

Stuffing her phone into her purse, she picked up the small gold hoop earrings she'd bought herself as a late birthday present and slipped them into her ears.

"Ready," she said, feeling a bit steadier now that he was there.

Simon's eyes were on her as they left the house, and as he opened the door for her. In the car, he found the sixties station he loved and turned the volume down until it was only a light buzz. "Aren't you going to ask me where I'm taking you?"

Allie blinked, realizing she'd been silent the entire car ride. As she gazed out the window at the last streaks of sunlight disappearing behind the tree line, she realized they had already passed Washington. "Where are you taking me?"

Simon's lips turned up. "I'd like to take you somewhere special. To celebrate your acceptance."

She frowned. Today was supposed to be a happy day. She had never expected to get into college, much less UMASS Boston. Her mom's dream of going to college—to UMASS—was one of the few memories she had of her. And the jerk from her past had just thrown a wrench into all her plans. How could she go to college now?

Simon had said something, and she had missed it.

"I'm sorry. What?"

"We don't have to go to dinner tonight if you're not up for it." Simon laid a hand on Allie's bouncing knee.

She glanced down before looking up to meet his eyes again. "No. I mean, yes. I want to go to dinner with you." She tugged a loose curl at the end of her braid. "It's just that someone from my past has caught up with me." She bit her lip. "Hey watch the road!"

Simon grinned and returned his gaze to the road but left one hand on her knee. She weighed the consequences of telling him the truth. If she had to cancel her plans for college and go on the run, she should probably tell him.

Actually, as her lawyer, didn't she have client confidentiality or something? And if she would have to take a chunk of money out of her trust and go hide on an island somewhere, she'd have to tell him something. *Okay, here goes*, she told herself.

"There's a detective who has been looking for me because he thinks I killed a man and now he's found me." She held her breath and looked straight ahead, terrified of making eye contact. When the forest to her right continued to roll by and Simon had said nothing for some time, she darted a glance at him.

Simon appeared to be wrestling with his own words now; his face contorted into several strange expressions before he turned to look at her.

"Who was the man?"

Could he have sounded any more disappointed? "He was one of my foster parents."

Simon's hand left her knee. In its cold absence, her knee started bouncing again.

"I didn't kill him."

"Why does the detective believe you did?"

Was she ready to tell him the rest of it? She wasn't. She really wasn't. But she'd said too much, and there was no going back now.

"He wasn't... kind." She swallowed. "The police were called several times during my stay because of complaints from the neighbors. He yelled a lot at both of us. There were two of us in the house and the neighbors reported signs of abuse more than once, so they came by several times. Every time, he would tell them new and terrible stories of things we had done. Every time, the cops believed him."

Allie wrapped her arms around herself. "Once, he was yelling; threatening to get his belt, and the faucet just started spraying water everywhere. He screamed at me. Called me a witch." She sputtered in nervous laughter, watching Simon's knuckles grow white on the steering wheel.

She cleared her throat a few times before continuing.

"So anyway, the neighbor heard it and called the police again. But when he leaned under the sink to shut off the water, the pipe..." Allie rubbed her arms. "I don't know what happened to the pipe, but he hit his head on it and when he came up, he was bleeding everywhere. By the time the cops arrived, he looked like he was the one being abused, and he told them I hit him with a bat.

"I tried to tell them I wasn't anywhere near him when it happened, but they didn't believe me. I was arrested. Taken to juvie that day. It was a nice break, actually. But then they let me out."

She paused, swallowing the bile rising in her throat.

"After that, he locked me in my room. He didn't let me out for days... He said." She bit her lip, watching Simon's knuckles grow impossibly whiter. "He said I was a witch and only one of us was getting out of that house alive. It was me or him."

Simon slammed on the brake, and the car slid to a stop on the side of the road. Allie tried to still her shaking leg, but her fingers trembled violently, making the effort useless. "I didn't kill him. I swear I didn't. I know how it sounds, but I didn't do anything to him." A tear slid down her cheek and she swiped at it.

Simon faced the road. One at a time, he pried each finger from the steering wheel. Indentations remained where his fingers had been.

Allie wrapped her arms around herself again, more tightly this time. The thrum of her heart was a hummingbird trapped in her chest. It prepared for whatever was coming next.

The air was thick with his rage, and it brought back every memory of a belt or a fist. She leaned into the passenger window, giving them space. He turned, slowly, and faced her.

"It's good he's dead. Because I would have killed him."

CHAPTER 3

Allie

Allie burst into tears. It wasn't the quiet crying girls did in the movies. Her sobs were loud. Snot ran down her face as her shoulders shook. When strong arms came around her, she flinched and her whole body shook.

"I'm so sorry he did that to you," Simon whispered into her hair.

Allie cried louder. She had thought his anger was for her. Knowing it wasn't should have made her feel better; instead, part of her soul had been bared, and it left her feeling raw, exposed. She hadn't told anyone this story. Even the detective. Even when it might have saved her from possible imprisonment.

"He's dead now. He can never hurt you again," Simon said as he pulled her into his warm embrace.

"I don't think I killed him," she whispered when her crying had quieted.

"If you had, I wouldn't have judged you for it." His words sent a fresh set of tears streaming down her face. How did he always know the exact right thing to say?

When her tears subsided, Simon released her, leaning back to look at her red, blotchy face. "Let's skip dinner. We can get take-out and go back to your place."

Allie swiped at her wet cheeks. "Maybe you're right. Take-out is probably best tonight."

Simon stared at her for one more moment before putting the car in drive and spinning it around in the direction of Bath, NC.

"It's too late to order anything in Bath," Allie said.

"We can pick up something in Washington. What about chicken and waffles from Waffle House?" Simon smirked.

"That doesn't sound good at all."

He frowned. "You love..." The words died on his lips.

"What do I love?"

"Trying new restaurants."

She made a humming sound in her throat. "Do I? I guess considering I spent most of my early life eating whatever boxed dinners my foster parents made me and the past six years eating whatever Ben brought home, that would be true. Everything is new."

"Remind me of Ben again. What did he do?"

Allie chewed on her bottom lip. She didn't like talking about her ex-boyfriend, especially with her current boyfriend. *Boyfriend*. Why did it sound so different in her mind this time? "He's in food services," she said evasively.

"Ah yes. I remember. He works at Subway."

Allie grimaced. "We had a lot of free food."

"I'm sure there's a Subway in Washington if you're in the mood for comfort food this evening."

Her eyes narrowed to slits as she turned her gaze on Simon. "Do you think you're funny?"

"I've been told I'm hilarious."

She punched him in the arm.

"Ow! Okay, sorry. Could you search on your phone? Find places in Washington that are more to your taste?"

Allie rolled her eyes, but she reached down and fished around in her purse until she found her phone. "New Message" was on the screen. She dropped the phone as if she had been burned by it.

"What's wrong?" Simon's light tone had been replaced by one of concern.

She picked up her phone, shivering. "I have another text."

"Read it to me?"

Allie swiped up, unlocking her phone. The new text was from a five-digit number. "Hmm. That's odd. It's an automated text." She opened the text and read: "*Welcome Freshmen! Student orientation begins next week. Check your email for updates and additional information about your first week. Text Y to accept messages or STOP to opt out of future messages.*"

"It's from UMASS." She huffed out a relieved breath. A lump formed in her stomach. How could she go to college next week? There was a detective on her trail, and now he knew where to find her.

"That's good news. What does it say?"

Allie tossed her phone back into her purse. "What does it matter? I can't go to college. If he found me out here in BFE, he'll be able to find me at school, where I'm registered. In a database."

Simon laid his hand on her knee. "When we get to your house, I want you to tell me all the details. Without evidence, all he can do is scare you. He can't arrest you. We will put an end to his harassment."

Allie took a deep breath. Simon was a lawyer. If anyone knew how to get her out of something like this, it was him. But... "What kind of lawyer are you?"

He laughed. "I'm an estate attorney, but I have a partner who handles criminal cases. I'm familiar with how the law works, Allie, even if I haven't worked criminal cases before. Trust me."

Allie bit her lip. She did trust him. How she had put so much faith in a person she had only known for a few months was unimaginable, especially considering all the people who had betrayed her. Everyone let her down eventually.

They pulled to a stop in front of a large yellow sign that read Waffle House.

"I thought I said I didn't want chicken with waffles."

"If you trust me enough to handle your legal issues, would you be willing to trust me enough to make a food choice for you? Just this once?"

Allie frowned, but Simon was turning large golden-brown eyes on her in that pleading way she could never refuse. "Fine, but we have to order something extra in case I hate it."

"Deal." Simon hopped from the car and before she opened her door, he was on her side, opening it for her. He was so fast sometimes.

"I can open my door," she said as she stepped out.

"What kind of gentleman would I be if I let you open your own doors?"

"A normal one."

Inside the small, yellow room, lit by garish luminescent bulbs, Allie read from the menu. None of the choices seemed appealing. She hated to admit it, but a few months of fancy dinners with Simon, and a stocked fridge, thanks to her influx of cash, had made her something of a food snob.

Simon stepped up to the counter and placed an order for two chicken and waffles.

Allie continued to scan the menu. "Just order a chicken sandwich, I guess."

"You want me to order you different chicken in case you don't like the chicken I ordered for you?"

"It's not the chicken I don't want to try. It's the chicken *with* waffles." Simon laughed, but placed her order, slipping a credit card on the counter before Allie could make a move for her wallet. "I can pay once in a while."

"Nonsense. You already pay me every day."

He had a point. She'd never considered looking into his rates. What if he was overcharging? But no, that was silly. Her thoughts had run away with her for a moment.

Simon stood at the counter, out of place in this dingy diner. The cashier eyed him and his flashy watch and leaned over the counter to whisper something in his ear, pressing her ample cleavage against his arm. Allie bristled, heat licking down her back. Simon laughed, glancing over his shoulder at her. His smile fell, and he reached out, pulling her closer to him.

At his touch, the flames died, and she relaxed, leaning into him, breathing him in. His skin was cool to the touch under her banking anger.

He turned to face her. "Everything alright, firefly?"

Silly little words. But they had butterflies exploding in her stomach and her temper wedging back into the box where all her unwelcome emotions lived. The cashier lifted her rack from the counter and backed up, getting the message, but

Allie hardly noticed. She wanted to kiss him, to tear his clothes off right here in this diner, and revel in the feel of his warm body pressed against hers.

Simon released his hold on her, and a fog cleared from her mind. The desire was still there, but the burning need to have him here and now had dissipated. She leaned into him again, pressing a kiss to his neck, and felt the steady, rapid beat of his heart. She looked up into his eyes, saw the wide dilation of his pupils and knew he was thinking all the same dirty things.

And with all they had done these past months, all the ways they had explored each other, it took little imagination to conjure thoughts of him now. She kissed his neck again, trailing kisses up his jaw to his ear. "Good thing we're getting this to go," she whispered.

"Order for Simon," a high-pitched voice said, sending Allie back a few steps, her cheeks burning.

Simon reached for the bag, pulling her after him out the door and back to the car. Neither looked back as they reached the car and Simon pressed her into it, sliding a leg between hers as he pressed the hard length of his rapidly growing desire against the thin fabric of her dress.

He kissed her neck, down to her collarbone, and trailed his lips along the sensitive skin there.

She wrapped her arms around his waist, finding the takeout bag still in his hand. "Maybe we should go to my house."

"Have I told you how hot you are when you're jealous?" Simon said in reply, pulling her braid to the side to give him better access to the sensitive skin at her throat.

His warm breath on her skin distracted her for a moment before his words registered. "What?" she pressed a hand to his chest and pushed him back. "I'm not jealous."

Simon chuckled. It was low and dark. "Oh, you were jealous, and it was so damn hot." His gaze was still unfocused as it fell on her lips.

Allie wasn't sure if she was mad or turned on. Both. She was both. "You were flirting with that cashier at the Waffle House. Did you want me to be jealous? Of the cashier?" She crossed her arms over her chest.

He leaned in again and kissed her cheek, smiling against her skin. "I can't help it if women find me irresistible."

She glared at him. "So you admit you were flirting with her?"

"I wasn't. I promise. But if the result is your fiery anger, maybe..."

"Do it and you better sleep with one eye open."

Simon laughed. "Come on, firecracker. Let's go home." He opened the door for Allie, and she dropped inside. He closed it behind her, unaware that his words had hit her like a punch to the gut. Home. Home.

Let's go home.

CHAPTER 4

Allie

Allie sat in silence as they drove the twenty minutes it took to get from Washington to her countryside mansion in the quaint town of Bath, NC.

Simon said nothing, probably assuming she was still mad at him, but he couldn't have been more wrong. Three little words had her thinking about things like forever and family. Dangerous thoughts.

Let's go home, he'd said, like it meant nothing. Like he didn't know what it meant to her to have a home of her own and a person to share it with. Maybe he didn't. She knew so little about him. Maybe things like home and family were normal for him.

"Are you cold?" Simon's words tore her from her thoughts.

"No. I'm fine." She glanced in his direction.

His lips were creased at the edges; turned down. "You have goosebumps."

She rubbed her hands along her arms, feeling the tiny bumps. "I'm just hungry."

Simon snorted. "Goosebumps aren't a byproduct of hunger as far as I know."

"I guess they're not." She chewed on her bottom lip. "I'm just thinking about Detective Blake," she lied.

"Detective Blake, the man who sent you a text. How long have you been running from him?"

"I wasn't running exactly, but when my foster dad died, he made my life miserable for a while. Are we talking about this now?"

Simon said nothing as he rounded a curve and turned into the drive, stopping in front of massive wrought iron gates. Allie clicked a button on her keychain and the gates swung open. Sinister gray gargoyles peered out into the night as the car rolled over loose gravel toward her house.

They pulled to a stop and Simon was out of the car and on her side before she could open her door. She wrapped her fingers around the to-go bag as she stepped out, avoiding Simon's outstretched hand.

At the door, Allie shuffled the bag into one hand while she fumbled with the old iron key to her door in the other. Simon lifted the bag from her hand.

"I had it," she grumbled.

"It's acceptable for men to help once in a while."

Allie twisted the key a second time and pushed the door open, calling over her shoulder, "Once in a while being the key phrase."

As the door swung in, a small blue bird flitted overhead and out into the night.

"What the hell! That's the third time a bird has been in the house! How do they keep getting in here?"

Simon stepped around her, into the foyer. The smell of vanilla and chicken wafted after him. "It's a big house. You can share some of it with the woodland creatures."

"No! I can't. That's disgusting."

Simon's laugh echoed off the hallway.

Allie stormed in after him, closing and locking the door before following him to the kitchen. "You think I should live with raccoons and opossums too?"

She stumbled to a halt in the kitchen as she took in the scene.

Simon was on his knees on the kitchen floor, propping Rhea's limp head in his lap, her body sprawled across the tile.

"Oh my gosh, what's wrong with her?" Allie breathed.

"She appears to have hit her head. Get some ice, would you?"

Allie rushed forward, propelled by fear. *Please let her be ok. Please. Please. Please.* She flung open the freezer, reaching for a handful of ice. It bit into her fingers, blisteringly cold, but she gripped the ice as she went to the counter and pulled out a hand towel.

Simon was murmuring something in Rhea's ear, leaning in. She stirred, but her eyes were still closed.

Allie brought the towel-wrapped ice to Simon and watched as he pressed the cold compress to the side of Rhea's head. She could see it now; mottled purple skin swelling along her temple. "What happened to her?"

Simon looked up. "We better get her to the hospital. It's worse than I thought."

Allie grabbed Rhea's hand, squeezing it.

"I'll drive. It would take too long to wait for an ambulance."

Allie nodded. "What can I do?"

Simon shifted Rhea's head gingerly as he said, "Get Rhea's ID would you and meet me in the car?"

She raced up the stairs, sliding to a stop in Rhea's room, grabbed her wallet from the bedside drawer, and darted back down finding the door flung wide.

In the already running car, Simon wasted no time making the circle around the drive.

Allie chewed on her lip, darting glances at Rhea every few seconds.

Rhea was pale and her lips, normally flush with color, were white. *Please be okay*, Allie thought again, reaching back to squeeze Rhea's limp fingers.

Simon was speeding, flying down the road, sliding around each turn at a dangerous clip. Allie hardly noticed. She trained her gaze on Rhea's chest, rising and falling. Was it growing slower? Her vision blurred. If anything happened to her friend, she didn't know what she would do.

There was no blood and there had been no broken objects on the floor that she had seen. Nothing to indicate there had been a struggle. The kitchen looked the same as always. Several of the new dishes Allie had bought were on a towel, face down, drying, but the sink was still half full of dishes. Allie groaned aloud.

"What is it? What's happened?"

Allie never took her eyes off Rhea as she said, "This is my fault. Rhea was washing my dishes when something happened to her. Maybe she spilled some water and slipped, or her knee was giving her trouble again and she fell. If I hadn't left those dishes for her to wash, this never would have happened!"

"Rhea washes your dishes every day, firefly. It's not what you might consider dangerous work."

Even through the haze of fear and guilt, Simon's nickname warmed her chest. Had anyone else ever given her a nickname aside from waste of space or trash?

"If she fell, it wasn't your fault. I promise," Simon went on.

She squeezed Rhea's hand and whispered, "When you're all better, I promise I will wash my dishes from now on. And we will schedule an appointment for your knee surgery. No more putting it off."

Simon rested his hand on Allie's knee. She hadn't known it was bouncing until his light touch stilled her nervous energy.

"The closest ER is in Washington. I'll have us there in less than fifteen minutes."

Two hours later, Allie was wedged into a very uncomfortable waiting room chair, watching Simon pace. They had heard nothing, seen no one since they had taken her behind emergency room doors. Allie was going to lose her mind if someone didn't tell her something soon.

Simon's phone buzzed in his pocket. He pulled it out, scanned the screen, and clicked it off. It buzzed again. He gave a frustrated huff and stuffed it back in his pocket. It was almost eleven pm. It couldn't be work texting him that late.

"Who is it?" Allie asked.

"No one. It's just a marketing blast."

"This late?"

"Allie, as much as I enjoy your jealousy, now isn't the time."

She bit back her reply, watching him continue to pace. He was more upset about her house manager than she would have expected. He hardly knew Rhea after all. But maybe it was just that he had a big heart.

A loud grumbling noise came from Allie's midsection, and she pressed a hand to her stomach.

Simon stopped pacing, dropping into the chair beside her. "I've been so thoughtless. We left our food and you've had nothing to eat all night." He reached for her hand, lacing their fingers together. "Let me go get us something to eat. If you hear anything while I'm gone, will you text me?"

She arched an eyebrow at him. Did his sudden interest in getting food have something to do with the text messages he'd just received, or was he genuinely concerned she was hungry?

"Tonight was supposed to be a date night. I still owe you dinner."

Allie eyed their clasped hands before looking up into his eyes. She blinked, feeling lightheaded. What the hell was that? For a moment, his eyes had been different. Cat-like. Gold?

"What is it?" Simon asked, squeezing her fingers. "Are you okay?"

Allie pulled her hands from his grip and stood shakily. "I'm fine, I'm just lightheaded. Maybe you're right. I need food." As if in confirmation, her stomach grumbled again.

"Sit, please. I'll get us something and be back in no time."

Allie sat, leaning into her chair. It had to be the stress of everything that had happened getting to her. First the text from Detective Blake, then Rhea.

"Okay, don't be too long."

Simon leaned down to kiss her forehead before striding for the door. She watched as he pulled his phone from his pocket, texting furiously on his way out the door. Her stomach dipped, a queasy feeling settling there.

"Miss Graves?"

A woman dressed in white with graying temples approached her.

She sat up straighter. "Yes?"

"Rhea is awake and asking for you. Would you like to come back and see her?"

Allie reached for the bag, and jumped to her feet, following the woman. "How is she? What was wrong with her?"

They turned right into a small, sparse room. Rhea was reclined against a raised hospital bed; her sallow skin was slick with an unnatural sheen.

25

"Rhea!" Allie squeaked and rushed into the room.

"Come sit beside me," Rhea said in a featherlight voice.

Allie sat, careful not to press any of her weight into her. "How are you feeling?"

Rhea cleared her throat a few times, touching her hand to the cotton bandages wrapped around her head. "They had to cut me open to remove a piece of metal in my head. Can you believe it? No idea how that got there."

Allie gasped. "A piece of metal?"

"I'll have to stay the night to make sure there's no more internal bleeding, but they said the biggest risk now is infection."

Allie scooted closer, reaching for her hand to squeeze it. "I'm sure you will be fine and tomorrow you're going to come home and rest. Whatever you need, we'll make sure we have it."

Rhea patted Allie's hand with her free one. "I'll be fine. The Lord watches over his flock."

Allie bit her tongue. She wasn't sure she believed in God or the afterlife, but if he was up there, she would pray that Rhea got through this.

"I'll leave you two for a while. If you would like to stay the night, Miss Graves, we can bring in a more comfortable chair," the doctor said from the doorway.

"Yes, I'd like that very much."

The doctor slipped out, leaving the two of them alone.

"What happened Rhea?"

"I'll tell you what I told the doctors. I was washing dishes, and then I woke up here in the hospital. That's all I know."

"You heard nothing before..."

"I didn't hear a thing. Hand me that bag on the counter over there," she said, pointing to a small Ziploc bag. Allie reached for it, inspecting it as she handed it to Rhea. "This was in my head. Can you imagine?"

It was bloody and small, only about two inches long. The metal curved slightly.

"Hand me the paperwork, would you Allie? I want you to read it. Make sure I'm not missing anything important."

Allie reached for the paperwork on the counter and scanned it.

Penetrating brain injury (PBI) is a traumatic brain injury (TBI). PBI includes all traumatic brain injuries other than blunt head trauma and constitutes the most severe of traumatic brain injuries.

Low-velocity penetration: Examples include a knife or other sharp objects.

Primary injuries occur immediately. Secondary injuries occur following the time of the injury. The final neurologic outcome is influenced by the extent and degree of secondary brain injury. Therefore, the primary goal in the emergency department is to prevent or reduce conditions that can worsen outcomes, such as hypotension, hypoxia, anemia, and hyperpyrexia.

Results: CT scan showed no signs of bone fragments, no intracranial air, no basal cistern effacement, no signs of brain parenchymal herniation, and no signs of transventricular injury.

Recommended next steps:

Patient should drink plenty of fluids, get rest, and limit mobility for six weeks with a checkup in one week. Antibiotics prescribed for 14 days. If signs of infection are present at one-week checkup, an additional 21-day dose may be prescribed.

If any of the following symptoms occur, contact your doctor immediately: nosebleed, fever, severe headache, body aches or chills, loss of senses including taste, touch, sight or smell. Inability to walk or loss of any motor functions.

Allie looked up from the paper. "This is serious."

Rhea chuckled. "It will take more than a bit of metal to bring me down."

Allie eyed her skeptically. "That thing was in your head. I can't believe you're awake. It doesn't seem possible. I had a foster sibling who was stabbed in the hand with a fork. He had pieces of bone everywhere in his hand. Someone stabbed you in the head and everything here says this is life-threatening, but you have nothing wrong with you."

Rhea leaned her head against her pillow and closed her eyes, clicking a button on the IV attached to her arm. "It doesn't feel like nothing."

Allie winced. "I'm sorry. I was just so worried about you."

Eyes still closed, Rhea squeezed Allie's hand. Allie gently extracted her fingers from Rhea's hand and reached for the Ziploc bag resting on the blanket. She lifted the bag and turned it, trying to get a better look at the object. Gray metal reflected the light in the places where blood had dried and scraped away.

"Can I rinse this off?"

Rhea mumbled something and she knew the morphine had kicked in.

She stood, opening the bag over the sink. She turned on the sink faucet and let the bag fill with water. She dumped the water out, pinching the bag so the tiny metal object didn't slip out, and repeated her actions several times. When it was free of blood and grime, she reached into the bag and pulled it out.

Now that it was clean, she could see it had a pointed tip and the back half of the curved cone was jagged, as if it had been ripped free from something. It almost looked like a claw.

She inhaled sharply, dropping it into the sink, and backed up.

CHAPTER 5

Simon

S imon typed the address he'd received into Google Maps. Three hundred and twenty-six miles. If he put in his order at Waffle House, he could get there and back in just under forty-five minutes, barring any complications with the job. He would have to chance it. He was already on thin ice with the angels, living in Bath three days a week instead of in his designated territory. They let him get away with it because of his incredible speed and the high likelihood Elizabeth would be back to finish what she started with Allie sooner or later.

None of them had known what gifts he would bring with him into his reash life. The angels told him it had taken them longer than usual to heal him, but besides retaining all his abilities, he no longer spent his days in Sheol. They didn't know if getting in was possible anymore and he saw no need to test it at present.

He'd happily agreed to the extra time tacked on to his sentence, all things considered.

With Elizabeth still missing and Gabriel absent, Simon was desperately needed on the mortal plane to help control a seemingly endless insurgence of demons. He had known Allie's reash life consumed most of her nights, but he'd never realized how taxing it was on everyday life, having to manage an entire territory by yourself. And she lacked his speed and other abilities.

He could not fathom how she handled it for six years. After three months on the job, the strain had begun to take its toll. When he wasn't dodging Allie's growing concerns about his evasions, he was missing work and struggling to make up the time elsewhere. While he may enjoy twenty-four hours a day on the human plane, a favorable change, he also now required sleep. An annoyance at best; complete havoc on his schedule at worst.

He opted not to take the car, hoping Allie wouldn't go searching for him in the parking lot. That would only lead to more questions. He had to take the chance, though; being gone any longer than necessary would draw suspicion from her.

He reached the Waffle House in just under a minute, placed the same order from earlier that night, and told them he would be back to pick it up in less than an hour.

He dashed out the door and flew into the night.

Setting one foot in front of the other, the world sped by. He'd been surprised to learn he hadn't been gifted with the third eye ability Allie had during her time as a reash and suspected the gift was unique to her and not given by the angels.

If that were true, it meant they had only given her the sword—now strapped to his back—the added ringing in her ears to alert her to a demon's presence, and the knowledge of demons' existence. Poor gifts for the one tasked with doing their dirty work.

He suspected she had been using her other abilities—the ones passed down through the Graves family line—all along. Perhaps it was why they chose her.

And tonight, he was certain she had seen something. Allie was an open book, at least for him. There was no expression, tone of voice, or small tick he couldn't read. After nearly one hundred years with her, she could hide nothing from him.

Simon stopped just half a block from his destination. His ears didn't ring, but he smelled the sulfur in the air and his enhanced hearing told him the complete stillness around him was unnatural.

Stuffing his hands into his pockets, he strolled, whistling a light tune. His shadow stretched as he walked toward the alley and split in two when he turned the corner. His shoulders stiffened, but he didn't slow his pace. The trick was to give the impression of nervousness, without confirming their presence.

Demons, like angels, needed some faith to be corporeal enough to physically harm a human. A healthy mix of fear and skepticism was the right cocktail for a demon to make its move.

The air pressure dropped, and Simon knew this was no low-level demon. Something truly bad was wreaking havoc in his territory tonight. So much for a quick job. He would have to come up with that excuse, after all.

CHAPTER 6

Allie

Allie reached for the small metal claw. She turned it over, examining the jagged edges where it had been torn away from its body. The unique color of the metal should have given it away sooner, but covered in blood, she hadn't noticed until now.

Someone had torn a claw from one of the metal gargoyles surrounding the estate. It was hard to imagine how anyone had climbed the ten-foot fence, let alone ripped a piece of metal free from it. Was that even possible? There had to be some explanation for it. But what?

Her stomach grumbled, reminding her Simon should have been back with food by now. *Shit!* She was also supposed to text him with an update on Rhea. She pulled her phone out of her purse. Midnight. Where the hell was he? Her temper flared, heat rolling down her arms to her fingertips. A blue spark leaped off her finger onto the metal claw.

She shrieked, dropping the claw on the bed. "What the hell was that?" Rhea gave a loud snort, but her eyes remained closed. Her head lolled to the side as she adjusted under the covers. Allie covered her mouth. When Rhea didn't move again, she stood, swiping up the claw from the bed. It was warm to the touch. *Probably because I was holding it,* she told herself.

She placed the metal object on the counter and swiped her phone up again. 12:03 am. Well. As promised, she would let him know Rhea was fine, and that they did not need him for anything else tonight. *She* kept her promises.

The door to the room swung open, and Allie's heart leaped into her throat. She had overreacted. There was a line at the restaurant, there was a long wait, he got a flat tire...

"I have a chair for you," a woman in blue scrubs said, dragging a large tan chair into the room.

"Thank you," she said, moving to help her drag it in. It scraped as they dragged it across the floor.

"If you need anything, just let me know. Have a good night."

The woman turned to leave, but Allie called, "Actually, is there a vending machine anywhere in this hospital?"

"Sure, come with me." Allie trailed the woman down a hall lit with bright fluorescent bulbs. "Here we go. The vending machines are to the right."

Allie thanked her again and faced the wall of machines. Alone, she let out a shaky breath as she scanned the options. She swayed on her feet, her ears beginning to ring. As she leaned into the vending machine to steady herself, a dull ache started behind her eyes. She must really be hungry.

"Allie."

She turned, leaning against the vending machine for support, and froze. "What happened to you?"

In the garish light, his wound looked horrid. Blood ran down the side of his face, staining the collar of his shirt. He moved so fast her addled brain was having trouble processing it.

"Allie, what's wrong? Are you okay?" He pressed into her side, lifting her into his arms.

"Put me down. You're the one who's injured. What happened to you?"

He set her down, not releasing his hold on her. "I was attacked in the parking lot. They stole my wallet, but luckily, they didn't get our dinner." He grinned, holding up the bag.

"You need to see the doctor. We need to report this, and you might need stitches."

Simon chuckled. "I don't need stitches. A bit of rubbing alcohol and I'll be good as new."

Allie gave him a skeptical once-over, but a drum pounded against her skull, and she was having trouble focusing on his face. She swayed again.

"Come on," he said as he guided her back down the hall. "They told me Rhea is conscious."

Putting one foot in front of the other as the hallway blinked in and out of focus—in time with her heartbeat—she moved unsteadily back toward Rhea's room.

Simon opened the door and led her to the seat in the corner. He went to Rhea's side, resting a hand on her forehead before returning to Allie.

"Let's eat something. It will help."

Allie wanted to protest. Simon needed medical attention, but the smell from the bag of food had finally penetrated the fog in her brain and her stomach violently protested any action that didn't involve putting food in her mouth. Her stomach gave another loud bellow before she relented and accepted the box Simon had removed from the bag labeled Waffle House.

She popped open the lid and stared at golden, crispy, fried chicken resting atop waffles. "I'm not eating the waffles," she said in a woozy voice.

"I won't force you." Simon laughed. "What did they tell you about Rhea's condition?" he asked, patting his face with a paper towel, and pressing it to his wound. He crossed the room, stooping to pick up his food. Now that the wound was clean, she saw the cut was shallow. Head wounds always bled the most. Her knowledge of that fact was borne from years of treating fellow foster kid's wounds.

"I left the paperwork on the counter. It's not good, but she's doing well, considering." Simon crossed the room, picking up the papers and scanning them. Allie bit into her chicken, moaning at the delectable flavor. This waffle place knew how to make fried chicken. Salty, crunchy flakes melted on her tongue as she chewed.

Simon chuckled. "If you like that, wait till you try it with the waffles and syrup."

"Gross. Never ask me that again."

Simon set the paper on the arm of the chair. "I'm sorry for leaving you here to deal with this alone," he said as he sat.

"Why are you sorry? I was here thinking the worst, and you were fighting for your life in the parking lot."

"I would hardly consider a mugging fighting for my life. The guy asked for my wallet and when I put up a bit of a struggle, he sliced me with his knife. In the end, he ran off with my wallet and I decided it wasn't worth the effort to pursue him. I would have been inside sooner, but the parking lot security guard came up just as he ran off and forced me to give a statement."

"Chase after him!" Allie said around a mouthful of chicken. She swatted him with one greasy hand. "You better not chase after criminals. Your wallet is not worth it."

Simon dodged her swipe. "I said I didn't chase him."

She narrowed her eyes at him. "You almost did." She wiggled her greasy fingers at him, giggling as he squirmed away from her.

"Sometimes, firefly, you are downright savage." When Allie had finished all her chicken, she eyed Simon's box. "You only get a piece of my chicken if you try it with waffles and syrup."

She pouted, sticking out her bottom lip.

"Your she-devil tricks won't work on me. If you want my chicken, those are my terms."

"Finneee," she relented. She parted her lips, letting him stuff the strange concoction into her mouth. "Oh. My. Gosh. Why didn't you tell me you had Heaven on a fork?"

Laughter rumbled up his chest. "That never gets old."

"What?"

"Your love for new foods."

She frowned, licking the sweet syrup from her lips. He said the weirdest things sometimes.

Simon picked up Rhea's paperwork again and read through it. "It looks like she was very lucky."

Allie chewed on her lip. "I thought so too. But... I need to show you something." She stood, crossing the small room. The pounding in her head had faded. "This is from the gargoyles at my house. I'm sure of it." She placed it in Simon's hand.

He scrutinized the small metal object. "You're right."

"And it was torn off. How could someone tear metal?"

Simon's lips pursed, considering. "From the right angle, and if you had the right tools, applying the right amount of pressure would make a tear like this."

Simon, the detective, the lawyer, and all-around perfect guy, had an answer for everything. She couldn't have come up with that. Tools and pressure and angles. She hadn't finished high school; knew nothing about math or physics. How did she hope to pass her classes in college?

At Simon's prompting, she had studied half the summer to complete her GED. That, coupled with the killer entrance essays Simon had helped her write and letters of recommendation from his friends in high places, were the only reasons they'd accepted her.

"I can't go to college next week." The words were out of her mouth before she knew she said them aloud.

"What do you mean?"

"Rhea is going to take six weeks to recover, at least. And someone has to be here to look after her. She might get an infection or need help. Not to mention there's a detective after me."

Simon grabbed her hand, pulling her into his lap. All her senses flared to life. Even after three months, every time he touched her, it sent butterflies dancing in her stomach. "You're going to college. We'll hire someone to care for Rhea, and I will check in on her every day if I must. I am not concerned with the detective. You would be in jail if he had any proof. I will get a restraining order if needed."

Allie relaxed into him, wishing it was that simple. "I can't just leave her to be cared for by strangers. And you don't know how bad this guy is. He's like a dog with a bone. It's been over six years, and he still hasn't let it go."

"I will find a home healthcare nurse tomorrow. Rhea will do nothing but relax and recover. You can come home every weekend until she's better."

It couldn't be that simple, could it? It was a two-hour flight. She really could leave every Friday and come back Monday morning.

"There's still Blake."

"Do you feel up to telling me the story tonight? Give me as much information as you can, and I'll have a solution for you tomorrow."

Allie yawned, her limbs feeling leaden. "Let's save it for tomorrow."

Simon wrapped his arms around her, leaning back to make her more comfortable. "Go to sleep. In the morning, we'll all go home."

There it was again. That declaration. She yawned, her eyes drifting closed. Wrapped in Simon's embrace, she slipped into sleep, her belly full and her heart warm.

CHAPTER 7

Allie

Allie cracked heavy lids open, blinking in the harsh false light. There was a stinging pain in her neck, and her foot was tingly. She peered around the empty hospital room and sat up. "Simon?"

The hospital bed was made, and the door was ajar. She stood stiffly and shuffled out the door into the hall.

"Allie," Rhea called from down the hall. Allie's chest warmed as she took in Simon ushering Rhea toward her.

She moved, stopping in front of them. "I was worried when I woke, and you were gone."

"Just stretching my legs." Rhea patted Allie's hand. "Simon was nice enough to walk with me."

"It was no trouble," Simon said, smiling affectionately at the woman. "The hospital has prepared the discharge paperwork. If you're ready, I'll get the car."

Allie took Rhea's hand and squeezed, meeting Simon's gaze over her head. "Thank you."

He winked before striding ahead of them and out the door.

"I'm feeling much better this morning," Rhea confided.

"That's good, but don't get any ideas about doing work when you get home. It'll be nothing but Netflix and chill for you for the foreseeable future, and on that note." Allie reached for a wheelchair and rolled it around to face Rhea. "Sit."

Rhea chuckled, dropping heavily into the chair and Allie slid behind her. They made their way through the lobby to the emergency room exit.

"I've been wanting to watch season three of The Witcher, but I haven't found the time." Allie patted her shoulder. "I won't be watching season four, though. Henry Cavill is the only Geralt of Rivia for me."

"You'll need to find more shows to watch than one season of The Witcher, Rhea. The doctor said you need to stay off your feet for at least three or four weeks. Possibly up to six, depending on recovery. You better be ready to binge Grey's Anatomy or the entire Marvel cinematic universe."

"I do love Tom Hiddleston." Rhea snickered.

Allie rolled her eyes. No one watched Thor for Tom Hiddleston, but she would let Rhea have her crush. A black Lincoln pulled up and Simon sped around the car, holding the door for Rhea.

She slid into the passenger seat and gingerly buckled her seatbelt, swatting at Simon as he leaned over her. "Leave me be. I can do it myself."

"Of course, Rhea." He closed her door, opening Allie's before she could manage it.

She wasn't surprised to find her bag already settled on the seat beside her. She supposed his endless chivalry would grow on her... one day.

Rhea reclined in her seat, resting her head against the headrest, and before long, stately evergreens were gliding by as they turned onto the highway.

"Should we stop to get breakfast?" Simon asked, glancing in the rearview mirror at Allie. Rhea was snoring again. The doctor had said the medication they gave her would knock her out for most of the day.

"I have plenty of food at home." Simon made a humming sound in response. "What's that supposed to mean?"

"Do you have anything you know how to cook?"

"I've been cooking for myself for nearly twenty years!"

"Was it edible?"

Allie punched Simon in the arm. "Ow. What was that for?"

"Calling me a terrible cook. You have no idea whether or not I can cook. You insist on taking me to dinner every time we eat."

Simon was slow to respond, but when he did, his voice was thick with emotion. "Would you like to make me dinner?"

Well, shit, when he said it like that, she wasn't sure. She cleared her throat. "I mean, I had to cook for myself for most of my life. It's not like someone was there to take me to dinner when I was hungry."

"And you were hungry often, weren't you?"

Allie looked up, meeting Simon's eyes in the rearview mirror, before glancing away to stare at the blur of green flying by.

"Being hungry isn't the worst thing a person might be forced to live through."

They drove in silence for some time, Allie lost in thoughts of her childhood, her parents, and her last foster parent, Dan. Try as she might to keep that part of her life buried deep, Detective Blake and his threats were determined to drag them to the surface.

She jumped when Simon said, "What can I do?"

"I'm fine, honestly. I have a good life now. Better than I ever imagined."

They pulled into the drive and waited for the gates to Graves Estate to open.

"You'll love college. Don't let the detective scare you. Let me handle him."

Allie said nothing, chewing on her bottom lip. College had never been her dream. It was her mother's. But never finishing high school was a shame she carried with her everywhere. Furthering her education—going to the school of her mom's dreams—felt like the next step.

The car pulled to a stop, and she pushed her door open, grabbing her bag and sliding out before Simon could get there for once.

She opened Rhea's door and Simon leaned in, pulling the sleeping woman into his arms as if she weighed nothing. She stepped in front of him, unlocked the front door, and pushed it open.

Simon carried Rhea straight through the foyer and up the stairs. Allie trailed after him, closing the door behind them. She poked her head into Rhea's room just in time to see him plant a kiss on Rhea's forehead. She melted just a little.

Simon wrapped his fingers around hers and pulled her with him as he left the room. "Come on, Chef Allie, let's go find something to make for breakfast."

In the kitchen, Simon sat at the butcher-block table in the center of the room while Allie bustled around the room, making breakfast. "She'll be okay; she already seemed so much better this morning. Don't you think?" She cracked eggs over a skillet.

"Yes, she's doing remarkably well."

A beep sounded, and the toast popped up. Simon stood.

"Sit. I'm making you breakfast." Allie wielded her spatula like a sword, swinging it wildly in his face.

He put his hands up and relaxed back into the chair. "Okay. I'm sitting."

Allie pulled two plates from under the counter and put two pieces of toast on each. Taking the plates with her, she went back to the counter beside the stove and pulled the lid off the butter, digging a knife into the soft yellow substance.

"That's not butter. Don't put any of that on my toast, please."

Allie gasped. "What! This is better than butter. It's 'I can't believe it's not butter.'" Allie dug her knife deeper into the plastic container, scooping out a large glob of the yellow goo.

"Do not put that on my toast."

"Or what?"

"Or I won't eat it."

Allie dropped the butter onto the first piece of toast and slid the knife back and forth, grinning wickedly as the not butter melted and soaked into the toast.

"That's your plate."

"Oh no, this is yours. If I had to try chicken with waffles, you have to try 'I can't believe it's not butter.'"

"I refuse."

Allie picked up the buttered toast and lunged for Simon, attempting to shove it into his mouth. He dodged her easily, and she stumbled forward, nearly dropping it. She swung around and tried again, but again he was too fast, and she crashed into the counter. "Hold still so I can feed it to you!" she demanded.

"I will not ingest those toxic chemicals."

Allie pouted, dropping the buttered toast back on the plate. "Fine. Don't ask me to try any of your favorite foods ever again."

She faced the stove and scooped out two eggs dropping them onto each plate. She placed several slices of bacon on the same skillet and laid them out next to each other, cramming them together to fit as many pieces as she could. Strong arms wrapped around her, making her jump.

Simon pressed his nose to her hair and inhaled. "You smell like eucalyptus and lavender. It's a lovely combination."

"Flattery won't work on me."

He chuckled, the sound reverberating against her back. "If it means that much to you, I'll try it."

She began flipping the bacon over in the pan, ignoring the man pressed against her. "It's your loss. I don't care."

"Oh, my little firecracker is upset about this."

"Nope." Allie slid three slices of bacon onto each plate and lifted them both, turning in his loosely circled arms and wedging one plate into his chest. "Here, I made you breakfast. Enjoy it."

He released his hold on her, taking the proffered plate. "Allie, where are you going? I said I would try it."

She ignored him, taking her plate to the living room, and slouched into one of the cerulean velvet couches centered on an enormous fireplace. The imposing gaze of Alexander Graves watched as she crunched bacon. She'd considered taking his large, framed portrait down, but he had given her the house, so it seemed impolite.

She spied Simon slinking into the room but didn't face him, staring instead at Alexander as she chewed.

Simon sat beside her, looking up at the portrait. "What are we looking at?"

"This generous and kind man who probably would have liked my cooking very much."

Simon sputtered and choked, coughing.

She turned her gaze to him, arching an eyebrow. "It's that bad, huh?"

Simon set his plate down opposite her and slid closer until their thighs were touching. He lifted a slice of toast from his plate and waved it in her face. "I'm trying the butter. See?" He took a bite and chewed. "Mmmmm, delicious."

A tingling sensation started at the apex of her thighs. *Stop*, she told her lady part. *We're mad at him*. But her lady parts only cared about the heat radiating from his thigh resting against hers.

"It's the most delectable morsel I've ever tasted."

Eyebrows slanting down sharply, she turned to face him. "You're not funny."

Simon leaned closer, licking the edges of her mouth. "It tastes better on you." She squeezed her thighs together, glaring at him. "I'm imagining all the places I'd like to lick this butter off you." He licked his fingers.

Allie slid away from his warmth and stood. "You can't just seduce me into forgiving you."

Simon stood pulling her close and whispered into her ear, "Sure I can."

Sparks of electricity danced up her fingers and arms and she leaned into him, kissing his neck, sliding her tongue along the pulsing vein that ran down his jaw and disappeared into his collar. She wanted to pull the collar aside, follow its path, and find out where it ended. But Simon had her fingers laced between his, and he wasn't letting go.

She bit into the sensitive skin just above his collarbone and his answering chuckle sent goosebumps rippling down her arms.

"Take your shirt off," she commanded.

"Forgive me, and you can have whatever you want."

She frowned. She wanted his shirt off, but some distant part of her mind didn't want to forgive him, even if that was the price. He pulled her closer, leaning to kiss the sensitive skin behind her ear. She shuddered and tried to pull free from his grasp again, but his grip was like iron.

He pulled her hands behind her back and trapped both wrists in one hand.

He brushed aside her hair with his free hand, exposing her neck, and trailed featherlight kisses down her neck. She squirmed in his grasp.

"Forgive me," he breathed onto her skin as he continued to trail kisses down her neck and collarbone.

She fought harder against his hold. "Let me go. I want to rip your shirt off and feel your skin pressed against mine."

Simon straightened, looking into her eyes. "Say the words and you can have all of me."

Allie began pulling in earnest, intent on getting free. One thought consumed her. *Have him, take him, make him mine.*

A popping sound followed by searing pain running down her arm cleared the fog in her mind, and Simon released her.

She was back in the present, aware of her surroundings and the scorching pain emanating from her shoulder.

Allie screamed, wrapping her good arm around the one hanging at an odd angle. It felt misshapen and wrong. Desire was replaced by agony.

Simon was looking at her with something like horror on his face, and he repeated something over and over.

She couldn't focus on it. The pain overwhelmed everything.

Simon reached for her shoulder and, too quickly for her mind to process, he wrenched it back into its socket.

There was a moment of relief. Then there was only blackness.

CHAPTER 8

Allie

The first thing Allie noticed as her consciousness swam to the surface was the warmth radiating at her back. It soothed the ache that grew more noticeable with each moment consciousness returned to her. The scent of lavender wafted under her nose, making her smile.

"Simon?"

The warmth at her back evaporated as the bed shifted and Simon sat up, staring down at her. "How are you feeling?"

She rolled her shoulder experimentally, prepared for the searing pain from before. Instead, there was only a dull ache. "Better than I expected. I don't know what happened. It was like I was a zombie and all I wanted..." She trailed off, her cheeks flushing.

"It's not your fault. I shouldn't have pinned your arms like that. It was stupid. Reckless."

Allie lifted a hand, touching his face. "Hey, you weren't the one flailing around like a wild animal. How can a person even dislocate their own shoulder?"

Simon stood and began pacing. "I should have eaten the damn toast when you offered it. None of this would have happened. I know better than to behave this way. It's an abuse of power."

"Okay, you're blowing things way out of proportion. I overreacted to the toast thing. I can admit I'm stubborn."

Simon crossed the room and sat beside her on the bed again. "Allie, I promise I will never—"

"Hey, guys." Rhea's weak voice came from the door. Simon jumped up, going to her side, and ushered her into the room. She leaned on him, smiling. "I hope I'm not interrupting."

"Not at all," Simon said, as Allie said, "Of course not."

"It's kind of embarrassing. Allie, would you come with me to the bathroom? I don't want to pass out and hit my head on anything, but I've got to pee."

Allie sat up, surprised again at the lack of soreness in her shoulder. She had expected the pain to be horrendous after a dislocated shoulder injury, but unless Simon had drugged her in her sleep, it was surprisingly mild.

"Come to my bathroom. It's closer."

Allie took Rhea's arm and guided her into the bathroom, sparing one glance for Simon, shaking his head and mumbling, before she closed the door.

When she finished, Allie led her back to the bedroom, and they both sat on the large four-poster bed at the center of the room. Rhea looked better, the bright glow to her skin restored. There was one notable difference, though. Rhea's left eye, usually a rich brown, was black, the pupil blown wide, and rimmed in bright red, reminding her of the vampire eyes she'd read about in books.

"How are you doing?" she asked Rhea.

"I have a headache, and the medicine is making me tired, but otherwise, pretty good."

Simon came around the bed and leaned down, inspecting Rhea's eye. "We may need to get you an eye patch to give your eye time to heal."

Rhea gave a small laugh. "An eye patch to go with this head bandage. I'm a real catch."

"I don't think you'll be going on any dates for a while." Allie bit her lip to hold in her laugh.

Rhea patted her arm. "You're probably right."

"I'll make you some tea," Simon said, excusing himself from the room.

When he was gone, Rhea turned to face Allie. "What happened? I heard a bit of your conversation before I came in."

"I don't know." She rubbed her arms. "It was like I was possessed or something, and Simon was just messing around, pinning my arms behind my back, but I wanted to get free, and I pulled my arm out of its socket."

Rhea frowned. "Were you drinking?"

"No." Allie threw up her hands in exasperation, surprised again at how little the motion hurt.

"I'm not a doctor, but if you had pulled your arm out of the socket, you wouldn't be waving it around now like you are."

"I thought so too. If Simon wasn't so mad at himself over it, I would swear I dreamed the whole thing."

"It must not have been as bad as you thought."

Allie considered, remembering the popping sound and the pain that followed. She remembered Simon popping it back into place.

"It doesn't matter. What matters now is making sure you get better. How would you feel if I hired an in-home healthcare nurse? I can come home on Fridays and leave Monday mornings. Simon promised to come check on you as often as he can. But say the word, and I won't go. I can start next semester."

"You're going to college." Rhea cut her off.

"College will always be there."

"I'm fine, and if you want to throw money around hiring fancy nurses to wait on me, I will not say no. It'll be my turn to be waited on all day."

"I want you to feel comfortable. If you don't want a stranger to take care of you, I completely understand."

"Tea," Simon said, moving into the room, and handing cups out before sitting on the vanity chair.

"Simon, tell Allie she has to go to college. Tell her to stop being silly."

Simon looked up from his cup. "I won't tell Allie what to do, but I can have security installed to ensure Allie can keep an eye on you even when she's out of town."

"That's a bit much," Allie said at the same time Rhea said, "Good."

"Would you feel safer?" Allie asked, turning her gaze to Rhea.

"This big, creepy house has always freaked me out. If I'm going to be here by myself most of the time, I want all the security you two want to pay for."

Simon dipped his head. "It's settled then. I'll make all the arrangements tomorrow. And you"—he turned his gaze on Allie—"will stop putting off packing."

Allie opened her mouth to let Simon know what she thought of his bossy attitude, but Rhea squeezed her fingers, pulling her attention away from him. "Are you okay? Do you need to lie down?"

"I need to rest for a bit. Walk me to my room?"

In Rhea's room, Allie tucked her into bed and pressed a palm to her forehead. "No fever. That's good. I'll bring you something to eat when you wake up. For now, rest."

Rhea's eyelids began drooping before Allie had finished speaking. She stood and left the room, glancing over her shoulder once before gently closing the door.

Allie stopped in the hall, steeling herself before entering her room. She took a deep breath and stepped in. "I'm not—"

"Don't decide now." Simon cut her off. She closed her mouth. "You promised me a story before everything happened last night. Tell me what happened, and we'll find a solution. If he knows where you are, hiding at the estate won't keep you safe."

"Let's go down. We can talk in the living room."

Simon trailed her out of her room, down four flights of stairs, through the foyer and into the kitchen, where they stopped to grab platefuls of grapes and cheese before making their way to the living room.

She couldn't hear him, silent as he was, but she felt his presence at her back. Like a wraith, hovering just over her shoulder.

Settled on the couch, eyes pinned to her lap, she began.

"I was a senior. I only had to graduate and turn eighteen, and I would have been free. Vanessa and I shared a room. It was the only thing keeping us safe at night.

"Vanessa was at practice; I was in my room when he came in yelling, demanding I get my lazy ass up and help clean the house. Typical behavior, but I could tell he'd been drinking, and it was more than usual. It wasn't even five yet. Early for Dan.

"'Get in the kitchen and clean it before I get the belt.'

"I slid by him, giving him as much space as I could in the narrow hallway. He followed me to the kitchen and leaned in the doorway, watching as I picked up dirty plates and silverware."

An involuntary shudder rolled through her as she paused, taking a deep breath.

"The sink had just filled with water when I felt him. He pressed into me, wedging me between his thick body and the counter." She wrapped her arms around herself, digging her fingers into the soft skin on the underside of her biceps, and swallowed a lump rising in her throat.

"I tried to spin around, to push him back, but he was heavy and a lot bigger than me."

Allie looked up. Simon's brows were dark slashes drawn low over amber eyes. She took a few steadying breaths, trailing her gaze down his tailored black sleeves to the white-knuckled grip he had on the edges of his plate. "And then..." She swallowed again, clearing her throat.

"And then he pressed into me. I was suffocating under the weight of him."

She darted another glance at Simon's tight grip on the plate.

"He was unconscious. I mean, he was on fire. I don't know what happened. I don't know why he was on fire, but he slid down my back and slumped to the floor. I didn't think, just ran for my life out of that room, out of that house.

"Outside, I watched smoke fill the air. He didn't come out. I waited for... I don't know what I was waiting for, but I didn't go back in or try to save him. I just stood there on the lawn watching the flames swallow the home that had been my personal hell for almost a year.

"Neighbors came out of their houses, calling the fire department and the police. Vanessa came home. She asked me what happened. I think I was in shock. She asked where Dan was, and I said... I said I didn't know.

"That was the statement she gave to the fire department when they arrived. So they didn't go in looking for him. The whole time I said nothing. Maybe they could have saved him. Maybe they would have tried if I had told anyone he was in there."

Allie squeezed her arms, rubbing the goosebumps peppering her skin. She looked down at her lap. Her vision blurred. *I will not cry. I will not cry.* A weight fell on her, and Simon pulled her into his arms.

"It wasn't your fault."

A tear broke loose from her lashes and fell down her cheek. She steadied her breath before she said, "I wanted him to die."

Simon pressed a finger under her chin and turned her face up to his. "Wanting something and doing it are not the same. You couldn't have helped him."

Allie bit her lower lip. "If I had told the fire department or the police, they could have tried at least. I might not have set the house on fire—or him—but if I had told anyone he was in there..."

"It wouldn't have made a difference."

"It might have saved him and it would have meant I didn't look guilty as hell when they came to investigate." She unwrapped her arms from around herself and wiped a tear from her cheek. "Detective Blake came to my new foster house a few days after to ask questions. He made it clear he suspected arson. I was home, I lied to the police, and I had motive. As far as he was concerned, I was guilty."

"Suspecting something and being able to prove it are not the same. He has no evidence. This is good news."

"After he came to see me, I ran from the foster house they placed me in and hid in an arcade for a few days. That's where I met Ben. He gave me a place to stay. I didn't tell him what I was hiding from, and he never asked. Detective Blake must have assumed the worst when I ran. Why would I run if I wasn't guilty?"

"You did, and you weren't. You wouldn't be the first person." Simon laid a hand on her knee. It stopped bouncing; her nerves settled by his touch.

"Well, now you know my story. And why I can't go to Boston."

Simon stood, pacing. "First, it's not illegal to go wherever you choose if no charges have been filed. I'll find out if any have been. If not, he's harassing you, and I can warn him off. Either by addressing him directly or by bringing it to his superiors. I will bet this case has been put to bed, and he's only acting out of some personal vendetta. Has he ever contacted you after the initial meeting, apart from the text you received yesterday?"

"Yes. About a month after it happened, there was a robbery at the convenience store on the first floor of the apartment building Ben and I shared. The description the clerk gave matched mine. I had just reached the fire escape ladder when he saw me and called for me to stop. I recognized him and ran. Ben told me later I couldn't go back to that convenience store because they had sketches that looked just like me."

"Mmmm." Simon pursed his lips. "Were you guilty of that one?"

Allie sat up straighter. "No. Why would I steal?"

"No judgment; you were unemployed."

Allie's cheeks heated as a blush crept down her neck. "I didn't do it."

Simon held up his hands. "I'm only asking. This is a safe space."

She glowered at him. "I didn't steal anything... Anyway, after that, he staked out the convenience store for a few weeks.

"We only ever crossed paths one other time. A few years ago. I had gone to the lockbox Lily instructed the attorneys to advise me of. He was waiting outside. He asked a lot of questions about what I was doing there and where I had been for the past year and a half.

"I didn't answer, just kept walking, pretending I didn't hear him. I thought he would do something, hit me, maybe, but he let me go. I never saw him again after that."

Simon continued pacing. "A change of scenery is just what you need. I'll do some homework to find out if they ever filed any charges and get all the surveillance setup here, but the best thing you can do right now is get out of town."

Allie frowned. "What about Rhea?"

"The security around the estate will be enough to deter him if you're worried about the detective and I've made arrangements with the hospital. A home healthcare worker starts tomorrow. She will want for nothing."

"Except for a friend to care for her."

"Allie Graves, will you miss your house manager when you leave?"

She giggled, a bit of the tension riding her easing at his light tone. "I might."

"And what about me?"

"You're at work in your New York office more than you are here. I assumed I'd see you more in Boston."

Simon leaned down, reaching for her, and pulled her up into his arms. He spun her in a circle, dancing to some inaudible music. She laughed, letting him twirl her.

"Won't that be delightful?"

Allie's stomach dipped as he led her through some intricate dance that seemed to be from a time long ago.

And just like that, it was decided.

CHAPTER 9

Allie

"Are you sure you'll be okay? I'll be back on Friday and Suzanna has the list of all your instructions. She has my number and Simon's." Allie stood in the doorway scrutinizing Rhea.

"I'm fine. Get out of here before you miss your flight!"

"Call me anytime, seriously, even if I'm in class. I will pick up." She dodged a pillow as Rhea chucked it at the door.

"If you don't leave now, I'll eat all your ice cream while you're gone."

Allie laughed. "Fine, I'm going. Call me!" she called down the hall as she reached the stairs and descended. She hadn't been entirely sure about leaving Rhea with a stranger, but Suzanna had proved to be a more than capable home healthcare companion and she felt lighter knowing the woman would be there while she was gone.

In the driveway, she tossed her bag into the back seat of the Uber and slid in, resting her purse on the seat beside her.

"Alexandra?"

"That's me." She pulled her phone out of her bag. No messages from Simon. She'd known he had to be at work this morning back in New York, but she had expected at least a good luck text. On Simon's advice, she had blocked Detective Blake's number. She scrolled through her email, clicked on the flight confirmation, and reread it, confirming the time and terminal. Why was she so nervous? Yes, it was her first flight. Ever. But it was only a two-hour flight. The drive to the airport would be longer.

"Dropping at RDU?" the driver asked.

"Yes. Terminal two."

"Great. We'll arrive around ten am. Do you have a music preference?"

"Whatever you like is fine."

The driver nodded and turned on a pop music station. She scrolled through her email again looking for the one labeled Orientation Day.

"I know where you live, Miss Graves." She froze on the email, her fingers shaking. *Shit, shit, shit.* She hovered a finger over the title, chewed on her lip, clicked her phone screen off, and stared at the black screen. The face reflected at her was pale. He knew where she lived. Great for him. She wouldn't be there. Simon was right; she needed to get out of town. But what about Rhea? Would he go to the house, harass her, and get information out of her?

She swiped up, bringing her email up again, and clicked on the one from *him*.

"Do you think a little money is enough to buy your freedom? I will prove you did it. It's only a matter of time before you slip up again. I'll be watching."

She swore under her breath, clicking her phone's screen off again, and dropped it into her lap. Was he going to her house? Had he been there already? She picked up her phone again and swiped up clicking on Simon's name. She began typing.

"Do you think Detective Blake will hurt Rhea? Did you find out anything about him yet? Read this email. I'm sure it's from him."

She opened the email again and forwarded it to Simon. She stared at her phone, waiting for a reply. He was always busy when he was in the city, but surely he would answer something this serious. She tapped her nails against the armrest lifting her gaze to the window.

"Going somewhere fun?" The question brought her out of her thoughts, and she blinked, looking into the rearview mirror.

"I'm going to visit my boyfriend." She wasn't sure why she lied, but the idea of telling anyone her plans seemed like a bad idea. She was seventeen again, on the run, and she had to get out of there fast.

"That's nice. Going for the week?"

She inspected the driver more closely. Why was he asking her so many questions? "No, it's a quick trip. Just there and back."

He nodded, seeming to sense her mood, and said nothing else.

She glanced at her phone. It had been over half an hour and still nothing from Simon. She huffed. Where was he? Well, he wasn't the only one who could do research. She typed into her phone's search bar: "Detective Jason Blake."

Article after article filed onto her screen.

"Detective Jason Blake retires from Atlanta PD."

"*'Please Don't Shoot'* One witness account of the night Atlanta PD Detective Jason Blake shot youth, Raid Williams."

"Kayla Williams' tearful plea for justice."

Allie clicked the last one.

A Fox Five news video appeared on her screen. She watched as the reporter described the events leading to the fatal shooting of a thirteen-year-old boy. The shooter, identified as Police Detective Jason Blake, gave this statement. "It was dark. I had no way of knowing what he intended. He ran at me, and I fired."

The news anchor turned to Kayla Williams, who responded, tears in her eyes, saying, "It's been over six months and my son's killer is still free and walking the streets. While my son..." She paused, working to compose herself. "My baby will never walk the streets again."

Allie watched all of it. The additional details shared by the news anchor, Kayla's mournful cry for justice, and the five-minute montage of her son's brief life told through photos. Allie swiped a tear from her cheek as the video ended.

So why was he after her? She clicked the share icon at the top of the page and sent it via text to Simon. Where the hell was he? She spent the next hour and a half scanning the internet for any other information on Detective Blake. Most of the articles were from around the time it had happened and the immediate public backlash. Around six months ago, he disappeared. So why come looking for her now?

Her phone dinged. Finally! She swiped her screen open to find a message from a five-digit number.

"We look forward to welcoming you tonight to orientation dinner. Check your email for additional information. Reply Y to continue or STOP to opt out of future messages."

They pulled into the terminal drop-off lane, and she slid out, pulling her backpack with her.

"Thank you," she called to the driver as she closed the door. He gave a curt nod and pulled away.

The airport was large, but lines moved quickly and soon she found her gate and sat, sliding her phone out to check one more time. Nothing. Was she seriously going to board the plane without hearing from him?

"Now boarding flight five-one-seven with service to Boston, Logan International Airport." She stood, hoisting her backpack onto her shoulders. The line moved slowly and as she boarded; a thrill ran through her as she stepped into the narrow aisle. Finding her seat, she maneuvered past a mother and son and wedged herself into the window seat.

"Good morning. This is your captain. We have clear skies and perfect weather for flying. We'll be in the air shortly. Flying time is approximately one hour and fifty minutes. The weather in Boston is a cool thirty-seven degrees, so I hope you brought your jackets." The pilot chuckled into the intercom.

Good thing she had checked the weather before packing. Boston was having some sort of freak cold front and had hit a record low for August.

Allie reached into her bag and pulled out the brand-new AirPods Simon bought her. She swiped her phone up, searching for a new true crime podcast she'd begun listening to called *Going West,* and clicked on the most recent episode. Mary Lands.

"Mary left her home in two thousand and four and was never seen again."

Closing her eyes, she swallowed, doing her best to focus on the words rather than on her body pressing back into the seat as the plane rose. Digging her nails into the armrests, she dared a glance out the window, seeing nothing but white fluffy clouds.

Then they were leveling out, her stomach settling as the pull of gravity lessened, and she could almost imagine they were floating. Her shoulders loosened, dispelling some of the tension she'd been feeling since she'd received that text. Why was he after her? What did a disgraced police officer want with her after all these years?

She peered out the window again, spying dazzling azure blue sparkling in every direction, the occasional cloud barring her view of the vast ocean. She often forgot how close she lived to the beach. From up here, it was hard to imagine how anyone could forget that something so immense dozed nearby. A slumbering beast that might be woken at any moment to ravage the land and everything on it if it so chose.

Allie removed an AirPod in time to hear the pilot's announcement of their initial descent. She packed them in her bag and gazed down as the city came into view. In many ways, it looked like her current home. White sailboats, freight ships, and other boats dotted the vast blue horizon.

As the picture came into focus, she saw the differences. Where Bath was rural, with more trees than buildings, in Boston, buildings crowded together in every direction as far as she could see. As the ground rushed up to meet her, she noted the old-world style of many of the structures intermingled between newer, sleek ones. A network of gray lines weaved throughout them, all seeming far too narrow for cars from this height.

Something about it was beautiful, even from this distance, and for the first time since deciding to go to college, excitement blossomed in her chest.

As the plane touched down, she took her phone out and switched off airplane mode. She opened the most recent text from Simon. Nothing.

Unlike RDU, Logan International Airport was bustling with activity. All around, people seemed to be in a hurry. It was nothing like the leisurely pace she'd grown used to in Bath.

She loved it.

Pressing open the door to the outside world, she wrapped her arms tightly around herself as she was blasted by the frigid morning air.

She dropped her bag and dug through it, pulling out the flimsy jacket she had packed. It wouldn't be enough. She slid her arms in and zipped it to her neck, shivering at the chill clinging to her limbs.

She scanned the signs for arrivals then saw the Uber line and strode toward it, widening her steps.

"Need a ride, firefly?"

The smooth voice stopped her dead in her tracks, and she turned, squealing. "You're here!" She ran to him, flinging herself into his outstretched arms. He caught her, spinning her as they hugged.

"Did you think I'd leave you to handle your first day all on your own?"

"Is this why you were ignoring me?" She released him, stepping back.

Simon ran a hand down his thick black coat. "I wanted to surprise you." Simon wrapped his fingers around hers, pulling her close again. "Your fingers are like ice. Come on, let's get in the car." He led her to a black Lincoln town car and held the door, taking her bag.

He pulled the driver's side door open, tossing her bag into the back seat. "I was driving from New York when your texts came in. I don't believe in texting and driving. Aren't you happy to see me?"

She was happy. More than happy, and something about that grated on her. She had only known him a few months and already it felt like she needed to share every moment with him. It was her problem though, not his. She reached for his hand, lacing her fingers between his.

"Thank you for picking me up."

Simon squeezed her fingers, grinning. "Anything for you."

Allie rolled her eyes, but she knew he meant it. Every time she doubted him, he reminded her he could be trusted, and he wasn't leaving.

"Is this your first time in Boston?"

"Yes! I have no idea where I'm going."

"You don't have orientation until four. Would you like to see the city first?"

Warmth spread through Allie's chest. "Yes!"

CHAPTER 10

Allie

"I 'd like to take you to my favorite place in this city."

Allie nodded as they pulled into traffic.

She stared out the window, taking in every sight. An underground tunnel, lit only by flashing yellow overhead lights, opened to a new world. Gothic old buildings sandwiched between modern new hotels lined either side of the street. Once in a while, she spied slices of aquamarine glittering between buildings.

They drove into a second tunnel and emerged on the other side with a view of Boston's downtown. To her right, endless blue littered with white ships of various sizes dotted the horizon. To her left was a network of buildings surrounded by moats of cobblestone or brick sidewalks.

They passed signs for North End and West End and turned onto Newbury Street.

Shops and restaurants of every kind were wedged into old brownstone buildings as far as the eye could see. As they glided by, she tried to read each sign, but there were too many crammed together, fighting for space.

"This is Newbury Street. My favorite place in all of Boston," Simon said, grinning.

Allie saw why. A person might spend a week here and never explore every store or restaurant.

They stopped beside a tiny space between two cars along the narrow street as Simon expertly maneuvered into a spot.

Allie reached behind Simon's seat, grabbed her bag, and pushed her door open, smiling triumphantly, but scowled when Simon's hand came down and pulled her out.

"How do you always make it to my side of the car so fast?"

Simon winked and didn't release her hand when they exited the car. A slight pink warmed her cheeks as he clasped her fingers and pulled her along. She tried to shake him loose, but his grip only tightened.

"You will have to get over your aversion to PDA. I intend to ravage you in front of everyone."

Her blush warmed to a bright crimson as she averted her gaze from people passing them on the sidewalk.

"They heard you," she whispered.

"They'll see me too." He waggled his brows, a slight skip in his peppy step.

They moved briskly, but so did everyone else. In Boston, people had places to be. They stopped next to a fenced patio packed with patrons sipping coffee, eating pastries, and mingling with one another.

"It's freezing out here." Allie wrapped her arms around the thin fabric of her jacket, pulling her hand free from Simon's.

"It's fifty degrees. This is not cold weather for Boston, but we'll need to get you warmer clothes. You won't survive the winter."

Allie eyed him skeptically. "How cold are we talking?"

"No need to worry about it now. This week is a fluke. The weather will be beautiful next week. Seventies and eighties every day. Shall we find you a better jacket now, or would you prefer brunch first?"

"Definitely brunch."

They stepped into a cute coffee shop more crowded inside than outside and stood in a long line. Allie glanced around, taking in the room. A glass cabinet featuring brownies, mini cheesecakes, eclairs, and other desserts she had no name for stole her focus.

They found space on a brown leather bench with the smallest table she'd ever seen and slid in beside the other patrons.

When someone had come by to take their order and their food arrived, she leaned back, glancing around the room. "It's more crowded than I expected."

"It's just Boston. During the school year, there are two hundred and fifty thousand extra people here. It's always crowded, but at the start of term, it's bursting at the seams."

Allie shot her neighbor a withering look, but he didn't seem to notice as he laughed and spoke animatedly to his group. His flailing hands almost knocked her fork from her mouth when his story came to its conclusion. She tensed, preparing to say something when Simon slid a hand over her thigh, dragging his fingers dangerously high, and all her focus zeroed in on their path.

"We could always get a hotel room for your first night in the city. You don't have to sleep in your dorm."

Allie darted a look at the tables beside them. No one seemed to notice his inappropriate behavior, but it didn't stop the flaming heat that stained her cheeks and ran down her neck.

She grabbed his fingers, intending to pull them away, but sparks danced over her fingers and instead, she began pulling his fingers up, guiding them to the apex of her thighs where the burning had begun.

Tugging his fingers farther north, she slid the band of her pants down, but before she could do more, he pulled his fingers from hers and embarrassment flooded through her.

She jumped up, knocking the table aside, sending the last of her hot chocolate tumbling across the plate with her mini cheesecake on it.

"Oh shit. Sorry." She reached for it, but Simon got there faster, catching the cup before it clattered to the floor. "I'm sorry. I don't know what happened."

Simon turned away from her, taking the cup to a bin in the corner, and placed it on top of other dirty dishes. When he turned again, his face was set in some dark expression she couldn't read, but it smoothed as he reached her.

"Come on, let's find you a coat."

The heat of her shame crept up her neck, burning her cheeks. Had she really been about to slide his hands into her pants in the middle of a coffee shop in front of all those people?

Simon didn't wait to see if she followed as he strode from the coffee shop. He held the door, ushering her through, and gave her a wide berth, careful not to touch her.

What was wrong with her? Something about Simon always had her acting like a horny teenager.

Extreme bursts of jealousy or insatiable desire; she always burned hot when he was around. But he had started it, right? He had been the one to slide a hand up her thigh. Why was he mad at her?

She'd walked several blocks before she realized she had stopped noticing what stores she passed. She looked up. H&M. They would have jackets. She pulled the gold door handle, noticing Simon made no effort to help. He stood behind her, brooding silently with his hands stuffed into his pockets.

Fine. If he wanted to be mad, let him. He was the one making promises of ravishing her in public, and now he wanted to act all high and mighty. Like his covert touches were preferable to... whatever she had done.

She weaved through racks until she reached a corner full of jackets. Finding long white puffer jacket, she pulled it off its hanger and slid it over the thin jacket she already wore. It was a size small, but it was still big. Good. A large bubble jacket would put distance between them. She went to the register and stood in line.

"I'm sorry," Simon whispered in her ear, sending a shiver down her spine.

She turned to face him. "What are *you* sorry for?"

He pulled a hand from his pocket, running it through his chocolate locks, longer now than it had been at the beginning of the summer. *I like it longer,* she thought absently as she watched him struggle to find the right words.

"I was happy to see you, excited about you living closer to me. I got carried away."

"Next guest," the cashier said, turning her around. She slipped off the jacket and handed it over. "Did you find everything all right today?"

"Yes. Thank you," she mumbled as she dug in her purse for her wallet. Simon handed the cashier his card.

The woman gave him a brilliant smile swiped his card and passed the receipt and credit card back to Simon.

Allie rolled her eyes. "Let's go, babe."

Simon quirked an eyebrow at the new endearment, but followed her to the door, this time holding it open for her. She marched down the street, her stomach a tumult. Was he mad, was he not? She stopped at the passenger side of his car.

Simon came up beside her and pulled it open.

Had she just been standing there waiting for him to open it? "Stupid," she mumbled, sliding into the passenger seat, and tossing her bag and new jacket into the back seat.

Simon slid into the driver's seat and turned to face her. "Allie, this attraction you have for me; it's unnatural."

"What!" She flushed scarlet. "I thought..." She choked on her words. Her eyes stung, and she reached for her bag, leaving the jacket on the seat.

Simon wrapped his fingers around her arm before she could grab it. "Allie."

She wrenched her arm from his grasp. She had to get out of his car.

Turning away from him, she flung the door open and jumped out. She stumbled into a broad chest and looked up through bleary eyes.

"Allie. That came out wrong. I meant to say... I mean, can we just talk in the car instead of out here on the street?"

He wrapped his arms around her, but she backed up, working to get free of his hold.

"Let me go." She wriggled in his arms.

"Please," he breathed.

She sucked in a sharp breath. "I said let me go." She meant to sound confident, but it came out like a plea.

Simon loosened his hold but didn't release her. "Allie. I love you."

She blinked the tears aside, looking into his eyes for the first time since this fight began. "What?"

He searched her face. "I love you, and I want to be honest with you."

She swallowed. "Okay."

She was trembling, and he rubbed up and down her arms. "Please, get back in the car. Let's talk."

She was in shock, but even that hadn't been enough to curb the sudden spike of fear the words *let's talk* sent through her.

Simon pulled her door open, leaving one hand on her back. She slid back into the car, feeling a chill that had nothing to do with the wintery air.

Simon dropped into the seat beside her as she faced him, clasping and unclasping her hands in her lap. He reached for her fingers, taking them into his own, and pressed a kiss to each one.

He looked up, their eyes meeting. "It may sound odd, but I can think of no better place to start than at the beginning."

Allie's stomach did somersaults, but she said nothing as she watched him squeeze her fingers between his own.

"I was born in 1922."

A hysterical laugh bubbled up in her chest. "What?"

"I know how it'll sound but let me tell you everything and you will understand."

She had a hundred things she wanted to say, but her muddled mind couldn't form words, so she nodded.

"I was born in 1922, in Bath, North Carolina, and I died in 1940."

Allie ripped her fingers from Simon's grasp. "Is that supposed to be a joke?" She slid farther away from him in her seat. "Because it's not funny."

"I know it's hard to believe, but I promise you it's true. Magic brought me back to life."

"Magic?" she sputtered.

Simon turned in his seat, angling himself to face her. "Have you ever noticed strange things related to water when you're upset?"

"Strange things like what?"

Simon licked his lips. "Like, pipes bursting, leaks in sinks, rain."

"Rain when I'm upset. Seriously..."

"What about fire? Have there ever been any unexplainable instances of fire in your life?"

Allie's mind conjured images of a man slumped over her, burning. "You know there have," she whispered. Ice spearing her stomach. "Are you suggesting magic started that fire?"

"I'm telling you; you are a witch."

Allie stared for one long moment at the man she had thought she was falling for and knew now *this* was what she had been waiting for. The proverbial rug that he would sweep out from under her.

"I know it may be hard to accept, but I'm asking you to think about every strange thing that has happened to you. Can you say with certainty you experienced nothing strange when it occurred? No headaches, no heat in your veins?"

Headaches, she knew something about. Those had plagued her from childhood. Heat in her veins? There had been a time once when she had been berated and belittled at the table for fifteen minutes; when she was sent to her room to think about her actions, she'd stood, wrenching her chair back and black scorched fingerprints remained.

That was the day Dan started calling her... a witch. Her lip curled. "I'm not a witch." She reached for her door handle, the metal warping under her touch. What the hell? She stepped out of the car and sprinted down the street.

Hot tears stung her cheeks as she ran blindly. Was it true? Had she done that? Had she killed Dan? She staggered into a woman mumbling apologies. She slowed to a walk, swiping at her cheeks.

"Are you okay?" a man asked.

"She's fine," Simon growled from behind her.

She whipped around to face him, hovering a few feet behind her.

"Why are you following me?"

"You didn't let me finish my story."

"You accused me of murder!" A few people on the sidewalk stepped out of her path, glancing in their direction.

"Having the ability and having intent are not the same." Allie opened her mouth, but Simon said, "But if you had intended it, I would not have judged you for it."

His words from the other night came back to her. His promise to end Dan if he were still alive. The way he had peeled his fingers from imprints left behind on the steering wheel.

She gasped. "Are you a witch?"

"There are other things besides witches."

Ice ran down her spine, and she glanced around again. "What are you?" she whispered.

"I can't tell you that." Simon stepped in closer, leaning down to press his lips to her ear. "But it's nothing good."

She shivered. "If you're not good for me, I shouldn't be here with you."

"I didn't say I wasn't good for you." Yellow flames danced in his eyes. They were like liquid fire.

"Simon, your eyes... They're gold." Her breath caught as she stumbled backward.

His arm shot around her, too fast for comprehension, and he steadied her.

"What the hell was that?"

"You've been noticing things for weeks. I knew it was only a matter of time before your magic woke again."

"Again?"

He pulled her close to him and she let him, less afraid of his strange yellow eyes than she ought to be. A memory was niggling at the back of her mind, struggling to break free.

"It's called an Obscura spell. It's meant to block memories, but the spell has never been strong enough to hold your memories back forever. Your magic is too powerful."

He wasn't making any sense, but she tasted the truth of his words. "Let's say I believe you. I am a witch. If you died eighty years ago, what does that make you? A ghost?"

He chuckled low in his throat. "Something a bit more corporeal."

"A vampire?"

"It wouldn't be the first time you called me that."

"It wouldn't?"

Simon shook his head before dipping to her ear again, whispering, "I meant what I said before. I love you."

His words burned in her chest, searing her lungs, making it hard to breathe.

A moment ago, she was sure he had accused her of murder. Now she thought he might be some undead creature, but he loved her. This strange, beautiful man loved her.

She slid her hands into his hair and pulled his mouth to hers. Their lips met, and hers parted for him, letting him drink her in. Someone shouted a curse at them. She ignored it.

This man, whatever he was, was hers and he loved her.

CHAPTER 11

Allie

Simon pulled back, his yellow eyes meeting hers. She felt a bit dazed. His kisses had never left her this light-headed before. Her vision blurred and light danced across her face, tiny sparkling particles floating in the air. She watched them swirl lightly in the breeze.

Without thinking, she lifted a hand and twirled her wrist. All the tiny sparkling dots spun into a whirlwind around her fingers. She puffed her cheeks, releasing it, and watched them form into the shape of a heart. It was as easy as breathing.

Simon's lips parted. "I should have mentioned your air magic first."

Her gaze focused, returning to his face. The beauty of his smile was blinding. Something in her chest ached to look at him.

"You're alive."

Simon's movements calmed to a predatory stillness. "Rebecca?"

She blinked. "Who?" Simon opened his mouth, choking on some unspoken words. Was this what flustered Simon looked like? No, he was afraid. "Who is Rebecca?"

His features settled into the mask he wore when he didn't want to tell her something. "Just an old friend. Why did you say I'm alive?"

Her brow furrowed. "You told me you died in 1940. I'm looking at a living, breathing man."

His intake of breath was slight, but she hadn't missed it. Something she said had scared him.

"Let's go back to the car. You're shivering."

She let him lead her through the growing crowd, watching as he moved confidently between them. He stood taller than most of the people they passed, but then, so did she.

They reached the car, Simon holding her door for her, and she dipped her head, dropping into her seat. She rubbed her arms for warmth. In less than a second, Simon was opening his door, sliding into his seat.

"Okay, I'm not imagining it. You move really fast."

Simon gave her a wide grin. "I knew you could see my true form again!"

"What do you mean again? Why do you keep saying that?"

He reached for her fingers, wrapping his hands around them. His warmth trailed like lightning up her arms. He dropped her fingers, leaned behind his seat and pulled out a pair of gloves. "Here, put these on."

She eyed the gloves. "You could turn on the heater."

His smile fell. He slid his key into the ignition and the car purred to life. "It will take some time for the car to warm up. Please, put them on."

She reached for them, sliding them on, feeling the soft leather between her fingers.

He pulled one gloved hand into his lap, lacing their fingers. "This part may be hard for you to believe," he began.

She squeezed his fingers. Should she tell him it was *all* hard to believe?

"Alexander was my creator and your great-great-great-grandfather. He was a witch. Besides creating me, he also placed a curse on your family line that wiped your memory of all magic. I've known all the women in your family for the past eighty years. Each of them fought his curse and eventually remembered they had magic. For each of you, it was always just a matter of time."

Allie swallowed. He was really invested in this story.

Something about his words soured in her mouth, though, tasting untrue; not a lie, more of an intention to mislead. "You said you weren't a ghost; what are you?"

Simon's eyebrows dipped low. "I know I'm asking a lot, but there are some things I can't share. Can you trust me when I tell you I'm not a witch, but I'm not dead?"

She resisted the urge to pull her gloved fingers from his grip. He was still keeping secrets. "Can you tell me why you can't tell me some things, but you can tell me others?"

She stared at him. Those strange yellow eyes that had not returned to their natural dark amber should have unnerved her, but somehow, they seemed more at home on his face than his brown eyes ever had.

"It has to do with my job. The people I work for require complete anonymity."

"Are they magicians?"

Simon squeezed her fingers tighter. "I cannot breathe a word about them."

Allie pursed her lips. "So you're not my lawyer?"

Simon blew out a breath, his accompanying chuckle ruffling the curls around her face. "I'm your lawyer. I've had my practice since 2008."

"Are they clients, then?"

Simon released her fingers, twisting his wrist to check his watch. "I wanted to show you more of Boston before orientation today. Can we drive while we continue this conversation?"

Allie nodded and Simon put the car in reverse and backed up before putting it back in drive and wheeling out of their compact space.

They passed a sign for South Station, and Simon pointed to it. "This is where you'll need to go when you want to take the train to New York." He glanced over at her before he said, "If you still want to see me."

They turned onto Beacon Street, and she peered out the window to her right as a swath of green appeared right in the middle of the city. Her heart sank as they passed the park and turned left. Soon, they pulled into a parking garage and parked.

Allie scowled at Simon as he appeared at her passenger side door, swinging it wide and holding his hand out to her. "So, you're not going to pretend to move at human speed anymore?"

"I always moved at this speed. You just didn't notice before. Your senses were dimmed, as most humans are to my kind."

"And what kind is that again?"

Simon smirked. "I would tell you if your very soul wasn't at stake."

Allie rolled her eyes. "You're so dramatic." She took his hand, letting him pull her from her seat.

When they stepped into the bright sunny day, her light jacket was enough to hold the receding chill at bay. It was warming to a beautiful day.

"You brought me to a cemetery?"

"Not just any cemetery. This is the third oldest cemetery in Boston. The earliest burial here was in 1660."

"*Fascinating.*"

"Come on," Simon said, pulling her up to a plaque in front of the ancient-looking cemetery.

She sucked in a breath. "Are you buried here?" A sick feeling twisted in her gut. Seeing a gravestone for the man holding her hand might be too much.

"The last person buried here died in eighteen-eighty. I'm not *that* old." Simon laughed. "I brought you here to show you something you might find interesting, though. Do you see that headstone right there? The tall dark gray one pointed at the top?"

Allie stared at the sea of faded, gray, broken headstones. "Um. Maybe."

He leaned over the low chain, pointing again. "Right there."

She peered left and right before stepping over the chain and onto hallowed ground.

She looked over her shoulder, raising an eyebrow. "Coming?"

Simon hesitated a moment before following her, carefully stepping around the places where bodies rested deep below.

"You won't squish them." She laughed.

"I was buried once. I have an appreciation for their plight."

Allie stared down at her feet, dread pooling in her gut. She stepped around the patch of earth she was on, careful not to step where a person's remains might lie.

When she reached a tall gray headstone, she stopped beside it. "It's too faded. I can't tell what it says."

Simon wiped a hand across the stone, running his fingers over its marred, faded surface. "This one belongs to one of your ancestors."

She leaned closer. "I can't read it. Is it a Graves?"

"Your ancestors are from Greece. You probably don't know much about them but having spent many years with your great-great-great-grandfather, I learned a bit about your past. Before they became Graves, your family name was Gravas and before that, they were called Gavras.

"Yours is an ancient bloodline. It dates back to the Byzantine Empire. They were considered royalty once. But as with most royal families lost to history, they were nearly wiped out. Killed by rival aristocracy. Those who survived escaped to Greece and Turkey and changed their names. The ones who went to Greece took the name Gravas and later Graves.

"Those who went to Turkey adopted the name Kavraz. This tomb"—Simon rested his hand on the cold stone—"marks the resting place of a Kavraz."

Allie moved closer, but the words were not discernable to her eyes. "How can you tell?" she whispered.

"Alexander did extensive research on his family history and sometimes sent me to track down leads. I can assure you; this was much easier to read fifty years ago."

"Fifty years ago." She gaped. "What else did he learn about them?" She moved around the headstone to stand beside Simon.

He reached for her hand again, pulling her closer. "Come, let's leave the cemetery. My favorite park in Boston is just this way." They walked in silence, both careful not to disturb the dead.

When they crossed Park Street, they stepped into a manicured park with circular paths leading around a historic-looking fountain. People sat on blankets, sunning themselves or reading, others played Frisbee or walked their dogs; everyone was enjoying the sunny, warming day.

"Alexander hailed from the Greek side of his family. They were widely known for their adeptness with water magic. But Alexander's relative, Nicholas Gravas, did not possess that skill. He had fire magic and made his way to Europe to study there, honing his craft, but the magic he practiced was dark. He experimented with blood magic and—" Simon choked, coughing.

"Are you okay?" Allie asked, patting his back. They stopped in front of a large pond while he worked to catch his breath.

"It seems I can't say more about it." He sucked in air, wheezing.

"You mean the magic won't let you?"

"My employers."

She bit her lip. "He practiced dark magic. Leave it at that. What else can you tell me about my family?"

"Nicholas married Linda and together they had a daughter. What Nicholas didn't know, would never know, was that Linda's family, long ago, came from the Kavraz line. One legend said the original Gavras family carved their place in history through the use of magic. They were believed to have incredible abilities, not only fire and water but also earth and air. The four elements combined could be used to manifest unimaginable feats.

"When the family scattered, so too did their gifts."

Allie pulled Simon to a bench and tugged him down. "Let's sit. This seems like it's going to be a long story."

Simon swiveled his wrist around, checking his watch again. "We have about an hour before we need to leave. I don't want you to be late for orientation dinner."

Allie slid back in her seat. "Will this story take an hour?"

Simon wrapped an arm around her shoulder and squeezed. "I'll be quick."

Allie's lips tipped up. If there was one thing she knew about Simon, it was that his stories were never quick.

"So as I was saying, Linda's family descended from the Kavraz line in Turkey. Her side manifested air and earth abilities, with the occasional person showing some abilities with water.

"When Linda gave birth to Adalaide, it shocked them to discover her magic seemed boundless. She could manipulate air, mold earth, control water, and her strongest gift of all, fire, eclipsed her father's by far. While Linda adored her child, Nicholas was jealous. Ada had everything he wanted and more. Even with enhanced abilities due to his practice of dark magic, she surpassed him.

"At sixteen, her powers were so great, they began to draw unwanted attention. More than that, Nicholas's jealousy was becoming an uncontrollable rage. When Ada nearly died at her father's hands, Linda took her and hid.

"In 1842, Ada had twins. If she knew who the father was, it was never documented, and the babies took their mother's last name. In 1845, Nicholas found Ada and Linda. According to Alexander's note, Ada killed her father. There is no record of Linda after that. Alexander assumed she had died that day too."

Allie shifted uncomfortably in her seat. "My ancestors killed each other?"

"I think Nicholas was a terrible man, made worse by the corruption of the—" He choked again. "Dark magic. They had a family heirloom that amplified their abilities. Alexander believed when Ada killed her father, she acquired it."

"What was it?"

"I can't say. But I will say that I don't believe it's the heirloom that made him bad, merely his use of it." He gagged a little on the last words, frowning.

"Let's get something to drink," Allie suggested.

Simon nodded, attempting to clear his throat as he stood. She wrapped her gloved fingers in his, realizing she hadn't taken them off. She reached for the glove, pulling at the tips of her fingers.

Simon reached for her hand, stilling it. "Leave them on for a bit."

"I'm not cold anymore."

"Please, firefly, just a while longer."

She relented, letting him swing her hand between them like a pair of children. She attempted to smother the grin working its way across her face but couldn't hold it back.

"Adalaide had the object, and she gave it to her son, John. John kept it until 1905, when Alexander visited him on his deathbed. That was when Alexander obtained the heirloom. That and the old journal Nicholas found and continued writing in."

Allie stopped walking, turning to face him. "So Alexander was evil too?"

Simon furrowed his brow, pursing his lips. "He was not a good man."

"Did he make you carry out his evil plans?" She quirked her lips into a grin, but Simon remained grave as he continued.

"His purpose for making me was in search of his eternal immortality and nothing more. I was a byproduct of that quest."

"Then he did it. You're immortal, right? Is he still alive too?"

"He was never sure of how he made me. He didn't know how to duplicate the process on himself."

"So you're the only one? The only immortal, whatever you are."

Simon opened his mouth. Closed it. He tried again. "I can't."

"I don't understand why you can't tell me about this. What does it have to do with your employers?"

Simon continued walking, pulling her with him. "What indeed."

They stepped off the sidewalk, left the park, and crossed the street. He pulled her into a corner convenience store, and she took in the shop. It was the cutest convenience store she had ever seen. Not one square inch of space was wasted. Narrow aisles were overflowing with snacks, treats, and drinks.

The entire back wall was laden from floor to ceiling with a diverse wine selection.

She left Simon trailing a hand along the bottles, thinking it would be nice to buy one to share with her new roommate tonight, whoever she might be. The selection here was impressive, crammed into the small space and exponentially better than what she would have found in the old convenience store she frequented in her neighborhood in Atlanta.

She stopped in front of the Pinot Noir section and scanned the top shelf. She had learned all the best options were at the top. The cheap options, the ones she might have perused just three months ago, already tasted foul when she attempted them. How had she become such a snob in only three short months?

She selected two bottles, one from California and one from France.

Simon came up behind her, resting a hand on her waist. "You're buying wine from California?"

She turned, her narrowed eyes taking in his expression. "Just when I think I'm becoming too snobby, you remind me I could always be worse."

He laughed, pulling the bottles from her grasp. "As the lady wishes." He turned, taking the bottles to the cash register.

"I'm paying for those." She called after him. "Those aren't for you!"

Simon ignored her, tapping his card on the card reader as she reached the counter. She rolled her eyes, swiping the paper bag holding her purchases from the cashier.

"Thank you," Simon said to the cashier as she stalked to the exit.

He reached for her paper bag, but she ducked away from him, dashing back to the parking garage and, turning the corner, sprinted for the car. She arrived at the passenger side door at the same moment she heard it beep, signaling it was unlocked, and shuffled her bags to her left hand, reaching for the door handle. She ripped it open and dropped into her seat.

Simon was sitting in his seat when she looked over. "You're the only woman I've ever met who would make it a game to avoid my help."

She beamed at him triumphantly. "I won. That's all that matters."

He patted her knee, turning his yellowed-eyed stare on her. "Are you ready to see your new school?"

CHAPTER 12

Allie

A llie peered around Simon as she got her first glimpse of her new school.

"You're missing the best part. Look out your window." Allie swiveled her head to stare out her passenger side window.

"It's just the ocean. I've seen more of the ocean since arriving than I have in the past fifteen years."

"Don't you think it's nice, though? Water surrounds your campus on three sides."

"I guess." She turned back to her left, staring at the rows of buildings. "Look at that. It's all glass. It looks like a four-story staircase."

They turned into a parking garage and followed arrows in a circle until Simon found a spot. Allie flung her door open before he finished putting the car in park and leaped out. "I win again."

Simon moved around the car at dizzying speed and kissed her cheek. "Good job."

Wrapping his arm around her waist, they left the garage and followed signs for Campus Center.

"Beacon Beginnings" and "Welcome Students" banners hung overhead as she stepped into the main campus building for the first time. People in blue and white shirts littered the hall, greeting those in normal clothes, directing them this way and that. She found a registration table and stopped in front of it.

"Hi, I'm here for freshman orientation."

A perky-looking blond girl smiled brightly and handed her a packet. "There's a map inside with directions to everything you need on campus. Orientation will be held in Ballroom B. Orientation begins at four and dinner will be at six." She turned her attention to Simon. "Are you here for orientation too?"

"I'm just here to support my girlfriend." Allie's stomach did a little flip.

"I'm sorry, only students are allowed at orientation. You can meet her after dinner."

"I won't get in the way. I'll just wait at the back." Simon gave her a wink and one of his more charming smiles. The girl smiled back, her cheeks growing pink.

"Students only. But you can hang out down here."

Allie squeezed Simon's arm, pulling him away from the table. "Could you keep your flirting to a minimum on *my* orientation day?"

Simon turned that same smile on her. "I was only trying to get into your secret orientation meeting. What do you think they'll do in there that's so private?"

"You've only succeeded in getting yourself an invitation to her dorm room. Knock it off." Simon's eyes were bright. "Are you sure no one else can see your eyes?" she whispered, eyeing students as they passed by.

"Unless there are any other especially powerful witches here today, we're safe."

She slid her gaze over his shoulder to a student who had stopped and was staring at them. "Keep your voice down," she hissed.

Simon gave her a lazy smile, but Allie wasn't looking at Simon. She was watching the girl who was staring at them. "Shit. She's coming over here. She heard you." Simon turned. "Don't look!"

Allie froze as the most beautiful girl she had ever seen stopped in front of them. She had emerald green eyes that sparkled as if she knew a secret, and it delighted her to keep it. Long golden-brown waves of hair tumbled down her shoulders, obscuring the light dusting of freckles splashed over her face and arms. Her bronze skin, a much deeper tan than Simon's, made her appear sun-kissed even in this cold place.

To say she stood out among the sea of bleached masses would have been an understatement. She gleamed like a radiant beacon and now that Allie had caught her breath—regaining some of her composure—she noticed she wasn't the only one who had noticed her. All around them, people stole glances, and some openly stared. She was oblivious to it, though, confident as she held her shoulders straight. Allie realized the girl was nearly as tall as she was. The three of them stood taller than most of the other students in the hall.

"Hello. Are you going to orientation?" Her strange accent was melodic, capturing Allie in its enchantment.

Simon was eyeing her warily, his dark brows drawn low. "Allie darling, can I speak with you for a moment?"

"Mm-hmm," she said absently, not moving. Simon tugged her arm, encouraging her to go with him.

"I'm so sorry. I haven't introduced myself. My name is Sophia."

"I'm Alexandra."

Simon tugged harder. She backed up a step, but her gaze never left Sophia's face. *Sophia.* It was like melting sugar on her tongue. Sweet, addictive. She wanted to drink it and feel the taste of it as it rolled down her throat. *Sophia.*

Simon stepped into her line of sight. Allie blinked, her eyes watering. Her head pounded, and she stumbled back. Simon caught her, holding her tight as he led her out of the building, into the fresh air.

She took a strangled breath before she began sucking in lungfuls of air, her chest heaving as if she was swimming upstream, fighting for air. "What the hell was that?"

"That was a witch." Simon rubbed circles on her back as her breathing returned to normal.

"What did she do to me?"

"It's called a siren song. Only a very powerful witch can do it. I have no doubt you could if you learned to harness your magic. It concerns me, though, that she will be here with you on campus."

Allie leaned into him, breathing in the scent of lavender. It calmed her. "Well, I'm not going back in there without you. What if she does *that* again?"

"She can't call you unless you make eye contact. Don't make eye contact with her, and you'll be fine."

Allie eyed Simon, eyebrows raised. "Is that supposed to be my plan for the next four years? Keep my head down. Don't make eye contact with anyone."

Simon wrapped his arms around her, squeezing. "You've worked too hard to get here to let one witch scare you away. My girl wouldn't let another witch chase her away that easily. I can teach you a few tricks to help you avoid her."

"Maybe we *should* get that hotel room tonight."

He pulled back, tucking a stray curl behind her ear. "Were you still debating? I thought I had convinced you to stay with me tonight."

Her stomach dropped, and she took a step back. Memories of that morning in the coffee shop flooded her. "I honestly didn't know what you wanted to do after this morning. You were... upset." She swallowed the lump rising in her throat.

He slid a hand along her cheek, cupping her neck, and pulled her closer. "I was never upset with you. I was upset with myself." He breathed the words along her neck and kissed the sensitive skin just above her collarbone. "How could I ever be upset with you?"

She crooked a finger under his chin and pulled his mouth to hers. When he kissed her, it felt like he meant the words he'd said earlier in the day, and for this moment; she let herself believe it.

When Simon pulled away, his lips were swollen and pink. She ran a finger over his soft skin, marveling at the warmth of them. Definitely not a ghost.

Simon's lips parted, and he nipped at her finger. "You'll be late for orientation." She shuddered, dropping her hand, and looked over his shoulder. The hall, previously filled with students, was now deserted. No sign of the witch who had ensnared her. "I'll be right here when you finish. Just avoid the witch for the next few hours, and we'll come up with a plan."

Allie smiled, watching his beautiful puffy lips as they moved. Of course, she could do this. She had faced far worse monsters in the foster system. She could handle one girl. One striking, dangerous girl.

She reached for her bag and pulled out her phone. The screen read 4:16 pm. "Shit. I'm super late. Okay, see you after!" She sprinted away from him into the building. The perky girl in blue and white watched her sprint by.

"You're late."

Gee thanks, she thought as she ran. She found ballroom B and flung the doors open. She stepped into a room silent except for the woman standing at the podium.

A resounding clang boomed through the room as the door crashed shut behind her and every eye in the room turned to her. Heat radiated up her neck and crept up her cheeks as several hundred sets of eyes fell on her. Her shoulders hunched, shrinking under their scrutiny. A few students snickered.

"Take your seat," a voice erupted from the microphone at the front of the room. She jumped, moving to a seat at the back and sliding into it. After another pregnant pause, the speaker continued, and Allie buried her head in her hands.

"Don't worry about it. No one will remember that tomorrow."

Allie lifted her head. That strange melodic accent could only belong to one person. She cast her gaze to the floor immediately. "Don't talk to me," she hissed.

"I'm sorry about earlier. I didn't mean to trap you. I was just so excited to see another witch at this school. I don't have complete mastery of my gifts yet."

Allie kept her eyes trained on her shoes, studying the laces. How did this work? How sure was Simon she couldn't be ensnared if they weren't making eye contact? She fumbled around in her bag, pulled out her phone, and found Simon's name in her chat history.

"Please, can we start over, Alexandra?"

Allie's fingers hovered over the keys. One text from her, and Simon would burst in, prepared to rescue her. Was that really what she wanted? Not only because it would be the second embarrassment on her first day, but also because she wasn't sure she liked this new Allie she was becoming. Since when did she need a man to save her? She didn't need him to fight this battle for her.

"I go by Allie," she whispered, still not making eye contact.

"I go by Sophia." A hand slid into view just below her nose.

She reared back, looking up and accidentally making eye contact with the witch. "Shit," she seethed.

"Allie, I promise you, you don't need to be afraid of me."

"Fool me once, shame on you. Fool me twice, shame on me."

"I shouldn't have been able to ensnare you so easily. Has no one in your coven taught you protection spells?"

Allie's head snapped up again. Sophia's dazzling smile caught her focus. She dropped her gaze to her shoes. Why had she fallen for that?

"It's time to pair into groups by major," the presenter at the front of the room announced. Allie darted to her feet, staring straight ahead. "Sciences will go with Brooke," she was saying. Allie trained all her focus on the presenter, blocking out any peripheral images of the tall, tan girl beside her. "Undeclared and general studies are with Brian." Allie stepped into the aisle and moved to stand with a group of other undeclared majors.

She slid her gaze to the left and felt her stomach drop as she spied wavy golden brown hair brushing against her jacket sleeve.

"I don't know about a major," the voice whispered conspiratorially as if they were in on this cosmic joke together. Allie ignored her, facing Brian.

He started moving, and the group followed. Allie raced ahead of a red-haired student, putting space between herself and the other witch.

They took the stairs to the second floor as Brian explained that each of the buildings on campus was connected through a catwalk on the second floor. Allie looked to her left, watching waves roll across the darkening water.

"It reminds me so much of home."

Allie stumbled, before regaining her footing and kept her focus on the window, gritting her teeth. "I'm not your friend. I don't want to be your friend. Please leave me alone."

"I see. You are not one to trust. What can I do to prove to you we can be friends?"

Trust? Trust! Where Allie came from, you didn't trust someone after they attempted to siren you. She picked up her pace. Sophia did the same.

"Look, I don't need a friend like you," Allie said, whirling to face her and stopping in the hall.

Several students staggered to a stop behind them as Sophia stopped too. When the two didn't continue with the group, the other students moved around them.

"Someone must have really done a number on you," Sophia said, planting a hand on her hip. "Haven't you ever had a mistake? I don't get any other chances. It was just the one?"

Allie bit her lip, but she mirrored Sophia's stance, placing a hand on her own hip. "It's *made* a mistake."

The line of Sophia's brow smoothed as the corners of her lips turned up. "Made. Right. I must have sounded terrible." She huffed a soft laugh.

Allie's eyes crinkled at the edges, and she grinned. That one minor slip had reminded her this girl, dangerous or not, was in a new place and probably just as nervous as she was.

She was trying, and Allie had been nothing but rude. "Let's start over. I'm Allie. We can be friends if you promise not to siren me again." She held out a hand.

Sophia took it. Her fingers, rougher than they looked, gripped Allie's tightly as she shook her hand. "Sophia, and I promise." They grinned at each other; hands clasped.

"Ladies, the tour is this way," Brian called from the end of the hall. Allie released Sophia's hand and turned to catch up with the group. Sophia strode beside her, matching her pace. Allie flitted another glance at the girl.

Had she just made her first friend in college? And it was another witch?

CHAPTER 13

Simon

"I want answers, Zophiel. I did not agree to this." Simon paced the roof of the residence hall. It was the tallest building he could find where he would still be within hearing range of Allie should she need him. He wasn't sure why Allie had been able to ascend when she needed to speak with the angels during her time as a reash and he wasn't, but climbing a tall building was as close as he could get.

He ran a hand through his hair, snagging a finger in his tangled locks as he dropped his hand to his side again.

"We agreed if you were to continue to interact with Allie, you would be forbidden from sharing certain information. You accepted that."

"I consented to not mentioning you, Gabriel, or the other angels. I guess I understand why demons are part of the bargain, but you've restricted me from sharing basic information about her past. I never agreed to that."

"It is too dangerous."

Zophiel's white robe fluttered on an invisible wind as she hung suspended a few feet above him. He swatted at the cloth as he marched by. "How am I expected to protect her, to keep her safe from the dangers in this world if I cannot arm her with any relevant information? Just today, she met another witch."

Zophiel dropped lightly to the ground, resting a hand on Simon's arm. "You can tell her anything you like about her magic, just not the demons who have the potential to power it. That includes the amulet."

Simon crossed his arms over his chest. "When is Gabriel returning? I need to speak with him. I've seen no trace of Elizabeth these past three months. She's planning something. I'm sure of it."

Zophiel's ethereal beauty didn't mask the concern marring her features. He was fairly certain she couldn't lie. Or perhaps she simply wouldn't. Either way, that she had not disclosed where he was, was troubling. Three months ago, he was so ingrained in Allie's life she dreamed of him. Now, when her life was in real danger, he was nowhere to be found. They were hiding something from him. But damned if he knew what it was.

"Simon, you are more than capable of protecting her."

"I can't be in three places at once," he cut in. "You have me chasing down every demon within a five-hundred-mile radius, and I have her to watch over at night, and my business to run during the day."

"She will be much easier to protect now that she is in Boston."

"Yes, but I'm still watching Rhea as well. That makes four places I have to be at once."

"We will lighten your reash duties until Rhea recovers. This I can offer you."

Simon rubbed a hand over his face. "I need Gabriel here, watching my back, watching over Allie, in case Elizabeth returns. *When* Elizabeth returns. You know it's only a matter of time."

Zophiel sighed. "Heaven knows he would be here if he could. I will speak with Raphael. He may be able to lend a hand."

Simon gave a curt nod. "If he would keep an eye on Rhea, I'll handle the rest."

"I will see what can be done. But Simon, you must teach her how to protect herself. Her best defense will be in her ability to use her magic." Simon nodded again. He turned, prepared to depart. "Simon, it has been only three months. You cannot continue like this. You will not survive eighteen years. And you can protect none of them if you are dead."

CHAPTER 14

Allie

Allie spied his tall, dark form casting its shadow across the sidewalk before the blackness of the ocean swallowed it. She bolted for him, a skip in her step. He caught her with ease, spinning her around, before pressing a soft kiss to her lips.

"How was it?"

"There was a lot of dancing and singing, but I got to see the library. It's huge. It puts the one at my house to shame, and the dining hall was massive, but the food choices weren't great. I'll be stocking up on lots of snacks at the grocery store."

Simon smiled as she told him about her evening, but it didn't reach his eyes. "What's wrong?"

"I'm just tired." He cupped her cheek. "I'm glad you had a good evening. No more trouble from the witch?"

"About that. She's not as bad as I thought. She offered to help me create a defensive spell. It will protect me from any other witch's compulsion." Simon's grip tightened on her arm. "Ow. That hurts." She pulled free of his grasp.

Something in his eyes sparked, but he released her. "I'm so sorry. I didn't mean to hurt you."

"It's okay." She rubbed her arms. "Let's just go to the hotel. It's getting cold."

"Shall we drop some things in your dorm, or would you prefer to do that tomorrow?"

"We can do it tomorrow. Right now, I need a hot shower and a glass of wine." Simon slipped his fingers between hers as they made their way back to his car.

Allie followed Simon through the bright lobby into the elevator. As the doors closed, he pulled her close. She rested her chin on his shoulder, breathing in the scent of lavender and Simon. He brushed the hair from her neck. "I'm proud of you." His soft breath tickled the edge of her ear.

She twined her fingers through his hair and pulled his head up, brushing a kiss across his lips. "It'll be nice knowing you're so close," she said into his mouth. "I'll miss Rhea though…" Rhea! How had she forgotten to check on her all day? She released Simon, stepping back to dig through her bag. She pulled out her phone and found Rhea's name on her contact list as the elevator dinged. Simon stepped out, grabbing her bag. She followed as she pressed send and listened to it ring. Once, twice, three times, four.

"Hey, it's Rhea. Leave me a message." She dialed again. On the fourth ring, it went to voicemail.

"She's probably sleeping. I'll check the camera feed when we're in the room," Simon called over his shoulder.

Allie dialed again. "I haven't heard a word all day. She would have texted if she was going to bed for the night." She tapped her foot, listening to her phone ring.

Simon slid the room key into the door and pushed. Allie followed him in, hanging up as Rhea's phone went to voicemail for the third time. "Wow." She stopped at the door, taking in the space. Slanting windows devoured half the wall on two sides. A central fireplace stood between a study and a dining room with a TV mounted above it. Large, tasteful art pieces hung around the room.

"Did you rent the penthouse?"

Simon chuckled. "No. Just a suite."

"Why? We're only here one night."

"I thought I might stay for the week. I can work from here this week."

She stepped into the room and spun in a circle. It was the most beautiful hotel room she had ever seen. She crossed to an enormous set of double doors and slid one to the side. "One bed," she called.

"Did we need a second?"

She grinned over her shoulder. "I suppose not." She stepped into the bedroom and flung herself on the bed, sinking into white mountains of cotton and goose down. "Why didn't I think of getting a new mattress for my bed?" she shouted.

A blur moved across her vision, and Simon was above her, leaning in before she registered the movement.

"Shit, that was fast," she breathed.

"You have no idea how fast I am." His smile was devious.

She pressed a hand to his chest and pushed. He dropped beside her on the bed. "Have you been holding back? Acting more human for me?"

"Why don't I show you?"

Allie rested a hand against his chest once more, pressing him back. "Hold on Romeo. I need a shower and wine."

"I think you smell wonderful just as you are, but if it's wine you want." He was gone before she could reply. In moments, he had returned, two glasses in hand. He twisted the top from the wine bottle and frowned at it. "This is what you get when you buy wine from California."

Allie laughed, swiping a glass from him. "Fill me up. I'll be the judge of this wine's caliber." Simon quirked an eyebrow, pouring a perfect six-ounce pour. "Come on, we're not in a restaurant." She made a clicking sound and tipped her glass. He obliged, pouring another several ounces into her glass.

When he had poured for himself as well, they clinked their glasses. "To your new adventure," he said as he dropped beside her once more, not spilling a drop of his red wine. "Let me check the camera feed from today. Have you heard from Rhea?"

Allie swiped her screen up. "No. I'll try her again." Simon set his wine on the bedside table and tapped furiously on his screen until he was viewing footage of the various access points to the house. Allie leaned into him, watching as he sped through scenes. "You can't possibly see everything that happened today when you scroll through it that quickly."

In response, he began scrolling faster. The screen blurred into a dark blob. She gave up and rolled to her stomach. She pressed Rhea's name again, listening to it ring on the other end of the line.

"Hello?" Rhea's sleep-addled voice sounded far away.

Allie blew out a breath. "You're okay! I was worried about you. I haven't heard from you all day."

"Mmhhmm."

"Are you sleeping?" Allie sipped her wine, a grin breaking over her face.

"No. I'm awake." The faintness of her voice and its distance from the phone told Allie all she needed.

"Okay, go back to sleep. I'll call you tomorrow." Rhea's silence on the other end of the line confirmed it. Allie laughed, ending the call.

"Only Suzanna, the healthcare worker, in or out all day. All clear at the Graves' Estate," Simon said.

Allie peered over her shoulder at him. "Well then, get over here and make good on your promise."

With exaggerated slowness, Simon set his wine and laptop on the bedside table and twisted to face her. She giggled, biting her lip as she peered over her shoulder at him.

He lifted a hand; trailing light fingers up the back of her calf. Even through her pants, shocks of electricity danced over her skin. His light touch continued north, making her shiver. He reached the bare skin between her shirt and pants, slid his hand under her shirt, reached for her waistband, and flipped her over.

She wasn't prepared for it and her glass flipped with her, but Simon caught it with one hand and set it on the bedside table beside his own glass.

"Now you're just showing off." She laughed.

"You asked me to show you what I can do." He pulled her onto his lap, sliding his hand into her pants, warm fingers inching beneath her panty line. His touch heated her skin, sending sparks down her stomach straight to the apex of her thighs.

She leaned back, giving him better access. The feral grin that spread across his face had wetness pooling in her panties. Her breath caught as he moved with unimaginable speed, pulling her pants off and burying his head between her thighs too fast for her to track.

A groan escaped her as he slowed, rolling his tongue languidly over her sensitive skin. Her eyes closed as she fell back, lost in the sensations he elicited from her. Strong arms slid under her thighs as he cupped her butt in his palms, pulling her to the edge of the bed. She wrapped her legs around his shoulders, rolling her hips in time with his tongue. His hands slid around to her hips and dug into her soft skin.

She bucked against his hold, creating more friction between her legs. The sensitive nerves at the apex of her thighs buzzed to life. As pleasure built, threatening to explode, his speed increased, and his name spilled from her lips as the sensation carried her over the edge.

"More," she groaned. "Show me more."

Her legs dropped to the floor as Simon disappeared, the lights in the room going out. He was back in an instant, his weight pressing into her as he kissed along her stomach, sliding her shirt up to kiss the small scar below her breast.

She pulled at her shirt self-consciously, attempting to cover it.

"Don't hide yourself from me," Simon said, gently tugging her hand free. He pressed his lips to the uneven flesh, sliding a hand down her thigh and slipping one finger into her warmth. She gasped, fisting his hair, and pulled him up so their mouths met. He slid his tongue inside her mouth as his fingers slid in and out of her. He added a second finger, circling his thumb over the already tender nerves at her core.

Her discomfort ebbed away as she sucked on his bottom lip, digging her nails into his shoulder. The taste of her own arousal lingered on his lips, adding to her pleasure. He lifted himself, breaking their kiss.

In the dark, she felt rather than saw as he stood, nudged her thighs apart and dropped his pants. Only his outline was visible, the blackness swallowing the details she longed to drink in. Yellow eyes blinked up at her, unearthly and new.

She only had a moment to consider them before he was on her again and the hard length of him plunged inside her, filling her, and making her moan.

What began as a slow, gentle rhythm quickly moved into a dizzying pace. Her moans turned to screams of pleasure, but he kept up his brutal pace, and she felt herself falling into ecstasy only to reach a climax again.

When her body was numb, every ounce of pleasure wrung from her, her throat dry, she sighed, contented. She had never been sated so completely in her life.

Simon dropped beside her on the bed, pressing a kiss to her shoulder as her eyelids drifted closed. He wrapped his arms around her, nuzzling his nose against her neck as he pulled her against him.

"Good night, firefly."

Cold air prickled Allie's bare flesh, rousing her, and bringing her back to consciousness. She was on top of the sheets, naked. She cracked her eyes open, blinking into the darkened room.

"Simon?"

No one answered.

CHAPTER 15

Allie

*M*oonlight filtered through branches, casting eerie shadows across the girl's face. The thin sliver of light drained the world of color in the gray of night, leaving only the yellow of the child's eyes. Allie watched as she approached, stalking closer. As she moved, her shadow stretched and grew. The child before her, only seven or eight, was bleached white, and pale straight hair hung down her back.

Allie tried to move, to cry out, but her limbs were stone. Terror like she had never known gripped her, piercing through her chest. As icy tendrils trailed up her spine, she tried to open her mouth; to scream.

The child closed in, her fingers lengthening into claws. Her shadow became a living thing stretched into the shape of some dark creature, its eyes glowing bright red. The shadow's clawed hand swiped at her shadow, and she stared down in horror as red beads of blood welled on her arm where the shadow being had struck her shadow.

Ripping her arm free of the invisible hold, she flung up a hand, casting a blue ball of fire, and flung it at the girl. Her small, doll-like features contorted into a cruel smile, and she stalked closer. Allie spread her fingers wide and another ball of blue flame erupted at the center of her palm. As she widened her fingers, it grew.

The pale being halted, wary now. Allie's gaze moved from the child to her monstrous shadow. She looked to her own shadow, watching as the ball of flame in *her hand shimmered in her shadow's hand and the blue leached from her palm, dripping onto her shadow's hand.*

The girl's grin fell away as she whipped her head between Allie and her shadow. She turned to run, but Allie flicked her wrist, and her shadow did the same, sending the ball of flame into its dark counterpart.

Unearthly screams erupted from its black lips as it shriveled and winked out. On the ground, the child huddled in a ball, transforming before her eyes. Where the girl had been, a woman lay curled, moaning in pain. Allie lifted her palm again, this time wielding a spear of water. She plunged it into the woman's chest, watching as she convulsed and choked on the ground.

The woman shook, smoking, and the smell of acrid flesh invaded Allie's nostrils as a new shape emerged from the haze. Blackened and charred, a creature unfurled to its full height.

Allie lifted both hands, balling them into fists. The ground shook, and the creature staggered before straightening and lurching forward, stumbling over writhing branches as they erupted from the earth until tree roots surrounded it.

It clawed and screamed, but as some roots wrapped themselves around it, others speared its limbs and body, holding it in place. Its cries gurgled and died as root after root punctured charred flesh. It slumped, its head lolling against a tree branch.

As its mouth fell open, dark, insubstantial mist poured from between cracked, bleeding lips. The shape solidified into a grotesque, misshapen form resembling a woman. As it gained shape, red eyes narrowed to slits and a banshee's howl tore from its lips.

It hurtled itself at Allie. She twirled her wrist, blowing fiercely, and a blustering gale tore through tree branches catching the creature. It spun in place, trapped within the walls of her wind tunnel. "I willlll killl yoooouuu!" it screamed.

Allie flew up in bed, drenched in sweat, her sheets soaked. She blinked, looking around the room. Blinding daylight streamed in, reflecting off every surface. She held up a hand, shielding her eyes, and looked at the indentation on the bed beside her, her forehead creasing.

Had she dreamed that she'd awoken in the night to find him gone?

Wiping a sheen of sweat from her brow, she pulled a damp tendril of hair loose. On second thought, maybe it was a good thing he wasn't there. She slid from the bed, groaning at the wet outline she had left behind. Hurriedly, she began ripping blankets and sheets off the bed and crammed them into the corner, tossing the duvet cover over the pile.

Had the sweat soaked through the sheets? *Ugh.* She ripped the liner from the bed and shoved it under the duvet. Then stumbled into the bathroom and turned the shower faucet to its hottest setting. When the mirror fogged, she stepped into the shower, turning it down just a touch, and let the heat roll down her sticky, sweaty skin.

Her phone buzzed in the next room. She ignored it, reaching for a mini shampoo bottle. The scent of roses permeated the steamy space. A vision slammed into her like a punch to the gut, doubling her over.

She slouched into the wall as she was dragged under.

She was in her room at the estate, propped by pillows, knees bent. Pain such as she had never known ripped through her as she leaned forward in the bed, breathing hard. A nurse sat beside her, rubbing circles on her back.

"Deep breaths," the nurse encouraged. Her back seized as another wrenching pain tore through her. "It's time to push," she said.

Allie lifted a shaky hand, reaching for the nurse's and squeezed. Tears streamed down her face. She drew in unsteady breaths, preparing herself for the next spasm. If the recurring shocks of pain searing through her hadn't given it away, her round belly would have been enough of a sign she was in labor.

She screamed as the next contraction sent scorching flames of pain down her back, and she dropped her head on the pillows, sweat sliding along her temple.

"Push now, Rebecca," the nurse coaxed.

Through the haze of pain, the name registered in her mind. Rebecca. Was it a coincidence?

Her thoughts scattered as another contraction stole her breath and pressure built between her legs, threatening to overtake all conscious thought.

"Almost there, Rebecca. Give us one big push."

She pushed, straining muscles in places she didn't know she had, and a shudder ripped through her followed by sweet relief. She rested against the pillows again, on the verge of mindless oblivion, when a wail pierced the air, rousing her.

"It's a girl," the nurse said, and she pressed a warm, swaddled object into her arms. Allie peered down at the miniature human trapped within her arms and felt a tear in her heart. Never had there been anything more perfect, more pure.

"My immaculate child," she said without meaning to. She spoke again. "I will name you Sarah."

Allie blinked, pressing a shaking hand to the shower wall. Cold droplets pelted her pruned skin, waking her from the dream. She staggered, her knees knocking together as she pressed both hands against the wall. She twisted the faucet, a chill racking her the moment the water stopped.

She swayed on trembling legs, stepping onto the plush rug outside the shower, taking deep, steadying breaths. Reaching for a towel, she wrapped it tightly around her pebbled skin, grabbed a second towel, and wrapped it around her head. She stumbled to the bed and fell onto it.

Echoes of the immense pain she had suffered clung to her like a second skin. She slid a hand between her thighs, prodding tentatively at the sensitive flesh. Although it was tender, it was nothing she couldn't chalk up to her activities last night. No torn skin or blood.

The air in the room changed, the hairs on her arms rising and a slight ringing began in her ears. She froze, listening. Everything told her there was danger here, but she couldn't say what it was. The faintest scent of sulfur hung in the air, and she had the sudden feeling of déjà vu.

Slowly, she slid her hand from between her legs, scanning the room for anything she could use as a weapon.

"I brought breakfast," Simon said as he slid the doors to the bedroom apart. She let out a breath she hadn't realized she was holding. The sulfur smell dissipated, overwhelmed by Simon's lavender scent. The ringing had intensified though, and she pressed her fingers to her temple, rolling them in a circle. Simon dropped

97

onto the bed beside her, his features etched with concern. "What's wrong? Is your headache back?"

She nodded. "Could you close the curtains? It's too bright."

Simon stood and a blur of motion stopped in front of the windows, sliding the first set of curtains closed. He continued at that speed until the room was plunged into near darkness, the only light seeping through between cracks in the curtains.

"Thanks. This headache is killer." She reached for the bedside light, twisting it until her side of the bed was dimly illuminated. Simon returned to her side and wrapped his fingers around hers.

"Your skin is like ice."

"Something strange happened in the shower. I had a vision or a daydream or something where I was having a baby." Her mouth twisted in a humorless grin at the implausibility of such a thing. "But," she said, pressing her teeth into her bottom lip, "in my daydream, they called me Rebecca." She looked up, gauging his reaction.

His face was blank. *A mask.* He was only ever *that* devoid of emotion when he was hiding something. Her brows pinched as she continued. "When the baby was born, I held her and felt... I can't describe it. It was like nothing I've ever experienced. When I spoke, it was like someone else was speaking for me. She, I, named the baby Sarah." Allie rubbed her bare arms. "Then I was back in the shower and the water was cold. I must have been in there for a while."

Simon pulled her into his warm embrace, wrapping his arms around her. Her shudder wasn't entirely from the cold as the image of that perfect cherub's face swam into focus and seared itself into her mind.

CHAPTER 16

Allie

Allie waved to Simon as he sped away. She would need to figure out public transportation in this city at some point. She couldn't rely on him forever. Swinging her bag over her shoulder, she strode for the steps. Although regular classes didn't begin until the following week, she'd expected at least some people to be hanging around on the second day of orientation. Where students had littered the sidewalks and grassy areas yesterday, today the silent stillness as she moved up the steps had her stomach doing somersaults.

She pressed the doors to the Campus Center building. They didn't budge. She pressed harder, wedging her shoulder under the edge of the door handle. Nothing. She stepped back, craning her neck to peer up. She yanked the doors, but they were stuck tight. Had she gotten it wrong? Did day two of orientation take place somewhere else off campus?

She pulled her phone out of her bag. An unread message waited on her screen. She pressed her finger to the five-digit number and read, "*In an abundance of caution, due to unforeseen circumstances, all activities are canceled today. All campus buildings apart from student dormitories are temporarily closed. Check your email for additional details.*"

She closed her texts and opened her school email account. There, she found several Beacon Alert emails. She scrolled through each.

"6:13 a.m. - BeaconAlert - Police Activity in and around the Healey Library building. Please avoid the area."

"7:17 a.m. - BeaconAlert Police Activity in and around the Healey Library building is still ongoing. Please continue to stay out of the area until further notice."

"8:31 a.m. - BeaconAlert - Dear Students, due to events on campus around the hours of 5:30 a.m. - 6:00 a.m., all campus activities will be closed until further notice. Please continue to monitor your email for updated information. Orientation activities will be postponed until further notice. Student dormitories will remain open, including dining facilities and study pods. On campus, students may not have visitors or guests and it is advised that students seek alternative housing if possible. All on-campus residents will be restricted to the areas deemed resident housing only and a curfew of 8 p.m. will be in effect effective immediately. Should grief counseling services be necessary, please contact 617-252-1900.

Thank you,

Chancellor Suarez-Orozco"

"Excuse me. You can't be here."

Allie looked up to see a police officer approaching at a clipped pace. She dropped her phone into her bag.

"I'm sorry. I just saw the messages. I didn't know the campus was closed today."

"You'll need to return to your dorm, ma'am," he said, ushering her toward the residence halls.

She turned from the officer and strode to the East Residential Hall. Now was as good a time as any to check out her new room.

She stepped into the building, assaulted by the sounds and smells of bodies packed tightly into small quarters. The floor was crammed with students huddled in groups, staring at phone screens or laptops. She passed them, edging around students lying on the floor or sprawling across chairs and stepped over bags strewn across walkways, to the elevator, and pressed the button for the seventh floor. It was just her luck that they'd placed on the top floor.

Seven-oh-one. At least she had the closest room to the elevator bank. She slid her access card into the reader and waited for it to turn green. Pressing against the door, she jumped back when a bag swung at her head, dodging out of the way with reflexes she wasn't aware she possessed.

"Hey!" she shouted.

Emerald green eyes grew round as tanned arms fell slack and Sophia rushed forward, crushing her in a bear hug. "I'm so sorry. I thought you were the killer coming to get me."

Allie struggled for breath. "The... what?"

Sophia released her, stepping back. "Come in. Close the door."

Allie moved into the room, closing the door behind her. Sophia backed up, jumping up onto her bed. "I've been going mad in here by myself. Thank goodness you came. I was worried I'd have to spend the night alone with a killer on the loose."

"Killer. What are you talking about?"

Sophia ran her fingers through long strands of hair, brushing her mane over one shoulder. "You haven't heard about the murdered student?"

Allie gaped at Sophia. "No. I just got here and found the doors to the Campus Center locked. What happened?"

"I don't know the details, but students are being asked to stay in the dorm rooms today while they investigate. This morning at breakfast, one of the TAs told us a student was murdered last night. They found her in the library."

Allie covered her mouth. "Do they have any idea who did it?"

"I don't want to scare you, but I believe it was a witch."

Allie pursed her lips, glancing down at her shoes. She trusted Sophia not to use compulsion on her again, mostly, but the word reminded her she shouldn't completely let her guard down.

"Why?"

"The TA said the police described the student's death as a drowning."

Siren. The word came to Allie unbidden. What weapon would a siren use to murder someone if not water? She looked up, locking eyes with the green-eyed witch.

"We're roommates."

Sophia blinked. "Yes. I knew that when you told me your name. Didn't you get the email with my information when you were assigned the room?"

Allie chewed on her bottom lip. "I'm not the greatest at reading emails."

Sophia laughed. It was a deep, rich sound that matched the timbre of her voice. "I never checked emails before coming to school."

Allie moved to the bed across from Sophia and sat. "How did someone drown in the library?"

Sophia pulled a strand of freshwater pearls from under her shirt. "They said it looked like the girl was brought in from the bay."

Allie's nose wrinkled. "Why would someone bring a body inside after killing them?" She wasn't an expert, but if she'd learned one thing from her true crime podcasts, it was that people usually tried to hide their victims, not bring them to a public place where someone could find them.

Sophia shrugged, giving an involuntary shudder. "Why kill them in the ocean rather than using a gun or knife if they wanted everyone to know it was a murder and not an accident?"

Allie's lips twitched. Was Sophia into true crime podcasts too? "Well, being roommates will make it easier for you to teach me how to protect myself from compulsion. If there's a murderous witch on campus, I had better get started right away." Sophia's answering smile lit the room.

Allie wiped away the sweat trickling down her neck. She bit her tongue, trying again. Sophia made it look so easy. Effortless. She closed her eyes and concentrated on the ember she felt deep in her chest. She had never noticed it before, but now that she focused on it, following Sophia's commands, she wondered how she had ever missed it.

It pulsed in response. "How will I know when it's working?"

"You'll feel it expand until it coats every inch of your skin."

She grunted, giving another push. It swelled, warming her chest, then shriveled again. She let out a breath in frustration.

"I need a break. Let's get snacks." She stood, stretching out her legs, the tingles in her toes stinging as she hopped from foot to foot. They had been at this for over two hours, and the only thing she had managed was the mild warmth in her chest that receded the moment she stopped trying. How Sophia pranced through life with her protection up all the time baffled her.

Sophia stood, smoothing her long skirt.

Allie had only been in this city for two days, but she knew already Sophia stood out. Tan, where everyone else in the city seemed starved for sunlight and unusually tall for a woman. Her style of dress was also not suited for New England.

She wore a tiny crocheted top laced behind her back, no bra, and a white broom skirt with small teardrops cut out around the hem. A long strand of freshwater pearls was double-looped around her neck and stopped just above her exposed belly button. In the building, she would be warm enough, but if they ventured out, Allie feared she might catch frostbite.

Allie pressed the elevator button, glancing over her shoulder at the empty hallway. "Where do you think everyone is?"

"Hiding in their rooms, I suspect. It was chaos this morning."

Allie didn't blame them. She wasn't feeling too confident herself. The only thing that had stopped her from texting Simon was the knowledge that he would have come right back to pick her up.

As much as she enjoyed his company, the idea of spending the day trapped in the hotel room with him while he spent his day on calls was enough to have her taking her chances with a killer.

She was glad she had stayed. Spending the day with Sophia was turning out to be much more enjoyable than expected.

The girls stepped into the elevator and rode it to the first floor. When the doors opened, she frowned.

A crowd of students pressed into her, vying for space. She pushed back, grabbing Sophia's arm and tugging her forward. A shock zinged through her at the touch, and she glanced back at Sophia. She fought the crowd as its number swelled the farther into the room she moved.

Squeezing between bodies, she broke free into the larger space of the dining hall. In the center of the room, a man stood atop a table, holding a microphone to his mouth. "...are still unclear, but they said she was probably dragged in from the bay," he was saying to the crowd.

"Who did it?" someone shouted.

"What was her name?" someone else called.

Voices spoke over one another in a loud buzz. She stopped in a thin pocket of bodies, dropping Sophia's arm. An energy she hadn't realized was coursing through her drained away at the lack of contact. She darted another look at Sophia, who was wholly focused on the man speaking. She hadn't seemed to notice the strange energy.

"We don't know much, but I heard the police telling the chancellor there will be no activities on campus this week," he said into the microphone.

"What about next week?" someone asked.

"What about this semester?" The buzz grew louder as students spoke to one another.

"I don't know anything about classes, but I'm sure the chancellor will send out updates. If you have somewhere else to stay, I recommend going there for the rest of the week."

Allie spied a counter with just a few bags of chips and apples remaining. "Come on," she said, poking Sophia in the side. Sophia followed, weaving through the crowd. They reached the counter, finding it mostly empty, and grabbed what items remained. Sophia opened a cabinet door and found several bottled waters. They edged around the side of the room and slipped back out into the hallway.

"There's no way we're going to make it back to the elevator. The crowd is growing."

Allie lifted to her tiptoes, peering over the mass of bodies. "We probably shouldn't stay here, actually. We'll run out of food soon and getting in and out is going to be a problem." Sophia nodded, and together they pressed into the throng. "I can't get through on this side."

"Me either," Sophia called back. "Hang on, I have an idea." She cupped her hands around her mouth and called out, "Choriste ti thalassa!"

Allie's mouth fell open as the sea of people parted, leaving a path to the door open for them. Without realizing it, her own feet shuffled sideways into the crowd. Sophia grabbed her, causing another jolt to run through her, but it also cleared her mind and got her feet moving.

They strode through the swarm as it regrouped around them. Sophia pressed the door, and they stepped into clear, cool air. "What the hell was that?" Allie demanded, rounding to face Sophia.

"It was compulsion. We would not have been able to leave otherwise."

"You said you wouldn't do that again. You said it was an accident."

"I have been working to teach you how to block it all morning." Sophia arched an eyebrow. Allie opened her mouth to argue, but what could she say? It had accomplished their goal, and she *had* been trying to teach her.

"What was the electric shock when I touched you?"

"It is the call of one witch's power to another. Have you met no other witches?"

It was Allie's turn to raise her eyebrows. "Does that happen any time a witch touches another witch?"

"Like calls to like."

"Is that a yes?"

"Witches who can power share will always draw energy from one another. We share at least one elemental gift. Do you know what yours are?"

Allie thought of her conversation with Simon from yesterday. It felt like a lifetime. "Maybe fire and water?"

"Ah ha! I, too, have water. It is my strongest gift." Allie's emotions felt wildly out-of-balance today as the pendulum swung from kinship and trust to wariness and confusion. Some part of her rational mind fought against the idea that witches were real, even after everything she had experienced these past few days. She'd put that conversation with Simon in a box that she wasn't quite ready to deal with yet.

Still, she could think of no other explanation for everything and the more time she spent with Sophia, the less she could deny it.

"Let's get lunch," she suggested. She pulled out her phone, typing one of the few places she knew in Boston, into her Uber app. A chill wind whipped her hair in a cyclone of air, making her shiver. She looked up at the girl beside her, trailing her gaze along Sophia's bare arms. No goosebumps dotted her flesh. "Aren't you freezing?"

"The protection I explained to you insulates me from the heat or the cold." Sophia lifted a shoulder in a quick shrug.

This protection was creeping up on Allie's list of priorities. She pulled her cardigan tighter around her, wishing she had brought her new jacket. They made quite the contrasting pair, her with her porcelain skin, raven curls, and blue eyes, wrapped in a sweater and jeans, and Sophia dressed for the beach, sun-kissed skin, dusted in freckles and bright green eyes, with golden brown hair.

A black Mercedes pulled up beside them, the Uber sticker visible in the passenger side window. The pair slid into the back seat.

"Yeah. I already told you I'd have it by three. No, I don't have the numbers. I'll have them by three. Lenny. You're not listening." The girls exchanged glances, as they had no choice but to bear witness to the Uber driver's meeting. "Fine. Fine!" He tossed the phone into his passenger seat before swerving into oncoming traffic. Allie grabbed Sophia's hand as she let out a squeal.

Fifteen heart-clenching minutes later, they tumbled out of the car as he pulled up in front of Thinking Cup, yelling something into his phone about three p.m. They hooted with laughter as they dodged traffic and crossed the street to safety.

"I think I'm taking public transportation from now on," Allie said.

Sophia wiped a tear from the crease of her eye as they stopped in front of the tea shop, peering in at the tightly packed space. "Let's see what other options there are on this street."

Allie nodded. One crowded room was enough for today. They stopped in front of a pizza shop a few blocks later. "Pizza?"

"I love pizza!" Sophia exclaimed. They pushed in as the smell of tomato sauce and spices assaulted them. Allie stared at the menu for an eternity, chewing on her lip.

"Let me order for us," Sophia suggested. Allie dipped her head, turning her gaze to Sophia as she scanned the menu. "We will have the margherita pizza," she told the cashier. "And two limonta San Pellegrinos."

Allie slid forward, ready with her credit card for once. She handed it over, smiling smugly. Sophia didn't appear to notice. She had moved down the counter and was eyeing the pastries.

Grabbing their number, Allie led them to a table by the window.

Sophia placed her hand on the table, palm up. "Give me your hand."

Allie eyed it before meeting Sophia's green-eyed stare. "Why?"

"I'm going to show you how to power share with another witch. This is the most basic thing we learn from infancy."

Allie placed her hand on Sophia's. The shock was immediate, coursing up her arm. Where the first touch had been warm, this was frigid. It reminded her of stepping into the ocean on a balmy day. Cool, refreshing liquid streamed up her arm, running under her armpit.

A spike of fear shot through her when she felt it fill her chest, beating in time with her heart before it spread to her stomach and trailed down her right leg, then her left. It ran along her side, tickling up her ribcage before it chilled her left armpit.

It raced up and down each finger, up her arm, over her elbow, to her shoulder. The hairs on the back of her neck rose as it crept up her spine into the base of her skull. Her eyes widened, and she attempted to wrench her hand free, but Sophia gripped her fingers tightly.

Cerulean, sea foam green, and deep azure blue exploded across her vision as the world was momentarily submerged, everything cast in shades of blue and green.

As the film of color receded, returning her world to its more diverse palette, she tasted salt on her tongue and could swear the ground swayed.

Everything settled, and she refocused her gaze on Sophia. A light mist coated her skin and clung to her hair, making her look as though she had just stepped in from the rain. Sophia's lips stretched wide, dimples playing at the corners of her mouth. "You have been blessed with immense water abilities."

Allie dropped her gaze to their clasped hands, gasping. "Our hands are glowing." She snatched her hand back. This time, Sophia released her easily.

"No one can see it but us."

"Your first lesson in power sharing is this. Never release your connection with another witch while the magic seeks its path through you. If the circle is not complete, the magic will find another outlet."

"What do you mean?"

Sophia dropped her voice to a conspirator's whisper. "My cousin once severed her connection before the magic made the circle. She was throwing up ocean water for an hour." Allie drew back in horror. Sophie chuckled. "Don't worry. I'm strong enough to redirect it if you're with me. But be warned. Magic always demands balance. I may save you from such a fate, but someone, somewhere, will have to pay."

Allie blanched. "You're not really selling me on the merits of power sharing." Their phones buzzed, and they both reached for them, scanning their screens. Allie looked up first. "Classes start next week." A few days ago, the idea of delaying classes would have excited her. Now, she couldn't imagine returning to Bath to wait for news of school to resume.

Sophia lifted her gaze to Allie's. "They're still advising students to remain off campus for the rest of this week, though. Will you return to your hotel room?"

A woman stopped at their table, sliding a pizza between them, and dropped a pile of napkins. "Here you go. It's hot."

Allie thanked the woman. "Why don't you stay with us?" It was impulsive, reckless even. But leaving her alone in a strange city with a possible murderer on the loose seemed cruel.

"I don't know. Your boyfriend wouldn't like it."

Allie chewed on her bottom lip. "He won't mind. It's a big room. There's plenty of space. You can sleep on the couch in the living room."

Sophia reached for a slice of pizza. Allie reached for a slice but pulled her fingers back, hissing, "It's hot!"

Sophia smirked. "Learn to cast a protection over yourself and it will not burn you."

Allie scowled. It was going to take her more than a few hours to master that spell, but once she could, the possibilities were endless.

"I don't think I should stay with you," Sophia said around a mouthful of food.

"Why not?"

She looked up, her brows pinched as she considered her words.

"Allie, I know what he is."

CHAPTER 17

Simon

Simon tapped his foot impatiently, waiting for a reply. He pulled his phone out and checked again. Nothing. He was done waiting. Sliding his chair back, he strode for the door.

"Simon. I received your text."

He whirled. Only an angel could sneak up on him like that. He felt nothing when they appeared. It was almost as if they were a void, an absence rather than a presence. "We have an issue," he said.

"What is it?"

"Allie had a breakthrough memory. She had a memory of her time as Rebecca. You told me your gifts did not work like Alexander's spell. You told me she wouldn't remember."

Zophiel paced, her elegant white suit sleeves folding softly at the bend in her arm as she clasped her fingers behind her back. "Humans are unpredictable creatures, witches even more so. While we did not cast a spell to hold her memories back as Alexander had, the bubble we placed them in remains housed within her mind. Should she want the truth enough, she may find it."

Simon released a long breath through his nose. "I cannot keep her safe if she remembers all the things that hunt her. Can we try to refortify the hold you placed on the memories?"

Zophiel stopped in front of Simon. She gazed down at him, her iridescent eyes swirling beneath white lashes. "This is not a spell that one can simply cast and recast. We have crammed over eight decades of life experiences into the darkest corner of her mind. Getting her to Boston and away from things that may trigger memories was a good start, but if you want to ensure long-term success, you must remove as many reminders of her former lives as you can."

Simon returned to his chair, sitting. He unbuttoned one shirt sleeve, rolling it to his elbow, and repeated the action with the second. "I can't think what might have triggered the memory. And there's more. I need to speak with Gabriel."

Zophiel pursed her lips. "Gabriel cannot help us now."

He pushed back his chair, standing again. "Why not? Why all the secrecy? What aren't you telling me about him?" His nerves were frayed at the edges, all his careful months of planning and preparation deteriorating just when he had thought she would be safe.

"You know I cannot share the details with you. Would it be so bad if she remembered who she was?"

"Wouldn't it be bad for you?"

Zophiel raised an eyebrow. "You chose to remain in her life. You could have protected her from afar, and the risk of regaining her memories would have been vastly diminished. I'm afraid, with you in her life, there is a strong likelihood she will eventually remember her past lives."

"Not if I can help it." His jaw strained as he bit back his next argument. What good would it do him? She was as tight-lipped as ever and as little help as he had come to expect. "Before I forget, Elizabeth, or one of her minions, was at the estate. I'm confident they meant the attack on Rhea as a warning. To me or both of us. The metal object used on her was one of the gargoyle's claws. Elizabeth's calculating, I'll give her that. She chose a gargoyle beneath the mansion. If we had trapped a demon there, it would have slipped through the wards, given enough time."

Zophiel nodded, accepting the information, but offering none in return. "I will tell the others. Any update on her potential whereabouts may give us the advantage we need." Zophiel's form shimmered at the edges.

"One more thing," Simon said, stopping her before she could vanish. "I believe the memory Allie had was important. I'm no longer confident she has survived Alexander's death curse. I may need to make a trip to Europe, to the old Fellowes estate, where Alexander's uncle first found the book of dark magic to search for an unbinding spell."

Zophiel nodded once and disappeared. Simon turned to his computer. He had already told Allie he would stay the week, so he selected dates for the following week and searched for flights to London Heathrow. Just a short seventy-seven mile run from the Fellowes estate in Peterborough, he hoped to find what he needed and be back within the week. His phone buzzed. He pulled it from his pocket.

On my way, the text read. She was early. Orientation must have ended earlier than expected, or perhaps she had ducked out early to spend time with him.

She hadn't said the words yet, but he knew she was falling for him. Even with her memories gone, this was always their path. He was always destined to love her and she him. He just had to ensure she survived this time.

CHAPTER 18

Allie

Allie reached for Sophia, pulling her out of the car. Now that they had synced, as Sophia called it, she no longer felt the zap when they touched, instead, cooling liquid magic ebbed and flowed between their connected hands.

Sophia leaped gracefully onto the curb and fingered her long strand of pearls, mouthing something as she stepped into the hotel.

"What was that?" Allie asked.

"Just a bit of protection."

"I told you; you have nothing to worry about. Simon won't harm you."

"It never hurts to be cautious." Sophia tapped Allie on the nose as she strode past her into the elevator.

Allie pressed the button for her floor, eying Sophia. "I know we don't know each other that well yet, but if you trust me, you can trust Simon." Sophia said nothing, rolling a pearl between her fingers as she watched her reflection in the elevator mirror.

They left the elevator in silence, and Allie stopped in front of the room, digging in her bag for her access card. The door swung wide, and she looked up to find Simon grinning broadly. His gaze swiveled between the two and the corners of his mouth drooped.

"You didn't mention you were bringing someone with you." His gaze lingered on Sophia, nothing in it suggesting he was happy in the least to see her.

Allie pressed her palm to his chest, forcing him back. "Simon, this is Sophia. We met her yesterday. She's staying with us for the rest of the week. The campus is closed. Someone died."

Simon swallowed whatever he had intended to say and took another step back. He rubbed a hand over his chin, never breaking eye contact with Sophia. Allie waved a hand in front of his face.

"Did you hear what I said? Someone died at school today."

Simon turned his focus to her and wrapped warm fingers around hers. "Come in. Tell me what happened."

Allie let him pull her to the couch beside the fireplace. She glanced over her shoulder to find Sophia still motionless in the doorway. "Sophia, come in."

Sophia wasn't staring at her though, her gaze was locked on Simon. The subtle way she had widened her stance told Allie she was readying herself for a fight. She wasn't sure how she knew. Maybe all those old kung fu movies Simon made her watch.

"Sophia."

Sophia clutched her pearls, whitened knuckles straining against tan flesh. The stillness in the room was oppressive, weighing on the space, making it hard to breathe.

Allie squeezed Simon's fingers, finding him staring at Sophia again too. "Hey. Guys. What's going on with you?" She tried to infuse her tone with an airiness she didn't feel. Suddenly, she wondered if Sophia had been right to be concerned about coming here. Allie stepped into her path, blocking her view of Simon.

Sophia blinked; blinked again. "I... What?"

Allie reached for Sophia, feeling the rush of cool energy flow up her arm as she pulled her forward. "Come on, let me introduce you." They stopped in front of Simon. "Sophia, this is my boyfriend, Simon. Simon, this is my new roommate, Sophia."

She stared between the two of them as they eyed each other. Simon broke first, holding out a hand. "Nice to meet you, Sophia."

Sophia dropped her gaze to his outstretched hand and mumbled something in another language, spitting into her own before placing it in Simon's and shaking roughly. Simon grimaced, but he didn't pull his hand from her grasp.

Allie swallowed her snicker.

Simon released Sophia's hand and motioned toward the couch. "Please, Sophia, make yourself comfortable." Allie attempted to control the smile working its way across her face. He had resisted the urge to wipe the spit from his palm, but discomfort was written across his face.

Sophia moved stiffly, sitting straight-backed. Allie struggled to reconcile this version of her with the girl she had spent the day with. As she moved to sit beside her, Simon fell into a chair across from them both, relaxing into a slouch. Clearly, it would be up to her to relieve the tension between them.

She slid forward, resting her hand on Simon's knee. "When you dropped me off this morning, the whole campus was shut down." Simon wrapped warm fingers over hers. "I went to the dorms, thinking it would be a good time to check out my room, but it was a madhouse—Everyone crammed in, talking about what happened. I went to my room and found Sophia. That's when I learned we were roommates." She glanced at Sophia, who had settled back in her seat.

"How did the student die?" Simon's brow furrowed as his fingers tightened on hers.

"She drowned."

Simon darted a look at Sophia. "What do you know about this?"

Sophia shot to her feet. "Nice. Blame the witch when the devil himself sits with us. Just a stone's throw from the place it happened."

Allie stood, turning to face Sophia. "How dare you call him a devil!" She dropped a hand to her hip, squaring her shoulders to block her path.

Sophia swung her gaze to Allie, narrowing her eyes. "How can you share a bed with him? Knowing what he is? It happened in the early hours of the morning. Was he here this morning?"

Allie ground her teeth. A vague memory of waking sometime in the night to an empty bed drifted into her mind, but it was hard to grasp. It might have been a dream. "Of course he was with me."

Sophia's eyes widened, and she gasped. "You don't remember! Your sight is blocked. By him, no doubt. I should have seen it sooner." She lifted a hand, pressing her thumb to Allie's forehead, and shoved, mouthing something incomprehensible.

Allie stumbled back feeling as if she were falling. Her back hit water and then she was submerged, sinking, down, down, down, into the dark.

Images flew by. As she reached for one, it caught floating above her and she watched as a scene, foreign, and yet so familiar, played in front of her. It was her, skinnier, dirtier, wielding a sword. She slid it through a dark, inky substance, and green liquid sprayed the wall as the dark creature evaporated. The bubble popped, flooding into her mind.

Another hovered, blurry. It came into focus as some version of her from a time long past stretched her fingers over the grass in the orchard at the Grave's estate and small butterflies slid between them, exploding in a riot of color, shooting for the sky. It popped and bled into her mind.

She was shifting gears in a classic GT as she took corners on an unpaved road at speed. The bubble popped and was sucked in. More bubbles, more images. They surrounded her and displayed snippets of a time, a life that didn't belong to her and yet it did. All of them popped and flooded her mind.

Then she was choking, sucking in salty water, in desperate need of air. Her lungs filled, pressing her down, sinking her further into the cold dark. She flailed her arms in vain, waiting for the darkness and water in her lungs to take her. But as she continued to sink, bubbles surrounding her, feeding her new information, she recognized the panic for what it was and slowed her racing heartbeat, taking in calming lungfuls of water.

She touched the floor.

Bubbles swarmed her, coming so fast she couldn't see them, knowing she didn't need to. Knowing they would seep in and return to her. These were her bubbles. Her memories. They had lived within her, waiting to be discovered, restored, revived.

She sat up, sucking in even the tiniest bubbles, letting none escape, and peered around the room with fresh eyes, knowing this moment was inevitable. Knowing she would always get to this point again. And someone had tried to keep her from it.

Her eyes narrowed to slits.

CHAPTER 19

Gabriel

The darkness threatened to consume him. It was everything and nothing. The absence was enough to drive anyone to madness. It would have driven a lesser being over the edge already.

Why did I do it?

The question ran through his mind for the millionth time. His only companion in the dark.

In all his immortal life, he had never chosen wrong—not even the first time, when the pain of his choice was one-hundred-fold anything he experienced in this place.

Of all the rules imposed upon angels, there was only one that truly mattered. Yet in the moment, when the choice was clear, he had chosen wrong. He had chosen *her*.

A scraping, grinding sound began; the only method for counting time in this wretched place. Another day had passed. His tormentor approached. What new creative torture had he thought of today? It mattered little. No ache held a candle to the pain he felt every day from the absence of his Father. The myriad of creative tortures devised here were mere sufferances when compared to the complete and absolute severance of his Father's light.

A low chuckle rumbled from the dark. "You grow more pitiful by the day, Gabriel."

Gabriel's wings, once pristine, curled protectively around his battered form. His one small mercy in this place was that he could not see the sad, reduced state of them. They were often the greatest source of enjoyment for *him*.

"That's right, use those wings to defend yourself. And why you were given leave to keep them only Father knows and would never deign to tell the likes of us." The hiss of his words betrayed the split in his forked tongue. The mark of a liar. A fate awaiting any angel who told an untruth. One which had only ever befallen the one before him now.

Gabriel pulled his wings tighter, taking what comfort he could from the press of blood-slick feathers against torn, burned flesh. He had thought himself so strong, righteous even, but after ninety-seven days of punishment at the hands of this sadist, he knew the truth.

He had always been destined to fall, just as Samael had. He was no better than the being who stalked the edges of his waking nightmares.

"Still unwilling to speak to me, brother? Do you think yourself better, even as you huddle in this sorry state?" Gabriel curled his lip, a flicker of his old resolve bubbling in his chest. He *was* better than his fallen brethren.

Samael chuckled again, closer this time.

"I can almost hear the wheels turning in that thick skull of yours. But, before you cast a stone, ask yourself this; Did your Eve deserve the fate awaiting her, had you not interfered? And why does this treaty bind you to your eternal fate, while the demon who sought to harm her, even now, seeks his reentry to the mortal plane to finish the work he started?"

Gabriel stiffened but remained silent, biting his tongue hard enough to draw blood. He would not be baited. Not by *him*.

"Perhaps she will join you soon. What a comfort. I do hope she does, for your sake, brother." The scraping chains, forever bound to the fallen, signaled his departure.

When the sound blinked out of existence, he knew he was alone again. Alone in the dark, with only his thoughts of that night in the Graves' basement and of the woman whose life he had saved.

CHAPTER 20

Rebecca

"Simon!" she screamed. The rage pouring off her drenched the room, coating every surface. She pinned him with narrowed eyes. "You tried to keep me buried!"

Simon's pleading eyes did nothing to soothe the fire burning in her chest, her heart.

"Please," he breathed as he knelt beside her.

She threw out a hand, a wave of air slamming into him, sending him sliding back several feet. He stood, taking a step back.

Sophia dropped to her side, grabbing her hand. "I'm so sorry Allie, I didn't know." She wrenched her hand free, pushing to her feet.

Ignoring Sophia, she stalked toward Simon, who was backing away. "I thought you were dead." She choked on the words. "I thought..." She wrapped her arms around herself, swallowing the words.

"Please. I never meant to hurt you." Simon reached for her.

"Don't you dare touch me!"

"I'll leave you to...," Sophia began, but her words died as Rebecca swiveled her gaze in the girl's direction.

"You will stay." The power lacing her words rattled the lamp beside them, knocking a wineglass to the floor. Sophia stilled, dipping her head in silent affirmation.

Rebecca returned her gaze to Simon, who was looking anywhere but at her.

"*You* will leave. *Now.*"

"Rebecca."

"Get out of my sight!" The glass, drenched in its own dark stain, shattered as a shockwave rolled through the room and the kitchen faucet whined. Everyone turned to stare as a geyser erupted from the sink.

Sophia lifted one hand as she drew a circle around it with the other, and they all watched as the geyser wheeled and refocused its spray into the sink. The circular motion of the spray, now caught in a vortex, continued to spin above the sink and drop, draining away.

"Impressive," Rebecca said, giving Sophia an appraising once-over.

Sophia smirked, flicking her gaze to Simon. "What are we doing with him?"

The temperature in the room ticked up as Rebecca returned her focus to the man she had trusted for all her eternal life, the one who had hurt her more deeply than any other.

"I told you to leave."

Simon's tortured yellow gaze never broke from hers as he stepped closer. "Please Rebecca, just let me explain. I was only trying to protect you."

"By lying to me!" Blue sparks danced over her fingers. "By attempting to hide the truth from me!" Simon's gaze dropped to her hands and then flew up, darting between her cold scowl and the flames dancing over her fingertips.

"I only wanted to keep you safe."

"You wanted to keep *Allie* safe. You wanted a woman who took no shit from anyone; you got her." She lifted a hand, forming a ball of blue flame in her hand. Simon raised an eyebrow.

"Are you going to use your magic on me, Bec?" His playful tone said he didn't understand how serious the situation was. She expanded her fingers, letting the ball grow. The smugness on his perfect lips faltered. "Rebecca. I never meant to hurt you."

She stretched her palm flat, blue flames dancing in her periphery. "Well, you did." She flung the ball, aiming for his face. He dodged with the preternatural speed she knew he possessed, darting from the room, leaving her staring at the door as it swung shut.

Rebecca dropped onto the couch, heaving a deep sigh. Tears hovered, threatening to break free. It took every ounce of her will to hold them back. Sophia dropped onto the seat beside her.

"I wasn't aware he had stolen so many of your memories, Allie. I'm sorry."

Rebecca slanted her gaze to the bronzed girl. "He didn't. He wasn't the one who stole my memories. But he tried his damndest to ensure I didn't get them back." Sophia inched closer, her thigh pressing against Rebecca's.

"What do you mean?"

Rebecca slid away, giving them space. "I appreciate your help, but that doesn't mean I owe you any answers about my past. If you think I'm going to accept that you happen to be my roommate, you're mistaken. I asked you to stay because I want some answers from you as well."

Sophia's blue-green eyes glinted with amusement. "And the she-wolf is revealed. It's nice to meet you."

"How did you know what Simon was?"

"My coven has many legends of the night-beings. I didn't expect to meet one in my lifetime, but we know what they are. *Demons.*"

Rebecca's gut twisted uncomfortably. As much as she hated him right now, she would never assign him that label. "What have you learned about them?"

"That they have inhuman abilities, and until now, we believed them to only walk the mortal plane at night. Curious that your demon does not adhere to those rules." Rebecca bit her lip. Sophia slid closer again. "They're killers. They seek to further the agenda of the demon master."

Rebecca snorted. "You mean Satan?"

Sophia wrinkled her nose. "A Western name for the most powerful being in the underworld. The one who gives demons their power."

Rebecca reveled in the cool flood of magic running through her at Sophia's contact. The positive ions buzzing in the air from the waterfall she had created soothed some of her anger. She settled into the couch, letting water magic rush through her, a balm to the fire stoking just beneath the surface.

"I've never power shared with another witch before. Is this something exclusive to your coven?"

Sophia quirked a thick honey-brown brow. "This is standard for all witches in covens. What coven did you belong to before the demon took your mind?"

"The only witches I've ever known are the ones in my family. I wouldn't consider us a coven." She frowned. "And Simon didn't take my memories, as I said."

"Ah yes, a secret someone stole them. Not the demon you shared your bed with."

Rebecca narrowed her eyes. "I'm sensing you have something to get off your chest. Say it."

"I cannot accept that my coven is the only one who tells the legends of the night-beings and the dangers associated with them. How could you have shared your bed with one?"

Rebecca crossed her arms. "Listen, witch, I've known you for two days, and you being here is no coincidence. Either you came for me or Simon, but whatever it is you're here for, just tell me. I'm in no mood for more secrets today."

"I can see the naive girl I met yesterday is gone, and I am dealing with the real woman now." Sophia rested her hand on Rebecca's forearm, sending a cooling flush up her arm. "I will tell you what brought me here."

Rebecca's threadbare nerves were like live wires, sparking at every turn, ready to detonate at the slightest provocation, but Sophia wasn't using her siren gift and everything about her disposition spoke of someone being honest.

"I'm listening."

"I am from a coven of witches whose primary gift is water magic, but my gift, the one my coven prizes, is that of a seer. I had a vision that spoke of the end times, the end of humanity. The fate of our souls rests with a witch born of the Taurus constellation. I believe that witch is you."

"The fate of humanity rests with me?" Rebecca scoffed. Sophia watched her impassively. "And how am I expected to determine this fate?"

"That is not clear to me." Sophia lifted one shoulder and dropped it.

"So, let me get this straight. You've come to Boston looking for a Taurus, who's also a witch, who will determine the fate of humanity, and you think I'm that witch?" Sophia opened her mouth. "And," Rebecca continued, "you managed to get yourself into the same college I'm attending and into my same dorm. I'm guessing you're here to help somehow."

When she said no more, Sophia said, "I believe I was shown the vision because I will play a role in its outcome."

Rebecca pursed her lips. "There are a lot of Taurus's in the world. What makes you so sure it's me?"

"One of my sisters spoke with the ocean and it pointed me here, to Boston, to you. It is hard to explain things that you should have already learned in your coven."

Rebecca squeezed her arms more tightly across her chest. Were there truly whole covens of witches, teaching each other how to use magic, rather than hoarding all their secrets and leaving each other to fend for themselves?

"I'll need time to consider everything. School is canceled this week, and I need to go home and check on a few things. Stay here, take the room for the rest of the week. I'll see you back on campus next week."

"Now that the cards are on the table, Allie, I prefer to stay together as much as possible. Any scenario could affect the outcome of this war. You may need my visions to navigate the coming weeks."

Rebecca frowned. "If we're going to continue hanging out, you'll have to stop calling me Allie. My name is Rebecca."

CHAPTER 21

Rebecca

Sophia stood, striding into the kitchen. Rebecca watched as her hands wove an intricate pattern, reminiscent of knitting needles, and slowly, the water spraying into the air receded until it was only a small drip. She turned, facing Rebecca.

"This is all so much more complicated than I expected. I did not see the night-being or your memory loss in my visions." She crossed the room, returning to where Rebecca reclined on the couch. "I saw a great battle. One which ended either in the eradication of demon kind on earth or this plane being overrun with them. In either scenario, bodies litter the earth. Death reigns. It will be for nothing if you choose not to fight before the fight begins."

Rebecca blinked, tensing as Sophia slid onto the seat beside her again. Sophia reached for her hand, wrapping cool fingers around her fiery ones. Simon would have called her firecracker and told her to calm down.

That thought scorched a line of pain across her chest. If only Allie had known Simon's endearing nicknames were for her. But even as he tossed them carelessly at her, he fought at every turn to stop her from remembering who she was.

Sophia continued. "We need you, Rebecca. We stand no chance without you on our side."

It was meant to boost her ego, to placate the vain part of her that sought a larger purpose: meaning in her long life. It was working. She could feel her resolve bending. Who didn't wish to know they held the very fate of the world in their palm?

"I have responsibilities this week. The fate of the world won't be decided before Monday." She pulled her hands from Sophia's grasp.

Sophia's siren gift rose to the surface, but just as she had claimed, Rebecca blocked it. It surprised her that Sophia's water gift, singing to her very soul, was not unlike her father's gift, albeit in a smoother, cooler form. The shields she had constructed to block his fiery coercion worked equally well on Sophia's gifts, even though Sophia's primary gift differed from Alexander's.

"Well, look who's come out to play," Sophia smirked.

Rebecca scowled, clenching her fist tightly.

Sophia spluttered, choking, before Rebecca released her hold on the air she had pulled from her lungs. Sophia thumped her chest, sucking in a breath.

"Interesting," she choked out between coughs. "You possess water magic, fire magic, and air magic. I've never met a witch who possessed so many of the elements. If you tell me you can control earth, I'll bow at your feet."

Rebecca snorted. "Save your pagan idol worship for your coven. There are things that would have you rethinking your atheist ways."

"A belief in magical hierarchy and a lack of belief in God are not synonymous, Rebecca. We believe in God. We also believe that what he created, he created with a purpose."

Tool. The word stuck in Rebecca's mind, reminding her Gabriel had not reappeared after their face-off with Elizabeth. If she had not been so distraught over Simon's death, she would have asked Jophiel more about it. Now, the question hovered at the forefront of her mind. Where was he?

Rebecca stood, grabbing her bag. In three long strides, she reached the door, flinging it open. She glanced back at the other girl. "Stay here or go back to the dorms. It's up to you. I'll see you next week." She stepped through the door, stopping at the sound of Sophia's voice.

"You forgot your backpack."

Rebecca swore, turning around. She swiped for her backpack, but Sophia reached it first, holding it out. She looked up, meeting sea-green eyes swimming with some inexplicable emotion. Her breath caught.

Shaking her head, she snatched the backpack from Sophia's grip. "Your siren tricks won't work on me."

Sophia's mouth quirked up at the corners. "I wasn't using my gift."

Rebecca stepped back, letting the scent of the sea air clear from her nostrils. "Why do you want to come with me, anyway?"

Sophia's throat bobbed as she swallowed and said, "I have seen other things; things that suggest you are in danger."

"Tell me something I don't know," Rebecca scoffed. "And you want to protect me?"

"The fate of our world is no small thing. If you die, we all do."

Rebecca considered her words, chewing on her bottom lip. Sophia's blue-green eyes gave nothing away. She wanted to trust her—wanted to believe this girl's intentions were noble—but a lifetime of learning just what trusting others meant was a hard pill to swallow.

With the latest betrayal settling uncomfortably in her chest, she was not yet ready to trust another person.

"Sorry, not this time, witch. See you Monday." She spun on her heel, ignoring the tug in her gut urging her to turn around.

CHAPTER 22

Rebecca

Rebecca stared at the wispy clouds filtering her view of Boston's Harbor and the growing expanse of blue stretching across the horizon. White puffs thickened, blocking the scene, and she dropped her gaze to the phone resting in her lap.

She read the message for the ninth time, swallowing down the emotions threatening to surface. Did he think a simple apology would suffice? His actions were the deepest betrayal she had ever known. The ache suffused every muscle and tendon in her body, opening a deep chasm in her chest where eighty years of love and longing once lived.

Alone with her thoughts, free of the siren's oppressive presence, she felt it more keenly. Hadn't he promised her forever? Hadn't he promised he would always bring her back? She read the message for the tenth time.

"Rebecca, I never meant to hurt you. I was only trying to keep you safe. I'm sorry."

The screen cracked, a spiderweb of black lines trailing down its center. "Liar!" she said a bit too loudly.

People across the aisle eyed her, some outright staring. She sucked in a breath through her nose, breathing out slowly, counting to five. She repeated the action several times. Her grip on her phone loosened, leaving behind indentations where the heat rolling off her had melted plastic.

He didn't want her back. He wanted *Allie*.

A flight attendant came by holding a trash bag out to her. She dropped her phone into it, along with four empty mini bottles of vodka.

"Can I get four more?" she asked.

The flight attendant frowned but said nothing. Had she heard that outburst too? *Whatever.* It wasn't her job to judge. It was her job to get the bottles of vodka. She dug in her purse, finding the M&M's she'd picked up at the airport, and popped a few in her mouth. They were her favorite, and Simon never liked them, which made them even better.

She closed her eyes, letting the sweet chocolate coat her tongue.

"Here, honey. He's not worth it." Rebecca blinked her eyes open, staring at the bleary outline of the flight attendant.

She snatched the bottles from her outstretched hand, glaring up at her. "No one asked you." She twisted the first lid, wrenching it free from its cap, and took a long swig. The attendant gasped and a few of the surrounding passengers mumbled something to one another. The attendant stalked past her, making her way into the coach section of the plane.

Rebecca's gaze fell on a couple one seat back to the right. They were staring, blatant disapproval written on their weathered faces. She glared at them. The woman brought a hand to her chest, while her seat companion gripped her shoulders, whispering something into her ear. They both turned their gazes to the window.

Good.

The surrounding space blinked in and out of focus as she leaned her head against the window, twisted the cap on the second bottle, and took another swig. The burn coating her throat stung as it reached her belly and deadened some of the pain. She pressed the bottle to her lips, sipping. When it was empty, she tossed it onto the seat beside her and opened the third.

A crackling voice blared over the intercom, startling her and causing her to spill some of the precious liquid. She swore, licking vodka-drenched fingers.

"Good morning. We have begun our initial descent. Local time is eleven-fifteen a.m. It's a beautiful sunny eighty-eight degrees, and we should be on the ground in fifteen minutes. Welcome to Raleigh, North Carolina, and thank you for flying American Airlines."

Around her, passengers were shuffling in their seats, folding trays into their armrests. She tipped the bottle to her lips, drinking the remaining scorching drops in one gulp, feeling the plane sway back and forth.

A flight attendant stopped beside her seat. "Would you like some water, ma'am?"

She mumbled a reply, but when she looked over, the attendant was gone.

Her stomach swooped as the plane dipped, tipping toward the earth. She reached for her phone but remembered she'd tossed it in the trash. She would need to get another one when she got home. One with a new number, so Simon couldn't text her anymore of his lies.

Everything tilted, and she grabbed the seat in front of her. Darting a glance around, she saw no one holding onto anything and took a few deep breaths.

The plane touched down on the runway and she rocked forward. As the plane slowed to a stop, her stomach churned. *Shit.*

"Excuse me," she called, but it was too late. Her stomach heaved, and she turned, dumping the contents of her breakfast into the seat beside her. Garbled voices around her muttered disapprovingly, but she spared them no notice as she wiped the back of her trembling hand across her mouth.

The smell hit her and threatened to send her stomach into another purge, but she held it in, regaining some sense of her surroundings long enough to see that the people around her were standing, reaching for suitcases, and stepping into the aisle.

Unbuckling her seatbelt, she pulled her purse out of the place it had been lodged between her seat and the window and reached for her backpack under the seat, wrenching it free, and stumbled into a man in the aisle. "'Scuse me," she mumbled.

He stepped back, giving her space, and she moved into the aisle, leaning into the seats as she went. A flight attendant handed her a stack of napkins and a bottle of water. She took them both, then continued into the hallway.

She stopped—leaning into the wall as people moved around her—and wiped her mouth with a napkin before twisting the lid to her water and taking a long drink. The cool water washed some of the sour taste from her mouth.

"Ma'am," someone called from behind her. She pushed off the wall and started forward again. "Ma'am. You left your backpack." She turned, finding a flight attendant behind her, holding it out. She grabbed it, napkins fluttering to the ground. "I know it's none of my business, but things are never as bad as they seem."

Rebecca glared up at the unhelpful woman. "Things are worsss than thaay seeem. Every time. Juss wait till someone crusshes your soul and ruins yurr faith in humannity." She turned away, stumbling down the hall.

Glaring lights shone down on her as she zigzagged through the expansive airport.

She reached the door, pressed into it, and sighed as a light breeze caressed her cheeks. Spotting the Uber line, she changed direction, stumbled into a woman, and dropped her backpack. "Sorry, sorry, sorry." She giggled. That was too many sorrys. She leaned down to grab her backpack and toppled to the ground, laughing out loud. Her purse slid down beside her.

Arms reached under her and pulled her up, lifting her backpack and purse with her.

Even in her inebriated state, she sensed him. She would always feel him, in every part of her being.

"Le-mme go," she demanded.

"Rebecca, let me take you home," he breathed in her ear.

She wrenched herself from his grip, pulling her purse strap over her shoulder, and stumbled away from him. "You don't get to do anything for me. Yurr a traitor. A liar!" Her voice rose and people around them stared. She didn't care.

Simon stood rigidly, holding her backpack, looking as though she had crushed his dreams.

"Please."

It was one word. But it twisted in her stomach like a knife, sobering her thoughts. "Wheeere was my chance to beg when you left me in the dark?" She wrapped her arms around herself, swaying.

"I was always going to help you remember yourself. I just needed time."

She backed up. "Time with *her*!"

"Time to track down Elizabeth."

"You slept with her!" She turned, bumping into a group of girls who had their phones out, shamelessly recording the whole thing. "Get out-ov my way!" She shoved through them and wrenched open the door to the next Uber in line.

"Bath. Can you take me?" Simon reached the door, pulling the handle as she pressed the lock button. He held up her backpack.

"Rebecca, be reasonable. Come, I will take you home." His words were distorted through the glass.

"I can take you. There'll be an extra fifty-dollar trip charge for the distance, though."

"Iss fine. Just go."

The car pulled out into traffic, and she slumped back in her seat. Every fiber of her being urged her to look back, but she would not give him the satisfaction.

A light patter of rain started against the windows, and she closed her eyes, letting the sound and her own blurred thoughts drag her into oblivion.

"Miss, I need an address." She cracked an eye open.

"One-eleven Graves Road, Bath, North Carolina." She closed her eyes again, a spinning sensation sending her back down into nothing.

CHAPTER 23

Rebecca

Rebecca's eyes fluttered open a moment before she felt a stabbing sensation in her shoulder. She pressed a hand into the side of the door, pushing herself up, and rolled her shoulder. The odd angle she had slept in left her neck feeling sore.

Eyes slitted against the burning glare of the sun, she held up a hand to shield them as she watched the blur of green, yellow, and red slow and form shapes. Stately evergreens, red maples—already beginning to turn in preparation for fall—and massive oaks lined the road.

The car pulled to a stop in front of the towering wrought-iron gates surrounding her family estate. Her breath caught as she fought to maintain her composure. Home was just on the other side.

"Is there a gate code?" he asked.

"No, sorry. Let me get it." She dug in her purse for her keys and pressed the button Simon had attached so she would never lose it. So *Allie* would never lose it.

The gate swung open, and they continued forward, rolling over loose gravel. The car stopped outside her family home, and she leaned back, peering up at the fourth-floor windows. They appeared dark, but it was hard to tell in daylight. She stepped out of the car into the midday sun and winced, steadying herself against the car. Still a little drunk then.

"Thanks," she called over her shoulder as she pushed off the door and took several unsteady steps toward the house. When she had scaled the steps, she grasped the old iron key and slid it into the lock, turning it in two full circles. The door clicked, and she pressed in as the loudest, most obnoxious sound blared to life, screeching through the expansive foyer.

"Shit!" She pressed her hands to her head. "Shit. Shit." She backed out the door, dropping her purse to cover her ears.

"Who's there? I called the police!" The voice from inside the house was barely audible over the noise.

"It's me!" she yelled.

The blaring noise halted.

"Allie? Is that you?"

Rebecca ground her teeth, leaning down to swipe up her purse. She stepped into the blessedly silent space and halted in front of the petite woman, reduced by the passage of time. "It's Rebecca."

Rhea's face gave nothing away, but a slight tremor in her hand was enough to let Rebecca know *he* hadn't warned her. Rhea stood up straighter. "Well, get in here and close the door. You're letting in flies."

Rebecca stepped through the door, closing it, and whirled to face Rhea. "How could you go along with this, Rhe?" She hadn't meant to sound so hurt. But now, in her home, the place where she should feel safe, the sting of rejection burned.

She would have expected Rachel's old nanny, *her* old nanny, to have been on her side.

"Oh child, I'm sorry." She spread her arms wide, and Rebecca stepped into them, letting the woman's small frame curl around her waist. "We thought it would keep you safe a while longer while Simon sorted things for you."

"Don't say his name. I never want to hear his name again."

Rhea released her, stepping back. "You don't mean that."

Rebecca wiped her cheek. "I do. He lied. He didn't want me to remember who I was. He cheated on me with *her*."

136

Rhea reached for her purse, pulling it from her fingers. "Come on, I'll make you some tea and you can tell me all about it."

Rebecca started forward; stopped. "How much has he told you?"

"He's told me what he can. His bosses don't let him say much."

Rebecca nodded. "It's better you don't know." She looked around the space, spying white metal devices in each corner. "This extra security is obnoxious. Have there been any more intruders?" Rhea set her purse on a side table and continued into the kitchen. Rebecca trailed after, noting the slight limp in her step. "I can make tea. You should sit."

Rhea darted a glare over her shoulder. "I'm not an invalid."

Rebecca stepped around her, placing a hand on her shoulder. "Sit, Rhea. It's only been a few days." She took another step before sagging into a chair and some of the color returned to her cheeks. "Where's your nurse? She shouldn't have let you out of bed."

"I sent that pestering fool home. She wasn't fit to care for a goat."

Rebecca snorted. "I'll call the hospital and find you a replacement. You will not stay here in the house by yourself."

"You're going back to college, then?"

Rebecca reached under the counter, pulling out two cups, and moved to the electric kettle, flipping the switch. "For the first time in my life, I'm unburdened by poor health, a controlling father, and responsibilities at home. I can finally begin living."

The kettle beeped, and she lifted the pot, pouring steaming liquid into each cup. "Sugar?" Rhea nodded, and she dropped a cube in each cup, adding two more to her own.

Bringing the cups to the butcher block counter in the center of the kitchen, she slid a mug to Rhea and leaned both elbows on the table, breathing in the sweet scent of mint. They sipped in silence and a throbbing began pulsing at the base of her skull.

Why had she drunk so much? *Because the love of your life is an asshole who loves someone else*, a nagging voice reminded her. She scowled into her cup. "Did you really think it was better having her around than me?"

She peered up from beneath her lashes at the frail woman across from her. Rhea's red bloodshot eyes watered. Whether from the pain of her injury or her actions, Rebecca couldn't tell. Rhea stretched a hand across the table, holding it palm up. Rebecca bit her lip, placing her hand in the woman's smaller one, squeezing gently.

"I don't pretend to know everything your family gets up to, but I know Simon has always had your best interests at heart. If he thought it was best you not remember for a bit, I have to believe it was for a good reason."

A wet tear clung to the edge of Rebecca's lashes before breaking free and sliding down her cheek. "I could have been looking for Elizabeth. I could have been helping. He can't have thought I would be better off knowing nothing."

"I don't get involved with things above my pay grade."

Rebecca pulled her hand from Rhea's grasp. "He was dating her. Taking her to dinner, buying her gifts. None of that was for me!" She pushed off the table, taking a step back. "You told her what to wear, how to style her hair. For *him*."

Rhea pressed a hand to the bandage on her head. "He loves you; you love him. I was just trying to help."

"Trying to help Allie."

Rhea winced, pressing both hands to her head. "I love you, all of you, no matter what you call yourself."

Rebecca paced the kitchen, pulling one of her loose curls and twisting it between her fingers. She glanced over at Rhea, whose head was propped between her hands. Something tugged at her chest. Rhea may have worked for their family for more than a decade, but she was human.

She crossed the room, coming to stand behind her, and wrapped her arms around her. Rhea started as if she had forgotten anyone was in the kitchen with her. "Come on Rhe, let's get you back to bed."

"I'm sorry," she croaked, her voice thin.

"Shhh. I know. It's okay. Come to bed." She helped Rhea stand and led her up the stairs.

They went slowly, each step more laborious for the woman than the last. When they reached the fourth floor, a sheen of sweat dappled Rhea's forehead and her cheeks had lost their color.

Rebecca bore most of her weight as she moved to the bed and Rhea dropped onto it. She smoothed Rhea's hair back from her face, tucking a silver strand behind her ear.

"Rest," she whispered, taking a step back, but Rhea's paper-thin lids were already closed, a light snore burbling from her lips.

In her room, she dropped onto her bed, wrapping her multicolored blanket around herself, and groaned. The dull throb in her head had begun pounding in time with her heartbeat, making her vision blur at the edges. *I'll just close my eyes for a moment*, she thought, resting her head on her pillow.

CHAPTER 24

Simon

Simon set Rebecca's backpack down inside the door and hesitated at the entrance. He wanted to go to her, to tell her she was wrong, that he had done it for her, to protect her, but he knew it was at least partially a lie. Perhaps not for the reasons she thought, but she wouldn't accept his apology now.

A light moan sounded from upstairs, and he bolted for it, damning the consequences of her anger. The sound came again as he stopped at the door to the yellow room. Rhea turned over, whimpering softly. He moved into the room, reaching her side, and pressed a hand to her temple. He whispered the words that found their way into his mind, watching as a soft white light radiated from his fingers.

The vee in Rhea's forehead smoothed, leaving only the permanent lines that marked her natural progression through life. He traced a finger along the deep line that ran through the center of her brow, marveling at the smaller ones bisecting it. So many tiny lines that told a story of her years on this earth.

The scars he once bore—marking his passage through time—were erased when the deal with the angels was struck. Now the only scars he carried were the ones that rested upon his soul.

Rhea twisted again, rolling away from him and he stood, running a hand down his pant leg. "Sleep," he whispered, backing out of the room. Going back down the hall, he intended to leave, but some invisible force pulled him toward her.

She had demanded space, and he owed her that much, but the pull was too great, and he found himself standing in her room and then beside her.

In sleep, she was so like the others; peaceful, unburdened by the world and all it had thrown at her. Could she ever understand he only wanted to give her respite from the tragedies she had endured? He had hoped to spare her from it this time, but Rebecca, fierce, defiant Rebecca, never played by anyone else's rules. And it was only a matter of time before she realized one of her father's curses, the deadliest of them, might yet plague her.

Was it selfish that he had wanted to spend a bit more time with the version of her that was blissfully ignorant of her curse and the creatures who stalked her? Perhaps it was, but he would give up his own eternity if it meant she would one day look like the woman in the next room, wrinkles telling the story of a single human life.

He pressed a light kiss to her forehead, inhaling her lavender and eucalyptus scent. A smile lifted the corners of his lips but never reached his eyes. "I will stop it," he promised, leaning back to take her in one last time.

He sped out of the room, down the stairs and into the receiving room before pulling his phone from his pocket and texting.

Zophiel appeared in the blink of an eye. "Yes, what's happened?"

Simon tucked his phone into his pocket, striding to the couch. He waved a hand toward the navy velvet couch, but Zophiel declined with a shake of the head. He remained standing too. "Rebecca has her memories back."

"Which ones?"

"Maybe all of them. It's hard to say. She isn't speaking to me at the moment."

Zophiel's wings twitched, the only sign of her agitation. "I had thought we would have more time to prepare."

"You wanted this," he reminded her.

"I only said it was inevitable."

141

Simon stuffed a hand into his pocket and paced before her. "I need to go now while she doesn't want to see me. It's the perfect time to search for a spell to reverse her father's curse." Zophiel opened her mouth, but Simon continued. "And she's going to start asking questions about Gabriel soon. You had better be prepared with more answers than the ones you gave me because if you think she will accept them, you're mistaken."

Zophiel slid a hand into her white pantsuit pocket and pulled out a small white stone. "I need you to give this to her." She held the stone out in one smooth palm.

"What is it?"

"It's a binding stone. It will restrict her from any mention of us."

"Good luck with that." He choked on an incredulous laugh. "Rebecca won't take any gifts from me right now. And if you think she'll hang on to any mementos I give her, you're wrong."

"She only has to touch it once for it to work."

Simon backed up. "Looking to kill two birds with one stone by handing that thing to me? You have me wrapped tightly enough for my liking. If you want her to have it, give it to her yourself."

"It would be unwise to meet with her now. There is a chance she does not remember us."

Simon ran a hand through his hair. "I'm sorry, but I draw the line at binding someone else on your behalf. If you want to silence her, this is something you'll have to do alone."

Zophiel's wings fluttered at her back, shimmering around the edges, a faint glow circling her head and running along the edges of white feathers. "You swore an oath of allegiance to us. You are required to comply." She set the stone on the edge of one cerulean couch arm.

"I called you here to tell you I need to leave sooner than expected, not to take on more responsibilities for you." Simon stepped back, away from Zophiel and her stone. "I'm leaving tomorrow, and I'll be back just as soon as I find something to help her."

He darted from the room, using his preternatural speed to put distance between them, stopping only at the door to fling it wide.

CHAPTER 25

Rebecca

Rebecca's eyes flew open, all senses on high alert. Shadows lengthened across rosy walls as the last rays of sunlight reached for the sky, battling encroaching darkness in the few final moments of daylight.

As the room was swallowed by night, her ears rang, telling her what had woken her.

She sat up, listening for any sound that might give away its presence, but the house was eerily quiet. She stood, tiptoeing to the door, and peered across the hall, hearing the faintest sounds of Rhea's snoring. At least Rhea was safe on the fourth floor.

She stepped out, casting an image of herself and sending it forward, down the first several stairs. She moved with it, watching. On the third floor, her image paused, looking left and right. When nothing happened, her replica stepped forward, and she went with it, continuing down the stairs. On the second floor, her image stopped again. The ringing in her ears was growing stronger, but she didn't smell sulfur. It must be a powerful demon, farther away than she thought.

She stepped forward and was knocked off her feet, landing hard on her back at the edge of the third-floor landing.

She threw up an air shield a moment before the second attack came. A form slammed into the wall of air, bouncing off and recovering quickly. A dark-haired woman solidified above her, beating her fists against the shield at dizzying speed.

Using her free hand, Rebecca cast a ball of blue flame and expanded her fingers, working to enlarge it. The yellow-eyed creature flinched at the sight of it but continued pounding. Her wild-eyed gaze met Rebecca's and for a moment she thought she saw terror in the woman's eyes, but it was gone too fast to be sure.

As the woman raised a fist to start again, Rebecca dropped her air shield, hurling a ball of flame into her face.

Agonized screams pierced the air as the woman's entire head erupted in flames and skin slid down her face. She fell on Rebecca, scratching and tearing at anything she could grab. Rebecca cast a second ball of flame, pressing her glowing fingers into the woman's blood-stained, sagging cheek, and gasped in horror as her fingers slid through skin, touching wet sinew and tendons.

Her second hand, still alight with blue flame, dug into the woman's charred scalp, scraping bone. She gagged, but held firm, pushing her magic into her fingers.

The woman's wails died as her hands went slack and she collapsed on top of Rebecca. She rolled onto her side to slide out from under the still form. Her fingers trembled as she wiped globs of something wet and sticky from her face and neck.

She sat up, wiping an arm across her mouth. A salty and acrid taste coated her tongue and she spit, trying to rid herself of the foul taste. Bile burned up her throat, threatening to spill from her lips, but she swallowed hard, holding it back.

"Allie, is that you?" A thin voice called from the fourth floor.

"It's Rebecca," she said, pushing to her feet. She trudged up the stairs grimacing and stopped in front of Rhea's door. "Everything ok, Rhe?" She hoped her form, shadowed in the doorframe, didn't look as disheveled as she felt.

"I thought I heard something." Rhea's words were cut off by a round of coughing, and she tried to sit up.

"Don't sit up," Rebecca chided, coming into the room. She stopped beside Rhea's bed, wiping dirty fingers against her leg and lifted a cup to the woman's lips, tilting it gently. "Better?"

Rhea nodded, her eyes fluttering closed. She set the cup down and watched the rise and fall of Rhea's chest as it slowed. When she was sure Rhea was asleep, she walked on light feet to the door.

The skin just above her knuckles tingled as if it had been rubbed raw. A shower was desperately needed. "Sleep tight," she whispered and stepped into the hall.

CHAPTER 26

Rebecca

R ebecca inhaled deeply, breathing in the eucalyptus and lavender scent permeating the air as sticky globs of the night-being she'd destroyed slid down her body. She turned to face the shower head, letting it pelt her skin as scalding drops loosened any remaining bits from her hair and eyebrows.

She opened her mouth, letting blistering water cleanse her lips and tongue. If she never had to face another of Elizabeth's foul creatures again, it would be too soon.

When her skin burned and she felt clean, she stepped out, reaching for a forest green towel and wrapped it tightly around her lean frame. It would have made more sense to clean up the mess before showering, but she couldn't spend another moment with that foul taste in her mouth.

Dressed in a pair of Allie's black leggings and a sports bra, she swung her hair into a high bun and reached for a sword that wasn't there. For one fleeting moment, she wished Simon was there to help.

After checking in on Rhea, she bounded down the stairs to the third-floor landing, where the remnants of her battle stained the floor. She surveyed the scene, blanching.

Tentatively, she reached down, lifting one slack arm. A shudder rolled through her and she dropped it. It hit the floor with an audible thud. How had the angels cleaned up all her messes? Would they come if she called them?

"Gabriel!" she whisper shouted. A noise from Rhea's room made her wince.

She bit her lip and dropped to a squat, resting both hands on the creature's prone form and spread her fingers—pressing her magic into her palms—then watched as the creature's remaining scraps of clothing caught in her blue flame. Before long, it was engulfed.

The pungent smell burned her nose, making her eyes water. She glanced up again, straining for any sound in Rhea's room. A dark cloud of thick smoke wafted up and drifted toward her open door.

Rebecca stood, flinging an air shield across the door just as the thick plume of smoke reached it. It hit the invisible wall and drifted up, continuing along the hall. Spinning her hands into a sphere, she constructed a tunnel, barricading all the doors on the fourth floor and ran to the end of the hall, flinging a window open, leaning her head out to breathe in fresh air. Acrid black smoke began funneling out into the night.

She turned back and swore. Her blue flames burned at a far higher temperature than a natural fire and very little of the body remained, but the fire had leaped to the banister and was trailing downward at a rapid pace.

She raced back to the third floor, pulling on her water magic. It was her weakest element, and she wasn't prepared for the surge of water that came when she pulled it from a third-floor bathroom. A rush of soothing cool liquid flooded her veins as the stream became a flood and water burst from the wall to her left, rushing toward her.

She braced, throwing up an air shield as the force slammed into her shield and flowed around her. Bits of bone tumbled down the stairs as water continued to pummel her shield and a whine started farther down the hall. *Shit.*

Dropping her shield, she gritted her teeth against the flood as she attempted to mimic the complicated pattern Sophia had woven when she had redirected the spray back in the hotel room.

The water's pressure eased before redoubling, slamming into her with force. She widened her stance, trying again. Again, the water slowed, but in a moment, it slammed her again.

"Allie?" Rhea called from the fourth floor.

"Stay in your room. We have a leak," she called back as she ducked to the side, avoiding the brunt of the spray, and ran to the first floor.

Standing in the pooling water, she pulled the front door open, watching as water and the remaining bits of the night-being streamed out and followed the flow out the door and around the side of the house to the main water shut-off valve.

She twisted, muscles straining against the pressure until it stuck tight, and leaned against the side of the house, wiping her brow. She sucked in a few calming breaths before straightening and turning to go back inside.

In the doorway, Rebecca stepped over a large bone, splashing through the foyer.

"Hello? Allie, are you there?" Rebecca ground her teeth.

"I'm here Rhea. There's a mess downstairs. I need to use your phone to call a plumber," she called, taking the stairs two at a time. She groaned as she passed a deep scorch mark on the third floor but continued up.

She found Rhea reclining in her bed, wide-eyed, hands trembling, and crossed the room to sit beside her. Taking her hand, she patted gently. "Nothing to worry about. It was just a burst pipe, but I'll handle it. Rest." Rhea's frail fingers curled around hers, as the trembling subsided.

"I'm sorry I called you Allie again. I keep forgetting." She closed her eyes. "When is Simon coming back?"

Pain speared Rebecca's chest, stealing her breath for a moment. "Where's your phone, Rhea? I need to make a few calls."

Rhea lifted her free hand, waving at her bedside table. Rebecca stood, gently releasing Rhea's hand from hers, and slid the drawer open, reaching for the phone encased in purple. A gift from Simon, no doubt. She left the room, doing a quick search for local remediation companies, and dialed the first one.

An hour later, Rebecca set Rhea's phone down on the butcher block countertop and turned, pulling open the refrigerator door. Her stomach ached, and she couldn't remember the last time she'd eaten more than M&M's.

Pulling out strawberries, yogurt, and granola, she closed the fridge and grabbed a bowl. She opened the drawer, sighing. No clean spoons. She wrenched the drawer as far as it would go, searching the very back. *Ah ha!* Her hand landed on cold metal and her stomach dropped.

Rebecca was sucked in, falling fast, and landed hard, grunting as she turned to face Jophiel. Jophiel handed her a cup. What was this? Not a memory she had ever seen before. Not one of Claire's. Had she made her own memory, knowing the angels would steal it from her? She turned away from Jophiel, moving to the sink to fill her cup with water. It flowed freely, not in the present, then.

"I'm sorry Allie," Jophiel said to her back.

She turned to face her. "For what?"

"I did what I could for Simon."

Rebecca swallowed. This was after the attack. When Jophiel had appeared to take her memories instead of Gabriel. Why didn't she remember this part? What had she wanted to remember?

"Where's Gabriel?"

"As I said before, Gabriel would be here if he could."

Rebecca arched an eyebrow. "Why can't he be?"

"Allie, he crossed a line. He broke the one rule that truly matters to our kind."

Water spilled over the side of Rebecca's cup as her hand shook. She stilled it, looking down at the spoon still clenched in her other hand. She remembered this part, but this was not how it had gone. Jophiel came to take her memories, told her Simon was gone and healed her. She looked up.

"What happened to me? How was I injured?"

"Alexander attacked you. You should be dead."

"But Gabriel stopped him. He stopped a demon?" She eyed Jophiel, wondering how much the ethereal being would tell her.

"Yes."

"You're going to take my memories, anyway. Just tell me what happened to him."

Jophiel crossed the room, peering out the window at the dimming orange light. "I must go soon. The Nasdaqu-ush who released Alexander's demon form escaped when Gabriel stopped him from killing you."

"The what?"

"Nasdaqu-ush. It is the name for Elizabeth's kind."

Rebecca laughed. It was a cold, bitter sound. "She's still out there, hunting me, and you're just going to wipe my memories and leave me defenseless. I thought you protected humans."

Jophiel's mouth twisted into a grimace. "We would not leave you defenseless. We have selected a new reash who will be tasked with hunting not only demons but also any Nasdaqu-ush found in the territory."

"So that's it. You'll tell me nothing else before you wipe six years of my life away and replace them with some fabrication."

Jophiel gave her an inscrutable look. "We must wipe your memories now. We cannot risk tipping the balance."

"What balance? What does that mean?"

Jophiel's lips pinched. Rebecca sipped from her cup. Perhaps she had misjudged the angel, and she would say no more. She drew a breath to try again as Jophiel opened her mouth. "As you know, humans have free will. Our Father wishes for all of you to choose the side of good, but several tests throughout your lifespan determine which path you will follow. When the first human was tempted by one such test, Primoria was created as a place of punishment when they failed. But the test was for both the angel and the human.

"When the angel failed, his punishment was banishment to the very place created for humans. Lucifer has never forgiven his father for that decision. Instead, he made it his mission to turn all God's children to the dark.

"Demons were never meant to be, but Primoria is a place that exists in the absence of light and God. Where some souls wither and fade, others, the darkest of them, grow into something else. Something we now call demons. These creatures possess the ability to cross over the mortal plane.

"In the early days of man, they came in droves, wreaking havoc on the world, raping, pillaging and inciting war. And though his warrior angels—Gabriel among them—fought, demons were winning.

"Humankind was doomed, and the terror that threatened to consume the world meant all who remained were destined for Primoria. Our Father looked at what his children had become and wept.

"In desperation, he came to the human plane, as a man, to meet with his fallen to negotiate for the souls of humanity. For thirty-three years, he entreated with Lucifer, and for thirty-three years, Lucifer refused him. But our Father on earth, living among humans, performing miracles, reviving faith, was turning the tide.

"Recognizing this change, Lucifer agreed to a meeting. At a dinner, on the last night of our Father's human life, a deal was struck. As with the very first human, Lucifer's children would be given free rein to test the humans, but no demon could inhabit a human's body.

"In exchange, no angel could sabotage a demon's tests. If a demon broke the rule inhabiting a human, angels could vanquish that demon back to Primoria. However, if an angel harmed any demon who had not broken the rule, that angel would be sent to Primoria.

"They sealed the deal with a sacrifice, and it would be up to humans to pass the tests Lucifer's beastly children created. On that very night, Lucifer's most trusted demon, in the body of a man, led a legion of monsters to claim their sacrifice.

A bead of sweat slid down Rebecca's temple as her heart thrummed in her chest. Gabriel had broken the rule. She knew now why he hadn't come.

CHAPTER 27

Gabriel

I mpossibly, his vision *had* adjusted to the complete darkness of this plane. Samael said it would, but the vitriol that poured over his pierced lips, spilling along that forked tongue, could not be trusted.

He looked around the space, much larger than he'd assumed, wondering again how many days it had been since he had last been visited. Was the Fallen growing bored with him or had something diverted his attention elsewhere?

He pulled his shattered wing in close, cradling it against his shoulder, shuddering as a wave of agony rolled through him at the touch. It was healing, slowly. On day ninety-nine, the torture had ceased, but so had the visits. Now, he had no way of knowing what day it was, no way to count the endless torment that awaited him. Perhaps it was a mercy.

He would have considered it so if Samael's last prevarication had not sent a bolt of fear through him. But that was all it could be. Samael, playing on his worst fears, seeking fresh forms of torture.

He stood, balancing on one leg. The first had grown back remarkably quickly, but the second, taking slightly longer, was still not strong enough to put his full weight on. He had no doubt that his brother would soon be back to remove them again. For now, he used this time to his advantage, leaning heavily on his right leg as he hobbled to the corner.

Not a true room, but a cave, with endless tunnels leading out. Primoria was an ever-expanding realm, he knew, stretching to accommodate its inhabitants, just as Alaxia did. These tunnels might stretch for unfathomable distances and likely led to countless foul beings.

That his presence here was still a secret was the only thing keeping him from being tortured by its residents. Leaving the room was a risk, yet, if any part of Samael's story held truth, Rebecca was in danger—more danger than she knew—and it was likely she would not survive it. He must find a way out of this place.

CHAPTER 28

Rebecca

Rebecca set her cup down on the counter and paced the room. "Why can a reash vanquish demons if we serve angels?"

"Reashes are still human. Even with their enhanced abilities, it breaks no rules to enlist their assistance."

"But you can vanquish the Nasqush?"

"Nasdaqu-ush," Jophiel corrected. "It is a Sumerian word meaning 'kissed by death', although it can also be translated as witch or sorceress." Rebecca shuddered. Her sister, Elizabeth, fit the description well. Perhaps it was an ancient word for necromancer. "The first Nasdaqu-ush lived over three thousand years ago. She was famed in her time for her ability to speak with the dead. Her name was Sanura, but most knew her as the Witch of Endor. She spent her days in Sheol, the place you call the in-between, and her nights on the mortal plane.

"When a king in her time sought her help to consult with the prophet Samuel, she contacted a demon instead, sharing secrets no human should be privy to. It was decided that her kind, the Nasdaqu-ush, possessed an ability too powerful to exist.

"Our Father tasked Gabriel and me with wiping them from this plane of existence."

The edges of Rebecca's vision darkened as Jophiel reached for her.

"Wait, Rebecca, he needs you. Help him."

The world blackened and then she was standing in the kitchen, her feet soaked, holding a spoon.

Rebecca collapsed into the soft cerulean blue cushions of her couch and sighed. Warmth radiated from the place where Jophiel had clasped alabaster fingers around her wrist. How had she done it? Not once, in any of Claire's memories, had someone known she was visiting and not the person she pretended to be.

But Jophiel *had* known. What had she risked in sending her that message? How did she think Rebecca could help him? If he was trapped in Primoria, the only way in was death. Wasn't it? As a reash, Allie could enter Alaxia. Did that mean she could have entered Primoria as well? But she wasn't a reash anymore. And the only reash she knew...

Her lip curled. *No.* She would not ask him for any favors.

Something glinted in her peripheral, catching her eye. She leaned across the couch to get a better view of the polished stone resting atop deep blue velvet. It sparkled, refracting rainbow hues in some imaginary light. *Magic.* It must be. But where had it come from?

She knew better than to touch it.

Glancing around, she spied her backpack on a chair in the room's corner, the one she'd left with Simon. Of course he'd been here. Probably while she slept. Had he left it as some sort of peace offering? But he didn't possess any magic. It was more likely one of Elizabeth's minions left it. Even more reason not to touch it.

She couldn't leave it out for Rhea or some unsuspecting maintenance worker to find. The spoon also needed a new home. She wondered absently who had stuffed it at the back of the silverware drawer, but that was a problem for another time. At present, she needed a good hiding place for the spelled objects.

Ten minutes later, Rebecca had hauled a red weekender bag down four flights of stairs and dropped it on the couch. Several of the objects inside clanked against one another, making her wrinkle her nose.

She opened the bag, careful not to touch any of its contents, and made a bubble of air, which she sent under the stone. It didn't budge. That shouldn't have happened. She'd lifted entire bodies with that trick. A tiny stone should have been nothing. She dropped her bubble of air and tried again. Nothing.

She frowned at the small object. Someone must have spelled it against magic. She would have to do this the old-fashioned way. She went to the kitchen, grabbed a dirty spoon from the dishwasher, and reached under the sink for a pair of cleaning gloves. Better safe than sorry.

Gloves on, spoon in hand, she tried to wedge it under the object. She frowned, trying again. Spreading her legs wide, she bent both elbows and pushed with all her might. The stone didn't budge.

What the hell kind of magic was this? Sophia might know. Did she want to ask the witch for help? It would mean inviting her to her family home and into her personal space. At the moment, she was out of options, though, and workers would arrive in the morning. There was no telling what this object would do to them.

She placed the red bag on top of the stone, obscuring it from passing glances, and picked up the spelled spoon, dropping it inside.

Grabbing her backpack from the chair. She pulled out her brand-new MacBook Pro, a gift from Simon—for Allie—and logged in. She opened her school email account and, just as Sophia had said, she found the email with her roommate assignment and contact info.

Typing out a quick email, she chewed on her bottom lip. The reply was almost immediate: '*Tell me the address. I will be there on the next flight.*'

She typed her reply with instructions for the nearest airport and opened a new screen. Next, a phone.

Rebecca jumped, her laptop tumbling to the floor as a loud buzzing sound rang through the house. She'd fallen asleep on the couch reading articles about the strange weather patterns across most of the eastern coast of North America. Soft yellow streamed in from the hall windows, casting warm patches of light across her face. The buzzing sound rang again.

"I'm coming," she grumbled, setting her bare feet down on the still-damp rug. That would have to go.

She pressed a white button beside the door and said, "Yes, who is it?"

Crackling sounded back then a voice ""Morning ma'am. We're here with Entrusted to remediate your water damage."

She pressed the button below it opening the gate.

A few moments later, cathedral bells sounded through the house and she flung open the door as a man in overalls, with five-day-old stubble, turned to face her. She slid back, waving a hand to usher him in.

He stopped just inside the door and two other men stepped in behind him. "Well, shoot ma'am. Looks like you had a real serious leak."

She nodded, wiping sleep from her eyes.

"Can you show me where the water's coming from?"

She led the man in overalls up the stairs. The back of her neck tingled at the sensation of eyes on her. "The water came from two places," she said, turning as his eyes drifted from her midsection to her face. *Jerk.* "This wall"—she motioned to dark patches of drywall, torn away in places—"and the bathroom here." She walked backward, giving him no chance to ogle her ass again.

He tipped an imaginary hat as he stepped past her into the room and let out a low whistle. "Seems like the problem is these old pipes. Old houses like these always got old pipes." When she said nothing, he continued. "Well, ma'am, I'll need to take a moisture reading of the walls and floors everywhere the water touched. Did the leaks come from anywhere else?"

"No." She crossed her arms.

"I'll check the other floors too, just in case. You never know where invisible leaks might be." He grinned exposing one jagged broken tooth.

"Be my guest but stay off the fourth floor. People are sleeping up there."

She turned, eager to get away from him. Taking the stairs two at a time, she stopped at the door to Rhea's room and poked her head in. Rhea was propped against two large pillows flipping through TV channels.

"Can I join you?" Rebecca asked.

Rhea patted the seat beside her, scooting over. "Come on."

Rebecca dropped lightly onto the bed beside her and reached for her hand. "How are you feeling today?"

"Fine. My eye isn't giving me trouble, so it's a good day."

Rebecca squeezed her hand and leaned closer, pressing some of her warmth into the woman beside her.

Her mind wandered as Rhea continued to scroll. She wasn't sure how much to tell Sophia, but she needed to get her magic under control, and after yesterday, she wouldn't use water magic again until she had a better handle on it. She wondered what it would be like to power-share fire magic.

Sometime later, the loud buzzing sound signaling the gate rang and she sat up. "I'll be back, Rhe. Do you need anything?"

Rhea waved a dismissive hand. Rebecca pressed a kiss to her forehead and bounced down the stairs to open the gate.

Flinging the door wide. Sophia waved to the Uber driver before turning to face her. Her mouth fell open as she surveyed the scene behind Rebecca. "I see why you reached out."

Rebecca moved back. "You could have warned me."

Sophia stepped in and a buzzing started, the positive ions vibrating in the air. Rebecca swiveled her gaze around the room. She could *feel* the surrounding water with Sophia present.

"How are you doing that?"

Sophia flexed her fingers at her side. "When you have power shared as many times as I have, the water strains to be near you."

Rebecca chewed on her bottom lip. "So the more times I do it, the stronger the magic will become?"

"May I set my bags somewhere?" Sophia asked, shouldering her large bags.

"Oh, I'm sorry, let me take one of those." Rebecca stepped forward, taking one large duffel bag from Sophia's shoulder. Their hands brushed against one another, sending a cooling calm down her arm, making her shudder. "It'll be best for you to stay on the fourth floor. They're working on the other three floors."

Sophia followed as they made their way up four flights of stairs. They stopped at the door to Rhea's room. "Hey, Rhe. This is Sophia. She's a friend from school."

Rhea looked up. "Nice to meet you." Sophia waved.

"That's my room. The next one is the brown room if you want to be close to us."

Sophia peered in. "Does it have a bathroom? I prefer a bathroom if that's an option."

"No, only the red room, my room, and the green room have their own private bathrooms."

Sophia giggled. "The rooms are color-coded?"

"Something my father found amusing," Rebecca said, her brows dipping.

Sophia schooled her features. "I'll take the green room if it's available." Rebecca led the way to the room at the opposite end of the hall. She'd considered moving to this room once. It was her favorite color, but in the end, she stayed in the room that had always been hers, throughout all her lifetimes.

"Here we are. The water won't be turned on until the plumber comes to repair it, but it should be later today."

Cathedral bells rang again. Rebecca groaned. It would be a long day.

CHAPTER 29

Rebecca

When the remediation company had set annoyingly loud fans out on the first and third floors, promising to return the next day, the plumber had come and gone, her phone and several Amazon packages had been delivered, and the new home healthcare worker had left for the evening, Rebecca fell into the cushions of her favorite velvet couch and stared up at her father's portrait.

"Well, Dad, you didn't see any of this coming, did you?"

"That is your father?" Sophia asked from the doorway.

"That's him. Alexander Graves."

"May I join you?"

Rebecca waved her arm at the expansive space beside her. "Please." Sophia moved into the room, sitting on the opposite couch. Rebecca's stomach grumbled. She eyed Sophia, who was taking in the grand room. "Are you hungry? I'm ordering dinner." Sophia nodded.

Pulling her phone from her pocket, she texted Rhea, asking for her order from Blackbeard's Tavern, and swiped open the menu. She passed her phone to Sophia. "Pick whatever you'd like."

Sophia scrolled through her phone for several seconds, made her selection and passed the phone back to Rebecca.

"What is the red bag beside you?" Sophia asked.

Rebecca glanced at the foul bag, grimacing. "It's part of the reason I asked you to come. You seem to know more about other types of magic than I do." She lifted the bag, revealing the smooth white stone, and Sophia gasped.

"A blessed object."

"What?" Rebecca dropped the red bag to the floor.

Sophia stood, coming to sit beside her. "This is from the Heavens. How did you come by it?"

Rebecca's brow furrowed. "I found it right here, but I can't move it. What do you mean it's from the Heavens? Like from angels?" She swallowed. Had Gabriel somehow sent her a gift?

"Objects from the Heavens are meant to be worshiped. We have several in our temples back home. This one has found its way to you. We must place it somewhere sacred. Do you have any place like that?"

Rebecca huffed. Someplace sacred in her house? This was the house of a thousand horrors. Her lips pinched. "What do you think would happen if I touched it?"

Sophia's eyebrows drew together as she examined it. "If it was meant for you, it must be a gift to help you on your path."

Jophiel must have left it; she had found it right after the memory with the message from Jophiel to save Gabriel. She snatched it up. The stone came easily, as if it weighed nothing. It was warm in her palm, sending a light humming sensation flashing through her body before the stone went cold.

Sophia watched her. "What did it reveal to you?"

Rebecca's lips dipped at the corners. "Nothing." She waited for... what? But nothing else happened. She dropped the stone, letting it bounce on the couch. It was no help at all. "Maybe you can help me with some of my other questions."

Sophia's chin dipped. "If I have the answer, I will share it."

"You mentioned the Heavens. But what do you know about..." She gagged, choking on her next words. She coughed, beating her chest. "What do you know about..." She coughed again.

"Are you okay? Do you need water?"

Sophia sprung to her feet, running to the kitchen. Rebecca sputtered on a choked, "no," but Sophia was already gone. She returned with a cup of water and held it out. Rebecca took it, letting the cool liquid run down her throat. Somehow, she felt inexplicably tied to water in a way she never had before. Was it how all water witches felt? She had never felt such a strong tie to any of her elemental gifts, though. It must be due to the power-sharing, and if she could find others, her power would only grow.

Sophia dropped beside her. "Better?"

She glared at the rock. That bitch had left it for her, knowing she would pick it up and be unable to speak to anyone about the angels.

Thirty minutes later, when dinner had arrived and the girls had served themselves, Rebecca chewed her slice of pizza, pondering this new predicament. She had been on the verge of asking Sophia for help with Gabriel and now she couldn't say anything about it. Did the gag order extend to writing? She hopped up, raced to the second-floor library, and grabbed a pen and paper from the desk.

Downstairs, she pressed her pen to the page and wrote. The pen halted as she formed the letter a. She pressed harder, but the pen wouldn't budge. She screamed, pressing her weight on the pen. It snapped in two.

Sophia stifled a snort. "Are you well?"

Rebecca glared at the witch. "I'm fine, and when I find that...," she mumbled, letting the words die on her lips. What could *she* do to an angel?

Sophia balled her napkin up and dropped it into the Blackbeard's Tavern bag at their feet. "Come, we have several days until school resumes. Let me teach you to control your water magic so there are no more instances like yesterday."

"I've had a long day. Let's save the lessons for tomorrow." Rebecca stood, feeling the strain in her back. She must have been up and down the stairs at least a few dozen times today. Sophia yawned.

"Perhaps you're right. We start the day fresh tomorrow." She nodded to herself, scooping up the paper bag beside her and holding it open. Rebecca tossed the empty pizza box in and patted her belly. She would pay for that overindulgence later, but it had been worth it.

The girls moved up the stairs one last time for the night, Rebecca stopping to check in on Rhea. Light snores emanating from the dark space settled something in her chest. Rhea had seemed better this evening, even asking for ice cream. Little by little, she was recovering.

Elizabeth stepped out from the dark, casting her shadow across Rebecca's path. Yellow eyes glinted in the dim moonlight, and her small mouth stretched into a wide grin. "Have you missed me, sister?"

Rebecca squared her shoulders. "You don't frighten me, Elizabeth."

Elizabeth raised one hand and the surrounding ground trembled and shook. Rebecca steadied herself and drew in a sharp breath as hands shot from the ground, bending at odd angles, digging into the earth, and soon heads, followed by bodies, emerged. She peered around at old, worn, cracked, and broken headstones. It was like the cemetery Simon had taken her to in Boston.

Disjointed figures jerked and stumbled toward her, some little more than bone and rags. Rebecca raised her hand, casting a ball of flame, and Elizabeth's smile grew.

"Do your worst, sister."

Rebecca flung flaming balls, one after another, at the bodies as they drew near. They caught fire but didn't stop, edging closer. Elizabeth laughed and her shadow lengthened, reaching for Rebecca's. She continued pelting bodies with blue flames as Elizabeth's shadow wrapped dark fingers around hers. As it strangled her shadow, she reached for her own throat, gasping for breath, desperate for air.

She flung her ball of flame at Elizabeth, but it fell short. As she fell to her knees, she let her hand expand and looked at her strangled shadow as it mirrored her movements. Slowly, the flames in her own palm bled into her shadow's. The shadow smashed blue flame into its counterpart and an unholy scream rent the night.

Rebecca sent another ball of flame into her shadow's hand, and it flung the flame into Elizabeth's shadow. The shadow writhed and smoked before winking out. Elizabeth now lay in its place, huddled and shivering. As she watched, her sister's form shimmered, morphing into a woman with dark auburn hair.

Rebecca stretched her hand to the ground, beckoning the earth. It rose, meeting her palm in the shape of a spear, and she brought it down on the woman, crushing her into the ground, burying her beneath it. She called on vines and tree branches, wrapping them around the woman until she was no longer visible beneath them.

A hand broke free, broken nails digging and clawing as vines snapped and roots bent. Rebecca lifted her palm, sending fireballs raining down before the woman could escape. She flailed madly, screaming in rage as her limbs burned with blue fire.

A cloud of smoke swallowed the woman. When the screams died, Rebecca curled her fingers into a fist and the fire winked out, leaving only the charred outline of a beastly creature.

Lips cracked as the creature wheezed, mumbling some incoherent phrase.

Rebecca raised her hands to the sky, bringing down a spear of water, and drove it through the beast. It crumbled, flaking away to nothing as thick black smoke rose from the ashes.

Red eyes formed in the mist, narrowing to slits as it lunged for her. She threw up her hands, spinning a cyclone of air at the beast.

Rebecca's eyes flew open as she gasped for breath. She had had this dream before. But this time, she knew who the girl was. Elizabeth.

Streaks of pink bathed her walls as morning light filtered in through sheer curtains. The smell of lavender hit her, hollowing her chest. She sat up, throwing the blankets aside.

She padded lightly to the door and listened. Low, muffled voices drifted from Rhea's room. She raced across the hall, pulling the door open. Rhea looked up from her place on the bed, turning her TV down. "What is it? What's wrong?"

Rebecca smothered her frown. "Nothing, I thought I heard..."

Rhea gave her a knowing look. "He would be here if you called him."

Her lips drew into a thin line. "No."

"Suit yourself." She pressed the volume button on the remote, making it unnecessarily loud. Rebecca backed up, closing the door behind her. A new smell assaulted her. She bounded down the stairs, her heart thrumming in her chest, and slid to a halt in the kitchen.

Sophia looked up from the stove, spatula in hand. "Good morning. Eggs?" Rebecca stepped into the room, schooling her features into neutrality. "How did you sleep?"

"Fine, you?"

Sophia's eyes gleamed as her lips parted in a broad smile. "This house is full of so many stories. I could spend every night here!"

Rebecca's brows dipped. "What do you mean?"

"My visions come as dreams. Most tell me future stories, glimpses of what will come, but the sight is not always what is to come, but what has already been. This house tells a lot of stories."

Sophia's long hair was untamed, spilling down her back. Her bare feet—ringed by several silver anklets—danced from one to the other, making a light jingling sound. She wore only an oversized T-shirt that did little to cover her long, bronzed legs and down the back of her left leg was a series of star tattoos, seemingly in some constellation pattern.

"I have strange dreams. How do you know when they're a vision or just a nightmare?"

Sophia lifted her frying pan and deposited two eggs, sunny side up, on a plate. She cracked two more eggs in the pan and danced on the balls of her feet as she watched them sizzle and pop. "It is something you feel in your soul. When you know it is not just a dream, but something more."

Rebecca considered her words. "Is it a rare gift?"

Sophia looked up, giving her an appraising stare. "Only one per coven has the gift, but visions may come upon any of us, when necessary."

"I'm not part of any coven."

"You are a part of my coven."

Rebecca choked. "What? I never agreed to join your coven."

"A witch can only power share with witches of their coven. When you power shared, you became a member of mine." Sophia blinked up at Rebecca, her eyes wide and innocent.

"You tricked me."

"What is the issue? You didn't have a coven. It is an honor to be invited into one you were not born into."

"I was fine on my own."

"A witch is never *fine* without her coven. You sought comfort from a night-being. I knew you needed my help the moment I saw you with him."

"You weren't helping me. You played me." Rebecca crossed her arms.

Sophia slid the spatula under the eggs. "Was it not helping to release your memories?"

"How do I leave your coven?"

"You may leave at any time." Rebecca's shoulders sagged. "Provided you have another coven to join." Heat licked down Rebecca's spine, her fingertips lighting with tiny sparks of blue. "Or," Sophia went on, sliding the eggs onto a second plate, unfazed by Rebecca's flames, "if the coven votes to have you removed." She pressed the plate into Rebecca's chest.

"Great. Let's get them on the phone," Rebecca said, taking her plate to the butcher block counter.

Sophia tsked again. "The elders cannot simply be called on the phone to discuss a matter as important as the removal of a coven member. It requires a tribunal."

Rebecca blew out a hot breath. This was a problem for another time.

They ate in silence, Rebecca considering her next move. Her two competing concerns now were Elizabeth and Gabriel. She couldn't fathom how to stop one without the other and, much as she was loath to admit it, she was worried about him.

Something about that dream nagged at the back of her mind. She looked up at Sophia.

"I had a dream last night." Sophia set her fork down and waited. "I've had it twice. In the dream, I'm fighting a night-being, and she uses her shadow to attack me."

"Did you die?"

"No, my shadow conjured fire, my fire, and used it to destroy her shadow." Sophia's brow dipped.

"How do you know it was *your* fire?"

"It was blue."

"Are you the only witch with blue fire magic you've met?"

Rebecca scowled. "Do you know other witches with blue flames?"

Sophia's mouth quirked into a wry smile. "I am not asking to make you angry. In a vision, everything is a clue, but it can be misinterpreted. I am only clarifying the details."

"I'm sure it was mine. The flames bled from my palm to my shadow's. That was how my shadow defeated the night-being's shadow. Do you have any idea what it means?"

"Is there more to your dream?"

Rebecca nodded, sharing everything she could remember.

Sophia placed her hand palm up on the table. A swirl of water formed and separated into several tiny drops floating in place. They reminded Rebecca of the constellation tattooed on Sophia's calf. "The pieces are coming together. Rebecca, *do you* possess all four magical elements?"

Rebecca swallowed. "No, I have mastery of fire and air magic, and you know I have water magic, even though it's weak but I've never had control of earth. I can do other things, create illusions, and I think I've always had some form of sight."

Sophia hummed. "Illusory abilities are merely a combination of air and water magic. These are not elemental gifts. Every coven has one with the gift of vision. You would have been your coven's Pythia."

"Pythia?"

"It's the word for oracle or seer. I am Pythia for my coven."

Rebecca peered at the tiny drops of water hovering above Sophia's palm. "What is this?"

"This is the Hyades cluster. It makes up the brightest point within the Taurus constellation. It lit the night sky every night I dreamed of the end." She pointed to one drop at the center with her free hand, and it glowed red. "Aldebaran, though a member of the Taurus constellation, burns brightest in winter. Yet, on May 6th, its bright red glow burned with such intensity even our neighboring covens called a meeting to debate its meaning. It was on that night I dreamed of a great battle. Lives lost on all sides and in the middle, a bull.

"His hooves struck the earth with such force; the rumble was felt all over the world and on the center of his forehead was a glowing red eye."

"You dreamed of a..." She gagged, swallowing the unsaid word. For the love... She couldn't say demon either? "Something not human," she finished.

Sophia's gaze roved her face, some unknown emotion playing across her features before continuing. "The red eye represents Aldebaran. The third eye placement is the sign for a witch."

"So a witch, born in May," Rebecca said, leaning back in her chair.

"Precisely, and with your vision, we also know this witch must possess all four magical elements. Such a witch has not been heard of in centuries."

Rebecca *had* heard of such a witch, though. Adalaide. "What if you're wrong?"

"The visions are never wrong."

"What if you misinterpreted them? There was someone with all four elements. My ancestor. And she had children. Isn't it possible one of her children could have also possessed this gift?"

"Have any of your ancestors been born in the Taurus constellation?"

Rebecca blew out a breath. "My father kept meticulous family records. He was researching his history. He might have their birth and death dates recorded somewhere." This would be so much easier with Simon here. He would know where to find the information. She brushed the thought aside.

"It's good that we have the rest of the week here to find it." Sophia winked.

Rebecca pursed her lips. "What if I have another ancestor with a Taurus birthday? How does that help us?"

"More will be revealed as we move closer to the answer."

She arched an eyebrow. "Fine, let's divide our time between searching my father's records and lessons in water magic."

Sophia nodded her affirmation and the drops of water hovering in her palm fell, splashing over the tabletop.

CHAPTER 30

Simon

S imon stuffed his phone into his pocket, running a hand over his face. He had been sure the last message would at least get a response from her. He had poured his soul into it, but still no reply. She had completely shut him out. What was she doing now? Was she thinking of him? He could check. For her safety, he should, but he knew she would consider it an invasion of her privacy to watch her in her own home.

He'd opened the app only twice, once when the alarm went off, and he'd watched her stagger inside to her bed and once more to be sure she was still sleeping before he brought her backpack inside. He wouldn't do it again. No matter how much he wanted to.

He stood. "Excuse me," he said, stepping into the aisle. The woman who had spent the better part of fifteen minutes organizing and reorganizing her bags in front of him seemed no closer to deboarding now than she had when she stood. He slid around her, narrowly avoiding tiny snapping teeth as her small dog attempted to take a piece of him as a souvenir.

"Well, I never," she grumbled as he broke free of her and exited the plane.

"I apologize, ma'am," he called over his shoulder.

All around him, throngs of people moved, blocking his path. He slid another frustrated hand through his hair and wished he could fly or levitate or something more useful than move quickly. Any of Rebecca's abilities would have come in handy. Thinking of her left an ache in his chest.

It was wrong not to tell her. He saw that now. He had enjoyed the time he spent with Allie, even if this version of her, the one that never became a reash, never hunted down demons for six years or died alone in a gymnasium, didn't have the same hard edges she once had. Couldn't empathize with the trauma of remembering her own death.

He was no stranger to the ever-evolving Rebecca, though.

And he loved her, imperfect as she was, the orchestrator of his friends' and lover's demise. What would he give to see any one of their smiling faces right now? Rachel's rebellious spirit, Sarah's shy inquisitiveness, Allie's fiery temper. His firecracker.

And yet, he didn't love her any less for taking them all away from him. She had always been jealous of them. The ridiculousness of it would have made him laugh if there was room in his heart for any emotion apart from pain.

And after everything, she had shut him out of her life.

He stepped through the door into the brisk morning air. It was a welcome reprieve from the stifling heat of North Carolina in August. Pulling the second strap over his shoulder, he placed one foot in front of the other, putting the airport behind him, and sped toward the only hope he had of saving her life and winning her back.

Simon slowed as he reached the edge of the Fellowes estate. It was nestled on the edge of Peterborough, just inside the district of Cambridgeshire on twenty acres. It was an impressive piece of land for the time and spoke of the wealth the family still possessed that they had not parceled it away over the years.

He ran a hand down his shirt, smoothing it, and rang the bell. His phone buzzed and his heart seized as he fumbled in his pocket for it. *Thank you for flying with us. American Airlines invites you to complete a brief survey telling us of your recent experience.* His stomach dropped as he slid the phone back into his pocket.

Was this how it would be now? Every text, every call, sending his heart soaring, only to plummet when it wasn't her?

He rang the bell again, schooling his features into polite neutrality, and pasted a smile on his face. He heard heavy footsteps approaching long before the door creaked and slid open.

"Good day. How may I help you?" a balding man asked in a heavy Yorkshire accent.

"Hello, I called ahead about the article I'm writing. John Fellowes said I was welcome to stay at the estate."

"Ah, yes. Please, come in, sir." The man stepped back, ushering him inside. "May I take your coat?"

"No need. If I might be shown to my room, I will leave everything there."

He nodded. "Right this way. I will let the Viscount know you've arrived."

He stepped in, following the balding man down an expansive marble hall. It hadn't changed a bit since he'd been here last. Even the paintings hung in their original positions. Of course, none of the inhabitants here would remember him now. Most were likely not born the last time he visited, apart from the oldest Fellowes resident, Victoria. She must be in her eighties, but he hardly expected her to remember him after all this time.

"Your room is here, sir. Tea is at eleven. The Viscount will meet you in the parlor."

Simon dipped his head, bowing, and the balding man did the same. He checked his watch, already adjusted for local time. A meeting at eleven left him plenty of time to do some snooping.

CHAPTER 31

Rebecca

Rebecca blew out a breath, dropping to her knees. "I'm done. I'm over it."

Sophia chuckled. "We've barely begun."

"It's been four hours."

Sophia tsked. "Rome wasn't built in a day."

Rebecca wiped her sleeve against her brow. "It's hot. I'm hungry, and we still need to search my father's records today. I'm going in." She stood, dusting her knees, and started for the door. A blast of icy water hit her in the back. She spun on her heel. "What the hell is wrong with you?"

"I cooled you off. Now we can continue."

Rebecca ground her teeth. "We still need to find out if any of my ancestors was a Taurus, remember?"

"Reading is for the night. Daylight is for physical labor. We practice." She lifted her hands, sending another blast of water at Rebecca. She threw up an air shield, blocking it. "You have this one. We are practicing water magic. Take control, bend the water to your will."

Another blast of water barreled toward her. She lifted her hands, attempting the complex patterns Sophia had forced her to practice all morning. The cooling liquid in her veins surged as she felt it respond to her pull. The water slowed, hovering in front of her.

"Good, send it back to me."

She bit down on her lip as she framed her fingers around the water, working to shape it into a ball. It drooped, slipping through her fingers. Sophia swatted her hand and cold liquid splashed her face, dripping down her collar into her shirt, soaking her bra. "Bitch," she grumbled.

Sophia laughed, covering her mouth. "I am keeping you cool."

"Where are you even getting all this water from?"

"The pool." She said it as if it were obvious, but the pool was around the corner and out of view.

"This is easy for you. Water is your primary element. Water is my weakest."

"You are wrong about that. I felt it in you when we power-shared. Your water magic is not weak, it was merely dormant. I woke it."

Rebecca grumbled a few choice words under her breath. She blew out another breath and widened her stance. All she had to do was bring the water from the pool to her. Simple. She leaned into the feelings that always seemed to bring water to her before.

Simon's feelings for Allie, the way he touched her, held her, kissed her. The water in her veins hummed to life, thrumming under her skin. Their last night together. Images of his lips against her fevered skin, *Allie's* skin. The hairs on her arms rose.

"Rebecca," Sophia said.

His head, buried between her thighs as he wrung every ounce of exquisite pleasure from her. Blue veins running down her arms bulged under her skin.

"Rebecca."

Every moment seared across her brain, a brand that would never fade. Static electricity buzzed around her.

Sophia spun, throwing her hands in the air just as a tidal wave rushed toward them. She threw her hands wide, and the water parted, shooting left into the orchard and right into the wall of the house.

Rebecca fell to her knees, sucking in lungfuls of air. What had happened? She had never lost control like that, never let her emotions overtake her so completely. Her skin still buzzed, the rush of liquid magic making her feel bloated and puffy.

When she looked up, Sophia was dropping to her knees beside her. "Rebecca, your eyes."

Rebecca rose unsteadily to her feet. "What's wrong with them?"

Sophia stood, holding her arm out. "Let me help you."

Rebecca leaned against the other girl, sighing as the rush of magic slowed, feeling as if it were being siphoned away until only a thin trickle ran through her. They walked slowly as Rebecca regained her sense of calm.

Inside, they stopped at the first mirror in the hall and Rebecca stared in wonder at the ring of deep azure blue now rimming her irises.

She turned her head from side to side. At the center of each eye was a deep blue starburst erupting from the iris of each eye, bleeding into their normal glacial blue. It was beautiful.

"I've seen nothing like it," Sophia breathed. "We need to call Yia-Yia."

Settled on cerulean blue velvet that now more closely resembled the color of the starbursts at the center of her eyes, Rebecca chewed on her bottom lip as she watched Sophia speaking into the phone.

Sophia's tone sharpened, her words growing more rushed. Rebecca sat forward, a thrill of anxiety racing through her. She picked up the white stone beside her absently, rolling it over her clammy palm. "Xero. Xero. Yia-Yia prosecho." She dropped the phone into her lap and looked up. "She says it's the mark of power."

"So it's good news?" Sophia pulled a strand of hair, twisting it between her fingers. Rebecca hadn't seen Sophia fidget before. She was always calm. Her stomach swooped. "Bad news?"

Sophia turned, facing her. "It means one of two things: either your magic has been unnaturally enhanced through some dark magic or you're dying from some unnatural cause and the use of this much magic is speeding the process."

Rebecca's heart seized in her chest as she struggled for air, the room going black at the edges. Sophia's voice came through a tunnel as the world spun. "No," she breathed. A sharp pain pierced her chest and her breathing grew ragged. *Not again. Not again.*

Something cool and soothing touched her back, rubbing in circles. The cooling magic bleeding into her calmed her racing heart. She pulled in a breath then another.

When she was breathing normally, racing thoughts tumbled into her mind. She was dying. Her father's curse wasn't broken. She had two years if this recent surge of power didn't kill her sooner.

"I can't practice anymore."

"You just need to learn to control it. If you get it under control, it will not hurt you." Sophia placed a hand on Rebecca's arm and the soothing rush of her liquid magic flowed into her, easing the nervous thrum of her heartbeat again.

"No. I'm dying. My father placed a curse on me, a death curse. I thought... I thought I was free of it."

"Curses can be broken, Rebecca." Rebecca tore her arm from Sophia's grasp.

"What do you know about it? I've lived with this curse all my life..." Her voice trailed away.

"We will discontinue practice for now until we have more answers. I will call Yia-Yia again tomorrow. She will know what to do." Rebecca swallowed the lump rising in her throat. With Sophia's calming touch gone, the panic was rising again, threatening to consume her. Her heart raced, making her lightheaded. Was this her last life? Would she die for real this time?

"I need some time." She stood, bracing herself against the arm of the couch as she skirted around it and left the room.

In her room, she pulled out her phone, pressing the numbers she knew by heart. She held it to her ear, listening as it rang.

"Hello." Her lower lip trembled. His voice made something inside crack and a sob escaped her. "Hello, Rebecca? Is that you?" A soft whine broke free as she began to cry in earnest, saying nothing, sobbing into the phone. He listened, his quick breaths a balm. "What can I do?"

She sniffled loudly, sucking air between wracking sobs, working to compose herself enough to speak. "I'm... I'm dying." Her voice broke. "I'm still dying."

"I'm coming."

"No... don't." The silence that followed was deafening. She owed him more than that. "I'm not dying now." A soft whimper escaped her. "I have some time. I just wanted to tell you, to hear your voice one more time."

"Rebecca. We'll fix this. We can find a solution. Together."

"No," she cut him off. "This is my problem." She wiped her slick cheek. "I just... wanted you to know." She hung up the phone before he could say more. She knew it was cowardly, but his words were too tempting. It would have been easy to fall back into old habits. Let him rush in. The knight in shining armor who always wanted to save her. But she was tired of being the damsel, and she hadn't survived more than one hundred years by lying back and taking it.

She would be her own hero. She would break this curse herself.

CHAPTER 32

Gabriel

Gabriel stretched his wings, feeling the tender places where they had not completely healed. It was progress. The days ran together, endless nights giving no indication of how long it had been now, but his legs were healed, and his wings would be strong enough to fly in just a few days.

He scraped a white X over the passage, stepping back to survey this side of the cave. Three caves left to explore on this side, then he would move on to the next set. A tremor rocked through him, and he stumbled against the wall.

Someone had just been bound by one of his stones. Who? Why? Had something happened to Simon? Were they replacing him with yet another human? Another poor soul, tricked into bargaining away their freedom for a few more years on that merciless plane.

Why anyone would choose Earth over Alaxia, he would never understand. But what did he know of humans and their strange obsession with the place? Even the demons he found crammed into mortal bodies, in a desperate attempt for one more day up there, baffled him.

If something had happened to Simon, Rebecca truly was in danger. Without her guard dog to watch over her, Elizabeth might make her move, and she would be wholly unprepared.

He righted himself and stepped into the next passage. In absolute darkness, he should have had to rely on touch alone, but the longer he remained in this realm, the better he was able to see, and with each day, as the world around him grew brighter, the less it felt like Hell.

Strange flowers sprouted from cracks in the rocks. Where at first, he thought they existed in shades of gray and black, he now saw the myriad of deep indigo, wine, and plum that made each one unique. He quickly learned the blossoms, or lack of them, signaled danger. Where they grew thickest, the path was clear. Where they were most sparse, some vile thing dwelt.

This made clearing passages a much simpler task. He set out on a path and followed it until the flowers became scarce. When there were none left, he returned to the original cave and marked it as unsafe.

On his first trek, he had ignored the signs, nearly walking into a den of wispy creatures using one another for sport. Their own twisted machinations had distracted them too much to notice him.

The second time, he was on his guard and as the last flower bloomed in his path, a thunderous roar sounded ahead, beating hooves against the earth; warning him of its impending approach. He had turned and run, thankful his left leg could bear his weight.

As he moved deeper into the tunnel, he noted the petals growing lighter, some a deep burgundy. He stopped at a fork. To the right, flowers bloomed in abundance. To the left, fewer dotted the path. He scratched an arrow pointing right and followed that route, trailing his fingers along the petals. His chest warmed, buzzing as if a swarm of bees had taken residence there.

He continued forward, catching some light sound. It was melodic, pulling him along. He hummed as he plucked a petal from the nearest flower. A biting sting cleared his mind, and he looked down. Golden liquid, blindingly bright in the dark tunnel, slid from his finger, dripping to the floor.

The humming sound grew louder, drowning out his thoughts. He moved, seeking its source. Flowers crowded his path now, narrowing the tunnel until he had to crouch to continue. They pulled at him, snagging hair, scraping skin. They were a light annoyance, a mild sting, easily ignored. He pressed on, fighting their oppressive hold.

He broke through, stumbling into a room much larger than his and stood, swaying as the strange melody overtook him.

In the center of the room, a massive bathing pool dominated the space. A lithe figure rose, displaying full breasts, rivulets of water running down her bare flesh and below the dark surface obscuring her lower half.

She hummed, beckoning him forward. His feet moved, and he found himself at the edge of the pool. Her opalescent skin glowed in some unseen moonlight as she draped an arm over his shoulder, running a finger along his healing wing. He shuddered, a deep throbbing sensation beginning between his thighs.

She wrapped a second arm around his neck and pulled him close. He leaned in, glimpsing the black water still concealing the most delicious parts of her. He wanted to see those parts, desperately, urgently. Nothing else mattered. He dipped his head into the pool.

Stabbing pain tore into his shoulders as he was hauled into the dark liquid with more force than should have been possible.

He swallowed water, choking on it, reaching for the surface, but taloned fingers held him down with such force he could not escape.

When the panic lessened, he opened his eyes, peering around in the murky dark, and a muffled scream escaped him. All around bloated, distorted figures lay speared to the floor. The same purple flowers protruded from their chests, arms, legs, and necks. Each wore an expression of misery more profound than the next.

His mind cleared, and he fought to break the surface as a biting pain drove into each wing. He glanced left then right to see trails of golden blood floating to the surface. In the center of each wing blade, enormous purple and red flowers bloomed. He reached over his shoulder, tearing at the petals as a black blade tore through his arm, pinning it to the rocky wall beside his wing.

He screamed in rage, bubbles drifting from his lips and floating to the surface in this new prison. A dark shape filled his vision and Samael swam into focus. A deep maniacal chuckle escaped his pierced lips.

"Dear brother, I see you found my siren."

CHAPTER 33

Rebecca

"I'm fine... I'm great." She lifted one shoulder, watching the nonchalance in her reflection's gesture. Was it believable? *She* wasn't buying it. "So I'm dying. I have time." She spread her lips in a wide, toothy smile. *Too much.* She picked up her under-eye concealer, running it under each eye. It was doing nothing to hide the red rim circling each eye, but it masked some of the puffiness.

Blowing out a breath, she said, "It's not the first time I've died." She chewed on her bottom lip. That would be the right approach if she was going for the shock factor. "I will find a way to beat this."

A knock at the door startled her. "Yes?"

"It's Sophia, can I come in?"

She exhaled slowly. "Sure, come in." She turned from the vanity to face the door as it cracked open.

Sophia's honey-brown mane gleamed under the lights as she stepped into the room. "Are you all right?"

"I'm fine. It's not the worst news I've ever had." She winced. That wasn't even one of the lines she'd practiced.

Sophia gave her an appraising stare. "My mama texted. She thinks we should go to Greece. The coven has many skilled witches who could work to unbind your curse. I think she's right."

"We can't go to Greece. We have school on Monday."

Sophia arched an eyebrow. "If you believe you're dying, do you not think saving your life takes priority over school?"

Rebecca stood. "I have time, and I need to do some research here. It's my father's curse, which means the key to undoing it is likely here in this house. I'll stop practicing magic until I find the answer." She hoped she sounded more confident than she felt. Why had she said school?

Sophia gave her a curt nod. "I will help you."

"Great, but first, I'm starving."

"Me too," a voice called.

Rebecca and Sophia stepped into the hall and leaned their heads into Rhea's room. Rhea slung her legs over the side of her bed, lifting herself gingerly.

Rebecca rushed in, holding up an arm as Rhea leaned on it, patting her arm lightly. "Thanks. Help me downstairs?"

"Rhea, I can make you something or the nurse can. Stay up here. I'll bring it to you."

Rhea swatted her shoulder. "I've been cooped up long enough. Help me downstairs or I'll go down myself." Sophia moved forward, holding out her other arm, and gasped.

Rhea and Rebecca turned their gazes to her as her eyes rolled back in her head and she froze in place. Rhea looked at Rebecca, who shrugged, extricating herself from Rhea's hold to move around her.

She touched Sophia's arm, but the girl remained motionless, the whites of her eyes staring at nothing. "Rhea, sit for a minute so I can check on her, would you?"

Rhea pulled her arm free from Sophia, and her eyes rolled forward.

She stared at the two of them blankly for a moment, then said, "You should be dead."

When Sophia had convinced both Rebecca and Rhea she was okay, they all went down to the kitchen, taking the stairs one at a time. Rebecca pulled a plush chair from the corner to the butcher block counter and helped Rhea sit.

She faced Sophia with her hand on her hip. "So. What was that?"

Sophia pulled out a stool and sat. "I had a vision."

"I thought you only saw things in your dreams."

"It was a daydream. They're not common, but they happen."

"What was it about?"

Sophia twisted a lock of golden hair between her fingers, coiling and uncoiling it as she gazed at Rhea. "She was attacked by a night-being. She should have died. Someone performed healing magic on her."

Rebecca shook her head. "That's impossible. Rhea doesn't know any other witches, and I don't know any healing spells."

"The vision only showed me that she would be dead now if not for the healing touch of magic."

"Did the vision show you who it was? Was it a young girl?"

"It was a man, newly made."

"What's a night-being?" Rhea asked.

Rebecca came to Rhea's side, lifting frail fingers into her own and squeezed them, stilling them. "Someone like Simon used to be."

Sophia dropped the curl she'd wound around her finger, letting it slide free. "Used to be?"

Rebecca schooled her face into a neutral mask. She hadn't meant to say that. It surprised her she could. Didn't it give too much away for the angel's liking? "I only mean, he was around only at night, before."

"I see," Sophia said. A chill ran down Rebecca's spine as she watched Sophia's too-sharp eyes trail over Rhea's healing wound and back to her. "Well, who's hungry?" Rebecca bit the inside of her cheek, frowning. Sophia stood, sliding by Rebecca as she opened the refrigerator and began removing items. "Where do you keep the dry goods?"

Rebecca surveyed the items on the counter. Tomatoes, green peppers, mushrooms, and an onion. "What are you making?"

"I thought I would make Bolognese. Everyone likes pasta." Rebecca led the way to the gutted and restocked pantry and switched on a blinding white light. There would be no more crawling things in her pantry. Sophia sighed dreamily as she surveyed the floor-to-ceiling shelves stocked with every pantry item imaginable.

In the quiet space, Rebecca leaned closer to Sophia and whispered, "Try not to scare Rhea too much. She's already been through so much."

Sophia reached for the salt then grabbed other items as she moved through the pantry. "You do her no favors by leaving her in the dark."

"She can't protect herself. Why scare her?"

"I remember a similar argument in a hotel room just a few days ago." She bumped Rebecca's shoulder as she moved to the door, pushing it open.

Rebecca's mouth fell open. It wasn't the same at all. *She* had abilities. *She* could defend herself.

Pushing open the door, she halted outside the pantry. Rhea stood beside Sophia, chopping a tomato.

"Rhea, you shouldn't do that. Sit." Rhea swatted a hand, humming to herself. She did seem to be feeling better. Was it too soon, considering the seriousness of her injury?

"Ms. Walker," a voice barked from the kitchen door, making them all look up. A middle-aged woman in purple scrubs marched into the kitchen, hands planted firmly on her hips. "You should not be downstairs. We talked about this. Your blood pressure was elevated this morning. You could faint and hit your head."

Rhea mumbled something under her breath and continued chopping tomatoes. Rebecca smirked at the flustered woman whose cheeks were growing pinker by the second. Sophia uncorked a bottle of wine and poured generously into a mixing bowl.

A loud bang startled the four of them as Rhea yelped and Sophia reached for her, supporting her weight. The home healthcare worker scurried into the room, crowding beside Sophia.

Rebecca moved around the group in the direction of the noise. "Everyone stay here. I'll go check it out." She tiptoed down the hall on light feet, feeling a light breeze she knew shouldn't exist. Another loud noise drew her attention as she pressed her fingers to the door leading to her father's lair. The hairs on her arms rose, and her ears began to ring.

Flicking her wrist, she conjured a ball of flame, sending it overhead as she stepped down into the dark. The ringing in her ears intensified as another loud bang sounded from below. She reached the bottom step as the metal door to the lair slammed shut in her face. A creak sounded behind her, and she whirled, palms raised, to find Sophia a few stairs above her.

"What are you doing?" she hissed. "Get back upstairs with Rhea."

Sophia took the final steps down until they were eye to eye on the dirt floor. "Rhea is not alone. What is this place?"

"Go back upstairs. You're not safe down here."

"And you are?"

In answer, Rebecca spread her fingers, and the room grew brighter, tinged in blue. Sophia smirked, lifting a hand as a low rumble started, and roots burst from the floor, forming a long wooden lance. She tore the weapon free, and the roots receded into the floor.

"That won't protect you from what's on the other side of this door. Only fire or a blessed blade can protect you."

Sophia looked at the metal door and then back at Rebecca. "What is it?"

"I can't say."

Sophia arched an eyebrow, and without waiting for further explanation, she stepped past Rebecca and her ball of fire and wrenched open the door.

CHAPTER 34

Rebecca

"Wait!" Rebecca called, but Sophia stepped into the dark, wielding her spear, and was gone. Rebecca mumbled a few choice words under her breath and followed, bathing the room in a blue hue. "Get down!" she shrieked as an inky substance dove toward Sophia's head.

Sophia didn't duck. She opened her mouth, and a sound such as Rebecca had never heard poured free. The substance halted, forming the shape of a creature that might have once been a woman. Dark wide wings sprouted from each shoulder in place of arms and its head, humanoid in some ways, had large bulging horns in place of eyebrows that swung low, hanging to either side of its elongated head. Glowing red eyes fixed on Sophia as it swayed, caught in her siren's call.

Rebecca worked to tune out the sound and make her limbs work properly. The sweet melody was alluring, much stronger than the first time.

Sophia's brows lifted as her gaze fell on Rebecca and she tipped her head toward the demon hovering less than three feet from her.

Right. Forcing her arms to obey, Rebecca flung her ball of fire, sending it crashing into the demon hovering before them. The creature didn't so much as flinch as flames collided with her chest, catching her dark form alight before she winked out of existence.

The melody halted, sending Rebecca's stomach plummeting. An aching dark loneliness swept through her, making her knees buckle. She tipped forward as Sophia caught her in the dark.

"Whoa, are you okay?" Sophia asked.

"Your song was really powerful." She steadied herself, lifting from Sophia's grasp. "But I think I'm better now."

"My song is strongest for those who have experienced true heartbreak. I'm sorry for your loss." Sophia touched Rebecca's arm, sending a cooling wave of liquid through her. She sighed. It felt like her heart had been beaten with a sledgehammer, smashed into a thousand tiny shards, and the cooling water sliding through her veins found each sliver and pulled them back into place.

She took one breath, then another.

"Come Adelfí, let's return to the couches so you can rest."

Rebecca stumbled forward, cursing her waning strength after such a small display of magic. She pushed the metal door open, leading Sophia up the long set of stairs to the first floor and into the light.

They paused at the end of the hall as the sound of raised voices met them.

"At least sit down."

"I've been sitting for a week. All I've done is sit or lay. I need to get up. I need to be useful!"

"Let me just take your vitals and—"

"I'll take her," Rebecca cut in, moving into the room to stand beside Rhea. She held out her arm and Rhea took it.

"Well, I don't think—"

"What was your name?"

"It's Marissa, but I was hired to—"

"Thank you, Marissa. I'll make sure she gets to her room. Why don't you go back to whatever you were doing when we found her alone in her room this evening?" Rhea's chin lifted as they passed the home healthcare worker on their way into the foyer, and she huffed a light laugh.

"You can be mean sometimes, Rebecca," Rhea said, patting her arm.

Swallowing a lump rising in her throat, she glanced down at the frail woman. "You think I'm mean?"

"Your grandfather raised you to be that way. You can't help it. Sometimes folks need someone who will stand up for them, even if it means they have to be the bad guy."

An ache tugged at her chest, and she cleared her throat, saying, "Come on, let's take a stroll outside."

In the clear evening air, Rebecca breathed deeply. They passed under her favorite tree, and memories of baby Sarah laid out on a blanket, making butterflies, swam into her mind. She pressed a hand to the rough bark. Blinking back tears, she ran a finger over the small heart carved into the wood.

"This was Rachel's favorite spot too," Rhea murmured. She leaned in, peering at the small carving. "She was convinced her parents left that heart for her to find. Came out here almost every day to talk to the tree." The corners of Rhea's eyes crinkled as she chuckled low in her belly. "So independent, that girl. When she left, I was almost certain she'd escaped this place and its curses."

Rebecca drew in a sharp breath, letting it out in a whoosh. "There's no escaping Alexander's curses." She tasted the truth of her words. Resignation settled over her, threatening to seep into her bones and take root.

No, she couldn't accept it. It would not be her fate to die again. This time, she would live beyond twenty-five. "Come on," she said, pulling Rhea away from the shade of the massive oak and into the orchard.

Rhea moved slowly, but her steps were steady, her breathing calm. She truly seemed to be healing quickly. If what Sophia said was true, what did it mean? Who could have healed her? Who had the power to do such a thing? She had never heard of a witch with healing abilities, but she was learning there were a lot of things she didn't know about witches.

They reached the end of the orchard and looked up at the massive wall caging them in. Rebecca chewed on her bottom lip, glancing at Rhea's bandaged head. How had she forgotten about the bit of claw used as a weapon? It was too small to have come from the fence.

It had to be from the gargoyles in her father's lair. But the demon this afternoon had been trapped down there, which meant someone had put it back. *Simon.* Of course he had. It was probably the first thing he did after getting Rhea to the hospital. Perhaps that was where he'd gone.

She could only imagine what might have happened if he hadn't.

The loud noises the demon had made were unusual for a demon. They were normally silent creatures. It was almost as if the being hadn't expected to be trapped. Had it somehow known the circle was broken? Expecting to catch them in the daylight hours, unaware and unprepared?

That could only mean one thing. Elizabeth was behind the attack on Rhea and had somehow harnessed the amulet to trap a new demon and she was finally making her move.

CHAPTER 35

Rebecca

R ebecca waved off Marissa's chiding as they came inside and sat around the kitchen counter, coming together to try Sophia's Bolognese. It was heavenly, reminding Rebecca of a time before prepared sauces and prepackaged foods. When each ingredient mingled together, bursting with flavors unlike anything store-bought.

She moaned, eliciting a few stares from around the table, but Sophia only grinned.

"After dinner, we will search for information among your father's things?" Sophia asked.

"Yes, but first, I need to check my email. I ordered some books, and I want to be sure they'll be here in time for classes." Rebecca pushed her stool back, taking her bowl to the sink. She bit her lip. "Thank you for dinner, Sophia."

Rhea made a choking sound, sending Marissa into a panic as she waved her off. Rebecca smiled and slid out the door, making her way to the second-floor library.

It was fully dark now, and she flipped switches as she went, lighting the hallway and the room as she stepped in. She had always loved this room. Although most of the books were purchased to stage the space, one bookshelf was dedicated to the women of the Graves' estate. It housed Margaret's old collection of classics, the books Sarah hadn't felt the need to hide, and Claire's murder mystery novels.

She ran a finger over dusty, cracked, well-loved spines as she read titles. The complete Jane Austen collection, Harriet the Spy, Watership Down. She stopped on a brown leather, unmarked spine. How had it gotten there? She slid it out, flipping it open to one of the dog-eared pages.

The blood of one, the lives of many, must endure. Speak the words, know thyself true or be damned. Flame of desire, gilded heart, protect what lies within. This Grave responsibility.

Below was the translation written in her father's hand:

The Graves family line is the key to maintaining control. Protect the amulet, keep the secret. Fire and gold are its cage. Speak the words to invoke it. Translation above: If I cannot bend Heaven, I shall move Hell.

Her father had translated the old passage to make sense of it, but what if his translation had not been accurate? Did this passage have something to do with Sophia's dream? She had never paid much attention to her father's research, or his zealous obsession with their family's lineage, but what if someone in their family had known of the prophecy?

What if that person was also a Taurus?

She continued flipping and stopped on a page with scribbles and scribbles of handwriting that matched the earlier writing.

A soul's great solace, recognizing an analogous umbra. It comes in the night, threatening all I love. It whispers in the dark, promising life evermore. Myne immolation or oblation? Shall it be as it was meant or do fates so entwined defy predestination?

She scrolled to the bottom where she read:

Five and twenty, the price I paid. Recompense for pneuma, I woolde gladly pay again. AG.

Rebecca gasped.

"What is it?" Sophia's voice in her ear made her jump, dropping the book.

"You made me lose the page." She stooped, retrieving the book from the floor.

"Why did you gasp?"

Rebecca moved aside, putting distance between them as she thumbed through the pages. Finding it, she pointed to the original passage her father had translated.

Sophia twisted a lock of hair around her finger. "You think this refers to the prophecy?" She reached for the book. Rebecca jerked back, hesitant to give up her family's secrets to this girl whom she still knew so little about. Sophia frowned but made no move to take the book. "Is there anything else in the book relating to this passage? It is vague."

Rebecca turned to the page with the other passage she'd just read, holding it up. Sophia couldn't know what it meant. *She* didn't know what it meant.

Sophia stabbed the page with her finger. "This is an ancient Greek word meaning Soul. Where did you get this journal?"

"It's an old family journal."

"Your family is Greek?" Sophia raised an eyebrow, pursing her lips. "I guess I can see it, in the eyes. Your skin is pale, though."

Rebecca rolled her eyes, her lips tipping up at the corners. "What do you think the passages mean? Do you think they're connected to your vision?"

"The first part 'The blood of one, the lives of many' is similar in some ways to my vision. To me, it means one bloodline in exchange for many or even all souls on earth. The rest makes little sense to me, but the second part, this is clearer. 'Analogous umbra' means soulmate. 'It comes in the night' is your night-being, I am sure. What comes after is not clear, but 'Recompense for pneuma' means in payment for the souls."

Rebecca chewed on her bottom lip. If it meant Simon was her soulmate, he had already paid that sacrifice. Twice. "Immolation and oblation are two terms for the word sacrifice, but they mean different things. I read this to mean: Is it offered freely or taken? But"—she paused—"immolation specifically means to destroy by fire for sacrifice. Oblation is a religious word that means to present in offering to God."

The girls stared at each other. Rebecca noticed the small brown and gold flecks dotting Sophia's eyes. They marked a starburst pattern not unlike the one she now had in her eyes. She leaned closer, trying to get a better look.

Soft lips brushed against hers, and she startled back.

"What the hell?" Warmth flooded her cheeks as she backed up another step. Sophia's eyes danced with amusement.

"Didn't you like it?"

"No, and I have a boyfriend."

"Do you?"

She bit her lip. Sophia's gaze fell to her mouth, and she released the flesh from between her teeth. "Maybe I don't, but I'm not looking to get into anything new right now."

Sophia's lips quirked at the corner. "Let me know if anything changes." Unnerving emerald eyes never wavered, penetrating in their intensity.

Rebecca huffed. "Can we focus? I need to figure this out if I'm going to find a way to break this curse. In case you forgot, I'm dying."

Sophia's grin fell. "You're right. We have more important things to think of than our carnal desires."

Rebecca's cheeks flushed an unnatural hue as she cleared her throat. "I'm not having any desires," she mumbled, turning to face her book. "As I was saying, it all seems to say a sacrifice will be made. If your visions are to be trusted, that sacrifice is for the fate of humanity. I'm just not sure what the sacrifice is or how Simon is connected. He's already sacrificed himself. Twice. But your vision came after both."

Sophia leaned back, pressing against a beam. "My family tells a story. It's why I knew the meaning of 'analogous umbra'. When humans were created, we had four arms and legs and a head of two faces, but our hearts and our souls were one."

"I've heard this myth," Rebecca interjected.

"Perhaps you have, but most people only know part of the legend of Zeus. In my coven, we tell the whole story. When the split occurred, the spirit, or the pneuma, could not be shared. It had to choose one to go with, leaving the other empty. When the empty halves withered and faded the halves with pneuma felt the loss and screamed for vengeance.

"Their rage was known the world over. They became beasts, half whole, and fought amongst each other until few remained.

"When Zeus saw what he had done, he ripped pneuma's umbra from their bodies, feeding it to their other half. It was a shadow of the whole, a piece of the soul, but it was enough to sustain life. With their other halves revived, humans scoured the earth, desperate to find their analogous umbra. The shadow of their soul, its mate."

"My dream," Rebecca whispered. Sophia dipped her chin. "But in my dream, my shadow had to hurt Elizabeth's shadow. I couldn't harm her until my shadow destroyed hers."

"Who is Elizabeth?" *Shit.* She hadn't meant to say that. It was becoming difficult to work with Sophia without telling her the truth. Could she trust her? She had never shared her past with anyone but Simon. But she could see no way around it if they were going to work together.

"Elizabeth was my sister. Now she's a night-being, and she's after me. She attacked Rhea, or she had someone else do it for her."

Sophia's face paled, her confident demeanor dimming. A hand went to her throat, where she ran a finger across her collarbone, searching for something that wasn't there. "Your sister is a night-being?" she breathed.

"My father made her."

"No. No, den einai dynato. It's not possible. A human cannot make a night-being."

Rebecca opened her mouth, coughing as she choked on her next words. She tried again and felt the air lodge in her throat. She sputtered, coughing again. "Yes," she finally managed. "He made Simon too."

Sophia pushed off the wall, pacing. "It doesn't make sense. Are you saying you knew your demon, Simon when he was alive?"

"Yes. He was alive when I was." *Shit, shit.* She hadn't meant to say that either. It was too late, though. Sophia's head had already snapped up, and she was eyeing her, appearing to work out some complicated equation in her mind.

"You are not dead. Nor are you a night-being."

"No."

"You are nekromanteia," she hissed. "Practitioner of the black magic." Her accent was growing stronger as she mixed English and Greek. She paced faster. "This is Kako, Kakia. I need to call Yia-Yia."

Rebecca raised her hands, and Sophia flinched back. "Wait, no. I'm not a necromancer. It's complicated, but it has to do with my father." She moved to the chair in the room's corner and sat. Sophia hadn't followed. She stood poised to exit, looking a little wild. Blowing out a breath, she pulled her phone out of her pocket. It was nearly midnight, but where did they have to be tomorrow? "Okay, I'll tell you about my family."

Sophia had stopped pacing somewhere between her second life and her third and had pulled out a chair to sit across from her. The noticeable distance was discomforting when the girl had always crowded her before, but she had visibly relaxed after Sarah's death and Claire's short time on this plane. Rachel's tale led to Allie's, and her chest burned as she stumbled over the parts of her childhood that had left some of the deepest scars.

She omitted Dan, and it didn't feel right to tell Simon's story, so she only shared basic facts about his past.

She halted abruptly, choking on words that wouldn't come. Of course, she couldn't say anything about Allie's death or the deal she'd made. She couldn't say anything about the angels. It hurt, skipping over Gabriel's appearance in her life, but she couldn't say why.

"And then you restored my memories," she finished.

"So it was your father who erased your memory. I'm so sorry I blamed him. Your lover."

Rebecca ground her teeth. She would like to tell her it *had* been him this time, but the angels had made sure she couldn't. He sounded like a hero. He wasn't.

Sophia slid her chair closer, reaching for Rebecca's hand. Rebecca stared down. "I don't have time for complications in my life right now."

Sophia pulled her hand back. "It was dumb, Adelfí. You are a sister. I was not thinking. Your pull is strong. You must know it."

Rebecca scoffed. "You're the siren."

"With water ability comes the siren gift. It grows stronger as your water magic does."

Rebecca gaped. "You shouldn't have any issues blocking my so-called siren gifts if you're shielding. According to you."

"We are power sharing. It makes it harder to shield from one another."

Rebecca's brows dipped. "You forgot to mention that."

"Oops."

She frowned. "I've just told you my deepest secrets. Your turn. Spill." She crossed her arms. Sophia yawned, leaning back in her chair. "Could we start again in the morning? It has been a long day."

Rebecca's mouth stretched on her own yawn. "You're right. Enough stories for one night. Let's talk in the morning."

Sophia stood, stretching languidly. "Not too early," she said, yawning again as she left the room. Rebecca trailed behind, stopping at Rhea's door, and leaned in. Rhea's light snores filled the room, settling some of her nervous energy. At least Rhea would be okay. Someone had saved her. But who? The thought hung in her mind, floating between all the other questions she couldn't answer.

She dropped onto her bed and pulled out her phone. She'd meant to check her email earlier, but with everything that had happened, she had forgotten. Swiping through her phone, she opened Gmail. A few announcements from school, a USPS update. Her books would arrive tomorrow. Perfect. Her finger froze on the next subject line.

'Welcome home Miss Graves.'

CHAPTER 36

Rebecca

Rebecca's fingers trembled as she clicked the email and opened it. There was no message, only a picture of the outside of her house, taken at night. She dropped the phone, ran to her window and flung it open.

"Come out coward!" Allie may have been prepared to run from this man, but Rebecca wasn't. Who did he think he was? Some disgraced police officer—accused of murdering a boy—threatening her.

"Stop sending me messages and face me!" No one answered. She saw no one in the dark and Simon's fancy new motion detection lights weren't picking up any movement either. She slammed her window shut and locked it.

She ran down four flights of stairs to the front door, checking if it was locked. Sprinting to the back door, she jiggled the lock. Down the passage to the servant's hall, the side exit was also locked. The only first-floor windows that opened were also in the back. She checked those too.

Blinking red lights in the corners reminded her she could set the indoor motion sensors from her phone. She darted up the stairs, checking in on Rhea, still sound asleep, and then went down the hall to the last door on the left, peeking in. The bed was empty, but the sound of the shower running let her know Sophia was in the bathroom.

In her room, she opened the Ring app and pressed the Home button. Opening her email, she clicked on the one from Blake and began typing.

"You don't scare me. If you want to talk, come out of hiding and meet me face to face."

She hit send and waited for a response, listening for any indication he was outside. Her phone buzzed.

"I have a few loose ends to wrap up here in Boston, and then I'll come see you. By the way, I hope you liked my present. I left her somewhere I knew you'd find her."

The image of the drowned student flashed in her mind. Could he have killed that student? No. He was a cop. Cops didn't kill people. She swallowed a lump rising in her throat. This one had. Hitting reply, she typed: *"What do you want?"* In the hall, she heard heavy steps approaching. She reached for her sword. *Damn.* She conjured a ball of flame, bathing the room in a soft blue glow.

"Rebecca?" Sophia called from the hall.

"Come in." The door swung open as she doused the flame.

Sophia stepped in, looking around the darkened room. She reached for the switch, flipping it on. "You could use the lights." She laughed.

Rebecca turned, pacing away from her. "There's something I left out of the story that seems to be important."

Sophia crossed the room, settling herself on the bed. "Tell me before I pass out from sleep deprivation."

"I might know who killed the student on campus."

Sophia sat up. "Who?"

"There's a man after me. He's been sending threatening messages. He's someone from my past. A detective. He stepped down from his job a few years ago when he killed someone, a teenager."

Sophia gasped. "Why would the police do this?"

"I don't know. I read a few articles about him. He claimed it was an accident, but after that, he left the police force and disappeared. Until he started messaging me two weeks ago. But tonight, well. Read it." She handed her phone to Sophia.

Sophia's brows drew together as she scrolled. "What is this guy's problem? He's taking credit for murder. He knows this could put him in jail. Why would he send it?"

Rebecca chewed her bottom lip. "I don't know. I have no idea what he wants from me." She flung herself on the bed beside the other girl.

"The security is on?"

"Yes, I set the motion sensors on the first two floors. Don't go down in the morning until I turn it off."

Sophia rolled onto her side, facing her. "There's nothing we can do tonight. In the morning we report him. Tonight, we sleep."

Rebecca nodded. She'd come to the same conclusion. Although her enemies were piling up, and she couldn't ignore the feeling of impending demise, there was nothing to be done about it at two a.m.

"We're not sharing a bed. Good night, Sophia."

Sophia rose, yawning as she padded out of the room. She followed Sophia to the door, closing it behind her. She needed a shower, but her eyelids were growing heavier by the second.

Dropping onto the bed, she felt for her phone and tossed it onto the bedside table. Her eyelids drooped and this time, they refused to open.

A brilliant white light, blinding in its intensity, swallowed the room and an ethereal voice spoke. "You have chosen well, Adalaide Graves, and for this, we shall bless you." She squinted, holding up a hand to shield her vision. "Your sacrifice will mean a great deal to the humans." She bowed her head as a flaming sword dropped to her side.

The glow in the room diminished, the sword's flame winking out. She reached for the handle, feeling its weight in her palm. Looking up, she glanced around the darkened room, giving her eyes time to adjust. She was surprised to find they did not need it. She could see perfectly in the dark.

The sword hummed, and it was her only warning before an inky black substance detached itself from the corner, red eyes blinking open as it dove. She swung without thinking, slicing through its middle. A thick spray of green coated her before the creature misted out of existence.

The world spun, settling on a new scene. She was dressed in black, her hair pulled tightly behind her head, sword slung over her shoulder in a matching black sheath. Her ears rang, and the sword hummed. But she needed none of these signs to know she was outnumbered, but hopefully not outmatched tonight.

The first demon dove, scraping a taloned claw along her jaw. It burned, but she ignored the pain, swinging her sword in an arc. It rose as a second demon sliced a claw down her back. Screaming in rage, she called her flames to her, suffusing both hands in blue. They licked up the sword, ringing it in fire. She swiped again, catching one by the tail. It burst into flames before disappearing.

A screech filled the room as the two dove for her at once. She swung for them both, sending the first back to Primoria, but the second wrapped its clawed hand around her throat, digging sharp nails into her neck. A fourth appeared, knocking the blade from her hand as it wrapped itself around her wrists.

A fifth demon thrust a pointed tail into her stomach, searing her insides. She closed her eyes, reaching for the blue ember in her chest, and shoved with all her might, roaring as the flame burst from her, drenching her from head to toe in blue.

Around her, the room exploded in chaos as demons were flung back from the force of her power. They had no chance to escape as blinding blue light eviscerated every dark corner of the room, sending them all back to Primoria.

Rebecca sat up, gasping as she reached for her stomach. She patted the smooth skin there, trying to catch her breath. When her heart slowed and her breathing returned to normal, she fell back on the bed, landing on cold, damp sheets.

Soft morning light spilled across her bed, suffusing the room in its glow. She ripped the sheets aside, peeling sticky material from her damp skin. A shower was a must. She slid from the bed, plodding to the bathroom before shedding saturated clothes on the newly tiled floor. She reached into the shower, letting the spray turn sweltering before stepping in.

Scalding drops pelted her skin, washing away the remnants of her dream. She ran her fingers down her throat, trailing them along her collarbone, between her breasts, down to the gaping wound Adalaide had felt in her abdomen. The burn from the demon's poisoned barb still lingered under her skin but was overshadowed by the warmth pulsing at the center of her chest where an immense well of power lay.

It was unimaginable to have that kind of power. And yet—the dream was real enough that she *could* imagine it. Was it real? With power sharing, it might be. What could she do with a gift like that? She lifted one hand, pulling from the source at her core and watched the small blue flame flicker to life in her palm.

Digging deeper, she expanded her fingers, watching the ball grow. Droplets of water sizzled as they met heat and evaporated. She pushed harder, forcing it to grow. It was the size of a basketball, but it hovered in the air above her cupped hand. To let it grow, she needed to feed it. She called it back to her, letting it settle on her fingertips and dropped her arm, watching as a streak of blue trailed up her body, undiluted by the spray of water showering over her wet skin.

It licked up her arm, reaching her shoulder before she paused. At her hesitation, it stopped, hovering inches from her neck.

She continued, allowing it to trail along her hairline, up her ear, and to the peak of her skull. When she was confident it wouldn't burn her, she let it continue its path over the other side, down her shoulder and arm until it reached her left palm.

A buzzing in her chest warmed her already heated skin, making her feel alive in a way she never had before. Was it possible fire magic fueled her instead of draining her life away?

What if Sophia and her coven were wrong? Nothing was depleting about this feeling.

She pushed harder, sending the flame down her thigh, over her knee, and down to her soaking wet feet. The flame was unaffected by her wet skin, alive with the magic she funneled through it. It leaped from her left foot to her right and trailed up the right side of her body.

When it reached her right palm, a zing of energy shot through her as the flame took on a life of its own, running like a circuit around her body.

The light buzz grew to a sharp sting and soon it burned. The heat was like radiation, cooking her from the inside.

She flexed a finger, attempting to lift her arm, but it was glued to her side, tied down by a current of energy pulsing around her in a steady rhythm. A whimper escaped her lips. The pulsing energy surrounding her picked up speed and with it, the sting became a raging inferno, searing through her.

As the pain intensified, her eyelids fluttered, and she tried once more to break the circle, calling on her water magic. The cold, soothing liquid washed through her, dousing the flames as she sagged against the wall and slid to the floor. She sobbed, wrapping her arms around scalding, tender flesh. The last of her flames winked out as she huddled into the corner, taking shallow breaths through lungs that felt charred from the inside.

"Rebecca?" Her name came from a distant place, but she couldn't respond, slipping from consciousness as the world around her blackened and disappeared.

"You did not say my sacrifice would continue beyond my own life."

"A sacrifice is something which is difficult to bear. You care little for your own life. I would not call that a sacrifice."

Adalaide stepped forward, baring her teeth. "I gave up everything for you and you ask more of me?"

Gabriel turned, grabbing her shoulders. "Do you think we ask this of you lightly? The fate of humanity rests with you. We ask a lot. Too much. If you weren't so selfless, it would have been simpler."

She scoffed, wrenching free of his hold. "If I were more wicked, my kin would suffer less?"

Gabriel stepped back, his wings stretching out behind him. The only sign of his distress. "I did not ask you to agree to this. You made the sacrifice, and I cannot help you now."

Her shoulders slumped, and she dropped her gaze to the floor. "It is my family,"
she whispered.

"Only the women. This much I could do for you." He leaned forward, wiping a
tear from her cheek. "Human lives are brief. You will see that much awaits you once
yours has ended." She batted his hand away, stepping back.

"You've all but ensured that, have you not? I will not see my boys grow up. I will
not see the men they will become."

"You will see them again." Another tear slid down her cheek. He reached for her,
but she continued backward until she was at the pearly gates, and then she was
falling.

"Rebecca?"

She blinked, breathing shallowly. Shards of glass lacerated her lungs as she
sucked in air. The room swam into focus as the face in front of her solidified.
Bright green eyes, round with concern, blinked down at her.

"Are you okay?"

She sat up, looking around. She was tucked into her bed, a towel slung over her
damp frame. "What happened?"

"You fainted. In the shower."

"I... I was trying to..."

"You were trying to burn yourself out. You're lucky I felt the pull when you
called on your water magic."

Rebecca ran a hand over her face. "I had a dream."

Sophia tsked. "Unless it was about Henry Cavill, there was no need to set
yourself on fire over it." Rebecca chuckled, but it turned to a fit of coughing, every
cough raking nails down the insides of her chest as she tried to get her breathing
under control again. "Only yesterday, we learned that using your magic could
hasten your death yet, today you attempt to pull more magic than your body can
handle. Do you have a death wish?"

She asked with such sincerity, Rebecca thought she might actually want an
answer.

When Sophia said nothing else, she bit her lip. Even that hurt. "I dreamed of my ancestor. Her power was immense. Like nothing I've ever felt."

"I spoke to Yia-Yia. She says our dreams are interconnected. We must tell each other everything. Only this way will we understand the full picture. Can you tell me your dream, or will you need time to recover?"

Rebecca swallowed. It was like swallowing hot coals. "You first." Sophia patted her arm.

"Let me get you some ice cream. It will help."

"Wait," she croaked. "The alarm." Sophia nodded, passing over her phone and Rebecca swiped her screen, finding the Ring app, and disarmed. "Okay," she whispered. Sophia hopped up from the bed and was gone.

Rebecca slid back, resting her head on the damp pillow. Her wet hair cooled her charred neck and back but did nothing for her crispy insides.

Adalaide knew Gabriel. She turned the dreams over in her mind. Adalaide had made some kind of deal with the angels. A deal that extended beyond her own life. Her fingers curled into a fist. She squeezed, feeling her nails dig into her tender flesh.

Adalaide was a reash; Allie had been a reash. What were the chances of that?

Gabriel never mentioned any of it, never told the scared, dying girl she wasn't the first in her family to make a deal. What did it mean that Adalaide's deal would save humanity, but the women of her family would pay for it? Rebecca had never been a reash before Allie, and neither had any of her previous incarnations.

What price were they paying if not reash duty?

Five and twenty, the price I paid. Recompense for pneuma, I woolde gladly pay again. AG.

The passage from Adalaide's diary came to her unbidden. She had paid with her life and the Graves women continued to pay for it. It wasn't her father's curse. It was a curse made by the angels. She opened her mouth, a scream of rage dying in her throat as raw flesh refused to produce the sound. She beat her fists on the bed.

She had died half a dozen times because of *Gabriel.*

CHAPTER 37

Simon

He had worn a path on the already threadbare carpet. It was the end of the week and there was nothing to show for it. None of the books in the Fellowes library had produced any useful information and its residents knew less.

He had interviewed every person, including the newest members of staff, and came to a dead end. Rebecca would return to school in two days if she hadn't already left, and he was no closer to solving her problem. Worse still, she knew about the curse. It would consume her thoughts as it had so many times before.

Each time she regained her memories—each time she returned to herself—her impending death was all she thought of. This time, he had thought it would be different. This time, he had thought they would have a chance at happiness, free from the oppressive burden of her father's curse. But stubborn, headstrong, Rebecca and that meddlesome witch had ruined everything.

Now she would spend her last two years of life in a state of distress. Why was she always so determined to learn the truth? Why, for once in her lives, couldn't she just leave it alone and trust that he would keep her safe? Perhaps because he never had.

Why put her faith in a man who had never protected her from anything life threw at her? In the end, she had always been the one to save herself.

"Mr. Graves?"

He stopped, turning to the door. "Yes?"

"Lady Fellowes has invited you to join her for tea this afternoon in the sitting room. May I tell her you accept?" A bead of sweat ran down the side of Byron's temple. It was the only sign the answer mattered to him. Was wily old Victoria giving her staff a hard time? Simon smirked.

"Tell her I'll join her shortly." Byron's shoulders relaxed, and he bowed—yellow lights reflecting off his bald head—and left.

Pulling his phone from his pocket, he checked the time. One-fifteen p.m. It would be just after eight in North Carolina. She might be awake. But what would be the point of texting? He had no news, no new information. Since she'd called, he'd wanted to text every day, every hour. Not to say anything; just to see if she would respond.

At first, he hadn't believed her anger would last. When he'd realized she changed her number, he feared Rebecca was lost to him. But in her most desperate moment, he was the person she'd called, the person she shared her pain with, and a tiny flicker of hope bloomed, taking root in his chest.

He slid his phone into his pocket, leaving the library. The empty hall felt more like a museum than a home as the sound of his steps reverberated off the walls and imposing figures in various costumes reminiscent of their era glared down at him. The sound of a throat clearing drew his focus as he rounded the corner, stepping into one of the more ornate rooms.

"Good of you to join me," Victoria said, her tone making it clear she did not appreciate his tardiness. He dipped his head, sliding into the seat across from her, and folded one long leg under the other.

"I apologize. The time got away from me. There is so much to see in your grand home."

She clucked her tongue, lifting one white-gloved finger as she sipped from china most would have reserved for a visit from the queen. He lifted his cup, noting the bitter tang, and surveyed the table for something to sweeten it.

"You've had your fill of our library, no doubt, and can have nothing further to say of us. I find it distasteful to bring the subject to light, but as my great-nephew cannot be troubled, it is incumbent upon me to advise you; you have overstayed your welcome in our home."

Simon set his cup down less gently than intended, drawing a sharp gaze from his host. She was a spirited old bat, he would give her that, but leaving was not an option. Not until he had the answers Rebecca needed. He cleared his throat.

She held up a hand. "You think me a fool because I am old, but I remember you, Simon Graves. A face like yours is not easily forgotten, especially for an unmarried girl in her twenties." She touched her embroidered neckline, running white-clad fingers along its design. "You were the most beautiful man I'd ever seen." She sighed wistfully. "Even if you only lurked about after dark."

Simon swallowed, leaning back, some of his composure slipping. He'd expected no one to remember him. It must have been sixty years ago. Victoria's wrinkled brow lifted, a mischievous twinkle lighting her sharp gaze. He lifted his cup, sipping as he considered his next move.

Before he had formulated a response, she spoke again. "I told my father I would marry the yellow-eyed man." She chuckled low in her belly. "He asked me what man I referred to." Simon's cup rattled. He set it down. "Did you not know I was a witch, or did you simply think I lacked power?"

The door to the room swung shut, followed by the shutters as the room was plunged into darkness.

CHAPTER 38

Rebecca

"I don't care. I'm going today. I won't be late for class on my first day." Rebecca dropped her backpack, loaded with books, onto the desk.

"You could have died. You said you think you *are* dying. School is not important." Sophia crossed her arms, widening her stance as she blocked Rebecca's exit.

"You've spent a few days in my life and suddenly you think you're in charge of any decisions I make." She picked up her phone, typing furiously. When she had ordered the Uber, she swiped up her backpack, shoving her shoulder against Sophia's as she forced her way into the hall.

"Rebecca. Wait."

She didn't wait. She stormed down the stairs, flinging the door wide. The Uber would not arrive for another twenty minutes, but she had to get out of the house. To be anywhere but there. Sophia's oppressive mothering would suffocate her.

"Rebecca."

Sophia's exasperated tone only made her move faster. "I've said I'm fine twenty times. My lungs don't hurt. I'm breathing normally. I know I can't use magic. What do you want?" Sophia stopped at the door, shielding her eyes. The hurt in her expression penetrated some of Rebecca's shell. She knew her concern came from a place of genuine care. "I'll be careful, but I'm going. The police asked me to make a statement in person. We talked about this."

Sophia's hand dropped to her chest. She twisted a strand of pearls between her fingers, sliding the beads over each finger. She had begun wearing it again after she learned of Rebecca's past.

Rebecca could only explain it to Sophia so many times. She was tired of having the same conversation. Sophia didn't understand, couldn't understand, that after a lifetime of living on repeat, she needed something new. If this was her last life, she wanted to make the most of it, and however unlikely it might sound to some, college was a dream she'd never fulfilled.

In every life before this one, she'd become a mother at nineteen. She'd stop living for herself and when the weakness and pain set in, any chance for a normal life had ended. By the time she regained her memories, she was usually so weak, there wasn't much left to do but wait for death.

How could she explain to an eighteen-year-old girl, who had her whole life ahead of her, that priorities changed for a person when faced with their own mortality?

Rebecca paced along the driveway, glancing down at her phone as it buzzed, and a new message appeared. Her chest tightened as she thought for one panicked moment it would be from Simon. It was the same feeling she'd had every time her phone buzzed since giving him her number. It was becoming ridiculous, considering she'd heard nothing from him since that night.

She'd told him she was dying. Yes, she was mad. Yes, she had told him she never wanted to speak to him again, but she hadn't expected him to give up so easily. Didn't he care that this may be her last life?

She had started a text to him an embarrassing number of times.

"I'm coming too. You will not leave me in this house." Sophia turned, disappearing. In a few moments, she was back, shouldering her bags. In her hand, she carried a brown, worn, leather journal. "We can bring this and continue searching for clues."

Rebecca nodded, sliding her sunglasses down her face to rest on her nose. "I hope you brought a jacket. It's colder this week than it was last week."

"I don't need a jacket. I have magic."

"Rub it in my face, why don't you?"

Sophia grimaced. "We'll sort it, and you will be able to use your magic in no time."

They wouldn't though, and she couldn't explain to Sophia that her problem was so much bigger than magic.

"Welcome to Boston," the intercom announced as the plane slid to a stop and passengers began standing all around her. Sophia had convinced a woman beside her to trade seats using her siren gift and she stood first, sliding out of the seat and grabbing her bags from the overhead compartment. She reached for Rebecca's bag next.

"I don't need your help," she said, stepping into the aisle behind her.

"I was being courteous, Rebecca. It is okay to accept help from others." Rebecca reached for her bag, hiding her wince as she pulled it down. She would never tell Sophia that some of the pain from her overuse of magic still lingered, especially in her chest.

"Thanks," she said, popping an M&M in her mouth as she sidled by the other girl, exiting the plane. Sophia rolled her eyes, pulling two large bags with her. As they exited the airport, a small part of her expected to find Simon there, waiting for them, but as she scanned the rows of cars, she knew this time would be different.

"We can take the train," Sophia said.

Rebecca arched a brow, popping another M&M in her mouth. "I haven't taken the train yet. Do know which one to take?"

"Yes, I learned before I came here." Not waiting for a reply, Sophia turned, marching toward the train station.

"Wait," she called, hurrying after. She stopped at a turnstile, looking for a place to insert her credit card.

Sophia gave her an exasperated look. "You need a pass. Here, use mine, and we'll get you one when we get to campus."

Rebecca pressed the metal bar, sliding through the turnstile. "Are you sure you know where we're going?"

Sophia snorted. "I came to Boston a week before orientation and rode the trains everywhere. There is nowhere in Boston you cannot go on the train." Rebecca shouldered her bag, giving the surrounding people a wary glance, but she relaxed as the intercom announced the impending arrival of the train. Sophia chuckled, leaning closer. "I will show you a different side of Boston."

An hour and two subway changes later, they arrived at UMASS. An Uber would have been faster, but the subway was a novel experience. Everyone boarding and exiting had somewhere to be, something important to do. They hustled into the train car, finding a place to sit or stand, and rushed out, shouting into their phone, or moving with purpose, on their way to somewhere important.

The city was alive. It buzzed with a nervous energy that spoke of the underlying current running through it. In one short week, she had forgotten how in love she was with this place the moment she'd arrived.

Sophia was right about one thing: the train was the lifeblood of the compact city, ushering a fresh supply to each organ, and she had become a part of it.

They had dropped their bags in their room, stretching out on their beds, but she was still thrumming with the energy of Boston. Spending the day cooped up in their room was akin to caging a bird.

"Do you want to go somewhere?" she asked, hopping off her bed.

Sophia looked up from her phone. "I could eat."

"Yes!"

As she stood, she slid her shoes on, giving Rebecca a once-over. "Why are you wearing such a large jacket?" Rebecca glanced down at her extra longer puffer.

"It was this or a cardigan."

"After we eat, we shop."

Rebecca squealed, a rush of joy shooting through her. Something about the cool temperature and newness of the city made her feel she might never sleep again. She wanted to see and explore everything.

"Newbury?" Sophia asked.

Rebecca stopped bouncing, pursing her lips. "It's the only place I've seen in this city. What about Faneuil Hall?"

Sophia's mouth quirked up at the corners. "I love it!"

She had had her doubts about how it would be when they got back, but Sophia seemed to accept Rebecca's decision, putting their disagreement behind her. For all her fussing and complaining over the past few days, she'd stopped treating her like an invalid, and they were once again two college freshmen in a new city.

A short train ride later, they stepped out into the blistering wind. Rebecca shoved her hands into deep pockets, grateful for her new winter coat. It was the first week of September, but it must have been forty degrees. Sophia slid out beside her in a midriff tank top displaying her belly button. She appeared unaffected by the chill.

A thrill of jealousy ran through Rebecca as she again wished she could use her magic to do all the things Sophia could do. But with the risk of a hastened death hanging over her, a bit of warmth wasn't worth it.

The girls walked arm in arm, sampling food, smelling candles, trying on scarves and hats, tripping over cobblestones where they jutted at odd angles, smiling, and laughing. It was the happiest Rebecca could remember being in a long time. For one afternoon, she was a college student; no burdens or impending doom overshadowed her day. For one day, she could enjoy herself.

They stopped in a photo booth making faces, and Sophia conjured a circle of water around them, forming it into the shape of a heart. She tucked her print into her pocket, letting the feeling sink into her bones.

She glanced at Sophia, whose arms flailed wildly as she spoke excitedly with a man dressed in black and white. The man mimed his responses, not saying a word, but it did nothing to deter Sophia from her story.

Rebecca laughed, feeling an ache in her side, thinking this time, it may not be from an ailment, but instead, from too much happiness in a single day. Sophia glanced back, her eyes falling to the hand Rebecca pressed to her side, and her smile drooped.

She tossed a few dollars into the performer's hat and stepped back, grabbing Rebecca's arm. "Come on, we have a bit of daylight left."

They stopped in several stores before stepping into Boston Campus Gear where they found logoed items for all the big schools in Boston. Rebecca filled her bag with hats, sweaters, shirts, and sweatpants. Anything she could find with her school's logo. Sophia frowned as she moved to the cash register, handing over a credit card.

"What? I have to represent my school." Sophia shook her head, saying nothing. When the stores had closed and both girls were heavily laden with Rebecca's bags, they stopped for dinner. Sophia's eyes sparkled in true delight for the first time that day as they stepped inside.

Rebecca surveyed the menu as Sophia finished stuffing bags into the corner of her booth. "I'll have pizza," she announced.

"What! This is a Greek restaurant. We are not eating Italian." She waved a hand to the nearest server, shouting incomprehensibly as he approached. Rebecca watched as a fight ensued and their voices grew louder. He stormed away and Sophia turned to her, lips stretching into a wide smile. "There, I have ordered for us. It will be wonderful."

Rebecca glanced at the server speaking with his manager at the back. She wasn't sure if "wonderful" would describe whatever came next, and she wasn't sure how she felt about someone ordering for her without asking her first, but the new Rebecca was determined not to let her temper get the best of her. New Rebecca was open to experiencing life.

The food came, several plates at a time, and soon their table was piled with sauces, spiced meats, pita bread, salad, and grape leaves. "Is this for us?" Rebecca asked, giving the food a skeptical once over. This much food could feed a small army.

"I have invited the staff to join us." Sophia grinned. Rebecca eyed her room-mate, wondering if it was a joke, but didn't have long to wonder. Soon, two men sat, followed by a woman who popped a wrapped grape leaf in her mouth before sitting. Two more servers came and untied their aprons. The couple at the neighboring table pulled their chairs up beside the booth and dropped a bottle of wine between plates of food.

Everyone spoke animatedly, eating, pouring wine, and laughing. Rebecca wedged herself into the corner of the booth, giving the couple beside her space, but they only crowded closer, making space for a fourth on her bench. She peered up at Sophia, who had draped an arm over the man beside her and was pouring herself a glass of wine with her free hand as she cackled loudly.

Someone slid a glass of wine toward her, smiling. "Yia-mas!" he said, and everyone around the table repeated it, raising their glasses.

"Drink, Rebecca, drink!" Sophia said, clinking her glass against Rebecca's. She sipped her wine, marveling at the familiarity between strangers, linked by only their culture. Something in her chest buzzed to life, and she was transported to a dark, familiar street; she peered in at tables packed with strangers, eating, drinking, enjoying each other's company, while she moved silently through the streets, unseen.

Then she was back in the moment, warm bodies pressed in around her, speaking a language she didn't understand, and she had never felt more at home.

CHAPTER 39

Rebecca

She turned, checking her appearance again. She didn't want to go head to toe in UMASS-branded clothes, so she opted for a UMASS hoodie, plain white tee, and jeans. The laces said UMASS, but you couldn't tell unless you looked closely. Everything had to be just right for her first day.

A loud groan from the lump on the bed across from her drew her attention. She laughed, tossing a pillow at it.

"Stop. It's not funny. My head is cracking in two."

Rebecca moved to the side of her bed and yanked the blankets off. "Wake up! You'll be late!"

"Why are you screaming?" Sophia groaned, pulling the blankets back over her head.

"I'm not. Why did you drink so much the night before classes?"

"No one goes to class on the first day." Rebecca pulled the covers down again and went to the window, pulling the curtain aside. Dim yellow light streamed in, glinting off Sophia's caramel tangle of hair. "Noooo," she moaned. "Close it. I'll give you anything."

"Come on. You have Intro to Psych with me, remember? We talked about it last night. You told that girl you met how excited you were about this class."

217

"I was flirting. American women do this, no?" Rebecca picked up the bottle of water beside her bed, unscrewing the lid. She tilted it, letting a few drops fall on Sophia's cheek.

"Stoooooooop."

She giggled, tilting the bottle again. Sophia flung her hand out, sending the bottle streaming into Rebecca's face.

"Bitch! I already did my makeup." Sophia snorted, rolling over. Rebecca marched to the small table in the corner and pulled her makeup bag open. "You're lucky I can't use my magic. Otherwise, I'd set your bed on fire." Sophia mumbled something incoherent. "I'm leaving," she said, running a finger over her lips. Sophia made no reply. "Fine, bye."

She moved to the door, scooped up her bag, and yanked the door open. A blur of motion flew by her, knocking her back. "Sorry," a voice squeaked as it ran by, running past the elevators to the stairwell door. At least she wasn't the only one who would be late. But stairs, no way. At the elevator bank, she pressed the down arrow. In the silence of the empty hall, only the sound of the elevator approaching could be heard. Either she was early for class, which was great, or she was really late, which was bad.

A ding sounded, and the door swung open. Empty. She stepped in and pressed one. It couldn't be that late. She pulled out her phone. *Dead. Shit.* She had forgotten to charge it last night. Maybe she had drunk more than she thought. She felt great this morning, though. Nothing would stop her from attending classes on her first day.

The doors slid open, and a sense of déjà vu hit her. The crowd pressed in, leaving little room to step out. At this moment, she would have been grateful for Sophia's gift. She raised her arms, pushing into the throng. People paid her no attention, shuffling right or left into groups. Some whispered to one another, some sat together, holding hands or praying. A few were crying. Several were on their phones, their jumbled words difficult to make out.

Someone stood on a table at the front of the room, shouting over the milling crowd. "All I know right now." She shoved forward, making her way toward him.

"What do we do now?" someone called.

"Just like last week, we stay in the dorms unless we have somewhere else to go. That's all I know."

"I can't spend another week here. My roommate smells, and he refuses to shower." A few tittering laughs followed the student's declaration, but most were absorbed in their phones.

"What's happened?" she called as she approached the student at the front of the room.

"Class is canceled. Another death." The news was a punch to the gut.

"What do you mean?" The crowd's swelling buzz swallowed her words. A loud wail erupted from somewhere nearby, and several others murmured condolences or concern.

Another death. Another dead student. She should have gone straight to the police yesterday to give her statement instead of shopping. She had wasted the day on frivolous things and now someone else was dead. "When?" she whispered, but no one heard.

She fought the crowd, elbowing her way to the door, and stomping on toes. Loud grumbles of complaints and some who shoved back made her progress slow, but she reached the door to the outside world, bursting free. She gasped for air, sucking in deep lungfuls as leaned into the wall. The world was spinning, an ache forming along her brow.

Everywhere she went, people were hurt, people died. Where were the angels? Where was the reash who was supposed to be defending this territory? She was tired of waiting for something to happen.

It was time to do something about it.

She wrenched open the door to her dorm building. "Move!" she commanded, and the power lacing her words rattled the panes of glass. Several startled students jumped, moving left or right. "I said, get out of my way!" she bellowed, and the room parted, making space for her as she stormed through. Lights flickered as she reached the elevator bank and mashed her finger into the up arrow. It dinged, the doors sliding open, and she stepped in. Around her, the room had become eerily quiet, eyes darting toward her, only to look down or away. She pressed the button for the seventh floor, glaring at all of them, daring them to look back. None did.

On the top floor, she marched to the stairwell door and tore it open, taking the stairs up. She ripped open the door and stepped out onto the roof. Stomping to the edge, she eyed the distance and then darted forward. Her feet pounded the surface as she thought of her destination and leaped.

Some distant part of her was fearful she had just jumped to her death, but the moment her feet left the ground, she knew it had worked. Her ascent increased, sending the world in a dizzying rush and then she was falling, floating until she landed on a version of the roof most living souls had never experienced.

"Jophiel! Jooopphhiiieeelllll!" she yelled through the massive luminescent gates. No matter how you arrived, gates always appeared to block your path until you were granted entry. Was it the same in Primoria? Did some hulking black gate appear when one arrived? Probably not. If anything, she imagined a huge three-headed beast prepared to tear a soul limb from limb if they dared attempt to leave.

"Jophiel!" she called again. Did they still know when she was on their plane if she was no longer a reash? The glinting light reflecting off steel in her periphery was the only warning she had before a massive blade swung for her head. She leaped back, conjuring a ball of fire. A breathtaking male, bathed in a soft white glow, raised his enormous sword again, swinging for her middle. She danced back, glad for the lightness of her step on this plane.

She threw up her hands. "Whoa, wait. I'm here to see Jophiel." He held his sword out, the point a fraction of a millimeter from her throat.

"You do not belong in this realm." She touched her fingers to the edge of his blade, sliding it away from her neck.

"I used to work for Gabriel. I need to talk to Jophiel. It's about him." Not a lie. And better if she didn't try. Angels could sense lies, that much she remembered from her time as a reash.

One golden eyebrow rose on the sculpted face of the male in front of her. He let his sword fall to his side. "My brother is lost to us. What news have you?"

"I'd rather talk to Joph. Is she here?"

"She is not." Rebecca scowled. This would be harder than she thought.

"Look, people are dying. Gabriel is the only one who can help. I need to talk to him."

The angel shook his golden mane, shades of honey and sunlight glimmering as he moved his head from side to side. "He is lost, little lamb. Did you not comprehend my words?"

Did he just call her dumb? "No offense, goldilocks, but I think it would be best if I talk to Jophiel. If you could tell me where to find her, I would appreciate it."

He raised his sword again. "You may not trespass here before your time. You must return to your realm."

This guy was getting on her nerves. "What was your name?"

"I am Raphael, Archangel Raphael."

"Perfect, listen Raph, I will gladly leave when you tell me where I can find Jophiel." His gilded brows furrowed.

"I cannot..."

"For Heaven's sake, Raphael, I'm here," an ethereal tone cut in. Raphael stepped back, frowning at the pair before turning and spreading his wings wide. They flapped twice and his brilliant wings carried him over the gate.

Rebecca crossed her arms over her chest. "Thanks for coming." Landing beside her, tucking her wings behind her pristine white suit, Jophiel gave her an appraising stare.

"You are not injured?"

Rebecca pursed her lips. "I guess it depends on what you consider injured. Your... brother cursed the women in my family to die at twenty-five, and you put a binding on me that makes it impossible to share certain information with others who may be able to help me. So, I'm not feeling great."

Jophiel let out a small noise. "Where did you obtain that information?" Her words were halting and clipped.

"I don't have time to play games with you, Joph. People are dying, me included. How do we get to Gabriel? I can't use my magic until the curse is undone and if I can't use my magic, more people will die."

Jophiel crossed her arms, her brows pinching. "We cannot. He has committed the one offense angels are strictly forbidden from. He is in Primoria."

"How do I get to him?"

"For an angel, a trip to Primoria is one way. There is no returning from that realm."

Rebecca chewed on her bottom lip. "Forever?" She hated him right now. He had ruined her life, lives, but he had gone to Primoria for eternity to save her. What if she misunderstood the dream, vision, whatever it was? Sophia had said they could be misinterpreted.

Jophiel stepped forward, touching Rebecca's shoulder. "Only demons leave Primoria."

Rebecca stepped back, letting the warmth of Jophiel's touch seep away. "I could go see him though, couldn't I?"

Jophiel's smooth features wrinkled in concern. "You would have been killed upon arriving here had you been a normal human. What awaits a mortal traveling to Primoria is far worse."

"But I could... Travel there?"

Jophiel turned away, gliding toward the looming pearlescent gates. Her wings fluttered. She turned back, facing her. "Rebecca, I was wrong to ask you to help him." Her voice cracked. It was the most emotion Jophiel had ever shown. "The fate of humans would be put in jeopardy if an angel were to attempt to leave Primoria. We, the seraphim, could never risk that for ourselves."

"I'm not asking you to help me save him. I need to go there to ask him some questions. Tell me. How do I get there?"

Jophiel's wings fluttered again. She closed her eyes. "You must die."

CHAPTER 40

Rebecca

Rebecca blinked and sputtered a laugh. "You're joking. I can jump off a roof to get here, but to go to Primoria, I have to die?" She ran her thumb along her bottom lip. Jophiel's brows pinched again.

"No, you must die while intending to make your way there."

Rebecca frowned. "What do you mean?"

"Just as you do not arrive here every time you jump, you do not arrive in Primoria just because you die. You must focus your whole mind and intention on going there as you die."

"I see."

"Intention matters in most things. It determines..." Her words halted, her luminescence dimming. "I have said too much. Rebecca." She stepped forward, wrapping both arms around her. "Death is not the end. It need not last to be a successful endeavor. Go now, you must leave. You cannot stay where you do not belong." Her movements, like her words, were rushed, disjointed.

Jophiel pressed Rebecca back, and she fell, dropping back to the mortal plane.

Rebecca landed hard, feeling the impact of her fall more sharply than before. It was beginning. The deterioration of her body that inevitably led to one end. As she pushed the door to the stairwell open, she stifled the whimper that crept up her throat. She wasn't ready for death. It wasn't fair. Why was she carrying a curse from some ancestor she had never met? And to stop it, she'd have to die. That sort of defeated the point, didn't it?

She swiped her card in the door to her room, slipping in and dropped heavily onto her bed, sighing. The bed across from hers was still. Too still. She lifted herself up and ripped the pile of blankets aside. Empty.

She reached for her phone, remembering it was dead, and set it on the charger.

She dropped her bag, drumming her fingers on the table. The cramped space was suffocating, but stepping back into the madness on the first floor without a plan was pointless. What she needed was a list.

Reaching for her bag, she pulled out a notebook and pen and wrote across the top: *Things I know* and began listing:

Gabriel in Primoria

Must die to go there

Detective Blake killed two students

She scratched that out—she didn't know it for sure—and made a second list: *Things that might be true.*

Detective Blake killed two students

Gabriel cursed my family to die at twenty-five

Using magic will kill me faster

I'll die at twenty-five if I can't stop it

She crossed that out and moved it to the "Things I know list". Something else was bothering her about her recent interaction with Jophiel. The angel had a way of saying things without explicitly saying what she meant, and something about her words was niggling at the back of her mind. "*It need not last to be a successful endeavor.*" But what did that mean?

She had to die, but she didn't have to stay dead? How could a person not stay dead? Simon had died but hadn't stayed that way. But she had no interest in becoming like him, a night-being, even if the angels had given him back some semblance of a normal life. And she couldn't begin to guess at the magic her father had used on her to bring her back, nor did she want to know.

Her phone buzzed to life. As it did, it buzzed several more times. Messages from the school, she was sure. She let it continue to charge, returning her focus to the list. In the "Things I know" category, she added:

There are covens of witches

Sophia is her coven's seer—Pythia

In the "things that might be true category," she added:

I might be a seer

Does using that gift also kill me faster?

She chewed on her lip, staring at the question. She had no control over that gift, no way to stop it. Claire was dead at twenty-one. What if it had been because of her frequent use of magic and not because of Father's experimentation? He was an evil man, there was no doubt of that, but what if he *had* been trying to save her?

The door to her room flew open, startling her.

"Where have you been?" Sophia stepped in, bringing the scent of sea air and sunflowers with her.

Rebecca arched a brow, dropping her pen. "Did we have plans I'd forgotten about?"

Sophia closed the door, turning to face her. "Five students died last night. I've been looking for you everywhere. It's not safe here. We need to leave."

Rebecca's mouth dried, her tongue feeling thick and sticky against her teeth. Five? She pressed a shaky hand to the table as she rose to her feet. "He's doing this because of me. This is my fault."

Sophia crossed her arms. "I don't think one person did it. It was brutal. Some kids downstairs are sharing photos. A girl from our dorm found them. She took pictures." Rebecca gasped. How could someone take pictures of murdered people? It was unconscionable. "We're all in a text thread. Check your phone."

Rebecca lifted her phone from the charger. Did she want to see it? No. But some part of her had to see, had to know what they were dealing with. She swiped it open, tapping on the message button, and found several from the school, informing students that the school was closed until further notice. They would send additional details via email. Another notifying dorm students, they had one week to make alternative housing arrangements for the semester. Another directed students to contact the bursar's office for questions about refunds.

She wasn't prepared for the next one. It was from a number she didn't recognize, sent to hundreds of recipients. No words, just pictures. It was horrifying, but she couldn't look away. It was dark, masking some of the mutilation, but the blood was everywhere. On the walls, on the books, the floor, and streaked across the bodies that lay strewn across desks or slumped in their chairs.

As if they were so lost in their studies, they never saw it coming. It didn't look as though they had fought back; the carnage was meant to shock, to terrorize. It was meant to close the school.

She dropped her phone on the charger, looking up. "This was Elizabeth."

Sophia uncrossed her arms. "The night-being who stalks you?"

"I thought those messages were from Detective Blake, but this—" She waved a hand at her phone. "Elizabeth did this."

"Why would she do it? What does she want?"

"She wants me."

Sophia pulled a strand of double-wrapped pearls from under her shirt, rolling a bead between her fingers. "We should go to my coven. We will be safe there."

"I can't leave Rhea, and apparently anyone in my general proximity is in danger. I need to find Elizabeth and stop her before more people die."

The girls stared at one another, neither saying a word. Rebecca turned, pulling her suitcase from under her bed. "Might as well pack. You should go back home. Who knows when classes will resume if they do at all."

"I am not leaving you."

Rebecca spun around. "You aren't safe around me. She doesn't know about you yet. Leave while you still can."

Sophia turned, facing her bed, and pulled out her duffel bags. "I go where you go." She dropped the bags on her bed, unzipped them, and began tossing items in.

Rebecca watched her for a moment, considering. "Fine, I'm going back home to Bath, but first, I need to give the police screenshots of my phone. If there's a chance Blake is involved, they need to find him."

Sophia pulled open her tiny closet door, ripping clothes off hangers and dumping them into her bag. She zipped the first bag and started on the stacks of books on her desk, dropping them into the second bag. "I'm ready. Let's go."

When Rebecca had packed everything into her suitcase and backpack, they left the dorm, leaving the keycards on their desks. *Goodbye room. Goodbye college.*

They waited outside on the dorm steps. The oppressive air of all those sweaty, perfumed bodies mingling together was too much for her frazzled senses. She needed fresh air, space, and room to think.

She had gone over her options a dozen times, weighed Jophiel's words, and came up with one conclusion.

She pulled her phone from her pocket and typed, "Meet me at the house."

A sleek black car pulled up, and the trunk popped open before a man came around to help them with their bags. "Rebecca?" he asked. She nodded, slipping her phone back into her pocket.

"We have two stops to make."

"One Schroeder Plaza and then the airport." She nodded again.

The girls slid into the back seat and Rebecca stared out the window as they pulled away. The four-story glass structure gleamed, reflecting the sun's glare into her eyes. It had been so close, almost within her grasp, but this life, a normal life, would never be hers.

Sophia turned to face her. "Have you thought about what you will say?"

"I'm going to tell them the truth."

"How will that go? What reason does this man have for texting and emailing you after so many years?"

Rebecca chewed her bottom lip. She had a point. What if they didn't believe her, or worse, what if they thought she was involved? It wouldn't be the first time the police looked at her for a crime. And there was a file on her. But that was in Atlanta. They didn't know her here.

"Okay, I'll tell them he's been harassing me for years. It's true." Even if there was a break in harassment for a few of those years.

"As a reminder, you are walking into a police station with potential evidence connected to a five-person homicide," Sophia said.

The driver's eyes met Rebecca's in the rearview mirror before darting back to the road.

"Do you need to shout it to the world?" she hissed, pitching her voice low. "Maybe I should mail the evidence to them. Like a tip to put them on his trail."

"They would waste their efforts trying to track you down instead of the killer. What if you tell them he was your boyfriend?"

"I've had enough fake boyfriends, thank you." She rolled her eyes, slouched back in the seat, and pulled out her phone. No new messages. It hurt more than she'd expected, not that she'd ever expected Simon to ignore her.

He would have known what to say to the police. He was good at this sort of thing. She started typing, stopped. *You don't need him, Rebecca*, she told herself. Well, she did need him, but not for this.

"You could tell them he's your stalker. You have the picture of your house from him to prove it."

Margaret had always said honesty was the best policy. She smiled, remembering the last time she had seen her older sister. She was Rachel at the time, just escaped from the Graves Estate. Margaret must have been in her eighties. She was the only one of them to make it past...

The smile slid from her face as she sat up.

Margaret was the only one of her sisters to make it past twenty-five. How had she escaped the curse? She thought back on every journal entry she'd found in her father's records. Adalaide dead at twenty-five, her sister Mary dead from a rare heart disorder at age twenty-five, she and all her incarnations apart from Claire, dead at age twenty-five.

Since Adalaide, every woman born of the Graves line had died by age twenty-five. All but Margaret.

The Uber pulled to a stop outside BPD. She slid forward, pushing her door open. Sophia scooted behind her. She stepped out, turning to face Sophia. "I need to do this myself. Stay here. I'll be back."

Sophia's lips pursed as her brows dipped, but she said nothing, sliding back in her seat.

Inside, the station buzzed with activity, navy blue uniforms scuttling by, headed in one direction or another. The phone rang as she stepped up to a desk inside. The officer behind the counter picked up and answered in a heavy Boston accent. "Excuse me," she said, trying to get his attention.

He gave her a once-over and resumed his call.

"I have some information about a crime."

"Leave ya name and numba and someone will be in touch," he said and picked up a pen, scratching something on his notepad. "Ya. Ya, uh, huh."

He slammed the phone down as it rang again, and he answered. "Excuse me," she said more forcefully. "I have evidence related to the recent murder at UMASS."

He looked up. "I'll have to call ya back," he said, dropping the phone onto the receiver. "Let me get Detective Samuels. Have a seat right ova there."

She glanced behind her at the row of metal chairs against the wall. "I'll stand." He shrugged, leaving her waiting as he disappeared behind a glass wall.

After a very short wait, a middle-aged man, graying at his temples, tie loosened at the collar, appeared in the doorway to her left.

"Ma'am, come with me." They waited as the receptionist buzzed them through. He led her down a long hall, doors lining either side. They stopped in front of the last door, and he ushered her inside. As she sat, her gaze fell over his desk piled with papers, files, and photographs. He slid behind the desk, flipping the files closed. "I'm Detective Samuels, and you are?"

"Rebecca."

"You have some information you want to share with me about the UMASS incident, Rebecca?"

She cleared her throat. "Yes, I..." She coughed. "I have a stalker, and I think it may be related." She pulled out her phone, opening the email with the photo of her house first. "This was sent to me two nights ago. It's a photo of the outside of my house." She glanced up. The detective's face was a mask, unreadable. "And then he sent me this." She slid the phone to him. He skimmed the message, thick eyebrows raising into a crease on his forehead.

"And how do you know the person who sent this?"

She bit her bottom lip. This was the part she hadn't worked through yet. "He was a police officer." Detective Samuel's eyebrows crept higher, adding another layer of wrinkles to his forehead.

"I see. And what is his name? The officer."

"His name is Jason Blake. Formerly, Detective Blake, but he's not a police officer anymore. He resigned after a shooting incident where he killed someone." Detective Samuel's brows were in his hairline now.

"I'm sorry. Did you say how you know him? I think I missed that part." She swallowed.

"When I was in the foster system, he helped me find a new home after my foster father died." Hopefully, there was enough truth infused into that story to keep them off her trail.

"I see. Did you see Jason Blake at or around campus the night of the murders?" She shook her head, letting loose curls fall into her face. She could feel it growing warm. It must be blotchy and red. Did that make her seem guilty? Why did she feel guilty?

"I haven't seen him for over six years, but he's sent me messages, on and off, since then."

"Have you messaged back?" She wanted to say no, but she had.

"Just once."

"Would you mind if we kept your phone? Our cyber department could use it to trace the origin of these emails. Find out where they came from."

"I'd rather not. I can email them to you." The detective's mouth puckered.

"Is there anything else you can tell me, Rebecca?"

"I don't think so." He fished around on his desk and pulled out a rectangular card.

"Send the emails to me and leave your number so we can reach out if we have more questions. Do you have any plans to leave town?"

"Yes, I'm going home from here. School is canceled until further notice." He ran a hand over his chin.

"If you think of anything else, call me. If you see Jason Blake, call the local police right away and then call me."

Rebecca stood. This had gone better than expected, but her cheeks were flaming now, and her neck felt hot. She wanted to get out of this room before he asked her any more questions she didn't know how to answer. "One more thing," he said as she reached for the door handle, "did you know any of the murdered students?"

She felt a jolt run through her at the question. She didn't even know the names of the students who died. Would she have known any of them? Met them on campus? Had a class with them? Would she have gotten to know any of them this semester? She would never know now.

"No," she whispered as she grabbed the door and pulled it open.

In the Uber, she felt Sophia's sharp stare as she pulled the door closed. She said nothing, thinking of the students whose names she didn't know.

"Well?"

She glanced over at the bronzed girl beside her. "I gave the evidence. They said to reach out if I see Detective Blake or if I have anything else to share." She lifted a shoulder and let it drop.

"Hmph," Sophia said.

They rode in silence, each lost in her thoughts. Rebecca leaned into the window, watching her breath fog the glass. It was supposed to be warmer this week, but if anything, it was colder. Her phone buzzed. She pulled it out. *"BeaconAlert - check email for campus-related updates."*

She opened her email, finding one from Chancellor Marcelo Suarez-Orozco.

"Beacons, it is with a sad heart we report classes will not resume this semester on campus. This decision was not made lightly, but the safety of our students is our top

concern. With this in mind, we ask that you reach out to us if you are in need of counseling support during this difficult time.

However, we will offer remote learning on a condensed schedule beginning on the Fall-2 schedule beginning October 7th, concluding December 13th. All students wishing to enroll in online classes during the fall term may enroll during online Fall-2 enrollment beginning September 16th.

In light of recent events, we will offer a 25% discount on all online enrollments for the semester.

Thank you,

Chancellor Suarez-Orozco"

Rebecca looked up, watching Sophia as she read the same email. Sophia leaned back in her seat as she glanced up at Rebecca.

Rebecca's lips parted, stretching over her teeth as she grinned. "Aren't you excited? School's not canceled!" Her voice came out too high and a little like a squeal, but she couldn't help it. School wasn't canceled!

Sophia rolled her eyes.

CHAPTER 41

Rebecca

"Y**ou're the only person who would be excited by this news," Sophia said,
turning to stare out the window.

"You don't want to go to school this semester?"

"I don't want to go to school ever. I am here for you, Rebecca." Rebecca let out a small, defeated sigh. Youth was wasted on the young.

They boarded the plane, taking their seats at the back. It was all she could find on such short notice. She checked her messages one last time before placing her phone on airplane mode. Still nothing from Simon. She dropped her phone into her bag and leaned her seat back, closing her eyes. In four-and-a-half hours, they would be home and she could regroup.

She opened her eyes. Light turbulence was one thing, but the last rattle had been enough to wake her. She glanced around to find several passengers gripping armrests, looking as nervous as she felt. When the rattle came again, a few of the overhead compartments popped open, bags spilling out into the aisle.

"We've encountered a bit of turbulence, folks. We're going to try to get above it, so hang in there for just a bit. It might get a little bumpy."

Twenty minutes later, her jaw ached from grinding her molars together, and a baby wailed just a few rows ahead. By some miracle, Sophia had not so much as twitched through the entire ordeal. "We're clearing it now and it should be a smooth flight from here, folks. The storm wasn't on our radar today. Sometimes these things can't be avoided."

The pilot made it sound like the metal contraption hurtling through the air at five hundred miles per hour, rattling off its hinge, wasn't something to be concerned about. She missed the days when trains were the premier mode of transportation.

She slid open her window shade, staring out at the sparkling ground far below. In September, it should be lush and green. Instead, the world she careened over was bleached of color, a blanket of white dusting its surface.

She dug her nails into the armrest as the earth rose to meet them just a short while later and the pilot announced it would be a slick landing. Sophia cracked an eyelid, glancing over at her. "What's the matter with you?"

Rebecca choked on an incredulous laugh. "You didn't feel any of that?" She sat up, releasing her hold on the armrests. Sophia yawned loudly, unbuckling her seatbelt.

"I don't know what you're talking about." They stood, falling in line behind the other passengers, and exited the plane. The doors slid open, and they stepped outside to a world painted white. Frigid air scorched their cheeks, staining Rebecca's red.

They stopped in front of the Uber line and Rebecca opened the first, leaning in. "Can you take us to Bath?"

"Roads are iced over. Can't take you past Raleigh city limits." She slammed the door before he could say more, moving to the next car.

"Hi, we're going to Bath. Can you take us?" The driver shook his head. "No, can't." She scowled, shutting the door. She pulled her phone out of her bag, turning it off airplane mode. No new messages. Where the hell was Simon? She grabbed Sophia's arm, dragging her to the doors of the airport, pulling her inside.

Opening her phone, she pressed the Uber app on her phone and put in her destination address. *Finding your ride* flashed on screen. *No Uber drivers available.* She growled in frustration.

"I could convince them," Sophia suggested.

Rebecca's eyes found Sophia's, a hint of mischief dancing in them. "Yes!"

They marched back to the Uber line and Sophia leaned in, an otherworldly lilt coating her words.

"Take us to Bath, North Carolina." The driver nodded dumbly, and they went around to his trunk, lifting their bags inside. The driver sat motionless. They slid into the back seat of his car.

"One-eleven Graves Road," Sophia purred, and Rebecca leaned in, desperate to hear her next words. The driver pulled forward, and Sophia pressed her against the seat, whispering into her ear. "I'll need to keep talking to him to keep him under my compulsion. Can you try to fight it?"

She nodded, shaking her head to clear it. She focused on building a mental shield around her mind. It was like an air bubble in her head. She coated her brain with it, draping it over every thought. When she felt it was firmly in place, she nodded.

"It's so kind of you to take us," Sophia said, and the driver swayed in his seat, increasing his speed. She continued to murmur words of encouragement as Rebecca worked to keep her shield in place.

Two hours later, tires rolled over gravel as they pulled up to the massive gates of her family home. She fished in her bag, pressed the button on her key fob, and leaned back in her seat as they rolled forward. "Thank you for your kindness. Drive safely," Sophia said as they exited the car and pulled their bags out of the trunk.

The estate was transformed, sparkling white carpeting every surface. She crunched over fresh snow at least half an inch thick. She had never heard of snow in September in North Carolina.

As they stepped into the house, the air's stillness prickled the hairs on the back of her neck.

There was an absence of life here that spoke of a place unlived in. "Rhea," she called, her voice echoing unnaturally.

"It's a time capsule," Sophia whispered into the stillness.

"What do you mean?"

"Someone has frozen time here."

Rebecca's mouth fell open. Never in one hundred years of life had she heard of such a thing. "Who has the power to control time?" she breathed.

"Witches," Sophia said matter-of-factly. As if everyone knew this was an ability witches could possess. "The strange weather is something a witch can control as well."

"What?" She backed up, her ears popping as she stepped outside the bubble. She watched in fascination as Sophia remained frozen inside it and waved a hand in front of the girl's face, but Sophia remained still. Not even an intake of breath disturbed her frozen body. She leaned forward, pressing her head through some invisible wall.

"Weather is controlled by the elements. Witches control the elements." Sophia glanced back, noting Rebecca's change in position. She arched a brow. "It's dangerous to stand half inside, half outside of a time capsule."

Rebecca stepped in, the stillness overtaking her senses once more. "Time is not an element. How does a witch control it?"

"Sure it is. The earth moves, spinning on its axis, propelling us toward the next day. Fire is the element of kinetic energy in motion, a combination of air and the spark of life encouraging the decomposition of living beings. The sun breathes life into our world, pulling us forward through the control of a massive kinetic force. To control these three is to control time. A witch with mastery of earth, air, and fire abilities or perhaps, a few witches working together, could create a time capsule, temporary of course, but powerful enough to freeze the forward motion of the earth for a time, in one place."

Rebecca blew out a breath, feeling its disruption in this captured moment in time. Her heart rate ticked up, sweat beading along her temple.

"Brace yourself." As Sophia said the words, a pop sounded, and the world tilted precariously before it settled and the light reflecting off the hall mirror sat at an entirely new angle.

"It's dark," Rebecca gasped, spinning around.

"One cannot hold time without paying a price. We lost the amount of time the spell was in place." Sophia peered over her shoulder at the wall of windows down the left hall. "Judging by the dark, it's late. We must have lost several hours."

"Rhea," Rebecca said, running up the stairs. She slid to a stop in her doorway but knew before she arrived what she would find. The bed was empty, untouched for some time. She ran from the room, flinging open doors as she called into each room. In the orange room, she dropped to her knees beside the limp form on the floor.

"Marissa?"

Marissa moaned softly. A cut down the side of her head trailed down her neck, leaking blood onto the floor. "Marissa, can you hear me?" She lifted her head, gently prodding the wound. "Where's Rhea?" Marissa moaned again, but her eyes remained glued shut.

Sophia stopped in the doorway, letting out a breath. "She needs a doctor, Rebecca."

Rebecca looked up. Her vision blurred. "Rhea," she pleaded.

Sophia fell to her side, touching her fingers to Marissa's wrist. "Her pulse is weak. We must take her right away."

Rebecca nodded, setting the woman's head down gently. "I need to make sure Rhea's not here somewhere first." She stood, backing out of the room. "Give me five minutes. Take her to the car, and I'll check the other rooms in the house." Sophia's lips drew into a thin line, but she dipped her head. Rebecca turned, bolting from the room. She flung each door open with more force than the last. When she made it to her father's room, she shoved open the door to the back staircase and moved down the stairs, praying this wasn't the day they would collapse underfoot.

Rebecca cast a ball of fire overhead, damning the consequences of her use of magic, and surveyed the space. Rhea wasn't there. Some part of her had known she wouldn't be. Tears rolled down her cheeks. She had spent too much time pretending she had a normal life, pretending she could have anything for herself.

Her selfishness had gotten more people killed than she could count. If Rhea was next, she would never forgive herself.

She raced up the back stairs, wrenching open the door to the servant's hall, and ran.

She grabbed her bag at the entrance, threw open the door, and sprinted to Simon's car. Wrenching open the driver's side door, she slid in, looking back at Marissa lying across Sophia's lap. Her gaze traveled to Sophia. "Go. Her heart is slowing."

She had never taken the sharp turns on Graves Road so fast, and a new sprinkling of powder obscured her view, making it more dangerous, but she pressed on the accelerator and in less than fifteen minutes they skidded to a stop outside the ER in Washington and Sophia pushed open her door.

They carried Marissa inside, calling for help, and two men in scrubs dashed through a door, stretcher ready. They lifted her, pale blue sheets stained a deep violet as her blood soaked them. The men pushed the stretcher through the emergency room doors, and she was gone.

Sophia leaned into Rebecca, cooling liquid soothing her racing heart.

Suddenly, she felt bone-weary, her limbs leaden. She wrapped an arm around Sophia and ushered her toward a couch in the seating area. They slid down together, and she pulled her phone out of her pocket. New Message. She opened it.

"Did you get my latest present?"

She dropped her phone, a chill racing up her spine. Sophia lifted her head from where she had rested it against Rebecca's shoulder.

"What?"

"It's nothing. I'm just upset that Simon hasn't texted back yet."

Sophia's lip quirked as she closed her eyes. "I thought we hated him."

Rebecca picked her phone up, leaning forward, letting Sophia slump on the seat behind her. "I'm going to get something from the vending machine. Do you want anything?"

Not waiting to hear Sophia's reply, she left the room, stepping into the hall she'd been in all too recently when it was Rhea they thought might die. She stopped at the vending machine, remembering the way Simon had come in injured. She frowned. He'd faked a mugging in the parking lot to cover something up. But what? Her phone buzzed again.

"If you want your precious house manager back, I'm willing to make a trade."

Her heart seized in her chest. It was a trap. Of course it was a trap. Elizabeth had proven more than her match in their game of chess, but she wouldn't be caught by surprise this time. Gabriel would have been nice to have around. But he was gone, maybe forever. For some reason she couldn't name, the thought burned in her chest.

She needed his help, that was all. She needed him to tell her how to break his curse so she could use her magic, and if Simon wasn't responding, she would have to come up with another plan. Time was running out.

Think Rebecca. She had died. But she wasn't dead anymore. Was that why she could travel to Alaxia? Did it mean she could also travel to Primoria without dying again? Jophiel hadn't said how she could get there other than being dead. Was it as simple as wishing to go? She leaned against the wall, closing her eyes. *I want to go to Primoria.* She opened her eyes. Small red numbers glared at her from across the room.

Her phone buzzed again. *"Ticktock. What will it be, Allie?"*

Her fingers tightened around her phone, small spider veins running across its surface. There was no time for a plan, no time to find Simon, no time to go to Primoria and talk to Gabriel.

She slid to the floor, her head slumping between her shoulders. A tear clung to her lashes. She swiped it away, sniffling. If only she had earth magic, she could learn to freeze time. That would give her a massive advantage over Elizabeth and her kind.

What would Allie do? Old Allie, not the new version of her who had never fought demons, the version who never had Gabriel as her mentor. New Allie would have no idea what to do. *Damn Gabriel.* He really had been training her for this. Her phone buzzed.

She swiped up. *"Time's up."*

She stared at her phone as a new message flashed on her screen. *"Thirteen-twelve Cider Mill Lane, come get what's left."*

CHAPTER 42

Rebecca

The sound was growing louder. It was definitely sirens. She mashed her foot on the pedal as the car lurched forward. *I'm too late.* The words played on repeat in her mind. *I'm too late, I'm too late.*

Flashing red and blue lights blinked through the canopy of trees, lighting the predawn sky. Why hadn't she replied? Why had she waited? She took the turn more sharply than she should have and swerved as she came around the corner and her whole body went slack and the car decelerated.

Yellow caution tape bisected the road in front of her and continued in a large square. Half a dozen police cars were parked haphazardly around it, but garish yellow framing the blue and red glow of police lights was not what turned her stomach. The ground, streaked in red, littered with bodies, stole her breath, a cold stone settling in her gut. A strangled cry escaped her lips before she regained her faculties and slammed on the brakes.

The car skidded to a stop inches from a police car barricading the road. Rebecca flung the door open, stumbling out before her stomach heaved violently and the contents of her last meal erupted from her throat. She fell to her knees, her hands trembling as she retched again. She wiped the back of her mouth with one shaking hand, working to get her breathing under control.

On shaky legs, she stood, moving leadenly toward the scene. In front of her, the door to the closest police car hung open—torn from its hinges—a man wedged beneath it. She looked away, feeling her stomach turn again. Her eyes met sightless white orbs rolled back in the head of a man who couldn't have been more than twenty.

She turned, her gaze landing on a hand and some other indiscernible body part. Her vision glazed as the objects became unclear, and she stumbled between forms twisted at odd angles, some too disfigured to be called human. Maybe they weren't.

She'd stopped seeing faces. Her vision darkened at the edges and shapes tumbled together. Red, black, and brown all swirled into nothing as she swayed on her feet.

Something crunched underfoot and her stomach gave no warning as bile spilled from her lips, rolling down her chin. How many people had died in this place? How many people had Elizabeth killed while she chased shadows and dead ends? She met resistance as she continued trudging forward and pressed into an elastic yellow band.

It snapped, releasing her from the gruesome scene. Her chest was hollow, a gaping, wrenching hole where her once beating heart lay.

She slumped against a tree, trembling, her teeth clattering painfully.

Warmth bled into Rebecca's back as she lifted a stiff arm, pressing her hand into the rough bark. How long had she been there—alone in the woods—far enough from the metallic scent of blood and death that pine and loamy earth were all she smelled?

Along the horizon, glinting between massive trunks, predawn rays reached for a new day. Elizabeth could do no more harm for a few hours. It was a small comfort considering the carnage already inflicted upon the town and its people.

She spread her fingers, running them over the tree's trunk, feeling life thrum beneath its surface. Where so much death hung like a blanket, ready to suffocate her, its reassuring presence was her only solace.

She closed her eyes, breathing in the fragrance of damp earth and living, growing vegetation. It hummed, awakening some dormant part of her soul. She gasped, pressing her ear to the tree's trunk, but it wasn't something she could hear. It was a feeling.

Tentatively, she pressed her palm against the rough bark and stretched her fingers wide. Something tickled her skin. She lifted her fingers and marveled as tiny green shoots unfurled around each finger, wrapping soft green fronds around her middle and first fingers.

As she pulled her hand back, a green vine lengthened and turned brown, forming a solid branch with leaves sprouting from its end. She stepped back, and it followed, thickening as it lengthened. She curled her hand, making a fist, and brought it to her chest. A cluster of small blue flowers bloomed, slender stamens stretching toward her.

A tear slid down her cheek. In death, nature found rebirth. As she had, so many times.

CHAPTER 43

Gabriel

G abriel blinked in the murky haze, head listing to the side. Bubbles obscured his view as the siren's latest victim thrashed pointlessly against the only living thing in this bleak place. More bubbles erupted from the man's mouth, streaming toward the surface before he slumped, eyes falling closed, and his body convulsed. When his thrashing body fell still, he disappeared, leaving only smears of blood behind.

He envied humans their brief reprieve from unending torment. At least they had the luxury of dying, even if it only granted them a few moments rest before the torture began again. He might do unspeakable things for a moment like that. The dark thoughts creeping into his mind, his soul, sent a spear of dread through him.

He who had once been so steadfast in his beliefs, he who sought only justice and righteousness, questioned what a soul might do, given the right set of circumstances. The ache that never ceased, never relented, only burrowed deeper into his chest, was driving him over some invisible edge. He felt it. Where the pain of losing a limb dulled, faded; the absence of breath in immortal lungs never diminished.

Try as he might to put it out of his mind, it stole his focus; commanded all his attention. Even the piercing gaze of the woman who once plagued his dreams had diminished, sinking to the far recesses of his mind where faith and hope lived.

He closed his eyes, praying to a God he knew was no longer listening. A sharp pain wrenched through him as his eyes flew open. The dark shape of the mistress of this pool blocked his view as her face swam into focus, but it wasn't her face. It was the face of a headstrong woman whom he had thought of far too often. He gasped, but the action only sent fire raging down his chest as he let the warm liquid in. He coughed violently, sucking more water into his lungs, choking and gagging, a new round of pain wracking his body as he convulsed.

Unlike humans, he could not die. It was up to him to get it under control, to stop the involuntary intake of breath long enough for the liquid to settle in his lungs, burning and uncomfortable, a cough poised to explode from his lips; a battle of willpower he never knew he possessed before now.

Rebecca's face rippled, changing to that of the harpy who had trapped him here. Her lips pulled up into a languid smile, and she swam away. Just another of her daily tortures. Every day she tormented him anew and the tenuous grasp he held on his mind slipped a little more each time.

CHAPTER 44

Rebecca

R ebecca raised a hand, shielding her eyes as she stepped out of her car into the midday sun.

She'd gone much farther into the woods than she'd realized, and the trek back had left her weak and tired.

She stopped in front of the sliding doors of the hospital, catching her breath. She was no stranger to this feeling, though. She had lived it half a dozen times, over countless lives. Her true curse was gaining her memories just as the weakness and pain settled in her bones. How had she ever dared to hope this time would be different?

She slumped against the wall as Sophia darted forward to catch her.

"Where have you been? I woke up hours ago, and you were gone." Sophia stifled a sob. "Marissa didn't make it."

Rebecca could have sworn she heard a crack. Another line spider veining through her heart. She wasn't sure how much more death she could take.

"We need to go to Greece. I need to meet your coven." Her knees buckled as Sophia caught her, pulling her to the nearest chair to sit. Sophia squatted in front of her.

"Why did you change your mind? What happened?" Rebecca let her head fall into her hands.

"She killed them. All of them."

Sophia wrapped her fingers around Rebecca's, squeezing. "Who?"

Rebecca looked up. "I don't know. I don't know who any of them were. People from Bath."

"Rebecca, you're not making sense."

Rebecca's vision blurred, and she wrenched her hand from Sophia's grasp. "There are dozens of people dead, just outside of town. She texted me. Told me to meet her there to get Rhea back, but it was a massacre. Bodies everywhere. And the police must have come, but she killed them too." Her voice broke, fresh tears streaming down her face.

She had thought there were no more tears; thought she cried them all out in the woods. She twisted her hands together in some parody of prayer. "I have to go to Greece and power share with the other members of your coven. It's the only way to stop her."

Sophia stood, backing up. She wrapped her arms around her waist. "You could die."

"I'm already dying."

Sophia took another step back. "We can stop her. With all our gifts together, she will be no match for us."

Rebecca stood, pressing her palm into the arm of the chair to steady herself. "You came here looking for the girl from your prophecy. Here I am. I performed earth magic in the woods. Sophia, I have all four elemental gifts. I'm the one who has to stop her."

Sophia shook her head, tears brimming along her lower lashes. "Yia-Yia will know what to do."

Numbness settled in her chest as she moved unsteadily to the exit. Sophia trailed after. When she reached the car, she pulled open the door and dropped into the driver's seat. Sophia slid wordlessly into the passenger seat.

They drove in silence, the sun glinting off the colorless world around them, the slight tang of rust filling Rebecca's nose. She would not look at the dark stain on the back seat, the last trace of Marissa, a woman whose only crime was knowing her.

They pulled to a stop in front of the house, then silently climbed out. Sophia trudged up the steps into the house, not looking back.

A blur of motion sent fear spiking through Rebecca before solid arms wrapped around her, squeezing her in a familiar lavender-scented embrace. She melted into him, the fractures in her heart beginning to knit together.

He stepped back, holding her at arm's length. "Are you hurt? I smell blood."

She shook her head, glancing back to the car. "It's not mine." Yellow eyes searched her face. Tears threatened to escape, a whimper bubbling up in her throat. Steeling herself, she raised both hands, pressing him back. "Where were you?"

"I received your text and got on the first plane back here."

She wiped her eyes, crossing her arms over her chest. "You've been missing for... I don't know how long it's been."

"Rebecca, I was in Peterborough. It's not a short flight."

Her lip quivered, but she bit down hard, stopping it. "You could have texted; you could have said... something."

Simon ran a hand through his hair. "You sent me a one-sentence text asking me to meet you here, no explanation. I'm here. I came on the first flight. What were you expecting from me after your direction to never speak to you again?"

Straightening her shoulders, she stepped around him, striding for the door. He was in front of her, blocking her path in a blur. "Stop, I'm sorry. I don't know how to navigate this new situation."

She sidestepped him again and continued toward the door. He sped by again, framing the door. "Rebecca, please. Tell me what you need from me. Tell me what to do, and I'll do it."

Her lip quivered again. "You're too late!" She shoved him with all her strength. He slid backward and for the first time, she thought he might not have let her push him.

He gaped, looking down at the black streaks his shoes had left on her newly refinished floor. "What's going on with you?"

"I needed you twelve hours ago before Rhea was kidnapped. Before all those people died!" She stomped up the stairs, holding back the flood of emotion threatening to spill free. If she could just make it to her room.

"What do you mean?" he called from the bottom of the stairs. "Rebecca." She heaved herself up the last step, trudging into her room and slammed her door just before the dam broke and tears spilled down her cheeks.

She held a hand over her mouth, sobbing through her fingers. There was no hiding the sound from his keen ears, but she did her best, throwing herself on her bed, and crying into the pillow. Her shoulders shook as sobs wracked her body.

It turned her stomach thinking back to the moment she'd realized she would have to go back, to comb through the wreckage and be sure Rhea wasn't one of them. Images of torn limbs, bodies splayed at unnatural angles, and so much blood ran through her mind. And with each sigh of relief at discovering another body wasn't Rhea, guilt twisted her insides.

All those people had someone like her at home, worried about their loved one, not yet aware of the tragedy that had befallen them. They would never know it was her fault. Never know who to blame.

And she could do nothing for any of them. Even Rhea was out of reach. She was once again a pawn in Elizabeth's game, and she had no idea who the other players were. Was Rhea alive? Were they torturing her somewhere?

As the ache settled where her heart once beat, and her sobs quieted to a low whimper, she curled onto her side, cataloging all the pains in her body and soul, and shut her eyes against this new reality.

When she opened her eyes, she knew at once she was in a dream. She gazed around, taking in her surroundings. It was the estate, near the back of the property, by the Graves cemetery. She had been too focused on Elizabeth before, too gripped by fear, to notice the ring of beings surrounding them. They were so like the gargoyles circling her father's estate, but these creatures moved, pawing the earth, snorting. Tethered by some invisible force.

The world around them was cast in shades of gray, bleached of color, blanketed by snow. As she spun in a circle, she saw the gargoyles rimmed only half of the circle. The other half was made up of towering trees, water speckling their branches. Here and there, bright red, orange, and yellow flowers bloomed, and between them, a light breeze danced, carrying bits of leaves, water, and flowers with it.

Spinning to a stop, she came face to face with the shadow creature. It swiped, drawing a line of blood across her cheek. Everywhere her blood fell, green vines unfurled, rising to meet her. They wrapped around her legs, pricking her skin in places. Where blood welled, blue flowers bloomed.

She held out a hand, conjuring a ball of fire in her palm. As the flame grew, petals drooped and fell from the flowers at her feet. As she passed her flame to her shadow, she noticed its shape did not match her own. It was tall, broad where she was thin, and most notable of all, a pair of black shadows in the shape of wings sprouted from its back.

Her shadow caught the flame, flicking its wrist in time with her movement. Elizabeth's enormous shadow screamed as it shriveled and winked out. She stepped forward, knowing she would find a woman where the shadow had been. The woman moaned, gazing up, yellow eyes pleading, but she had no sympathy for the thing. She conjured a spear, calling it from the earth, and crushed the woman, burying her as she called on vines and roots to pull her under.

She was ready when the hand shot from the earth, and she called on her flame. It came, but it was a flicker of her usual power. She frowned, glancing down to see that all the blue petals around her were dead. She scanned the trees forming her half of the perimeter and called on them for aid. The wind carried petals to her, feeding her flame until it raged. It ran down her arm, leaping to her leg, growing in size and intensity.

Where it had once been blue, it was red, orange, and yellow, with the slightest hint of blue skimming along its surface. As the woman broke free, Rebecca sent the flame to meet her. The woman hurtled forward and as the sparks reached her, she was engulfed in a multicolored blaze.

Rebecca raised a second hand, calling on the trees. Another breeze sent petals into her palm, and she pointed one finger at the creature, strengthening the flames.

The yellow-eyed woman staggered, pressing forward. One foot pressed into the ground and broke free as she tried to step again. The second leg broke off at the knee as charred black limbs remained fused to earth. She tumbled forward, crumbling as she fell.

Rebecca raised her arms to the sky, calling rain down upon them. It pelted the creature, washing away the charred remains to nothing.

Thick black smoke rose from the ashes as a red-eyed demon formed in the mist.

Rebecca threw up her hands, trapping the demon in a cyclone of air. It beat against its cage, roaring. Fatigue weighed down her limbs, and she staggered back, holding up her hands. Vines reached for her, holding her up. Rough bark brushed her calves and thighs as the vegetation surrounding her leaned in, offering support.

Her back bent as the demon pressed against her magic. Wind whipped at her shoulders, pressing her upright. A tear slid down her cheek as she gritted her teeth, her arms like lead.

Her arms fell, and she gasped, stumbling to her knees.

The cyclone dissipated, and the demon lunged. She struggled to call for help, but none came. With her strength sapped; she watched helplessly as the demon dove for her.

A black shadow met the creature, blocking its path. She tipped forward, icy snow caressing her cheek as she peeled her eyelids open. She felt more than saw as the creature overpowered her shadow. Her eyes fluttered open. It was killing them both.

"Rebecca."

Her eyes flew open. The smell of lavender hit her hard.

"Get out," she panted, pulling the blankets around her.

"You were having a nightmare. You were screaming." Her chest felt as though a fifty-pound sack had been dropped on it.

Simon touched her cheek in the dark, making her flinch.

Her vision adjusted slowly, and she could make out his outline and the glow of his eyes, but not much else. "I don't need you to comfort me anymore."

Simon stood, pacing in the dark. "I'm trying Bec. I'm trying to give you space or whatever you need, but Rhea matters to me too. Tell me what you know, and I'll find her."

She took a few steadying breaths, rubbing sleep from her tear-crusted eyes. "You will not offer yourself up as another pawn for Elizabeth to use against me."

"Why are you treating me like I'm useless?" he asked, his voice laced with hurt.

"She caught you easily enough last time, remember?" She winced. That was a low blow, and she knew it. "Look, I do need your help, but not with Rhea."

"G." She gagged. Damn Jophiel and her binding. "There's a place I think only you can go."

Simon frowned. "Sheol?"

Why could he say Sheol, but she couldn't say Primoria? "No, the place people go when... *Seriously, I can't even say that?*" Simon smirked. "It's not funny."

He schooled his features into neutrality. "It's not easy, is it?"

"The only person I remember you wanting to blab to about it was Allie." *Shut up, Rebecca.* Breathing shallowly, she said, "Let me try again. There are three places. You said one of them, the Lakers go to another one, and then there's the last place."

"The Lakers?"

She bit her lip. "The Clippers."

"Ooh. Gotcha." He pointed to the ceiling.

"Right, but I need you to go there." She pointed down.

He sat at the end of the bed. "Why would I want to do that?"

"Because our friend Seth Gilliam is there."

"Who is Seth Gilliam?" Rebecca slapped her forehead. "It's your favorite show and the actor who plays him is Seth Gilliam..."

Simon's brows straightened, his forehead smoothing. "Riiiight. Father Stokes. The Walking Dead."

She sighed. "So Father Stokes is." She pointed down. "If you could talk to him, you could find out how to reverse my curse so I can save the world."

Simon scooted closer. "Bec, what does Father Stokes have to do with your curse or saving the world?"

"Wait," she said, ignoring his question. "Why were you in Peterborough? Never mind, it's none of my business."

Simon reached for her, pulling one hand from the blankets. "I went to find answers about your curse. I'm trying to help."

Her breath caught in her throat. He had dropped everything to help her, even after the way they'd ended things. "Simon, I..."

He squeezed her fingers. "I love you, Bec. I'll never stop trying to keep you safe." She sat up, wrapping an arm around him. He squeezed, pressing his nose to her neck. "I missed you."

When she pulled back, the skin along her neck was wet. "Are you crying?"

He swiped at his cheeks. "No."

She smothered a laugh. It felt good to laugh, and some of the pressure in her chest eased. "Simon, it was horrible. So many people are dead. She's killing them because of me. I have to stop her." Simon settled himself on the bed beside her. She leaned against him, resting her head on his shoulder.

"Why do you think Father Stokes can help?"

"I'm pretty sure he's the one who cursed me."

Simon sat up. "Alexander cursed you. The Clippers had nothing to do with it. I was there for all the experiments on Claire, remember?"

"Those experiments are what kept me alive. My death curse, the one responsible for killing every woman in my family at the age of twenty-five for two hundred years, has something to do with G... Stokes."

"What makes you think that?"

"I don't think it. I know." Simon relaxed into the pillow again. "I have visions. I'm a seer."

Simon chuckled. "Since when?"

"Since always, I just never had a name for it." She threw back the covers, sliding out of bed.

"Is that what your new friend told you?"

Rebecca moved to the door, flipping the lights on. "My *new friend* has been helping me in plenty of ways you never could. She's a witch, from a coven full of actual witches who know more about magic than I dreamed was possible. Is it so hard for you to believe I have visions?"

"Not at all, but your visions have always been repressed memories. They've never seen something you didn't already know."

"That's not true. I had visions of Margaret's life; some I had no way of knowing." The thought reminded her of her sister's long life.

Simon came to the realization at the same moment. "Margaret lived to be ninety years old."

"I know." She bit her lip, leaning into the bed. "But she's the only one. Adalaide, Mary, and all my incarnations; we all died at twenty-five. The rest died younger."

"Bec, I don't want to poke holes in your theory, but people, especially women, died young all the time back then. Surviving childbirth was a risk, not to mention limited access to medicine and all the myriad illnesses that a person could die from. It can't be a curse affecting your whole family if at least one person survived it. That's not how curses work."

He was right. The dream had seemed so real, though. She had been so certain it was a vision meant to guide her.

"Even if it wasn't something the Clippers did to me, it's real and every time I use magic, I get weaker." She sat beside him. "Look at my eyes." She leaned closer, giving him a better look at the new starburst rimming her irises.

He cupped her cheek, inspecting them. "What happened?" he breathed.

"Ever since I power shared with Sophia, my water magic has been unstable."

He dropped his hand from her face. "Power shared? What does that mean?"

She wrapped her arms around herself, looking at the door. "We synced our water magic. It strengthens my ability. I think it does the same for her."

"You gave the siren more power than she already had, Bec. Are you stupid?"

She flinched back. "No, I'm not stupid, and you're not a witch, so what would you know about it?" She slid back.

He moved too fast for her to catalog and pulled her into his arms. "I'm sorry. I didn't mean it." He pressed his mouth to her ear. "You're the most intelligent"—

he trailed his mouth down the edge of her lobe—"beautiful…" His lips found the pulsing vein at her throat, and he kissed it. "Clever woman I've ever met."

His touch lulled her, making electric sparks dance up her back. She leaned in, closing her eyes. Soft lips ran over her skin, resting on her collarbone. A memory flashed through her mind. Simon's kisses on the same neck, but it was Allie's neck. Allie's body bent for him, moving in all the ways he wanted.

"Stop," she said, shoving him back. "Keep your lips to yourself." Hurt flashed in his eyes, but he made no move to touch her again. "You can't be an asshole, and then use your gift to get what you want from me." She crossed her arms over her chest.

He stuffed his hands into his pockets, dropping his gaze to her bare thighs. She moved around him, climbing back under her blankets. "It's the middle of the night. You should go. We can talk tomorrow." His gaze flicked to the space beside her on the bed. Her eyes narrowed. "Go." His face, once so easy to read, was a mask she couldn't decipher. Finally, he turned to go. "Turn the lights off on your way out."

The room went dark, and she listened to the door close. He was soundless as always, a wraith.

Alone with her thoughts, she took a few shuddering breaths. It had been so easy to believe for just a few moments that things could go back to the way they were. Some part of her ached for his comfort, his touch. She closed her eyes, hugging her pillow.

It would be a long night.

CHAPTER 45

Rebecca

Rebecca crossed her arms over her chest. "Okay start at the beginning."

Simon's dark brow dipped low, but he smoothed his pant leg and sat. "I know what the necklace is."

Rebecca arched a brow. "What is it?" He glanced over her shoulder at Sophia.

"It houses a bone. A bit of bone dipped in gold."

Sophia snorted, but Rebecca sat forward. "Whose bone?"

"If the Fellowes heir is to be believed, the bone belongs to a witch, but not just any witch. *The* Witch. The first one in recorded history." Sophia slid closer to Rebecca, letting their pinkies touch. Simon's gaze darted to their hands, tracking the movement. He cleared his throat. "They called her The Witch of Endor."

Sophia gasped. Rebecca swiveled her gaze to the girl. "Do you know who that is?"

Sophia's bright green eyes widened as she took a steadying breath. "She is thought to be the mother of night-beings. She is the first necromancer."

Simon's gaze darted from her hand, pressed against Rebecca's to her face. "Who told you that?"

"It is known in our coven that night-beings are the children of necromancers; the only creatures who can pass beyond the mortal realm into Sheol and capture a soul before it departs to its final home." Rebecca stared at Sophia, tasting the truth of her words.

Simon shot to his feet. "Impossible."

"Who did you think made your kind?" Sophia asked.

"My maker was a witch."

"So Rebecca said as well, but night-beings can only be made by a necromancer."

Simon scowled sitting once more but lifted his chin, turning his gaze on Sophia. "How can you be sure?"

"I cannot say for certain. Most who encounter a night-being don't live to tell about it, but my coven has many stories of necromancers who dwell in Sheol, sifting through the souls there for their nefarious purposes."

Simon pursed his lips, his brows bunching between his eyes. "If she's right, Elizabeth was my maker," he said returning his focus to Rebecca. "She saved me when I arrived in Sheol, or she stopped me from going to... the place where the Clippers play."

A wrinkle formed on Sophia's brow as she darted her gaze between the two of them.

Rebecca patted her hand. "It's our code word for..." She rolled her eyes. "I can't say what it's code for."

"I don't understand," Sophia said.

"And we can't explain it." Simon's tone was clipped. He was staring at Rebecca's hand resting on Sophia's knee. She pulled her hand away. When had that happened?

"Elizabeth stopped you from crossing over to your final resting place?" Sophia glanced at Rebecca before returning her focus to Simon. He dipped his chin in a sharp nod. "She is a necromancer?"

"I didn't mention that when I told you about her before. Sorry."

Sophia twisted a lock of her hair around her finger. "But she is a night-being. Someone must have stopped her from crossing. How does she retain her powers after death?"

"I can answer that," Simon said. "Witches don't lose their power when they become like me. Their abilities change and become something else. Cybil controlled the element of water before she became one of us. When she joined our group, water froze at her touch." He said this last part to Rebecca.

"A bastardization of the elements. It makes sense."

Simon nodded at Sophia's words. "I don't know how a necromancer's power would be changed by the transformation."

"I have an idea," Rebecca said. "She could do more than bring back souls. She could soul hop."

Simon's eyes widened. "That's how she did it!"

Sophia's brows furrowed. "I'm lost."

Simon gave the subtlest shake of his head, so small Rebecca might have imagined it, so she pretended she had. "Elizabeth can move from body to body. She even occupies inanimate objects sometimes. But we freed her body from its grave, and I'm not sure she still can."

Sophia swiveled her gaze between Simon and Rebecca. "She can inhabit any body?"

Rebecca bit her lower lip. "No. I don't think so. She inhabits the bodies of the night creatures she created." She darted a look at Simon. "With their permission, but she could also squat in the gargoyles in my father's lair."

Simon's nostrils flared, but he said nothing.

"Those statues were crammed with magic. I meant to ask you about them," Sophia said.

"Could you feel it? The magic?"

Sophia nodded. "They are a magical conduit. Meant to enhance spells. A marvel of magical ingenuity."

Rebecca snorted. "My father nearly went broke having them made. They're made of a very specific metal compound. I always thought they were just meant to trap." She choked on the next words.

Sophia arched a brow before saying, "Their composition makes them ideal for channeling magic."

"I'm sorry. Can we go back to my news?" Simon stood, turning his back to them and pacing to the fireplace. He continued striding between them and the oversized portrait of her father for a time before he stopped, arm resting on the mantle.

Finally, he turned to face them. "As I was saying, the bone, gilded in gold, encased in the amulet, belonged to the Gavras family. I went to Peterborough to find information on your curse, but while I was there, I met with the current Fellowes heir, Victoria and she told me it was very old." Rebecca watched as he tapped his fingers on the mantle. "When her ancestor, John Fellowes, met your ancestor, Nicholas Gravas," he waved a hand at Rebecca, "he recognized the name from his family's old texts, knowing Gavras had become Gravas. He hoped returning the family heirloom to its descendants would unlock its potential.

"You see, he lied to Nicholas when he told him fire magic was all that was needed to open it. The amulet only ever worked for one family. The family who killed the Witch of Endor, stole her bone, and bound her to their family for eternity.

"Rebecca, the amulet doesn't trap the enemies of the Clippers. It trapped a witch. One with the power to pull the souls of humans back to our plane of existence."

Rebecca took in Simon's wrinkled suit; the dark circles under his eyes; his disheveled hair. "How do we know we can trust this Victoria woman you met?"

Simon blew out a breath, leaning into the mantle. He turned his yellow gaze on Sophia. "How do we know we can trust anything *she* says?"

Rebecca glanced at the girl beside her.

Sophia twisted a freshwater pearl between tanned fingers. "You have not said how the necromancer was pulled back from Sheol. You have told us fanciful stories of a necklace and, conveniently, a woman we don't know, who told you valuable information about your kind." She raised a single brow. "But I am the one being questioned for my honesty?"

Rebecca bristled. "Sophia."

Sophia turned her piercing gaze on Rebecca. "This is where you tell me Simon would not lie. Simon has our best interest at heart. But Simon was on his way to London the day we went to the hotel room. How did he know to go there before you ever told him about the curse?"

Simon moved in a blur, dropping beside Rebecca on the couch. "She's lying. She doesn't know my travel plans." Rebecca sucked in a breath. She glanced down at his hands now cupping hers, then to Sophia, who narrowed her eyes at Simon.

"Your computer was open when I came in. I saw what you were searching for. Tickets to London."

Rebecca's gaze swiveled to Simon. "Is it true?" Her voice broke, and she silently cursed her weakness. "Were you already going to London?"

Simon's eyes glinted. There was fear in them, the dishonesty written plainly on his face. "Rebecca," he pleaded. She ripped her hands from his grasp. "Rebecca, it's not what you think."

"Why were you going?" His lips flattened into a thin line, and he darted a glare over her shoulder at Sophia. "Don't look at her. Answer me." She blinked back the wetness pooling at the edges of her lashes. He gave her another beseeching look. She slid back, giving them space. "Tell me!"

His shoulders fell as he reached for her again. "Rebecca, please." His voice broke. "I'm trying to save you."

Her vision blurred as tears welled and spilled down her cheeks. "Why did you go?" she demanded.

"I... I was trying to find a way to break the curse."

Pain lanced through her, scorching her soul. He knew. He already knew she was dying. The shapes in front of her became hazy smudges as heat rose in her veins. Distantly, she heard Sophia and felt her soothing magic push at the edges of her own, but she was flame. She was a raging inferno.

The room lit with a fluorescent blue hue, then everything fell into darkness as consciousness swept from her.

A pulsing beat in time with her heartbeat sounded a rhythm against her skull. It beat against her head like a caged animal, seeking escape. Her eyelids blinked open, then closed, seared by blinding light. "Sorry," a muffled voice said.

When she blinked her eyes open again, the light had dimmed, suffused in coral. She squinted, letting the room swim into focus.

"Rhea," she croaked.

"It's Sophia."

She blinked again and the girl beside her solidified. She pressed her hand into the soft mattress, pushing herself up.

"Take it easy. You used a lot of magic."

Her vision swam as the pounding in her head increased, and she pressed a hand to her temple. She looked around her room. "Where's Simon?"

Sophia pulled her pearls out from under a hoodie—the first warm thing she'd ever seen her wear—and began twisting a pearl. "He left. He didn't think you wanted to see him." Rebecca winced as the pounding increased. Maybe that was true, but without him, her chances of reaching Gabriel were slim. "He healed you before he left. I think you might've been worse off if he had not."

Rebecca tried to process the words in her fuzzy mind. "What do you mean?" she asked, her mouth tasting like cotton.

"You used a lot of magic. More than I've ever seen. It took a lot out of you. He stayed for quite a while, feeding you healing magic."

"Simon doesn't have magic," Rebecca said.

"I watched him use it."

Rebecca frowned, that slight movement making the pounding in her head increase. "He doesn't have magic. He never has."

Sophia rested a hand on Rebecca's shoulder, letting cooling liquid magic flow through her. "Rest, Rebecca. We can talk about it when you have recovered a bit more." She tried to fight it, but her strength waned and the comforting magic washing over her eased the throbbing ache in her skull. She closed her eyes and slipped into a dreamless sleep.

CHAPTER 46

Simon

Simon was grateful to the angels for the first time since he'd made this deal with them. If he had not been restored to something like his human form, he might still have that twisted version of his gift, the one that ended life instead of restoring it. He couldn't reverse her curse, but he could slow its effects.

Saving Rhea from a fatal head injury was a delicate business, but nothing compared to the drain Rebecca's injuries caused on him.

She'd used a massive amount of power. More than he knew she was capable of. When the room had exploded in blue flame, it had taken him a moment to realize *she* was the thing on fire.

And the witch who'd caused them nothing but trouble since coming into their lives fought like some kind of feral cat when he'd picked up Rebecca and carried her to her bed, healing her as he went.

As if he would hurt Rebecca, could ever hurt her, even if she was too stubborn to see that everything he did was for her.

Rebecca didn't understand, not the way Claire had. He and Claire had shared a unique bond, one forged by the foulest of Alexander's torments. Claire understood the need for secrets. She had understood why Rebecca could never know what she suffered at her father's hands. In her moments of lucid clarity, she knew what had to be done. If he had had time to ask her, he was sure she would have agreed with his decision.

It was the one secret he would take with him to whatever end awaited.

Simon sighed, staring up at the soft yellow light coming from her fourth-floor window before he turned, racing away into the woods.

Rebecca flitted between lives, remembering none of it most of the time. It was up to him to make sure she was safe. His only life's purpose. Second Life, as Allie had called it. Dimples creased his cheeks, remembering the nickname. Even tough, resourceful Allie had seen how much she needed him in the end.

This was the first time she had treated him like he didn't matter. Like she could navigate this complicated world alone.

It would be up to him to remind her just how much she needed him.

CHAPTER 47

Gabriel

It had been one day, maybe two, breathing stale, blistering air, but his lungs rejoiced at each intake of frigid breath. "Kill him." The strange musical voice was a coax, not a demand. He could refuse.

He did.

"Kill him, or you go back in the pool."

Terror shot through him, and the human slumped before him, whimpered upon hearing the command. He drew himself to his full height, pressing his wings tightly against his back as he backed into the wall.

Her eyes narrowed, and he felt more than saw her gaze on him. She sat like a dark queen, her lithe naked body draped over a chair made of dark petals. Thorns curled away, unwilling to puncture the flesh of their sovereign.

"Kill him, or I make him suffer more." Gabriel glanced at the man on the ground. He could not end this man, but what if it was done only to stop his suffering? Was it a mercy? To what end? The man would only revive for her to torment him again.

"No."

"He speaks," she purred, rising from her chair. She moved suggestively, a provocative dance bringing her closer with each step, stopping in front of him. "Are you certain?" He let his gaze drift to the far wall, her form blurring across his vision. She leaned closer, pressing cold, wet lips to his mouth. He remained frozen. Moving would only earn him a spear through some vital part of his body.

She forced a cold, wet tongue against his lips, prodding her way into his mouth. Her forked tongue parted his mouth further. His wings twitched, but he remained still. Water poured over her lips, into his mouth, down his throat. He gagged, one leg falling back.

Pain shot through his calf as a vine tore through it and wrapped itself around his leg, holding it in place. She spread her webbed fingers on either side of his head, pressing slick skin against his temples, as she continued to pour cold liquid down his throat. He thrashed in her grip, choking, but her mouth was sealed over his. Water poured from his nose, leaking down his face. The water continued in an endless torrent.

He forced the panic down and held his breath. Her eyes opened; cobalt orbs bisected by a thin red slit. She released him, stepping back.

He sputtered and choked, expelling what felt like gallons of liquid onto the floor.

"You don't want to suffer that again, do you pet?" she asked, navy lips forming into a pout. When he had recovered enough to suck clean air into his lungs, he squared his shoulders, stepping back with his free leg. Her pout turned into an ugly sneer. Pain exploded in his chest and back and he let out a gasp as a dark vine burst from his midsection; a deep burgundy flower, lined in soft gold, bloomed across his stomach.

Her tail flicked left and right as she turned her back on him and faced the man on the ground. She slid a sharp nail under his chin, forcing his face to meet hers. "Please," he whimpered. "I'll give you anything." She darted a glance back to Gabriel. He let his vision become unfocused, blocking out the sight before him.

"Is that how your victims begged you before you killed them?" she seethed, sinking sharp teeth into his throat. She spit dark blood and chunks of flesh onto the floor. He choked on his own blood, a ruby pool darkening the surrounding earth. His limbs twitched. She smiled up at Gabriel, red teeth on full display. "You see, we're not so different. I seek vengeance for those who sin as well." She stood, sauntering toward him.

He swallowed. *I'm nothing like you*, he told himself. *I'm nothing like you*, he repeated in his mind again and again. He hoped if he said it enough, he would believe it.

Strong, wet fingers gripped his chin, forcing him to face her. Squeezing his eyes closed, he grimaced as her wet tongue slid over his bottom lip, catching on the seam before continuing to his top lip.

"Gabriel, I need you."

Rebecca's soft voice wrenched his eyes open, and he stared into black orbs slitted in red.

CHAPTER 48

Rebecca

Rebecca sat up, sighing heavily. She was tired of waiting for Elizabeth to make her next move.

She needed to come up with a plan to outmaneuver her, and fast. The problem was, in order to do that, she needed to power share with three other elemental witches. Her body still ached from her recent explosion of power and traveling all the way to Greece seemed like a daunting task.

A knock at the door brought her out of her thoughts.

"I brought you some milk and cookies." Sophia came to stand beside her, placing a tray table over her lap.

"Thank you."

Sophia dipped her chin, sitting at the end of the bed. "Rebecca," she began. "I think I've misinterpreted my dreams. I had another last night. It showed me something different."

"What did it show you?" Rebecca asked.

"It was hard to make sense of, which is saying something for me, but I believe it showed me two people instead of just you. I am no longer sure the dream is about only you."

Rebecca lifted the glass of milk to her lips, sipping as she considered Sophia's words. "Could the vision be changing?"

"No."

Rebecca wrinkled her nose. "You sound confident."

"A vision is not one path on many divergent ones. It is the catalyst for all future possibilities. As it is predestined, it cannot change. This is why visions do not show outcomes. They show pivotal moments that will ultimately lead to an outcome."

Rebecca bit into a cookie and chewed. Her brows furrowed. "If the vision can't change, how can the person in your vision no longer be only me?"

Sophia lifted a hand to her chest, twisting one oblong pearl between her fingers. "I told you before I saw a bull. But the bull was never clear. Always smudged at the edges. I knew this was telling, but thought it spoke of the relationship I was yet to form. Last night, in my dream, the bull was clear, but he stood on two hind legs and at his back, black wings stretched wide. As I watched, he split, one form solidifying into a live animal, the other growing wispy like smoke.

"The live bull, black coat shining, struck the earth with his hoof, and water seeped from the soil. Vegetation spreading undertow. The dark, winged half of him took to the sky, spreading wings that carried him higher and higher until he blocked the sun, its red glow framing him as if he were on fire.

"Together they charged, racing toward the battle, but with them, vines raced along the ground, life spreading to each hoof-marred crack along the surface. In the sky, the winged creature rained fire on everything, a gale at his back propelling him forward.

"Do you see, Rebecca? It cannot be you. The dark beast that blots the sun does not fight on the side of good. He brings evil. You can't be the bull; you can't be on the side of evil."

Rebecca swallowed, considering the similarities between her dream and Sophia's. What did it mean? It wasn't she who ended Elizabeth in her dream; it was her shadow. She had also thought it resembled a demon. What could it mean that her shadow, also winged, might be a demon? She remembered the story Sophia told of the soulmates torn from one another and tasted the truth in the story.

Could a human have a soulmate? Again, her mind went to Simon, wherever he was, but he was no demon, no matter how much she despised his recent actions. She blanched. Did she have a demon soulmate somewhere? Could that demon ever convince her to fight against humanity rather than for it?

"How do you know the flying bull is fighting for evil? In my latest dream, my shadow fought to save my life from Elizabeth."

"You had another dream as well?"

Rebecca took another sip of her milk. A loud thud drew both their gazes to the window. Something dark slid down the window, a trail of red following in its wake.

Rebecca lifted her tray, sliding out of bed. Sophia beat her there, peering out into the night.

A motion sensor flicked on at the corner of the house as Rebecca met her, scanning the grass for any sign of what had tripped the sensor.

Rebecca threw open her window as Sophia hissed behind her. "What are you doing?"

She turned, glaring at Sophia. "I'm looking for the asshole who threw something at my window." She turned back, shouting, "and then ran like a chicken!" A crash somewhere inside the house had her backing up.

Sophia darted from the room. "Close the window, Rebecca!" she called over her shoulder as she ran.

Rebecca wedged the window closed, turning the lock before chasing after Sophia. She halted, nearly colliding with the witch, who was waving a hand in the air as water burst from the restroom to their right and formed a wall in front of them, blocking the stairs.

"Seriously! I just had the house renovated," Rebecca seethed.

"There's a bloody creature being held back by my water shield. You're welcome." As Sophia said it, a creature drenched in blood crashed through her water wall.

Rebecca projected an image of herself forward and sent it down the stairs, running toward the door. He dropped mangled fingers, poised for attack, and turned to run after her illusion. Sending a gust of air after him, she slammed the front door shut.

Sophia sprinted down the stairs, locking it behind them. Rebecca stood at the edge of the third-floor landing, catching her breath. The gaping hole to the left of the door was his obvious entrance, so why was the door thrown wide?

She didn't have to wait long to find out. Another disfigured human blurred through the foyer, slicing a line of red down Sophia's back. She screamed as he spun, throwing up her hands and sent another wave of water—this time from the downstairs kitchen—bowling into the creature.

Rebecca conjured a ball of fire, sending it straight for the new creature. The being screamed in rage as flames hit her in the head, catching her hair and flesh on fire. She moved into Sophia's stream of water, letting it douse the flames, and screamed again as she charged Sophia.

Sophia doubled her efforts, pushing more energy into the water, pummeling the night being.

Raising her hands to the sky, she gritted her teeth and shoved the creature through shards of broken glass, out into the night. She wove her hands into a complicated pattern, looping water from the sink into a water wall, blocking the gaping hole beside the door.

Rebecca reached the bottom step as another blur shot by her, tackling Sophia to the ground. As the scene slowed, Rebecca watched, frozen in horror for one moment as a creature snapped at her face, flailing wildly.

Sophia pressed the creature back, her arms shaking with the effort.

Rebecca slid to her side, pressing flaming palms into either side of the creature's head and pressed with all her remaining strength, feeling bones splinter under the extreme heat of her fire. In moments, the creature slumped to the ground as Sophia rolled to get out from under her.

The girls sat back-to-back, panting, hands raised, waiting for the next attack.

A creature burst through the wall of water, startling them both. Rebecca's hand flung the first ball of fire before he materialized in front of them. He dodged the ball, and it fizzled out as it struck the wall of water.

Rebecca let out a soft whimper as Simon shook out his soaking hair.

"There are at least two of them out there," Rebecca said, wheezing.

"I took care of them." He glanced down at the remains of the woman who'd attacked Sophia. "I only counted three on the surveillance cameras. I got here as quickly as I could."

Rebecca stood on shaky legs, wrapping her arms around his damp form. He slipped his arms around her, and a warm sensation overtook her, infusing her with strength. She gasped, releasing him, but he hugged her tighter, whispering under his breath.

In moments, she felt nearly restored, almost as good as she had before the incident that left a ring around her irises.

Sophia stood, glass crunching underfoot as she left the foyer, and moved shakily toward the kitchen.

Rebecca pressed Simon back, and he released her, staring into her eyes. The moment stretched as they weighed each other, neither speaking.

The wave of water slowed and stopped, and Rebecca broke his stare, turning and striding into the kitchen.

Simon followed silently, her dark shadow.

Sophia leaned over the sink, picking glass from her forearm.

"Help her," Rebecca said, giving Simon a pleading look. He hesitated a moment before making up his mind and moving to Sophia's side, taking her arm.

She winced and pulled away. "I'm fine. Don't waste your strength on me." When she turned, Rebecca saw the dark line welling along her back.

"Simon." She tossed her chin in Sophia's direction.

He took her in, indiscernible thoughts rolling over his features before he dropped his gaze from Rebecca's and placed a hand on Sophia's back. As Rebecca watched, a soft light bloomed under his touch, and Sophia's skin knitted together, leaving a faint white line in its wake.

She wouldn't have believed it if she hadn't witnessed it with her own eyes. Simon had healing abilities. It wasn't anger she felt, but hurt, knowing he had a secret so big that he'd never shared with her. Did she have any secrets from him? She didn't think so. They were supposed to be in this forever. Once upon a time, at least.

Now she wondered if she had ever truly known him.

"They were Elizabeth's creatures. I went to investigate the murders at the edge of town. They'd been moved to the city coroner's office, but most of them were gone. Only a few were too injured to leave their steel tombs. I ended them. Their suffering was too great a torture to leave them like that."

Rebecca sucked in a breath. "Those people were horribly disfigured. I can't imagine how much they're suffering. What kind of monster could do such a thing?"

"The ones I came across outside were not much better. They would not have lasted long, a few nights at most."

A buzzing started in Simon's pocket. It buzzed three times, four, five. "I think you should get that," Rebecca said.

He ran a hand through his wet hair before pulling out his phone. "Damn." He dropped his phone back into his pocket. "There are several disturbances in the area. Groups of creatures terrorizing the town. I don't want to leave you two alone here. You're no match for so many of them."

"You can't win against that many either. Can't they send help? Are you expect-ed to take care of them all on your own?"

Sophia sat atop her stool, watching their interaction, saying nothing. Simon darted a glance at her before he reached for Rebecca, pulling her into the hall. "Excuse us for a moment."

In the hall, Simon pulled her into another embrace. "I'm sorry I lied. I know I have a lot to explain, but right now, I need to keep you safe. Your best chance will be if I take care of as many of them as I can tonight. I hate to say it, but you'll be safest in your father's lair. You can block the doors and if what Sophia said is true, the gargoyles will enhance your magic. I'll take out as many as I can and come straight back here. If any more show up, text me immediately. I won't be far."

She bit her lower lip. "You could die. There are too many of them."

His phone buzzed again. "If I do nothing tonight, Elizabeth will speak with them in Sheol tomorrow, and then we *will* be in trouble. Our best chance is destroying their bodies tonight."

Rebecca's vision blurred. "It's too dangerous."

"It's too dangerous not to." A tear slid down her cheek as she looked up into his yellow eyes. "Get some food, water, and I'll help you carry down books to block the doors. Don't come out for any reason before dawn. Is your phone charged?" She wiped her cheek.

"Yes."

"Okay. Meet me in the lair." He darted away as she returned to the kitchen.

Sophia slid off her stool. "What's going on?"

"We're getting food and water and our phones and going to my father's underground lair."

Sophia nodded. Her gaze held a distant expression, but Rebecca didn't have time to coax her through it now. She ran up the stairs, leaving Sophia to round up food. On the second floor, a blur solidified for just a moment as he planted a kiss on her cheek. He grinned at her before blurring away again, his arms full of books.

Rebecca reached her room, grabbed her phone, and froze. The window was open.

She darted around the bed, slamming it and twisting the lock. Something glinting in the moonlight caught her eye. She squinted into the dark tree line beyond the perimeter of Simon's new motion sensors and could just make out a white-blond mane streaking through the night.

"Simon!" He was there, beside her as she said, "I saw something."

Before she could say more, he was gone. In seconds, she spied his dark clad form disappearing into the night in the same direction the man had gone. It couldn't have been who she thought it was, though. It wasn't possible.

He'd been moving too fast.

CHAPTER 49

Rebecca

In her father's lair, Rebecca slid her chair beside Sophia's and nudged her shoulder. "Hey, we'll be okay. Simon is taking care of them. He'll be back soon." Sophia blinked, saying nothing. Rebecca was becoming concerned. "Are you thirsty?" She held out a water bottle.

Sophia stared blankly at the proffered bottle. Rebecca touched her arm, trying to mirror the actions she'd felt Sophia do so many times. A small trickle of liquid flowed between them.

Sophia sucked in a breath, the magic seeming to revive her. "I was wrong, Rebecca. I was so wrong."

Rebecca wrapped her arms around the girl, squeezing. "You're okay. We'll be fine."

Sophia's gaze snapped to hers. "I called him a demon. He protected us; saved our lives from his own kind. He killed them for us." Her green eyes were rimmed in red. "I would be dead now if not for him. A night-being saved my life."

Rebecca swallowed. She'd never considered what it meant to him to kill his own kind. Did it trouble him? The creatures in her home had been suffering, and she could imagine they weren't a burden, but what about the ones who were whole like him? And Elizabeth. Did he struggle with the notion of killing his maker? Not that he'd known what she was to him before.

Even as she contemplated all this, the newest lie in his recent string of untruths only fortified the wall she'd built around her heart.

"Sophia, how can a person have healing abilities if they aren't a witch?"

Sophia sipped her water. "They can't."

"Simon's not a witch."

"Have you not felt drawn to one another? A strong desire to be in each other's company, as you and I are?"

Rebecca's forehead creased, her brows bunching. "I have... but Simon and I have history. We... I mean, our past is complicated."

"Rebecca, I felt it too. He is a witch. Yours was a family of witches. A coven can only have one healer at any time. Like seers, the gift of healing does not manifest in the next witch in a coven until the previous healer passes. Someone in your coven was a healer. When they passed, Simon became the next. If it was recent, he may have just discovered his new ability."

Rebecca snorted. "I don't have a coven."

"You two are too close in proximity to say such things. It is natural for witches to form a coven through blood or proximity." Sophia slid back in her chair, taking another sip of water.

Rebecca swallowed. She would have known if Simon was a witch. He would have said something after one hundred years. But she couldn't deny what she'd seen him do in the kitchen, or how she felt. But the only members of her family who had been around less than a few decades ago were her father and Margaret. Margaret.

"Do you think a healer could prevent a death curse?"

Sophia shook her head. "A healer cannot perform miracles." She pulled her pearls out from under her torn hoodie. "A witch's magic is not indefinite, though. When they die, their curse fades until eventually it is nothing." Her eyes widened, and she reached for Rebecca's hand, squeezing her fingers. "We will stop it."

Rebecca couldn't tell Sophia that it wasn't a witch's curse. It was something much worse. It was a bargain made with angels. Beings who never passed on. Her phone buzzed, and she pulled it out of her pocket.

She swiped open her email reading: *"I've reconsidered. I'll give your house manager a choice. I'll ask her whether she prefers death or immortality. You have one hour to get here. If you have not arrived within the allotted time, I'll grant her wish."*

A link to a Google Maps pin showed an address less than fifteen minutes away. Her first inclination was to text the address to Simon, but she knew it was a trap. Sending Simon there would only result in his death and Rhea's.

Allie had been so certain the messages were from Detective Blake, but Rebecca knew the emails were from Elizabeth. Why then had she seen luminescent blond hair atop the shoulders of a large man darting into the woods outside her house? She'd only known one man with hair that white.

Were they working together? He was the kind of evil man Elizabeth might align herself with. She pressed a hand to her stomach as it flipped. Had she made him a night-being?

What might a man like that become with enhanced speed and strength?

A resounding clang against the metal door to her right brought her out of her thoughts. Sophia jumped to her feet, her limbs quivering.

"How do we use the gargoyles to enhance our powers?" she whispered.

Sophia glanced to her left, eyeing Rebecca. "You can't. Without Simon here to heal you, you'll be too weak."

"We don't have much choice. There is no water down here. We can't fight them without magic."

Sophia brought her hands up in front of her as something pinged against the door again. The vein in her neck bulged as she pulled at some invisible object. The door clanged again. This time, the books slid a few inches; the door cracking for a moment before slamming shut again.

Sophia's fingers curled as she grunted, still pulling at the imaginary thing. Rebecca looked around the room for any object that might work as a weapon. She spied the handcuffs wedged into the corner and smiled.

The creature on the other side of the door shoved once more and the stack of books slid forward, tumbling to the floor. This time, the door didn't close. Rebecca ran to the wall, hefting the handcuffs in each hand. Sophia balled her hands into fists as the room exploded into action.

A beast of a creature stepped into the room, followed by a wave of water crashing down atop it. The creature toppled to the floor, sliding several feet as a small wave swept through the room, soaking them. Rebecca moved, darting forward, but the handcuffs only went so far, and the creature jumped to his feet, neck bent at a strange angle as he charged Sophia.

Sophia shrieked, backing up. Rebecca cursed, dropping the handcuffs, and sloshed through the water toward them. Sophia pulled out her strand of pearls, wrapping it around the disfigured man's head, and pulled tight. Rebecca froze, watching slack-jawed as the pearls sliced cleanly through the creature's neck, severing it from its body.

"What the hell?"

Sophia bent, dipping her necklace into the water before wiping the strand against her leg. "It's spelled," she said, as if that explained everything.

"Come on, we need to get out of here," Rebecca said, pulling Sophia by the arm.

They trudged upstairs, fighting the tide rushing down the stairs. Sophia lagged, struggling to keep up. How had their roles reversed? Rebecca felt she could run a marathon, her health restored.

Her chest ached at the reminder that Simon could have helped her at any time, in any of her lives, but he never had. It didn't make sense. There was something he wasn't telling her.

They reached the first floor, and she groaned at the wet floorboards and line of water seeping up the walls.

"Sophia, I have to save Rhea, and there's no safe place for you. Coming with me will be dangerous, but staying here could be worse. I won't tell you what to do."

Sophia leaned against the wall, breathing heavily. "I'll come with you."

Rebecca nodded, sloshing through ankle-deep water to the front door and threw it wide.

In the car, she opened her phone, clicking the link to bring up her map. Sophia stared out the passenger window, sliding her deadly necklace along her neck.

"Why doesn't it cut you?" Rebecca asked.

"It was made as my shield. I can't hurt me."

The admission had Rebecca thinking of Jophiel's blade and its inability to hurt her. Was that because she'd been a reash? Was Simon safe from it now that he'd taken over her role?

She pressed on the gas. It was a problem for another time. What mattered now was coming up with a plan to save Rhea. If she drove straight there, Elizabeth would have a plan to immobilize her. She took a left, changing direction. Maybe if she circled around, coming in from behind.

The word shield had her thinking of the last time she'd seen Elizabeth when she'd used an air shield to silence her long enough to sneak up on them. It hadn't worked last time, but it might be enough to keep Sophia hidden while she went on this deranged mission.

"If I make an air shield for you, will you stay in the car while I go check things out?" To her surprise, Sophia nodded.

When she had pressed her bubble around Sophia, stashing the car along the side of the road, she encased herself in a bubble as well, and she marched into the woods to save Rhea.

The unnatural silence sent a chill down her spine. It was too much like the night she'd lost Simon or thought she had. She wrapped her arms around herself, pressing a little more air magic under her feet. Glancing back, she bit her bottom lip, wondering if any of Elizabeth's minions would notice the light tracks through the snow.

Circling back to cover her tracks would cost her precious time, though. Instead, she opted to sink into the ground and make tracks to the right, then lifted herself up again and circled back, moving lightly over the fresh powder.

The urge to drop her shield and listen for any sound that might tell her what she was walking into was strong, but she tamped it down. She pressed another puff of air under her feet, shooting up several feet to the branch of a low tree. Perhaps if she could just get high enough.

Movement at the corner of her eye sent a bolt of terror through her before she turned and spied a small red fox. It spotted her at the same moment and froze. The fox was a good sign. No woodland animal would be this close if there were a horde of night-beings close by. It pricked its ears, looking left, then darted into the woods in the opposite direction.

Rebecca sent more air under her feet, shooting another several feet up into the tree until she was deep within its branches. She scanned the ground, peering through the dense branches. Her phone buzzed in her pocket.

She pulled it out, opening her email. *Time's almost up Miss Graves. What will it be? Shall I send you her head in a box?* Rebecca scowled at the message. Wrapping her arms around the tree, she climbed.

When she reached the top, she peered along the canopy and gasped. It was breathtaking up here above the forest. A dusting of white settled on the treetops in all directions. It was the sort of view a person might only glimpse from an airplane window.

What if she could fly?

She'd tried nothing like it. If she failed, it would be a long fall. But air magic had always come as easily as breathing, and she was Rebecca Graves.

She set both hands on the highest branches and sent a puff of air under her palms shooting through the treetops. When her feet hovered just above the snow-dusted foliage, she pushed more air magic into her hands, tilting forward before she angled her hands to the back and pushed off.

She sailed unsteadily for a moment, dipping as the tree line sloped. Her stomach somersaulted as she passed over the first gap in trees and overcompensated by sending too much air from her palms. She rose several feet, her throat going dry.

As she leveled out again, her puffs of air sent snow scattering off the branches, leaving a trail in her wake. Good thing no one was up here to see it but the birds.

She moved closer to the break in the trees, hovering over the ones closest to the clearing. Movement below drew her focus, and she set down on a sturdy-looking branch high above her destination. She sucked in a breath, holding it before remembering no one could hear her.

Four night beings stood in a loose circle around a woman slumped against a tree. She was bound, her mouth taped shut, her limbs trembling. Rebecca's heart squeezed painfully. Rhea was still in her nightgown, poor protection against this cold weather.

None of the creatures were Elizabeth, no surprise, but they weren't the tattered, hapless beings who'd attacked them in her home either. They were well-dressed and clean. No visible injuries marred their skin.

She eyed the distance between her current tree and the one Rhea sat against. It was a long jump, even with air magic, but if she could get to the tree, her chances would improve dramatically.

Steeling herself, she lifted above the treetops once more and sent a powerful rush of air under her palms as she leaped off the treetop. She sailed over the clearing, squealing in her bubble as she dropped and sent another blast of air under her. She cleared the gap, crashing into the branches of the tree above Rhea.

No way they didn't hear that. She wrapped her arms around rough bark, squeezing as every muscle in her body froze. She stayed like that for what felt like an eternity, not daring to move an inch.

If they were scaling the tree right now, she wouldn't know it until the creature wrapped its lethal talons around her ankle and pulled.

Phantom fingers brushed along her leg, making her gasp. *Just my imagination, only my imagination*, she said until the feeling subsided. She released a breath and dared a glance down.

Her fingers slipped, and she dropped several inches before catching hold of a branch as she gaped down at the scene below.

Sophia stood in the middle of the clearing whipping a cyclone of white dust around her as creatures darted forward, only to bounce off.

Rebecca dropped her shield and growled in frustration. What was she doing? She was holding her own against them, but the element of surprise was gone. She dropped another several feet, but no one paid her any notice.

The vortex of crystals pelting anyone who got too close was a cacophony drowning out everything else. She dropped the few remaining feet to the ground, landing beside Rhea, and untied her, wrapping the woman in a hug before shoving her behind her and throwing up an air shield. The first creature had spied her and moved in fast, a blur rebounding off her shield only a moment before she'd thrown it up.

He shook his head and ran at them again, bouncing off. A second creature joined in, ramming her shield with so much force, she felt it reverberate down her arms. When they looked at one another, some silent decision passing between them, they backed up and charged her together.

She spread her fingers, shoving as much air magic into her shield as she could. One was slammed back, but the other dug his feet into the ground. She gritted her teeth as she watched him suck in a lungful of her air and step through her rapidly dwindling shield.

He had air magic. She was in trouble.

Casting a fireball in each hand, she charged at him. He darted around her, catching Rhea around the waist. She spun, screaming as he sucked in another great lungful of air, pulling it from Rhea's lungs. The frail woman dropped into his waiting arms.

Rebecca marched forward with her arms rimmed in blue, outstretched. He laughed, moving with preternatural speed as he disappeared into the tree line. She didn't have time to consider her next move as pain lanced through her shoulder and her fire winked out. She spun around, narrowly missing the next swipe of the creature's knife. Her shoulder burned where he had sliced it across her skin.

Glancing over his shoulder, she saw Sophia on the ground, pressing her hands into the face of one creature, its skin turning blue. Rebecca backed up, raising blue fireballs again.

Blindingly bright white flames burst through the tree line to her left, arcing through the sky, and then the creature before her split in two. The flames swooped in a circle, decapitating the creature under Sophia's fingers before it winked out and Simon was there, sliding Jophiel's sword into its sheath.

Rebecca flung herself at him. "You're here!" He wrapped both arms around her, squeezing her waist. "Rhea, he took her that way."

Simon released her, looking into the tree line. She winced, trying to mask the fresh pain radiating through her, but Simon missed nothing, and he wrapped her in his arms once more, murmuring strange words into her hair. She swatted him away. "He's going to get away. Stop him!" Simon furrowed his brows, but after a moment of hesitation, darted into the woods.

Rebecca rushed to Sophia's side, dropping to her knees. She threw her arms around the other girl, noting the chill in her friend's limbs. She was no longer maintaining a bubble of protection against the elements. "Come on, let's go to the car and warm up."

CHAPTER 50

Simon

Simon burst through the trees into another clearing and stopped. He tilted his head left, then right, listening for the sounds of the one who had gotten away.

After cleaving a path through Bath straight to the girls, he was certain this was the last one remaining. If he could finish him, they'd have time to regroup before Elizabeth's next assault.

Rebecca sure as hell wasn't leaving his side again. What Elizabeth had done was beyond comprehension. Worse, she seemed to be selecting her victims for their abilities now. Each one he'd come across displayed some variation on the four elemental gifts in its newly twisted form. He was sure the half-mad beings she let loose on the town were a distraction, but from what?

Were they meant to keep him occupied while she lured Rebecca into her trap? It would take more than a few dozen untrained creatures to keep him from her.

If what Victoria said was true, she must be after Rebecca for something other than her fire magic. Her blood. It was the only thing that made sense.

A sound to his left caught his ear. He moved stealthily. He'd already discovered he was faster than most all the other night-beings he came across. Was it because he'd been around longer? Most of them were new, and he'd never been able to catch Elizabeth.

He'd begun to fear the only way to catch her would be in Sheol. Now, though, with the new threat looming, it seemed riskier than ever to chance trapping himself there each day again. Rebecca needed twenty-four-hour protection. Demons were not bound by the same restrictions night-beings were.

Speaking of restrictions. A faint glow along the horizon told him the man he was chasing would need to get to wherever he was going soon. There was still a chance Simon could catch up before it was too late.

He stopped at the edge of the water, staring out at the expansive ocean. The night-being could have gone below, but a living woman would never have survived it. Not to mention the risk of all manner of ocean life nibbling on his body while he was away. It was a risk no night-being would take.

He scanned the docks, looking for any place to stash a body. It made no sense, though. Rhea could escape the moment he left his body for the day.

Sound in front of him drew his focus, and he peered up and up at the bow of a massive yacht parked just beyond the dock. How had he not thought of it? Adrift at sea by day, Rhea would be trapped and by night, they would bring it back along the coastline to wherever they needed to go.

Simon took a running jump and lightly landed aboard the deck. He cataloged each sound as the boat creaked, settling into the ocean's embrace. Another muffled sound from belowdecks had him moving around the stanchion.

As bright orange streaks painted the sky, he sped forward, wrenching the door wide.

A woman screamed, throwing a blanket over her body as the man under her shouted angry, slurring expletives. "I'm so sorry," he said, racing away from them, not waiting for a reply.

He leaped from the boat, cursing soundly. He had followed the wrong trail and now they were stashed somewhere for the day.

He was sure they had come to the water.

At least he had the full day to search the area. He turned, preparing to race back to Rebecca and regroup when pain pricked his neck.

He slapped his neck as a man stepped in front of him. *I've never seen hair that pale*, he thought as he sank to his knees and the world went dark.

CHAPTER 51

Gabriel

The wheezing, choking sound wasn't coming from him. It was her latest victim. Surprising only because his breathing grew more labored by the day. Had he thought drowning when you could not die was torture? He had been wrong.

His head lolled to one side, bringing the beautiful bouquet of dark dimensions blooming across his chest into focus. His night lady, as she preferred to be called, had lovingly cultivated the flowers just for him. They drew their color from the nutrients they ingested.

She had been delighted to find that her midnight purple and burgundy flowers lit up the space when fed a diet of seraphim blood. The unnatural glow radiated through the space, frequently drawing her attention to him.

She ran a dark finger down his cheek, purring. "You are my favorite pet. Have I told you?" His gaze fell to her lips. Deep blue, like squid ink, they stole his focus. His eyelids drooped, caught in the melody of her words. "Uh, uh, uh pet, don't drift away from me now. We're about to have so much fun."

He struggled against his lids, forcing them open. She slapped a cool hand against his cheek. Teeth gleaming in the bouquet's glow. "Good boy." She sauntered away, glancing back. He pried his eyes wide, not wanting to disappoint his night lady.

A man lay on the floor at the foot of her throne, struggling for breath. Gaping wounds in his chest dribbled blood, bubbles popping between rasps. She was prolonging his suffering. Letting him feel the pain so many others had felt at his hands.

When she'd explained it, it made sense. They were evil, vile creatures, and she was doing God's work.

His flinch when she thrust sharp talons through the man's neck—ending his suffering—was involuntary. Red slits darted to him, her lips curving into a frown. The man's body twitched for only a moment before he disappeared. She licked her fingers, never taking her eyes from Gabriel.

The man landed hard, something cracking as he hit the ground.

"Where? Where am I? Who are you?"

His questions were the same every time. This poor creature had no idea he'd lived this fate a thousand times. Part of her rehabilitation plan, she'd explained. The mind could only accept so much before it fled the body, leaving behind a shell. He could not be forgiven if he was too vacant to understand what he had done wrong. And so, she reset his mind each time, to give him the best chance to atone.

It was the most selfless thing Gabriel had ever heard. How she could subject herself to these repeated tortures to save wicked souls, he could not fathom. He should have made her an angel instead of this.

"I know, my sweet pet. It's unfair what's been done to me." She moved back to his side, leaning into his body. The cool touch of her slick skin stirred some emotion he could not name. "It's lust, pet." Was she reading his mind? She tittered in laughter, the sound musical and lovely.

"No, sweet one, you're speaking your thoughts aloud." She ran a hand over the luminescent flowers at his chest, slicing one free. "Now, I need you, pet. Are you ready to serve your night lady?"

CHAPTER 52

Rebecca

Rebecca stepped out of the shower, wrapping a forest green towel around her thin frame. The weight she'd gained over the summer was gone. She wasn't eating enough, but it was more than that. Her careless use of magic was depleting her, sucking the life from her bones.

She padded into her room, finding Sophia wrapped in her multicolor blanket, eyes glued shut.

The poor girl had not been able to keep her eyes open on the ride back to the estate. It made sense to sleep now, while Elizabeth and her minions could not reach them, but Simon had never come home, and worry gnawed at her, fraying her nerves. She never should have let him go after Rhea. They should have regrouped and come up with a new plan.

He wasn't restricted to the night anymore. He should have come back by now, but this new Simon wasn't like the man she'd known most of her life. He didn't return her texts; didn't come home every night. While some of that had been at her bidding, some had not.

She picked up her phone. No new messages. She was bone weary, but going to sleep while he was somewhere out there was unthinkable. If it was her, he wouldn't rest.

Sophia mumbled something in her sleep.

Rebecca went to her drawer, pulled out warm clothes and socks and stretched her new UMASS hoodie over the ensemble.

She glanced back again. Sophia hadn't moved an inch. In the daylight, and on the fourth floor, the girl would be safe. She left the room, tiptoeing down the stairs and stopped in the kitchen, grabbed a banana and a muffin and swiped Simon's keys from the counter where she'd tossed them upon returning that morning.

She would retrace her path to the meetup and search for clues to where he might have gone. He'd raced after the creature with Rhea less than thirty minutes before the sun rose. They couldn't have made it far.

Rebecca climbed out of the car in the same place she'd left just a few hours earlier. Where it had been lightly dusted in snow before, dazzling white blanketed the earth. She followed the most direct path to the clearing and stumbled to a halt. The creatures they had killed were gone.

Three sets of tracks were faintly visible in the snow. She followed them as they moved deeper into the woods, leading her farther away from the road.

Nearly an hour later, she broke from the tree line, crossing a road and losing the footprints.

Before her, the ocean sparkled in the morning sun. Frothing white waves crashed across its surface, disturbing the deep blue. It was beautiful; peaceful.

Some spark deep inside her flared to life at the nearness of so much unchecked might. In the core of her being, she knew she could harness the power of it, call it to heel at her command, but at what cost?

She drew her gaze away from the water, scanning the docks for any sign of Simon or Rhea. As she neared the ocean, it became a battle of will to control her need to tame it. She had never been so affected by her gifts before. Sophia had said it was strong within her, but she'd never felt its pull like this.

A yacht bobbed, tied to the nearest dock. Her gaze drifted farther out, catching on a ship anchored just offshore. It was peculiar to see a boat so close, not docked.

She spied a man in a small fishing boat preparing to depart. "Hey!" she called. He looked up, but pushed off, ignoring her. She sprinted down the dock. "Wait, don't go. Can you give me a ride?" she yelled. "I have money!" The boat stalled.

"Whaddo'ya need missus?"

"Just a quick ride to that ship," she said, stopping at the dock's edge. He cupped a hand over his eyes and peered out.

"You know the captain?"

She dipped her head in a nod. If it was Elizabeth's boat, then technically, that was true. He gave her a once-over before circling his boat around, bringing it back to the dock.

She hopped in, giving him no time to change his mind, and beamed at him.

"That'll be fifty bucks," he said. She gaped at him but reached for her purse.

"Shoot, I didn't bring my purse, but my sister will pay it when we get to her boat." He gave her another skeptical look. She didn't feel guilty in the least. Really, who did he think he was charging her fifty dollars for a ride to a boat not two hundred feet offshore? He circled again, giving his tiny motor a kick, and she fell backward as he zoomed toward the boat.

He pulled up along the stern, giving her easy access to disembark. She hopped off, waving in thanks. "Hey! Where's my fifty?" he demanded.

She ignored him and climbed the back stairs, taking her to the cockpit and out of view.

"I'm waiting right here for my money," he shouted.

She searched the deck, hoping she'd been right, and she wasn't about to be shot for trespassing.

No one manned the wheel, and there were none of the normal signs of life that she could see. No coolers of water or food. No music blaring. The boat was silent apart from the lapping wave slapping its sides. It was larger than it had appeared from the docks. No wonder the fisherman expected to get paid. Calling it a boat was almost an insult. This vessel was nothing short of a yacht.

When she was sure there were no passengers above decks, she found the companionway and slid open the hatch. "Simon?" she called.

A fast-moving object flew into her face, and everything went dark.

Rebecca blinked, the world coming into focus. Across from her, Rhea and Simon were tied together. Rhea's eyes were wide, darting glances to the left. Simon was slumped against her. His dark lashes were pressed together, but his chest rose and fell, loosening something inside her.

She swiveled her gaze to the left, feeling a dull ache at the base of her skull. By some small mercy, it was not yet night. Light streamed in through small portholes in a circular pattern around the small living space. She didn't see anyone else with them. Rhea gave another sharp jerk of her head, and Rebecca looked to the door leading to what must be a bedroom.

She shrugged her shoulders, and Rhea raised her eyebrows several times. Was she supposed to know what that meant? She shrugged again, twisting her wrists, trying to loosen the bindings behind her back. Rhea gave an exasperated sigh, which was surprisingly loud considering her mouth was taped shut.

The door to the bedroom slid open and Rebecca froze. Jason Blake stood in the doorframe, a wide, toothy grin stretching across his face.

"Hey, Allie, long time."

Her mouth formed an O, but no words came. He was no longer human, of that she was certain, but... what was he?

He ducked his head, stepping into the room. Rhea slumped back against the couch, eyes going wide.

"I hoped I didn't hit you too hard. It would have been shit luck if I killed you by accident before we caught up." The right side of his face drooped unnaturally as the left side hitched up into a poor imitation of a smile.

"What happened to you?"

The smile slid off his face. "You happened, bitch." Spittle landed on her cheek as he squatted down, getting in her face. The stench of decay wafted off him, making her gag. "What's the matter, Allie? You don't like her handiwork?" She leaned back, taking shallow breaths.

"This is what happens to people who are connected to you, even if they haven't seen you in years. She finds them and experiments until she gets what she wants. I thought she would let me die after I told her everything I knew." He snorted. "I mean, I died a few times." He ran a hand across his misshapen chin. "But she just kept pulling me back."

The red and brown wounds marring his face hadn't scabbed. They weren't healing, but his eyes weren't yellow, and it wasn't night.

"How?" she began, swallowing.

"How am I alive?" His tone was conversational, but his eyes promised death.

She kept her focus on him, not daring a glance at Rhea or Simon. He was only one man. Her chances with him were far better than they would be if this dragged on till night.

He leaned forward, giving her another strong whiff of decay. "She found this new way to do it. She stuffed a demon into my body and tortured me till I should have been dead. But she found me in that other place where they all go all day and shoved me out. Sent me into a body that didn't want me."

"I had to fight the demon for space in my own body." He fell back against the couch across from her. "It was me or him, so here I am!"

Rebecca pasted a smile on her face. "So here you are. Working for the creature that did this to you."

He reared forward and slapped her hard. When he leaned back, she tasted blood in her mouth. He smiled, that lopsided grin pulling hard on the left side of his face. It was as if he was wearing his own skin. Was it even the man she was talking to, or had the demon won?

She smiled again, showing red teeth. "You must be doing something wrong if she won't make you into one of her night-beings." She saw Rhea's eyes widen, the whites overtaking them, and it was the only warning she had before he stood, balling his hand into a fist and swung.

The next time she woke, it was dark. Her eyes darted to Simon and Rhea. Simon remained slack. He must have been under some sort of spell. The boat rocked, and Rhea also appeared to be sleeping. Jason Blake, or what was left of him, was nowhere to be seen, but neither did she see any of Elizabeth's other creatures.

She gazed around the space, her vision coming in and out of focus. Some dark object partially obscured her right eye and halos were circling the room. Her thoughts were muddled too, making it hard to think of her next move.

She was sure of one thing, though. If she didn't find a way off this ship soon, Elizabeth would be here, and with Simon also in her clutches, Elizabeth could ask for just about anything and she would be powerless to say no.

CHAPTER 53

Rebecca

Rebecca must have dozed. When she woke again, soft light filtered through the room, casting odd shadows over everything, making it appear to be tilting to one side. It took her a moment to realize *she* was on her side.

She pressed her elbow into the leather cushion along her side, trying to prop herself up. It was hard work with her arms tied behind her back and a sharp pain shot down her arm as she slid back onto her side.

Rhea and Simon were across from her, both asleep. Something was wrong with Simon. He had been asleep for too long. Even if Blake had knocked him out, Simon should have recovered by now. How long had it been? At least a full night.

She felt it then, the purr of the engine. The boat was moving. She listened for the sound of others moving about the vessel but heard nothing over the engine and the boat cutting through the waves outside.

She tried again to push herself up, wincing as she forced her elbow into an unnatural angle. Splaying her legs wide, she pushed herself into an upright position before bending her knees and bouncing to her feet.

She cupped her hands together, casting a small blue flame and held it against her back. The tang of toxic fumes wafted to her nostrils, and she tore her wrists apart, feeling the binding break. She stamped out the small bit of flame remaining on the synthetic rope at her feet and froze.

Heavy thuds resounded overhead. She dropped to the seat, flopping onto her side, and bunched the rope under her feet just as the door to the room slid open. She forced her breathing to slow as she let her eyelids rest along the rim of her lashes.

Daring to crack them open just a fraction, she peered through dark streaks of black as Blake stood with his back to her. He leaned over Simon, pressing a syringe into his neck. She stifled a protest as he slapped Simon hard across the face. Simon didn't flinch, didn't move a muscle.

Jason stood, turning his slow gaze around the room. She let her eyelids fall closed, working to slow her breathing. The hairs on her arms prickled as she sensed his nearness. On a whim, she reached for her third eyesight, wondering if she could use it even though her time as a reash had ended.

It flared to life, showing her faint trails of Simon's lilac path and in front of her, a deep charcoal gray outline pressed against the constraints of the man standing over her. Not a man at all, but not entirely a demon, either. The thing trapped inside decaying flesh was something new.

He was so close. He was... sniffing? His head dipped to her knees, traveling down to her feet. Shit. He smelled the rope. She brought her knee up with as much force as she could muster, driving it into his chin.

He stumbled back as she flew up, casting a ball of flame in each hand.

Charging forward, she planted both hands on his chest and reveled in the unearthly scream torn from his lips.

He shoved her hard and, too fast for a human, he circled behind her, grabbing a fistful of hair and wrenched her head back. The smell of burned flesh turned her stomach as he wrapped an arm around her chest, pulling her into him.

She pressed both burning palms to his forearm, and he hissed in her ear, but didn't release her. She pulled on the ember at the center of her chest, intensifying the heat until he bit out a string of curses, shoving her to the floor. She hit the ground hard, hearing something crack in her knee as the flames in her palms winked out.

In a moment, he was on her, slamming a rough hand into the side of her face, pressing it to the carpet. She struggled against his hold, but the weight of him and whatever magic aided the creature on top of her were too much. The man had always been a hulking beast, but the creature pinning her to the ground defied nature.

He wrenched one arm behind her back and then the other, pulling something from his pocket. She bucked her hips, wriggled under his weight, swore colorfully, but her arms were secured behind her back. He grabbed her hair, pulling her up by the head and looped an arm around her midsection, pressing oozing flesh into her shoulder as he pulled her with him up the stairs.

He said nothing as he shoved her down into the seat beside him. She rubbed her sweater against the chair, wiping gore from her sleeve. Her knee throbbed, and pain began at her elbow, radiating up her arm. She spied strands of hair wrapped between his fingers as he spun the wheel and knew they were hers.

Glaring daggers at the side of his misshapen face, she winced as she cataloged new aches blooming across her body. Her cheek felt tender and warm, and a searing pain in her shoulder told her something must have been torn. Along her right side, a dull throbbing had started, and each breath sent red hot daggers into her chest.

She slumped into the chair, a whimper escaping through cracked lips. If she could have curled into a ball and cried without this monster witnessing it, she would have.

Her gaze drifted from her captor to the surrounding sea, stealing her focus. In every direction, cerulean sparkled for as far as the eye could see. She glanced over her shoulder, wincing as pain shot up her neck. No land was visible in the distance.

The hairs at the nape of her neck prickled, and she turned, finding his dark stare already on her. The right side of his face had continued its southern trajectory, some of the skin hanging loosely off the bone. She could see red cords of muscle peeking beneath his right eye socket, and he truly smelled like something dead now.

"I always knew you started that fire," he said conversationally. "I would have never guessed all this was possible." He waved a hand down his body. "But I can always tell when a person's guilty. It's my special gift. The guilt wraps itself around them like a noose, choking the lies from their lips. That's why I was so good at my job."

Rebecca snorted, wincing at the pain in her rib. Jason glowered at her; the two halves of his face garish in their opposition. She looked away, her stomach threatening to heave its contents.

"Not going to contradict me? Make excuses?" He arched one eyebrow, the one that still had hair.

"Where are we going?" she asked, swallowing the bile rising in her throat.

He made a strange sound. His words were becoming more garbled, and she wondered if this new body had an expiration date or if he would continue to wear it until the flesh faded and there was nothing left but bone.

He pulled a phone from his pocket, fumbling with the keys. Cursing under his breath, it slipped between his fingers and bounced onto the ground below them.

"Pick it up."

She gaped at him. "How?"

"Use your special magic."

She stared at him blankly.

His eyes narrowed, and he shoved her off her seat. She tumbled to the floor, hitting her head on the footrest. She grinned up blearily and brought her knee down on the object, sending small cracks across the screen.

A shout of outrage was her only warning before his foot came down on her head and the world went black once more.

This time, when Rebecca woke, it was pitch dark. For one terrible moment, she feared her eyesight was gone after repeated bludgeons to the head. Her breaths coming in quick short bursts, she worked to calm her erratic heartbeat as stars danced across the blackness of her vision. She sucked in labored breaths, ignoring the sharp pain in her side. Something tickled her nose and mouth. Her heart rate ratcheted up as she sucked harder, ignoring the stabbing pains spearing her chest.

Calm down, Rebecca. Calm down. She repeated the mantra in her mind. Opening her third eye, she gazed around the small space. She was in a bedroom, on a bed. Ice ran down her spine as she cataloged every ache, searching for one that might suggest some other horror had befallen her.

Blessedly, nothing between her thighs was sore.

Wriggling her body until she was able to roll to her stomach, she held her head up, giving herself a moment to slow her breathing again as claustrophobia crept in once more.

Casting another ball of flame in her palms, she set fire to the plastic rope binding her and ripped her hands free, tearing the bag from her head.

She sat for a moment, sucking in great lungfuls of air before sliding off the bed and moving behind the door.

She'd love nothing more than to set fire to this whole boat, but with Rhea too weak to swim and Simon's limp form dead weight, she would have to find another option.

Jason was too strong to overpower, but if she could get her hands on the sedative he was using on Simon, perhaps she could use it to pacify him long enough to throw him overboard.

If that plan failed, well, she didn't have a backup plan.

She scanned the room, opening drawers and cabinets, looking for a syringe or vials of sedative. Nothing.

The boat rocked, sending her crashing into a wall. She leaned against it, holding in her groan. She ached in so many places she'd lost count.

Placing a steadying hand against the wall, she stepped forward, only to be thrown into the wall once more. What the hell was going on?

She inched along the wall to the door and slid it open, praying Jason wasn't waiting on the other side. Heaving a sigh of relief, she stepped unsteadily into the small living room as the boat continued to rock violently. Through the small portholes, she saw frothing water splashing against the ship.

She rushed to Rhea and Simon, untying them. If they were about to go down in a storm, she wanted to give them their best chance of survival.

Simon slumped over on the seat as Rhea threw her arms around Rebecca, squeezing. Rebecca wrapped her arms around the frail woman, releasing a shuddering whimper. The boat rocked, pitching them back as they fell against Simon. Rebecca slid forward, grabbing Rhea's shoulders.

"Stay here. I'm going up. Don't follow me no matter what you hear, okay?" Rhea's watery eyes blinked as she nodded. She looked as though she'd aged ten years since Rebecca had last seen her.

Guilt twisted in her gut.

Jason was right, everyone who knew her was in danger. At least Sophia was safe, far from this deranged creature. She ran a hand over Simon's smooth cheek, resting her finger against the pulse beating steadily under his jaw, and leaned down to press a kiss to his still lips.

"I'm so sorry I got you into this," she whispered against his cold mouth. Even when he'd existed only at night, his empty body had been warm to the touch. A spike of fear ran through her, but she pushed it down. She could do nothing about it now, and none of them would be safe until Jason Blake was dead.

She left Rhea and Simon, crossing the small space to a spear hooked to the wall. Pulling it down, she glanced over her shoulder once before moving unsteadily to the door.

The storm seemed to intensify above. Maybe her luck had finally changed, and she would find the waves had already tossed him overboard.

She pulled hard on the door, cursing her bad luck. Locked. Gritting her teeth, she yanked harder, working to get it open. A scraping sound from the other side of the door sent her stumbling back.

She lifted her spear.

The door slid wide as howling winds burst in, the world lighting overhead as streaks of white shot across the sky. Rain pelted the doorway and waves crashed across the deck, sending sea water sloshing down the stairs.

Rebecca took a step back.

A creak sounded, then another, as water whipped into the room in a cyclone spinning out, and Sophia stepped through the door.

Rebecca dropped her weapon, rushing forward to wrap her arms around the other girl. Sophia's arms came around her in a fierce hug, and they squeezed each other tightly.

Rebecca pulled back, scanning the small space over Sophia's shoulder. The sky had calmed, no longer lit with streaks of white, and the rain had stopped. Even the ocean seemed to have calmed.

Her eyes met Sophia's. "Did you do all that?"

Sophia wiped a tear-streaked cheek, smiling. "I had help. Come, meet your coven."

CHAPTER 54

Rebecca

It was a black, moonless night. Millions of tiny sparkling dots winked across the expansive Stygian sky. White frothing foam moved like seagulls over a black landscape, encircling them and stretching as far as the eye could see.

Rebecca's gaze landed on pale blond hair as Jason struggled to free himself from the hold of three powerful looking women. She lunged forward, hands raised as she conjured flames. Sophia stepped into her path.

She halted, blue flame winking out. "You should have killed him," she seethed.

"He knows where we can find Elizabeth."

"We need to get Rhea home. I'm not taking her into a battle with Elizabeth, and we're not ready to face her yet."

Sophia's brows drew into a flat line. "We found your friends, but there are others still missing."

Rebecca's stomach clenched. "Who?"

Sophia gazed around the deck and Rebecca trailed her gaze, noticing just how many people were aboard. There were at least a dozen women; many who resembled Sophia.

An ancient woman, a full foot shorter than them, stepped forward. She said something Rebecca didn't understand, and Sophia translated.

"This is Yia-Yia. She says it is an honor to meet you."

Rebecca dipped her chin. "You as well."

Yia-Yia said something else, and Rebecca's gaze fell on Sophia.

"She wants me to tell you we have lost ten sisters since Maria. Our sisters were taken by the night beings." Several of the women on deck mumbled in their language, shaking their heads. A few crossed themselves. "We cannot kill him until he tells us where to find our sisters."

Rebecca turned to Yia-Yia. "We would be walking into a trap."

Yia-Yia spoke, raising her arms in the air as a light drizzle began pattering the deck. Sophia held up a hand making a calming gesture as she spoke softly to the woman. Yia-Yia crossed her arms over her chest. Another woman, bearing a striking resemblance to Sophia, stepped forward, wrapping her arms around Yia-Yia, pulling her back.

Sophia spoke to the pair and Rebecca made a mental note to learn some Greek phrases as she watched, unable to make out any of their words. Finally, Sophia turned away from them, facing her.

"We will keep him alive for now. When the time comes, you may kill him." Rebecca arched a dark brow. "This is how things are done in a coven. The group decides, not the one."

Rebecca drew her lips into a flat line, glancing at Jason, who was, for the moment, sitting in silence.

She tossed her chin in the direction of the woman standing with Yia-Yia. "Is that your mother?"

"Yes, her name is Angeliki, and this is Helena, Phoebe, Nita, Georgia, Maria, Vassi, Thalia, Iris, and Cassia." Each woman dipped their head or waved as she pointed them out. Rebecca nodded to each.

"How did you find us?" she asked, directing her question to Sophia.

"Like calls to like," Sophia said. "And the ocean speaks to those with water magic. If you know how to listen, it will tell you many things."

"You all have water magic? And that storm. It was all of you?" Rebecca still thought their plan was a suicide mission, but the storm had been a thing of wonder.

"The power of many is great." Sophia winked. "Now, let's bring Yia-Yia to Simon. She can help him."

Rebecca swallowed, looking around the deck. "First, let's tie up Blake so he doesn't get free." She wished, not for the first time that she had the spelled restraints her father had made. She trailed her gaze around the deck, spying an enormous pile of rope and... snickering to herself, she crossed the deck, picking up a roll of duct tape.

Holding it up, she said, "This should do the trick."

When Jason Blake was duct taped to the passenger chair and several layers of rope were tied around him, she wiped her hands together, smiling.

They moved below deck, Helena following them. Helena stopped beside Rhea and pressed a hand to her temple, murmuring softly as shimmering white light burst from her palm.

"Healer," Rebecca breathed. Sophia nodded.

Yia-Yia sat beside Simon's limp form, resting a gnarled hand on his chest. She leaned down, pressing her ear to his rumpled black shirt. Speaking quietly, she unbuttoned the first few buttons on his shirt, pressing her palm to his bare skin.

Her milky eyes clouded as she drew in a breath and looked at Sophia. Sophia dropped to her side, and the pair whispered conspiratorially.

When Sophia looked up, her expression was unreadable. "He's gone."

CHAPTER 55

Simon

Of all the times to find out he could travel to Primoria, it had to be now, when Rebecca was in danger and Elizabeth had set her creatures on the town.

He was no stranger to the sensation of a needle prick. He knew what came next. If he ever woke, it would be to some unfathomable torture. No amount of selflessness could convince him to willingly wake to that reality. It had been his life for too long.

It had to be the reason he'd thought of going to Primoria when he fell under the sedative's pull. He would rather die than go back to a life like that. And if he was going to die, he could do this one last thing for her. Find a way to break her curse once and for all.

Now that he was here, though, he had no idea where to find Gabriel. It was dark and cold and vast.

It seemed to be a cave of endless tunnels. Wandering them had left him disoriented. Unlike Sheol, there were no rivers teeming with souls. It was empty and quiet.

With no way to tell how long he'd been here, and no way to know if the duration of his stay mattered, he continued, sometimes going right, sometimes left.

It was impossible to say whether it was day or night in the constant dark, but sounds in the distance seemed to indicate it was a new day and after hours of silence, this place was waking.

After stumbling over rocks and down narrow passages for what seemed like hours, never seeming to come any closer to the sounds in the distance, he came upon his first living thing. It wasn't a demon or a ghoul or even a lost soul. It was a flower.

Deep burgundy.

It was beautiful in a place so devoid of everything. It peeked from a crack in the wall as if to say hello. He took it as a sign to go right. A few feet further, he found another.

It became a game. When he came to a branching tunnel, he searched for a flower to guide his path. If the path carried on several feet with no flower, he doubled back and took the other.

One path always had a flower.

CHAPTER 56

Rebecca

R ebecca rested her hand against cool bare skin. Sophia had explained that Simon's soul was missing. His body was here, intact, but the soul had wandered.

It was night, though. When he'd left before, it had always been during the day, and his body had never grown cold while he was gone.

She sat with him late into the night, determined to be there when dawn broke.

The witches were bent on their mission to find their sisters. With much coercion, Jason Blake had admitted he was on his way to Bermuda. His only instruction had been to take the other night-beings to Bath, pick up Allie, and go to Bermuda to await further instruction.

Kidnapping Rhea was his idea. A way to draw her out. He'd needed to get her away from the crowded school campus and back to Bath where they could take the boat he'd left waiting to Bermuda. He'd played on her fears in the hope she would return to her house in Bath and be easier to catch. When threats from her past hadn't worked, he'd resorted to killing to get her attention.

The witches were most concerned with the change in weather and the location of their missing sisters. They feared the two were connected. Jason Blake claimed to know nothing about either.

Rebecca didn't believe a word that came out of his slimy mouth.

She also didn't agree with their plan to go to the place Elizabeth was expecting them, but the coven made all their decisions by vote. Not that she thought they were counting her votes. No one asked Sophia to translate what she said.

She ran a hand absently through Simon's dark hair, untangling silky strands. His body jerked, and she froze. Had she imagined it? She pressed her free hand to the pulsing vein at his throat. It was galloping at an unnatural speed.

"Sophia! Yia-Yia!"

Sophia poked her head into the doorway. "What is it?"

"Something's wrong with him. Where's Yia-Yia?" Sophia pitched forward, as Yia-Yia barreled down the stairs, dropping to the seat beside her.

She laid a gentle hand on Simon's temple before moving it to his bare chest. "Fevgei. Prepei na ton feroume piso."

Rebecca darted nervous glances between Yia-Yia and Simon. "What is she saying?" Her attention fell to Simon as his body convulsed again, and she stroked his cheek, her vision blurring.

Sophia faced Yia-Yia, ignoring Rebecca. "Pos boroume na ton sosoume?"

"Den to kanoume."

Sophia's brow furrowed.

Yia-Yia looked up at Rebecca. "Mono afti borei."

"Someone tell me what the hell is going on!" Rebecca demanded, her heart dangerously close to exploding as it matched the pace of Simon's, and he twitched again, less severely this time. She didn't know if that was a good thing or a bad thing.

"She says he is departing his body, and you must call him back to it."

"What? How?" She swiped at her eyes. His skin was growing colder even as they spoke. The women exchanged a few more incomprehensible words as Rebecca dropped her mouth to Simon's ear, whispering, "Please, Simon. Come back. Come back so I can be mad at you in person."

She pressed a kiss to his cheek. "Come back to me."

CHAPTER 57

Gabriel

He stared down through glazed eyes, some flicker of recognition straining against the confines of his mind to break free. Something about the man at his feet was familiar. But as his gaze fell on him, his vision blurred again.

"He's suffering, pet. End it." The words poured like honey, spilling from her lips into his mind.

His eyes found hers, the clearest blue he'd ever seen. In a millennium, they were the first eyes to steal his breath. He longed to fall at her knees, beg her for just one sweet touch. She was his light in an eternity of darkness.

A groan snagged his focus, pulling him back to the task at hand.

This man, like so many before him, was a killer. She didn't need to speak his crimes aloud but hearing them reminded him of his purpose. How had he spent so long watching idly as humans destroyed one another? He was a weapon, meant to cleanse the earth of all wrongdoing. It was why he had been made. Shelved so many thousands of years ago, to appease his brother's whims.

No more. In her, he had been remade. With her, he would remake the world.

"Tell me again, my lady, what are his crimes?"

She sighed and some part of him flinched at the exasperation in that sigh. Had he upset her? Made her angry? He raised one fisted hand, prepared to deliver a killing blow. Anything to appease his lady.

"Gabriel, wait. You're right. We must speak their crimes; allow them to atone." She stood; bare skin caressed the rigid muscles along his arm as she slid past him to stand beside the man at their feet.

"You, vile creature, have killed your fellow man, lied to your lovers, and made bargains with devils. Do you repent?"

The man's yellow eyes blinked open as he rolled onto his back. "Gabriel," he said through cracked lips. His familiarity was unsettling, scraping again at the far corner of Gabriel's mind. "Gabriel, she needs you." He coughed. "Rebecca needs you." The man closed his eyes, grimacing.

CHAPTER 58

Rebecca

Commotion from above deck drew Rebecca's focus for a moment before she returned it to the still form in her lap. His lips were tinged blue, and a strange dark pattern bloomed across his chest. Yia-Yia hadn't known how to call him back, only that Rebecca was his best shot, as their lives were so interconnected.

Was he fighting Elizabeth in Sheol right now? Could she harm him there?

If only she could use the power of all four elements to keep him safe. She bit her bottom lip. Could she preserve this moment in time? Sophia's explanation of kinetic energy and the earth's rotation gave her no clue how she would accomplish such a thing.

"Sophia." she called, afraid to leave him for fear her nearness was all that tethered him to the mortal plane.

Sophia slid open the door, separating her from the bedroom. Several of the witches had gone in to get a few hours' sleep, but Sophia was still awake. "What is it? Is he okay?" She rubbed her eyes, dropping onto the couch beside Rebecca.

"Can you teach me how to freeze time?" she asked hopefully.

Sophia gave her a sad smile. "That is magic beyond my ability."

Another loud thump from above had them both looking up at the ceiling. They looked at each other before Sophia glanced down at Simon. He hadn't twitched or convulsed in some time. Rebecca ran a hand over her face. "I can't leave him."

Sophia nodded, getting up and padding to the door. She slid it open and screamed as something rolled down the stairs, landing at her feet. She dropped to her knees as several other women poured out of the bedroom. "Nita," she sobbed, pulling the woman's limp form into her lap.

Angeliki dropped beside her, wrapping an arm around Sophia as Helena came up beside them, pressing a palm to Nita's neck. She shook her head.

The other women rushed past them, up the stairs and out onto the deck.

Rebecca watched the scene mutely, wrapping her fingers around Simon's. She darted glances between his shallowly rising chest and the door several times as shouts above deck made her fingers tighten around his, bones straining against the skin at her knuckles.

Yia-Yia ambled from the bed, dropping beside her, pressing gnarled fingers to Simon's chest. One of the women, Phoebe, dropped her head into the cabin, speaking rapidly. Angeliki and Helena exchanged a few words with her, and she disappeared again.

"What's going on?" Rebecca asked.

"We are in Bermuda," Yia-Yia said in heavily accented English. "And the demon man is gone."

Rebecca cursed under her breath. Of course he had escaped. And now, he would give Elizabeth the advantage. As if she didn't already have one. They'd only been able to extract the barest details from him. Elizabeth had instructed him to meet on Grace Island; one of the lesser of Bermuda's one-hundred-twenty-three islands. He hadn't shared how many night-beings were there or any of her plans for Allie once they had arrived.

The group voted in favor of plowing a path straight for Grace Island, hoping to beat him there. Rebecca voted to stop at the closest main island to gather intel.

Elizabeth wouldn't be there alone and if her night-beings were terrorizing the locals, people would be talking about it.

After a lot of yelling and arm waving, the witches had agreed to at least wait for dawn. She breathed a small sigh of relief, knowing they would be safe from Elizabeth for the day. If they could find her before nightfall, they might just stand a chance.

Helena had done a miraculous job of healing her, mending ligaments and bone, but the healer could only take on so much before she was spent and had to rest.

The whole thing smacked of déjà vu. And the last time she'd underestimated Elizabeth, it had cost her Simon. She touched his chilled flesh.

The blue tingeing his lips had spread to his cheeks. A human would be dead, but Simon wasn't human.

The witches gathered on deck as the sun's predawn rays crested a blue expanse of horizon, making the sea sparkle like diamonds. That strange pull had snagged in her chest again as she met them on the deck.

Georgia, Maria, Vassi, and Angeliki stood to Sophia's left, while Iris and Thalia stood to her right. Angeliki opened her mouth as a strange hum buzzed from her chest. The others followed suit and soon the waves swelled, crashing alongside the boat. She raised her arms as the sky darkened, black clouds materializing before Rebecca's eyes. Georgia spread her palms and streaks of white veined across the sky as fat drops of rain fell from the dark tableau, splashing them and soaking the deck.

Thalia pulled one splayed hand into a fist as thunder rent the air. Iris sucked in a breath, releasing it slowly as a heavy fog blanketed them.

Rebecca marveled at the sight of the witches working in concert to mask their approach as they prepared to skate by the royal navy.

Cool liquid raced under her skin, begging to join, to commune with her sisters. Adelfí, Sophia had called her. And she felt it, the call to be part of something bigger than herself.

Their ship sailed around the tip of the island, moving into Great Sound. They continued at speed, not slowing even as they approached a rocky, terrifying-looking shore. Crystal-clear water—even in the dark of the storm—made it abundantly obvious they would need a smaller boat to reach the island.

"Stop," she breathed. "Stop!" The ship swerved left at the last moment, sliding to a stop several feet from shore. As the group of women at the helm dropped their arms, heavy clouds dark with unshed rain scattered, some deflating like balloons as the last of the rain fell and golden light burst through the fog.

Her breath caught in her throat as sparkling aquamarine waves shimmered in the morning light. A school of fish leaped from the water in perfect formation, silver bodies glinting in the sun before diving below. She peered over the edge, watching them move in a zigzag pattern as they swam away.

Green shapes bordered by glittering azure dotted the horizon. White sand broke from the waves, stretching up to meet rocky coastlines shrouded in verdant foliage. It was paradise.

It might also be the place she died.

One by one, they crowded onto a small inflatable raft, several of the women carrying Simon, and sped for shore.

Ahead, a lone white structure stood at the top of the rocky cliff.

"How are we supposed to get up there?" Rebecca groaned.

Sophia bumped her shoulder. "We climb."

Onshore, Georgia and Vassi dropped back to help Rebecca and Sophia lift Simon and together hefted him—with the help of Rebecca's bubble of air—up the side of the side of a white cliff.

CHAPTER 59

Gabriel

His lady hissed a serpentine sound and her body rippled, transforming from the beautiful woman with raven hair who stalked his nightmares to the creature who had become his waking terror. Realization flashed in her red-slitted eyes at the same moment the name—clattering around his mind—crashed into a wall, shattering it.

Rebecca. Rebecca who must be in real danger if Simon was here.

The siren struck, but she was not fast enough, and her flowers couldn't save her now. He moved with a speed he had not possessed before, wrapping his fingers around her neck, cracking bone. She went limp in his grasp, transforming into the shape of a colossal viper.

Her scaled form slid between his fingers, coiling on the floor. Only her face remained humanoid, vacant eyes staring at nothing.

Gabriel reached down, holding his hand out to Simon. He grabbed it, pulling himself up. "I thought you were going to kill me," he wheezed.

"What happened to Rebecca?"

Simon dusted his pants, sucking in a breath. "I think Elizabeth has her. If she doesn't, she will soon." Gabriel growled low in his throat. The Nasdaqu-ush had escaped before, but she would not again. Simon squared his shoulders. "Rebecca has bigger problems than her sister. Did you curse her entire family?"

Gabriel's eyes slid left, gauging the reash's injuries. "I see you heal now. The deal you made with Dina benefits you." Not waiting for a reply, he stalked to the pool at the center of the room, pulling a man free from the vile flowers trapping him there. This one, she'd left to die repeatedly from asphyxiation. Each time he appeared in the same place, speared by the flowers waiting for his arrival and drowned in his own blood.

Simon trailed him. "Rebecca needs your help reversing her curse. She's dying." Gabriel moved to the corner of the room, tearing a man from the bed of petals holding him upright. The man slumped to the floor. "Are you listening to me?"

When every victim of the siren's snare was freed, Gabriel strode through the mouth of the nearest exit. The time he'd spent in that haze of delusion made one thing clear to him. One did not leave Primoria by dying or by searching for an exit. One left by putting an end to its king.

Gabriel turned left, following the ever-narrowing path. His form flickered, losing density. The feeling was wholly new. To be corporeal one moment and able to phase through walls the next was freeing. He stretched inky wings, feeling their cool touch against his back.

"Gabriel, wait! I can't go that way."

He tuned out the droning of the reash who'd found his rightful place in Primoria. Simon was not his problem. Simon had had one job. He'd been given a second chance and in exchange, he was meant to find the Nasdaqu-ush and end her. Instead, he had deposited Rebecca in her waiting grasp and left Elizabeth to wreak havoc.

Hearing his crimes aloud confirmed every conviction he'd ever felt about the creature. There was nothing worse than a liar. Simon didn't deserve her, had never deserved her love.

Had he been less selfless this time, he would have stopped Simon before he got his hooks into her. He would have taken his rightful place by her side.

Those were dangerous thoughts, though. His selfishness had been the thing to get her killed the first time. That and her deal. Foolish headstrong girl. But things were different now, and he would not make the same mistake twice.

Gabriel turned, stepping into a cavernous space. He knew it would be here; knew *he* would be here. From the moment he'd bent to the siren's will—caving to her depraved desires—spilling blood across packed earth, he'd felt the change. A tearing, rending at his core that could never be put right.

The incessant pull tugging him here only grew stronger as he drew closer.

A booming laugh resounded from the walls. The scraping sound marking his presence chafed, making Gabriel grind his teeth.

"Brother," the deep voice purred. "You are much transformed. I knew Asmodeus would help you find your way."

Gabriel bristled, feeling his dark wings flex. He spread his fingers, delighting at the sharp talons glinting in the near dark. He lunged for Samael, swiping a taloned hand only a millimeter from his face. Samael's lips stretched over teeth that gleamed in the dark, a low chuckle rumbling in his chest. Gabriel swiped again but missed. He stepped forward, reaching with both arms; still, his reach fell shy.

"What trickery is this?" he demanded.

Samael chuckled. "You cannot harm me, brother. Once you spilled blood in my realm, I became your Sovereign. I hold dominion here. Part of Father's agreement." He waved his hand dismissively. "And in keeping with my right, it's time I unchristen you."

Gabriel stepped back. "You have no authority."

Samael laughed again. "I assure you; I do." He raised a hand, fingertips lighting with a flame of deep crimson.

Gabriel strained against invisible arms holding him in place. He raged in silence as he found his mouth was also sealed.

Samael lifted his arm theatrically, swiping down Gabriel's chest. "I name you Azazel."

The invisible hold fell away, and Gabriel staggered back, touching a hand to three dark lines now marring his skin. They burned, blazing hot, as though the fire had scorched his very marrow.

"My name is G..." He stumbled over the word, feeling a sharp sting at the edge of his tongue as a split began to form. Samael had spoken true, renaming him and stripping the final vestiges of his sanctity. "Azazel," he said, as delicate flesh knitted closed.

His head fell, the burn lingering on his chest a pittance to the shame of being stripped of his God-given name.

"Go Azazel, begin your reign of terror. My kingdom is yours. Debauch yourself of my delights. Or should your tastes stray to livelier conquests, breach the divide, pillage and plunder. All the earth is yours. And when you are ready, return and rule at my side."

CHAPTER 60

Rebecca

Rebecca dropped onto her butt outside the building, heaving as she caught her breath. The others in her group had set Simon down in one of the church's many beds and marched away, unfazed by the treacherous climb up the rocky cliff wall.

That small bit of air magic had winded her.

Sophia dropped onto the sand beside her. "The others have searched the church and found no sign of Elizabeth or her night-beings." She rested a hand on Rebecca's knee. "Are you okay?"

Rebecca nodded, pasting a smile on her face. "I should be starving after four days with nothing to eat." She laughed at the absurdity of her statement. Worrying about food at a time like this. She swiped a trickle of sweat from her forehead. "But I just feel hopeless." She glanced at the girl beside her.

A cooling sensation ran up her thigh, emanating from the point of Sophia's touch. Sophia fished in her bag, breaking their contact, and pulled out a multigrain bar and a bottle of water. "I found these inside. Everyone took a few. Eat and drink. It will make you feel better."

Rebecca took them, smiling gratefully. Eating would restore her strength, even if she longed for nothing more than to crawl into a bed and sleep for the rest of her life.

"Skotos," someone said to her left, and then several others whispered or spoke at once. "Skotadi, kako, diavolos." Their words melded together, a chorus of ominous foreboding that sent a chill down Rebecca's spine. She didn't know what their words meant, but she felt their meaning.

She gulped water and swallowed dry bites of the multigrain bar, forcing them down before standing and moving to join the group.

Sophia grabbed her hand, clasping it tightly. "Don't look," she whispered, pulling Rebecca back from the edge. "There's no need to see that."

Rebecca pulled her hand free, leaning forward and swallowed hard as she got her first glimpse of the mangled bodies smashed against the rocks below.

The island was uninhabited now, but it hadn't been when Elizabeth and her creatures arrived.

Rebecca felt the crushing burden of guilt as she remembered how spectacularly she'd failed by giving Elizabeth everything she needed.

Except me. The truth of that thought tore through her. "I can't be here." She hadn't said it to anyone in particular, but several women turned their gazes on her. "I have to leave. Now."

Sophia squeezed her fingers. "We can stop her. This coven is powerful. You are powerful."

"No. You don't understand. She needs me. I am delivering myself to her on a silver platter."

Sophia's nose wrinkled as her eyebrows dipped. "What kind of platter?"

Rebecca pulled on one of her dark curls. "Blake kidnapped me and was bringing me here. She wants me here. I don't know why, but coming was a mistake. I need to get out of here."

Yia-Yia stepped up beside her, placing her twisted fingers in Rebecca's hand and doing the same with Sophia's. "Come, girls."

They followed silently.

Sophia pushed open the door to the church as she stepped in first. The cutout shape high overhead framed the light in the center of the room. It might have appeared like an X to mark the spot had it not been longer than it was wide.

They stopped less than a foot from the shape illuminated by the midday sun.

319

Yia-Yia pulled Rebecca around to face her. "Your path is written. You are chosen. But you must decide whether you will accept your fate or run from it." Her heavily accented words made it difficult to understand, but Rebecca got the gist. The fate of the world rested on her shoulders. Yia-Yia believed this was the moment in Sophia's dream.

She swallowed, wishing Gabriel of all people was here. He never wavered. He would have been steadfast in his conviction to do what was right.

Her gaze drifted to Sophia who had her hands clasped tightly together.

She'd found a kindred spirit in someone other than Simon and it restored just a bit of her faith in people. But what if Sophia's visions had never been about defeating Elizabeth? What if she was meant to face her sister, but not win? Her mind spun back to Adalaide's journal entry.

Myne immolation or oblation? Shall it be as it was meant or do fates so entwined defy predestination?

Immolation or oblation. A willing sacrifice or an unwilling one. Had Ada been a seer too? Had she seen the same prophecy but assumed it was for herself instead of for some future relative? What if this moment had always been about Rebecca? Was she meant to be a sacrifice?

But there was more to that entry. What did the analogous umbra have to do with any of this? Why was a soulmate important to the story?

She blinked, realizing she'd been lost in her thoughts for too long.

Yia-Yia and Sophia were still as statues. She waved a hand in their faces; neither moved.

She felt it then, the pressure in her ears. She was in a time bubble. Had she frozen time?

"Rebecca." A voice like a thousand harp strings strummed out her name, breaking the stillness. She started, whirling around.

Jophiel hovered high above, her glow, not unlike the cross illuminated on the floor.

Rebecca crossed her arms, slitted eyes tracking Jophiel's descent. "You finally show your face." Jophiel landed, padding closer. "Here to steal more of my memories?"

Jophiel's glow dimmed as she solidified. "Rebecca, I am here to give you grave news."

She rolled her eyes. What else was new? Angels never came with happy tidings.

"Gabriel." She paused. It was the first time Rebecca had ever seen Jophiel lost for words. "I never thought—" She broke off again. "He needs you."

Rebecca's insides twisted in discomfort. They had no right to ask her for anything. Gabriel, least of all. But she *had* meant to find a way to Primoria. She'd told Simon it was only to find a cure for her curse, but no one, not even Gabriel, deserved to be trapped there.

"I tried." Her voice cracked on the weight of her failure. "I tried to send Simon to talk to him, to see if it was possible, but..." She turned away, wiping a phantom tear from her cheek. "Simon's gone now too."

"They are together, Rebecca. You can bring them back."

Icy dread crept up her spine. Simon was in Primoria? How, why? "How do you expect me to save either of them from that place?"

Jophiel's wings twitched, the feathers vibrating in a strange rhythm. "You must die."

Rebecca blew out a breath. "So you said. Die but not stay dead. Whatever that means. Can you cut the bullshit for once and tell me something useful?"

A rare grin broke over Jophiel's ethereal face, her multi-hued eyes danced in amusement. "I do not believe anyone has ever spoken to me that way."

Rebecca's lips twitched, inching up before she remembered everything the angels had done to her. "I don't see why Gabriel is my problem."

"He sacrificed himself to save your life."

Something sharp and uncomfortably close to gratitude speared her chest. She shoved it down. "He probably had a reason that had nothing to do with me." The pain resurfaced, but she ignored it.

"He is damned," Jophiel cried. Stepping back, her face fell; the emotions playing across it were far too human for Rebecca's liking. When she had recovered, she continued, "He did not make that bargain with your ancestor. I did."

Rebecca gasped. "But." Her eyes stung as her vision blurred. "Why?"

Jophiel paced away from Rebecca. "I cannot tell you."

Rebecca wrapped her arms around her chest. Nothing she said would convince an angel to tell her if they didn't want to. "So I have to die to save them." It wasn't a question and Jophiel didn't answer.

"Please, Rebecca. Help him." Jophiel faded, and as she did, the room spun wildly, the sunlit shape of a cross sliding across the floor.

When it righted itself, Sophia sucked in a breath, looking around, and Yia-Yia leaned into her, tipping precariously.

"Did you do that?" Sophia asked.

Rebecca didn't answer. She couldn't. The binding wouldn't allow it. Instead, she said, "Sophia. I need your help."

Sophia glanced around nervously as if she knew they hadn't been alone. "Okay," she said hesitantly.

Rebecca squeezed her arms through the thick fabric of her sweater. On this island, where the abnormal chill hadn't reached, it clung to her skin, sticking to sweat-drenched limbs.

"Can you get Helena? I need to know if she can bring someone back from the dead."

CHAPTER 61

Simon

S imon landed on his hands and knees, cursing for the hundredth time as he felt the bite of rough stone cut into his palm. That overstuffed, self-righteous peacock had phased right through a wall and left him to wander the tunnels alone.

Was he supposed to be grateful Gabriel had spared him back there when the serpent woman asked him to kill him? It might have sent him to the earthly plane. He might not have done him any favors at all.

He crouched, ducking through a narrowing passage. Where was he going? He was headed in the same direction Gabriel had been going, but with Gabriel's new abilities and obvious new free rein of the place, the giant turkey could be anywhere by now.

The tunnel branched in three directions. The first seemed to widen, never a good sign down here. A foul-smelling breeze blew along the middle path, also a no, and to the left, the path was dark, cold, and narrow. *Seems right.*

A deep rumbling growl started somewhere behind him, and he picked up his pace. The chill had leached into his bones, stiffening his limbs, and he wondered if one could ever recover from a cold this profound.

The sound was getting closer, reverberating off the walls. He broke into a run, glad to know he still had super speed down here. The tunnel narrowed further, making him duck before it opened into an expansive space. He stopped, gaping around in a circle as he spied the luminescent veins of blue pulsing overhead. Deep striations wove a pattern, mimicking the constellations in the earthly night sky.

Far to the right, one seemed to wink brighter than the others. It stood out, in stark contrast to the other duller shapes. It was a bull and at the center of its forehead, a red stone twinkled, glowing brightest of all.

"Fascinating, isn't it?"

Simon spun, dropping his gaze to the wizened man, bent nearly in two. He clutched a staff, holding it as if it were a lifeline, and stared up at the canvas painted in glowing rocks overhead.

"Yes," he said warily, balancing on the balls of his feet, prepared to run. He hadn't fared well with his first local encounter. "What is it?"

"This is the divining room," the man answered.

Perhaps his question wasn't clear. "I mean, what does the picture represent?"

The man turned solid black eyes on him, and he felt as though they were made for peering into his soul, rather than the world around them. "That is a good question." The man shuffled forward, moving toward the brightest rock overhead. "I have been trapped in this room for more than five centuries. The picture never changes. Yet, I cannot divine its whole meaning."

"You have an idea, though?"

"It is Aldebaran. He sits at the great intersection of the planes of our worlds." The hunched man lumbered away, dragging a heavy chain behind him as he mumbled to himself.

Simon trailed after. "Who is Aldebaran?"

"Not who. What. Aldebaran, 'the follower' is one of the four royal stars. The hunter who stalks seven sisters across the night sky. Their chase makes up the bull humans associate with the Taurus constellation."

Simon's brow furrowed, knotting at the bridge of his nose.

"It's a common misconception that he was hunting the seven sisters. Aldebaran wasn't hunting the Pleiades; he was protecting them from Orion." The man reached a bench, sitting heavily, and motioned for Simon to do the same. Simon sat, giving them space.

The man pointed his staff at the constellation Orion. "Orion meant to take the sisters for himself. See how he overpowers them? But Aldebaran stands as their protector. Not chasing but turned to face Orion."

Simon nodded. Greek mythology was something he found quite fascinating. It was the catalyst for his deep desire to learn the language all those years ago. "But Orion is known for his mistreatment of women. Surely anyone would assume Aldebaran's role is as protector?"

"History is written by the mighty," the man said.

"You mean the victor."

His long gray beard brushed over his lap as he shook his head from side to side. "A victor's heart is true and sometimes the victor wins by losing."

Simon followed the man's black-eyed gaze to the outline of the bull, its glowing central eye more radiant than the rest.

The man continued, "Because Orion was mighty and defeated the victor, he wrote the history he wanted the world to believe, thus painting Aldebaran as the villain and himself as the hero."

Simon gazed up at the luminous rocks twinkling in their imitation of the night sky, considering what other historical inaccuracies the world might believe to be true.

CHAPTER 62

Rebecca

"This won't work, Rebecca." Sophia wrapped one honey-brown curl around her finger.

Rebecca tugged Helena's arm. "Translate for me, okay?"

A light sheen of sweat formed over Sophia's brows. "I don't think you should do this."

Rebecca settled herself on the bed beside Simon's still form. The unearthly chill had crept into his fingers and hands, frosty against her warm touch as she laced her fingers in his. "We don't have time to debate this. I have to get in and out before dark, so we are ready for Elizabeth and her army."

Yia-Yia shouldered her way into the growing circle of women standing over Rebecca. Sophia peered up at the woman, looking for support, but Yia-Yia said something to Sophia and she bit her lip, turning to Helena. Her words were rushed, incoherent, to Rebecca's untrained ears, but Helena gasped.

Yia-Yia jabbed her with a makeshift cane she had crafted from a branch she'd found on the island. Her words came out like a whip, and whatever she said, it jolted Helena into action.

Helena spoke softly, and Sophia translated. "She will stop your heart for two minutes. Anything longer would be too much to come back from." Sophia broke into another argument with Helena before Yia-Yia interceded again. When it was settled, she continued, "Two minutes and thirty seconds. Not one second longer. If you have not found them, they are lost. You have one chance."

Rebecca nodded, closing her eyes. Her heartbeat set a frantic pace as wild horses stampeded across her chest, and she attempted to calm her breathing. Soft fingers touched her wrist, and her eyes flew open as she gasped for air.

"Shh, Rebecca, it is only me." A rush of cooling liquid bled into her veins, slowing her heart. She sighed, taking deep breaths. It felt sluggish. She fought for consciousness as she felt a single thump in her chest... one more...

She sat up, panting in the dark. It was cold, so cold—seeping into her lungs—turning the air into crystals. She brought up one hand, forming a ball of blue flame. Thank goodness it worked here.

She tossed her flame overhead, gaping into the dark as it winked out. She opened her palm again, casting another ball of flame into the air. The moment it left her skin, it was gone.

Well shit. She formed a third ball of flame, letting it rest atop her fingers. Its warmth spread down her wrist, heating her veins. At least she wouldn't freeze.

She looked around, spying a network of tunnels leading in several directions. It seemed to be a cave, and she had landed in the center of... She looked down and darted left, breathing a sigh of relief as she gazed at the star now safely on her right.

What would have happened had that star been a spell to trap her here?

It wasn't worth considering. The star's points each directed her on a different path. One tunnel for each point of the star. She knelt, scrutinizing the shape. It was drawn in chalk or perhaps scratched into the rock. One central point appeared longer than the rest.

She took it as a sign and followed, moving as fast as she could over the uneven ground with only her flame's light to guide her way. The path curved and bent, sometimes doubling back, but soon she stepped into a large room. In one corner was a large chair carved from the stone surrounding it. Across the large space, she spied only one exit.

She darted through the room feeling a chill race down her spine. It reeked of demon essence.

Time felt as though it ticked by at a precarious speed, making her task daunting. She increased her pace. A light wind pulled at the frosted tendrils of her hair, beckoning her forward.

When she reached the small arched exit, she stopped, peering into the dark. Something was at the end of a long hall, but she couldn't make it out in the darkness.

"Simon?" Her voice echoed off the narrowing stone walls. "Gabriel?"

The wind grew stronger, sucking her toward it, and she released her flame, digging her nails into the grooves of the wall as she spread her legs, trying to find purchase. This didn't seem like the right way at all.

Her nails chipped off onyx stone as she lost her hold and slid forward.

A dark swirling vortex came into view.

The strength of its pull intensified. She dug her nails into the unforgiving stone and screamed, feeling the pull of her nails as they loosened from their beds.

"Gabriel!" she shrieked, jamming one leg against a protruding rock.

Ice-cold arms wrapped around her, yanking her backward, and she was pulled away from the dark hole trying to suck her in. Terror melted into relief as the scent of lavender washed over her.

When they stopped in a wholly unfamiliar room, she turned, throwing her arms around him, crushing him to her. "I thought you were gone forever," she breathed into his neck, squeezing her eyes shut.

Chilled arms enveloped her, and a frozen tear dripped and congealed on her cheek.

After a moment, he released her, pressing her back. "Why are you here, Bec? Please tell me you didn't..." The fractured hollowness in his words cleaved a hole in her chest.

She could only make out his glowing eyes in the pitch darkness. She raised a hand casting blue flame between them and his frozen face, lit with an unnatural pallor, reminded her of a corpse. She shuddered. "No. I mean, not really. I only have—shit—I have no idea how much longer I have. Where's Gabriel? We have to get him."

Simon's crystalline brows cracked, sending tiny bits of ice into his lashes. "He's... He can't come with us."

She frowned. "Why? Where is he?"

"Angels can never leave this place."

"No, Jophiel said..." She trailed off. She had said he was damned. But she had also said Rebecca could save him. Hadn't she? Damn angels and their memory bubbles. It was encased somewhere in her memories, but Jophiel must have locked it up. She could scream. "I'm not giving up on him that easily. We have to try. Where was the last place you saw him?"

"He was right in front of me, but he phased through a wall and disappeared. That was hours ago." He ran a hand over his face, wiping away some of the frost. "Hell, it could have been days ago. How long have I been here?"

Rebecca swallowed. "A while." A sharp pain tore through her chest, and she gasped, clutching her sweater.

"Bec, what's wrong?"

"Something's..." Her hands tingled, cold radiating up her left arm. "Something's wrong. Simon," she rasped through labored breaths. "Take my hand. Don't let go, no matter what. Promise—" She broke off again as another sharp pain scorched the entire left side of her body and her flame winked out leaving them in darkness. "Promise to go wherever I go."

She wrapped chilled fingers around him, feeling ice climb up her veins. She pulled him closer, praying this would work, breathing a silent apology into the dark space to Gabriel.

CHAPTER 63

Rebecca

Rebecca heaved in a breath, sucking until her lungs felt like they would burst. When she exhaled, it was slower, hitching as she winced around the icicles that had formed in her chest. The room blinked into focus as eyes of various shades of blue, green, and brown peered down at her.

None were yellow. She darted her gaze to the right. The space where Simon had been was empty.

"Where?" she croaked around a mouth full of ice. Sophia and Thalia leaned forward, helping her up. Their liquid touch thawed the chill that had settled in her veins.

"He said running fast would warm him up," Sophia said.

A whimper escaped Rebecca's throat as she sucked in another lungful of air and a dam broke, tears flooding her cheeks. She coughed, wishing her sobs weren't so embarrassingly loud.

Sophia pulled her into a hug, stroking her hair. "He is okay, Adelfí. He will be okay."

Her noises quieted to soft sniveling, and the tears slowed, stopped. Her face felt hot, and she knew it was blotchy and red.

Then he was there, wrapping warm arms around both of them, squeezing. Sophia squirmed uncomfortably, but he didn't release her.

331

"Thank you. Thank you for keeping her safe when I couldn't," he whispered.

Rebecca opened her eyes, noticing the other women's stares. Some hostile, others wary. She glared around at them, her gaze halting on Yia-Yia's. *She* was smiling.

When Simon released them, Angeliki reached for Sophia, pulling her to her side. Phoebe crossed herself, hissing something under her breath.

"He won't hurt anyone," Rebecca said.

Yia-Yia held out a hand, waiting for Simon to take it. A few of the witches gasped. He glanced at Rebecca, searching her face for confirmation, then, seeing it, took the elderly woman's gnarled fingers in his. Her lips spread into a wide, toothy grin. She made some proclamation that seemed to calm the others. Then, one by one, they laid a hand on him. Murmuring.

Sophia went last, pulling him into a hug.

Thalia gasped, then began chattering. The group all spoke over one another.

"What is it? What are they saying?" Rebecca looked to Sophia for an answer and was startled when it was Simon who said:

"They feel my earth magic."

The group huddled around them, pressing hands on Simon as they spoke animatedly over one another. He joined, sharing in the excitement. Rebecca sat back, huffing. Learning Greek had just risen to the top of her list.

Sophia slid back, bumping shoulders with her. "Look on the bright side. They could fear him, and he would not be welcome to join our coven."

Rebecca snorted. "We have to live through tonight before we make any plans for the long term." She felt more confident knowing Simon would be here with them, but they still hadn't solidified a plan. Relying on the ocean and a few minor earthquakes didn't seem like a bulletproof plan, not against Elizabeth.

"Thalia, Georgia, Cassia," Sophia said. Three women extricated themselves from the group, coming to join Sophia and Rebecca on the couch. Sophia faced

Rebecca. "Have you chosen to fight with us? Will you power share with each of the other witches?"

Rebecca's gaze trailed over the people milling around the room. Several witches stood in a circle, pressing their palms to one another. A bright sapphire sheen glowed to life in their hands, making it clear they were powering up for the evening's fight.

Helena pressed a hand to Rhea's temple as soft white light flared. Rhea smiled, sighing as she leaned back in her seat. Her focus shifted to Simon, who was watching Helena intently.

Eyes moving back to Sophia, she nodded. "I think so."

Sophia dipped her chin. "Good. I want to take it slow. Air magic seems to be the least draining. So, we will power share with Georgia first. Helena is nearby if it taxes you."

Helena left Rhea, who was asking if she could make dinner for the group. Several tongues clicked and brows furrowed. They seemed to understand *her* when she spoke. Still, Rebecca had to admire the respect these women had for their elders. It was uncommon these days.

Georgia came to sit beside Rebecca, and they faced each other, sitting cross-legged on a dusty leather couch. Georgia held out her hands, palms up. Rebecca clasped her open palms, sucking in a deep breath as the energy hit her.

Helena placed a hand on her thigh as she prepared to funnel healing energy into her.

Simon joined them, his gaze never leaving Helena's outstretched arm. He cocked his head, a question on his face. Helena spoke softly, and he nodded.

Rebecca returned her focus to Georgia, marveling as her hair lifted. She shifted positions and Georgia dug her nails into Rebecca's palm. "Ow. I wasn't letting go."

Sophia snorted. "This is my cousin. The one I told you broke her connection when she was learning to power share." She raised an eyebrow, and Georgia's cheeks flushed with a rosy hue.

In the next moment, the rush of energy stole her focus as it sealed its circuit inside her body and the world became a dazzling rainbow of refracted color, bending around an invisible blanket of air, coating the world. It dazzled her senses, making the bright green in Sophia's eyes twinkle and casting Simon in a soft purple glow.

Everything was suddenly more, and she could see how physical objects displaced the space they occupied.

When Georgia released her hold, the circuit broke, but a soft hum buzzed under her skin.

Everything was connected, and she could see how it looped and knitted together. They were not on this planet. They were of it, as intricately woven into the fabric of the world as the seas or the plants. Each living thing had its place.

Georgia rose as Thalia took her place.

"Wait. Let Helena check your vitals." Sophia nodded to Helena, who pressed two fingers against Rebecca's neck. Simon said a few words to her, and then he rested his fingers on the thrumming heartbeat at her throat.

Dimples indented his cheeks as he broke into a wide grin. "I can feel it. Bec, I can feel your life force." His grin faded. He dropped his fingers, swiveling his gaze to Helena, and they stood together. He said something that sounded sharp and demanding. Helena's reply was soothing. He paced away, and she followed.

Rebecca swallowed. "What did he say?"

Sophia pursed her lips. "He says your life force is weak."

Rebecca's stomach somersaulted. Of course it was. She was dying. They hadn't found Gabriel. She had no idea how to stop it, but Helena was making her feel better. Stronger. This would work. It had to. They would defeat Elizabeth and she would have two years to find a way to break Gabriel's curse.

She tried to ignore the panic rising in her chest, quickening her breath.

She nodded to Thalia, holding out her hands. "Come on, we don't have a lot of time."

Thalia darted a glance to Sophia, who nodded. She dropped warm hands into Rebecca's now slick ones. A burst of deep, earthy loam enveloped her senses. Inside, her womb grew heavy, and a sensation of new life bloomed in her chest. A deep green tinged the edges of her vision as the world around her took a breath.

A tiny spider raced toward her. Foliage brushing the windows pressed in, eager to devour her life-giving magic. A sour taste filled her mouth as she tasted the death surrounding them. Dead bark on the floors and walls, synthetic materials used to make furniture and clothes. She gagged. Thalia gave a sympathetic nod.

Sophia had explained that Thalia's primary element was earth. Was this how she experienced the world? Bursting with life and rotten with decay at the same time? When the connection broke, she leaned back, catching her breath.

Simon was there, pressing a hand to her cheek. It glowed, reviving her, but it also strengthened her power, making the stench of decay stronger.

"Stop," she gasped, and he flinched back, horror roiling on his face.

"Did I hurt you?" He was breathless, darting furtive glances between her and Helena.

Helena returned to her side, touching her neck. She said something to him in that same soothing tone, and he relaxed.

"It's just hard to experience all the death," she choked out, hoping the feeling would soon abate.

His brow smoothed. "I thought. I thought." He didn't finish, standing to pace the room once more.

Thalia rose, going to the kitchen to help the others as they worked in communion to make a meal.

Cassia slid into her place; a broad grin stretched across her face. "I do fire," she said proudly.

Rebecca grinned. "Me too."

CHAPTER 64

Simon

Simon buzzed with all the new information he had gathered.

He could sense a person's life force, and the moment he'd understood how it worked, he felt Rebecca's tether. Her cord, unlike Helena's, was already cut.

She wouldn't die today or tomorrow, but her death was determined. It wasn't hanging by a thread or even a coil of frayed edges. It had been cut with a blunt pair of scissors and there was nothing to reattach it.

There was no saving her.

Helena knew. She had known the moment she healed her the first time. But it was not a healer's place to share such truths. That's what she said. What a burden to carry. Did the others know? They couldn't.

Would he know everyone's impending death upon touching them, or did he have to search for it? The truth had nearly jumped out at him once he knew where to look. It seemed impossible to ignore.

Had he only known he possessed such an ability, things might have gone differently with Claire.

But then, when his gift had been twisted by Elizabeth, or by whatever magic gave her the power to drag their souls back from Sheol, he likely couldn't have seen her end.

Not a day went by that he didn't regret what he'd done to Claire. It tormented his soul.

But her endless suffering from Alexander's torture called to him in the same way his need to heal did now. To end her pain.

And it had to be done.

Rebecca deserved to be spared the knowledge of all that had happened to her at the hands of her father. It had been the only way to guarantee those memories stayed buried forever.

But now that twisted gift was made right, and he could heal instead of harm. He would heal Rebecca. If he could mend a physical wound, he could surely mend a curse.

After all, his abilities were far superior to the other witches.

CHAPTER 65

Rebecca

Sophia slid forward. "I think you need a break. Fire is your most volatile element. It will be a very different experience from the others."

Rebecca's mouth fell into a frown. "We don't have time for breaks. If our visions are right, I need all four elements to be operating at peak potential if we hope to stand a chance against Elizabeth tonight." She sat up straighter, feigning a confidence she didn't feel. She held out her hands for Cassia. Sophia leveled a glare at Cassia, who shrank back. "Wow, you'd think you were in charge the way they listen to you."

Sophia's chin jutted out. "I am."

Rebecca snorted. "What are you? Eighteen? No way you're in charge of this coven."

"I am Pythia. Pythia is in charge."

Rebecca gaped. "You're just a seer. You aren't even the most powerful witch in the coven. My money is on your mother. She was badass in that storm."

"Magical ability is not always the thing that makes you most powerful."

Rebecca crossed her arms over her chest. "Okay, I'll bite. What makes you the most powerful witch in this coven?"

"I see what has come, what is, and what will be."

Rebeca snorted. "You can't even decipher the meaning of your visions."

"I know more than you think."

Rebecca blew out a breath. "What aren't you telling me?"

Sophia's chin lifted. "I know what the visions really mean."

"And you haven't told me. Why? I have a right to know too."

Sophia arched one honey-colored eyebrow. "Some parts of the vision weren't meant for you."

Rebecca got to her feet. "That's bullshit. You said we had to tell each other everything to figure out what it meant. Was that just a lie?"

Something like pain flickered across Sophia's face and she darted a glance at Yia-Yia.

Rebecca tracked the movement, her temper flaring. "What is it? Tell me."

"You're going to die!" Sophia blurted. She looked down, breaking eye contact.

Rebecca leaned back, feeling Simon's warmth at her back as he sat. "I know that. I told you I was cursed."

"Tonight."

It was a whisper. She might have missed it if she weren't listening for Sophia's next words. *Tonight?* And Sophia had known all along.

Heat licked down her arms catching on blue sparks along her fingertips.

Yia-Yia stepped between them. She glanced at the group of witches gathered around the kitchen table who had stopped what they were doing to watch the altercation. "Come with me," she said, then turned, leaving Rebecca glaring at the girl who had called her sister.

Rebecca paced the small room, taking calming breaths. Every time she trusted someone, they let her down. Every. Single. Time. Sophia was no different. It hurt more than she would have expected. Betrayal was nothing new to her, but she'd been so sure Sophia was different.

She turned to face the pair. The familial resemblance was strong when they sat side by side. The old woman had probably put her up to it. Sent the young girl to college to befriend her and convince her they were in this together. But all they wanted, all anyone wanted, was to use her.

Even Gabriel. Especially Gabriel. Why was she thinking of him again?

She paced the room, giving them her back. If she took the raft to the main island, she could catch a flight and get the hell out of there before it was too late. Let these witches deal with Elizabeth.

She stopped at the door. She could get Simon and leave. Did he want to go? He fit in so well with them. She had thought she did too. The bunch of liars.

A loud rapping noise caught her attention. She turned to face Yia-Yia.

The woman stood, bracing most of her weight on a branch. She crossed the room, standing several inches shy of Rebecca's face, and pointed a finger up, pressing it into her nose.

"Listen to me, girl," she said, her words clearer than before. "You are selfish. Stubborn." Rebecca opened her mouth, but Yia-Yia silenced her with a look. "Any woman here would die for the rest of us. Not because we are family. Because pureness of heart is selflessness." Rebecca closed her mouth. "Pythia will not say it, but I will. You have a choice, child. Live for yourself or die for humanity."

Rebecca's cheeks burned. No one had ever chastised her so soundly. Was it selfish to want to live? To put her own life first? She thought of her sisters, all fleeing home at the first opportunity, leaving her to fend for herself. She hated them for leaving her alone in that house with her father.

And her father. She had thought he was the worst the world had to offer; that was before life as an orphan. Family could be cruel, but strangers were far worse.

In her very long life, they had all used her, all but one.

Her gut twisted.

Simon never had a chance to live his own life. He had dedicated it to her. And he was still by her side, plotting with her, and would die beside her. He gave no thought to his own life. How many times had he already sacrificed himself for her?

Maybe the world wasn't worth it, but he was.

Yia-Yia's finger fell, her frown twisting into a smirk. "I knew there was a good person in there," she said, patting Rebecca's cheek.

Warmth bloomed in her chest. A good person. When had anyone ever called her that?

Her gaze fell on Sophia. Sophia exhaled a shuddering breath. For all the girl's bravado, she was scared too. Rebecca hadn't considered what any of the others might sacrifice.

What else did Sophia know? Would they all die, or was it only her fate? She hadn't thought for even a moment about anyone's fate but her own.

Her chest seized as she considered dying for the final time. True death.

Yia-Yia and Sophia stood, leaving her with her thoughts. They had asked her for the impossible. Die for the rest of the world.

Her mind drifted back to her dreams of Adalaide. Ada had been prepared to die, knowing she would never return. Ada had been a willing sacrifice.

Could she be that selfless?

Rebecca followed the smell of seafood and garlic to the kitchen, finding a group, including Rhea and Simon, all seated around a long island at the center of the kitchen. They laughed, passed food, and touched one another freely. Some long-frozen part of her heart thawed at the sight.

Simon poured water into Cassia's cup, and for a moment, Rebecca could see it. If she wasn't here, making demands, consuming his time. He could be happy with one of them. Maybe Cassia, who was fiery, like her, and bold. Or Thalia, who shared his gift for earth magic.

She smiled, leaning against the doorframe as she let the scene sink in. There weren't many happy moments in her life. If she would die soon, she'd like to have a few to take with her.

Simon spotted her first, pushing back his chair, and coming to her side.

"I'm fine. It's fine," she said, pushing him off. "Go back to your seat. I want to spend some time with Rhea."

Rhea sat to Cassia's left, making broken conversation as Cassia tried her hand at English and Rhea pretended to understand. Her lips quirked in a half smile, knowing Rhea would be in good hands. Maybe she would learn Greek. Retire and spend her days on white sandy beaches, letting others take care of her for a change.

She slid into the empty chair beside Rhea and Georgia. Georgia dipped her head. She now recognized they did so in deference. Angeliki, Yia-Yia, Sophia, and she all received deferential treatment. It made her feel like a fraud. They all thought she knew and had been willing all along.

But whether she had intended to sacrifice herself willingly or been tricked into it, she knew she would do it.

CHAPTER 66

Rebecca

A fter they ate, everyone worked together to wash and clean up. All but Yia-Yia and Rhea. The others fussed and cooed over the women, setting them up in reclining chairs by the window, and bringing them tea and sweets. Rhea looked so uncomfortable, that Rebecca considered rescuing her, but it was well deserved, and, in the end, she left her to the gaggle of clucking hens who fawned over her.

Simon found her outside, watching the tide pull the ocean in, tucking their small island under its loving embrace before the night rolled in. He wrapped an arm around her, pulling her close.

She said nothing, breathing him in, feeling the warmth of the setting sun on her face. They stood, marveling at the beauty and might of Mother Nature.

"I've never told you how much I appreciate all you've done and sacrificed for me." Her words were quiet against the roar of the ocean, but she knew he heard.

"And you never have to."

She pulled free from his grasp, turning to face him. "Don't do that. Don't act like you don't matter. You do." He searched her face, his yellow eyes taking on the luminescence that spoke of darkness to come. Time was running out. She had to say it now before it was too late. "Simon, you should have had your own life. I asked you to give that up for me. It was unfair. It was horrible."

"Hey, I don't regret any of it."

He wasn't listening. She had to get through to him. There was no telling what he would do when she died if she didn't make him understand. "Listen to me." She pressed a hand to his smooth cheek and marveled at how perfect his skin was now that the angels had restored him, removing all the cuts and wounds he had borne for so long. At least she could be grateful for that. "I never should have asked you to dedicate your eternal life to me. It was selfish. You deserve happiness."

He pulled her close, hugging her.

The sun dipped precariously. There was no time.

"I love you. You are my family, and you deserve the world," she said, squeezing him. She hoped he would understand, but he wouldn't. Deep down, she knew he wouldn't.

She left him, making her way back to the church, and found Cassia. "Let's do it," she said.

Sophia caught up to them, and Thalia followed in their wake. Soon Georgia, Phoebe, and Vassi trailed behind too.

"I think you should do it outside," Sophia suggested. Her emerald eyes twinkled, a knowing smile playing across her lips.

They stopped just outside the church on an expanse of green rolling toward the ocean. Although the sun still reached for the sky, its dying embers setting the horizon ablaze, a white orb drifted overhead, signaling a full moon tonight.

Cassia held her hands out, grinning wickedly. "Ready, firestarter?"

Rebecca dropped her hands into Cassia's and exhaled as the rush of heat licked up her arms and over her shoulders.

It was nothing like the other power shares. Scorching heat seared her veins, boiling her blood, but where she'd charred her insides before, she felt alive now. A dangerous power thrumming below the surface. The world burned as her vision glazed in a red inferno.

Where earth magic and air magic showed her how everything was connected, her fire threatened to burn the world to the ground. This magic didn't come from the world around her. It was in her, of her.

She was fire.

The hands grasping hers were blistering. Cassia's eyes ignited orange and blue dancing in a mad circle of power, lust, and desire.

It crackled, sizzled. A bomb ready to detonate.

The hairs on her arms rose, sending electric shocks running down them to the ground. Several witches jumped back, shouting what she could only assume were expletives. But she didn't care; she was lost to the energy pulsing through her.

Blue and orange flames burst free, streaking from her arms to Cassia's. She closed her eyes, reveling in it.

Shouts erupted, a strange melody singing in her soul.

She pulled, lighting her very being aflame. The warm buzzing heat exploded into a sultry blaze. Her head lolled to the side, drunk with the energy spilling from her partner, feeding her.

Red-hot energy detonated as she felt her feet lift off the ground.

Something pulled at her, a dead weight, but it wasn't enough to suffocate the euphoria dancing in her veins.

Something inside cracked, releasing an invisible damper on her power then her vision went white; the world swallowed in an instant.

CHAPTER 67

Rebecca

The first thing she heard were the screams. They were incongruous with the blissful elation coursing through her.

Her eyes flew open, taking in the world. It was dark, apart from the cool blue hue lapping gently along her skin. Something darted by, letting out another scream. She flinched at the harsh sound.

Her gaze fell on a man with white-blond hair. *Blake.* Or... He had been a man, once. He ran faster than a man should. And the murky edges of his form were a dark stain against his sallow skin.

She moved, graceful and lithe, using the gifts at her disposal to get to him before he could harm another of the witches.

She reached him, wrapping a hand wreathed in flame around his neck. He bent; broke. Pitiful. *Human.*

A dark shape slid from his nostrils forming a beast she knew well.

"Father."

His dark brow—more horn than hair—dipped low over red eyes. "So you believed. So we both did." He grumbled in a deep otherworldly voice.

She lifted a hand and blue flames morphed into the shape of a spear.

His glowing eyes tracked this new power and as she launched it at him, he dropped into the shadows and was gone.

Before she could fully consider the meaning of his words, a scream drew her attention.

Two foul creatures were on Georgia, tearing, ripping. Then the witch fell still.

Rebecca moved again, reaching them faster than any mortal could, and calling on air and water, pulled the remaining bodily fluid and air from their husks, letting their bones smack the earth.

Around her, the witches fought misshapen night-beings, invoking their gifts, crying out for aid. Women she didn't know well, but who had risked their lives to save her and to save the others of their coven, reached for their gifts and called to the ocean, but there were too many night-beings and soon they were overwhelmed.

A dozen yellow-eyed creatures darted by.

Enough of these games.

She reached for the power no longer sealed away inside her and set the night on fire.

She thrust her arms overhead, tilting her head back to the night sky, and spread her fingers wide, basking in the melody of shouts, pleas, and dying whimpers as they fell at her feet. A crescendo of pops and sizzles accentuated their song. As the power tore through her, her toes touched the ground and a strangling warmth bled into her legs working its way up her chest. It reached her head and she gasped.

A new scream rent the air; one that begged. Begged her to stop.

Stop?

She was helping them.

But as she cast her gaze around the open space, she saw the truth. Her flame consumed them all. It would kill the night-beings, but it was killing the witches too.

She snuffed it out, letting the ember die and, as she did, the magic flooding her veins receded, leaving only the hollowed-out vessel of her body behind.

Simon dropped to Rebecca's side, pressing a hand to her chest.

She sucked in great heaving breaths. It was too much; she had used too much power.

"Rebecca. Bec." Simon's panicked plea swam through her sluggish mind.

348

Her gaze darted left, then right, struggling to take in the surrounding chaos.

In her immediate vicinity, several bodies lay charred on the ground. It was hard to say if they were witches or Elizabeth's creatures. There wasn't enough left to tell.

In the distance, shouts, screams, and the boom of thunder raged. She stood, her legs wobbling. "I need to help them."

She broke into a pitiful run, dragging her abused body toward the sound.

Simon stepped into her path. "You can't. You'll die. Stay here."

She staggered around him. "They need me. I need to find Elizabeth."

He moved, stepping in front of her again. "You are in no condition to fight."

A scream she recognized tore through the night.

"Sophia," she called, pressing her weight into him. He didn't budge. "Get out of my way. Sophia will die."

"I don't care about Sophia."

"Simon, you wouldn't let those women die."

His bright eyes met hers. Their hue a strange mirror to the moon's amber glow. "I would let the entire world sink beneath the ocean if it meant you lived."

She sucked in a breath. "Simon, please. They're dying."

Something in his expression broke. "It will never matter to you, will it, Firefly?"

Another scream sent a dagger of pain through her chest. "Please, please, let me do this."

Simon's steely gaze broke as he stepped aside.

Waves crashed over land, washing people out to sea. She couldn't tell who. Yia-Yia? Fiery Cassia? Sophia? She ran faster, letting her air magic carry her. It obeyed terrifyingly easily, lifting her into the night sky.

She landed hard, opening her palm to cast a fireball. Instead of a ball of flame, a torpedo of blue shot from her hand into the copse of trees, scorching them. She slid to a stop staring at the burning trees. *Shit.*

"Rebecca!" Sophia called, to her left.

She charged toward Sophia and a yellow-eyed creature who was quickly overpowering her. She raised a hand to the sky as she ran.

Lightning struck the earth only feet from Sophia and the night-being, and they both stopped fighting to stare at the charred earth.

Simon appeared at her side, then moved preternaturally fast, wrenching the creature off Sophia.

They disappeared in a blur and Sophia staggered to her side, leaning on Rebecca. "There are too many of them," she said between gasping breaths. "We are losing."

Rebecca glanced around, spying Phoebe as she fell to the ground, three creatures piling on top of her. Angeliki spun her arms overhead as wave after wave pummeled a group of advancing night-beings, but it seemed to do little to deter them. In the next moment, they were on her.

She turned her gaze to Sophia, who nodded. "You know what to do," Sophia mouthed.

Rebecca swallowed. She knew it would come to this, had accepted her fate, but couldn't still the tremor in her hand as she reached for that glowing ember inside her and tugged.

Sophia stepped back and turned, racing for her mother.

This time, when Rebecca pulled at the spark in her chest, all four elements burst free, weaving together, knitting themselves into a ball that encased her and consumed her. She tried to breathe, but the air was no longer under her control.

It didn't bend to her, it bent her.

Her back bowed, arms splaying wide. Water slid through her veins, curling her hands into fists, making her their puppet. All-consuming life surrounded her, making her heart pump faster, pressing her lungs in and out.

When they held her fast, a blazing heat began at her center. It licked along her veins.

A tear slid down her cheek as energy leached from her body, giving life to the flame.

In the moments before she was lost to it, lifetimes flashed in her eyes as she glimpsed all the moments that had truly mattered. Moments spent in quiet companionship with Margaret as a child, Simon in each of her lives, even the time she'd spent with Gabriel as he'd trained her, given her confidence where she'd had none.

Another tear slipped down her cheek.

Her eyes fluttered as yellow orbs blinked in and out of focus, closer with each blink, until a rush of healing energy hit her.

And then... nothing.

CHAPTER 68

Sophia

It was beautiful. It was as it was meant to be. As the power claimed her, swirling in a vortex of energy, Simon reached her, pressing his healing gift into her. She didn't need it. She was the most powerful witch Sophia had ever seen.

Just as her visions predicted, Rebecca consumed them all. Night-beings dropped all around her, leaving the witches intact.

Simon's sacrifice was unnecessary, but she had seen that nothing she said or did would stop him.

He wrapped both arms around her waist and they lifted, floating high above the earth. It was a macabre sort of dance. She spun, the magic using her as its conduit, as he funneled his own life force through her to lend it strength.

She had grown to care for them, even knowing what would come.

She hadn't believed the dark creature from her visions was Simon, but watching the scene unfold, it could have only ever been him.

When they fell, her heart fractured. From the day they met, she knew her friend would die, but knowing something and living it were not the same.

The earth reverberated with the impact. It was something no witch could survive, even with her immense power.

There was one thing that made little sense, though. The evil being from Sophia's vision—the one Rebecca was meant to sacrifice herself to end—wasn't here.

How could it be that she'd seen it all and still didn't know how it would end?

Around her, witches stood, limping, crying.

They had suffered a significant loss tonight. Yia-Yia, Georgia, Phoebe, Rebecca, Simon, and Rhea were gone. Likely others, they hadn't yet accounted for were gone too.

Angeliki met her at the edge of the clearing, wrapping an arm around her. "You were brave, daughter. I know you cared for her."

Sophia shrugged, something sharp piercing her chest. "It is a great burden to know the truth," she said, squeezing her mother's arms.

Iris and Maria joined them, then Thalia and Helena.

Vassi limped up, crying. "Yia-Yia is dead," she said.

Sophia pulled her into a hug. Yia-Yia had known. She may not be Pythia, but she had known she would be among the sacrifices tonight. Sophia grieved for her grandmother, but she was in a better place now. In Heaven with Yahweh and her other sisters and, hopefully, Rebecca, whom she had come to treasure as a sister.

"Hello ladies," a child's voice said from the dark. Sophia squinted, searching for the source of the sound. A girl of only seven or eight stepped forward. Her pale hair glimmered in the moonlight and her deep red gown, out of place in this century, was stained a deeper burgundy in several places. A long gold chain hung around her neck, too large for her slight frame.

None of that gave Sophia pause. It was the incandescent glow of saffron eyes that made her freeze in place.

She pressed a hand to her mother's side, stilling her.

"Elizabeth?"

THE END

353

EPILOGUE

R ebecca cracked heavy lids. The ache resonating through her entire body made her stomach turn. She blinked a few times; then, with great effort, opened her eyes.

It was a terrible decision. This new Hell far outweighed the oblivion she had experienced after the elements had overpowered her.

The room was dark and dank, decay heavy in the air. Worse, the essence of a demon's presence made her skin buzz, her ears ring, and the hairs on the back of her neck stand on end.

Was this Hell? Was she in Primoria?

She glanced around. Of course, Simon wasn't here. He was in Alaxia, singing his heart out with the angels.

If this was Primoria, why did every fiber of her being ache? And why wasn't it cold?

In fact, she had been to Primoria. This was not it.

She sat up, cursing. A heavy chain was cinched tightly to her leg, holding her in place. *What the hell?*

"Hey sis," a child's voice said from the dark. She ground her teeth. That was a voice she hoped never to hear again. Elizabeth stepped under garish yellow lights, the illumination casting her face into odd relief.

"Aren't you up past your bedtime?" Rebecca asked, silently chuckling in perverse delight as Elizabeth's creepy doll-like features twisted in rage.

"I saved you; you bitch."

Rebecca laughed out loud. "I doubt it."

Elizabeth moved closer, almost within reach. "I pulled you and your worthless lover out of that hole the witches left you in. You could thank me."

Icy dread shot through Rebecca. She saved Simon. Where was he? She bit her cracked lip, wincing in pain.

"Keeping us apart was a smart move. You could never overpower us together."

Elizabeth worked her face into a poor imitation of a smile. "Good thing we don't have to worry about him anymore, then."

Rebecca bit back her retort. Elizabeth was lying. It was what she did best. "You've been busy," she said, not taking the bait. "I killed a lot of your creatures last night."

The small creature's false smile fell. "No matter. I can make more."

Rebecca watched the girl's glowing eyes, running her tongue over her swollen lower lip. "How did you make them?"

Those bright eyes narrowed and a look of triumph appeared on Elizabeth's face. "You thought you were the last one who could open the locket, but I don't need your blood anymore. I have the blood of a Kavraz."

Rebecca's mind spun back to Simon's story in the cemetery. He'd said her family line originated as Gavras and while some had adopted the name Graves, some had taken the name Kavraz. But that had to mean the necklace was made before the line split. What had he said? The Byzantine Empire? That was over a thousand years ago. Her thoughts sped forward to the conversation with Simon in her living room. The necklace, according to the Fellowes heir, housed a bone belonging to the first necromancer. The mother of night-beings.

She trailed her gaze over Elizabeth's strange clothes to the necklace, too large for the girl, draped around her shoulders. How did Elizabeth—a seven-year-old girl—know the history of the necklace and what it was capable of? How was she always a step ahead of them? Something wasn't adding up, but her head was pounding and her body ached all the way to her bones.

"Hello? Can anyone hear us?!" The familiar voice cut like shards of ice. Sophia. Likely, they were all there. Her sacrifice had been for nothing. Elizabeth had them now.

A loud crash had both Elizabeth and Rebecca turning to face the dark hall to their left.

Elizabeth darted away, leaving Rebecca alone in her cell.

More noises came from the hall and Rebecca stood, moving to the bars to peer into the dark. She saw nothing, but the commotion set her heart on edge. Had Simon escaped?

She strained to hear, cursing her human ears.

Something dark materialized in front of her. She staggered back. *Demon.*

He solidified, two massive wispy wings forming at his back.

"Gabriel." She gasped. "What happened to you?"

Swirling red eyes narrowed. He pried the bars apart with unnatural strength. "Come."

She stood, rooted to the spot. "I... I can't." She glanced down at the magical cuff encircling her ankle.

He followed her gaze to the cuff. "Remove it."

"I can't. It's spelled."

He grunted, black wings twitching at his back. "You are Nephilim. The rules of humans do not apply to you."

THANK YOU

Thank you for reading Grave Prophecies. If you enjoyed this book, please consider leaving an honest review.

Amazon

Goodreads

C heck out all the books in this series and stay up to date on everything I'm working on at cassandraastonauthor.com

CASSANDRA ASTON

cassandraa
astonautho
r.com

GRAVE REVELATIONS

Prologue

2017

He dropped to the floor, cradling her head in his hands. "I'm so sorry," he breathed.

Her limp form was too thin, too frail. This life had been the one hardest to watch. She had wasted away to nothing, brought up in a system that fostered only cruelty and selfishness. Her kind soul had been hardened under its weight.

A featherlight touch on his arm drew his gaze from her blood-streaked face.

"Gabriel. I stand by whatever decision you make. I owe you that much."

"I know why you did it, Dina. It had to be done. Had they not hidden her from me so long, I might have stopped this needless suffering before it ever began."

She dropped her gaze to the girl nestled in his arms. "We have her now; we can protect her."

"I have no way of reaching her in Sheol. If she waits for her to return, there will be nothing I can do."

He leaned down, pressing his forehead to the girl's, and gently lay her head on the cold gymnasium floor.

She deserved so much better than this, but his ravaged soul couldn't survive if she were taken from him again. He could protect her this time. He *would* protect her.

"Are you sure we should do this?" Dina asked in a hushed tone, breaking into his thoughts. She dipped her head beside his, leaning over the crumpled form of the nearly lifeless girl on the floor.

A sudden intake of breath made his chest seize as a wheezing rattle emanated from her lungs, air sliding between her cracked lips. A red bubble popped, splattering blood across his face. Agony tore through him.

"We have little time. She's dying. It's now or never."

Dina's gaze met his, and she breathed, "He still might find her, you know. Perhaps we should bring her home now." She looked down at the too-thin girl clinging to life. "She's already suffered so much in this lifetime."

He ran a finger over her smooth cheek, smearing a line of blood across it. In that moment, he vowed to himself that he would never again hold her bloodied body in his hands while she slipped through his fingers only to be reborn in her cruel world once more. He would find a way to save her soul and bring her home with him.

"If we take her with us now, there will be no one left to stop him."

Another breath hitched in the girl's lungs; the exhale was much longer this time.

"Take my hand, Dina. We must do this now," he said as he reached for her.

The pair circled their arms above the body and began a rushed chant, their words growing in fervor until a slow, glowing flame burst from their encircled limbs.

Rising to stand, they increased their pitch, lifting their heads to the sky as the fire grew into a brilliant white-hot light arching through the night. A wispy blue spark sailed up the path of flame, following its trail until the light and the two forms standing over the dying girl winked out.

All that remained was a flashing red exit sign, casting the disfigured girl in garish repose between moments of complete darkness.

Present Day

A steady *drip, drip, drip* frayed her already strained nerves as she blinked in the dark, giving her vision time to adjust. Copper tang mingled with the scent of loamy earth and decay.

A chill ran through her, and it wasn't entirely from the frosty air. Death dripped from every surface, sluicing over the expansive stone table she leaned into to pool at her feet.

"Place your hand on the amulet and repeat after me."

"I won't."

Whimpering behind her drew her focus to the women huddled together on the floor.

"Let me tell you a story," the yellow-eyed demon said, drawing her attention back to the creature who had captured them all so easily. "The man who wielded this amulet before me only knew how to bind someone to him through magical spells and coercion. He failed to understand that to truly have power over something, you must get to the heart of it. Well," she pressed a finger to her pale lips, "the *soul* of it, really. You cannot hope to command obedience with a few simple binding spells."

The yellow-eyed creature pressed a small hand to her chest.

She flinched back. "Don't touch me, you beast."

"Uh, uh, uh. That's no way to speak to the one who holds your fate in their hands." The night-being curled her small fingers into a fist, and the witch gasped as her heart constricted in her chest.

Saffron eyes narrowed to slits as the creature's fingers uncurled, and she rested her hand against the witch's chest once more.

The witch panted, her heart regaining its steady rhythm once more.

"Now place your hand on the amulet, or you'll end up like the last two."

Chapter 1

Rebecca

"Gabriel, please. We have to go back."

"I don't care about them. You are all that matters to me."

"She'll kill them."

"They are nothing."

"What do you mean? Please, stop. Simon is back there, and Sophia. All the witches who helped me."

"Your dog is not with them."

Rebecca dug her nails into his shifting flesh. "What does that mean? Gabriel, please!"

"Don't call me by that name. Gabriel died in the icy pits of Hell. My name is Azazel."

Rebecca dug her nails in deeper, but each time she tried to tear through skin, it dissolved only to reform.

He chuckled, a deep rumble vibrating through her. "You cannot harm me, Light. You were made for me."

Was that a challenge? She'd weighed the consequences of using magic on him a dozen times. At this height, if he fell, she would die.

But Rebecca was never one to back down.

She spread her fingers, calling fire into her palm from the place deep within her chest. As before, it exploded from her fingertips, tenfold the power she'd ever known. Gabriel—Azazel, according to him—didn't flinch.

She pressed both hands against his bare flesh, staring in horror as his swirling black skin absorbed the cerulean flame, and a thin blue line erupted along the arm wrapped around her.

"No," she breathed.

Terror shot through her when the ember in her chest flared to life, and memories of the night she'd used too much magic resurfaced. Flames evaporated under her palm, and a sweat broke out on her brow.

"As I said, you cannot harm me. You are a part of me."

An image of her dream flashed in her mind: the dark shadow who shared her fire and his wispy black wings. "No," she whispered again.

Azazel dropped heavily onto a white, glimmering patio high above a small village, their view overlooking a sparkling blue sea.

"Where are we?" Her voice was a whisper against the pounding of her heart.

"Stay here while I deal with the necromancer. When I've taken care of her, I'll be back for you."

"You can't keep me here. I have to help my friends. Wait... When did you learn she was a necromancer?" The words died as he set her down on ivory cobbled stones. She looked up at him, seeing him in full daylight for the first time.

Her mouth fell slack as her gaze traveled down the length of him. In her sister's dark dungeon, she hadn't noticed how naked he was. She swallowed. How had she missed *that*?

Azazel's red and black swirling eyes glinted in amusement. "Like what you see?"

Her gaze shot up to his face, red staining her cheeks. "I... No. Where are your clothes?"

"They're an unnecessary obstruction. Stay here. I'll return."

Rebecca closed her mouth. If he were dumb enough to leave her, she wouldn't object. He turned, flapping shadowy wings, and gave her a full view of his bare ass as he flew away.

Why was she still looking?

When he was a speck in the sky, she darted for the stairs. Her foot hit the first step, and a sharp ache tore through her. She fell to her knees, wrapping her arms around her middle as it seared her insides. Breathing shallowly, she got to her feet, taking another step down. White hot pain stabbed her chest as her vision darkened at the edges.

What kind of vile magic was this?

She crawled backward, praying she wouldn't black out and tumble down the stairs. As she reached the patio deck, the pain receded until it was only a lacerating memory. She gasped in lungfuls of air, lay on her back, and stared up at the night sky.

Had he chosen that spot because he knew she would be trapped there, or had he somehow done it himself? What dark, twisted gifts did Gabriel have now that he was a demon? And what did it mean that her flames could not harm him? She'd taken out more than one demon with her fire magic.

Sliding to a sitting position, Rebecca rested her back against the cool stone lining the patio deck and craned her head to the sky. From this remote mountaintop, the stars nearly drowned out the dark with their flickering light.

As her breathing steadied and the remnants of pain faded, she gazed at the interconnected patterns between stars. A bright light streaked across her vision. She followed its trail, silently wishing that Simon and the other witches were okay and that Gabriel—Azazel—would save them.

Another star streaked by. She smiled; seeing two falling stars so close together was rare. She chewed her bottom lip, thinking of her wish. Another orb dashed across the sky, then another.

Rebecca sat up, rubbing her eyes.

A massive ball of flame hurtled toward her. She slid backward, ducking under the edge of the roof. Bright light filled her vision as the projectile crashed into the ocean, followed by several others.

Jumping to her feet, she wrapped sweat-slicked fingers around the handle of the sliding glass door and tugged at it. *Locked. Damn.* She wedged herself into the wall of the house, knowing it would do no good if any of the meteors landed too close.

Loud whizzing noises followed by splashes surrounded her, and when she dared to peek at the sky once more, it was ablaze.

The soft patter of rain began to fall, and Rebecca gasped as red streaked over ivory stone and slid toward her, pooling at her feet.

"What the hell," she breathed. Thick drops of red splashed her, staining her clothes. She pressed herself back against the wall of the building. It would be awfully convenient for Ga—*Azazel* to show up just then.

A tremor rocked the earth, making Rebecca stumble forward. Another rolling tremble shook the foundation, and she fell to her knees, the bite of rough stone slicing her skin.

When the ground shuddered for a third time, an enormous fissure opened before her, spider-veining across the patio and disappearing into the ocean.

"Gabriel!" she cried, scrambling back from the gaping chasm stretching wider before her eyes. "Gabriel!"

She wedged herself against the wall and screamed as a wall of sea foam green blotted the sky, barreling toward her.

Chapter 2

Rebecca

"Rebecca."

She cracked an eye, gazing blearily at the dark smoke hovering in her vision.

"Rebecca, wake up."

She opened both eyes. Gabriel's hulking form blocked her view as his wings curled around them.

"Am I dead?"

A cool hand settled under her neck, lifting her. "What happened to you when I left?"

Rebecca winced as pressure built in her head. She looked around at the smooth white stone bathed in soft light. "The world... it was bleeding, and there was a huge meteor shower and a tidal wave." She glanced down at her dry clothes. "I should be dead."

She sat up, wincing at the headache building at the base of her skull, giving herself space from the cool, unnatural feel of Gabriel's swirling onyx skin. He tucked his wispy wings behind his back, revealing blue skies.

Rebecca pushed to her feet, ignoring his proffered hand, and leaned over the patio wall, staring down at sparkling azure waves. Even from this height, the water was so clear she could see the white sandy bottom far below.

"I don't understand. A wave that big would have unsettled everything. I should have drowned. And it was raining *blood*."

Gabriel peered over the edge of the wall, hovering insufferably close.

She stepped back, stretching her neck up and up. "Were you this tall before?"

His brows dipped into dark slashes over his even darker eyes. "My form was not bound before. I chose to appear however I liked. Now, I am more confined in some ways, yet freer in others."

Rebecca gave him another once over, trying not to linger on the part that had captured her attention before.

His lips ticked up at the corners, a lopsided grin creasing one cheek.

"Please, explore," he said, stretching his muscled arms and lacing his fingers behind his head.

Rebecca choked on a retort, backing up further. "What happened to you? You were never... like *this*."

"I spent a few months in the bowels of the Forsaken's realm, tortured a few lost souls, and was relieved of my insufferable righteousness."

Rebecca turned away from him, gazing across the expanse of blue to a cluster of green in the far distance. "I guess you didn't find them," she whispered to the sea.

Cool fingers brushed along her arms, making her shiver, but she didn't turn, didn't want to look at what he had become.

She held a hand up, shielding her eyes as she searched for any sign of life beyond the horizon. Were they out there? She'd heard Sophia and some of the other witches in the dark cellar, too. But Elizabeth had said *he* died. She hoped desperately it wasn't true.

"Your reash did not survive, Rebecca."

She turned, narrowing her eyes and glaring into his swirling orbs. "You're lying."

"I don't lie."

A tiny fissure split down the middle of her heart, stealing her breath. It was true. Gabriel never lied. Her vision blurred, and she swiped her eyes. But this wasn't Gabriel.

"Maybe Gabriel didn't, but you've changed.

"You would know if I lied, Light."

"What does that mean?"

"You can sense a lie the same as any seraph."

Nephilim. The word clanged through her mind. So much had happened in Elizabeth's dark lair that she'd nearly forgotten the moments after he'd arrived. He had called her Nephilim and, as if saying it aloud was its own form of magic, she had simply reached down and broken her spelled bonds. No human could have done that.

But she was no angel. She had human parents and siblings. They had all lived and died, she more than once. She gasped.

"Is that the real reason I keep coming back?"

He shook his head, his wings shaking with the movement. "The reincarnation was your father's spell. A nasty bit of dark magic that kept you from me for nearly a century." He reached for her, wrapping cool fingers around hers.

She stared down at their contrasting hands, hers slender, warm, and pale, his cold and several times larger. By human standards, he would have been classified as a giant. She looked up, cataloging the similarities between the Gabriel she knew and Azazel.

"Why did you change your name?"

"I didn't."

She huffed, tearing her hand free from his. "One thing hasn't changed. Short answers that mean nothing to me."

He reached for her again, wrapping large hands around hers. "My brother, the Fallen, renamed me."

Rebecca tugged uselessly against his grip. Although gentle, his touch would have been akin to pulling her hand from concrete. What was it about this creature that calmed her flaming temper, soothed her breaking heart? Simon was gone,

367

possibly dead, and the others might be too, but a sense of calm settled over her when he touched her.

"So you're a demon now? Like the devil?"

Wispy wings twitched as he pulled her forward, wrapping an arm around her waist. She tried to back up to give them space, but it was useless. He was immovable.

"I'm not like him," he breathed against her hair, ruffling her curls. "He cares for no one but himself."

Rebecca's breathing hitched, her heart galloping in her chest as he pressed his mouth to her ear.

"And he doesn't have you."

Ready to read the rest of the story? Follow the link below to read the final book, Grave Revelations

ACKNOWLEDGEMENTS

I f you've made it this far and kept reading, a special thank-you to you. Readers like you are the reason I keep going!

To my mom, who continues to be my first reader, even the horrible first drafts, I'm so grateful our love of reading brought us even closer.

To my son, who tells everyone he meets about my books, sometimes to my embarrassment. Thank you for being my biggest supporter.

To Joqui, for listening to me talk for hours about the life of a writer and for always being supportive of my dream.

To my street team, for believing in me and being so willing to give your time and energy to share my stories with the world.

To HarbingerDesigns for another beautiful book cover.

To Owleyesproofsandedits for all your hard work on this one.

And to SCOriginal for all your art pieces.

Thank you.

ABOUT THE AUTHOR

Cassandra Aston grew up near Austin, TX on a ranch just outside the city. She's a lover of everything fantasy, especially the Fae. Although her first series Prophecies of Angels and Demons doesn't delve into the realm of the Fae, her 2022 NaNoWriMo project, which will be released in 2025, is an urban fantasy, stand-alone story that will take the reader deep into the world of Faerie.

Cassandra currently lives in Houston, TX with her family of four.

SOPHIA'S BOLOGNESE RECIPE

M ake Sophia's bolognese sauce using this easy recipe.

First, you'll need a large stock pan and the following ingredients:

- 1 tablespoon olive oil

- 1 tablespoon unsalted butter

- 1 ½ pounds (680 grams) 80/20 ground beef

- 1 ½ pounds (680 grams) ground pork

- 6 ounces paresan cheese

- salt to taste

- black pepper to taste

- 1 large onion

- 2 celery stalks

- 2 large carrots

- 5 garlic cloves, grated or finely chopped

- 1 cup white wine, or red if you prefer

- 3 1/2 cups good quality can tomato purée or marinara sauce

- 1 cup milk

- 1 cup beef stock

Instructions:

Start by chopping celery, carrot and onion into small squares.

In a large pot add oil and butter over medium heat and brown meat adding salt and pepper to taste.

When meat is browned, add onion, celery, and carrots; mix well and stir in the garlic.

Add wine, stir and allow to cook, and reduce slightly for about 3 minutes. Add the tomato purée, milk, and stock, and mix well.

Partially cover and simmer for 3 hours, stirring often to prevent it sticking to the bottom. If any fat rises to the top, use a spoon to skim it off.

If you find that the liquid is not reducing, remove the lid completely and make sure the sauce is bubbling. It may get messy.

When done, taste for seasoning and adjust to your taste.

www.ingramcontent.com/pod-product-compliance
Lightning Source LLC
Chambersburg PA
CBHW021131260626
47169CB00005B/1552